"To a most inter   at
her low-cut bodice   rs.

The fiery-haired beauty wanted him to finish his drink to
the last drop. He couldn't set it down after one sip! "To
. . . to love," she blurted.

Rhys broke out in amused laughter. "To love? I don't
think so, sweeting. To *making* love, I'll agree to."

Calypso could've smacked the sensual smile off his
handsome face. *To revenge,* she vowed inwardly as she
dashed the remainder of her drink down her throat. The
earl followed suit, draining the last of his as well.

Now it was only a matter of time. But how long? She
had forgotten to ask.

Nibbling her ear, he whispered, "You stir me, woman, in
a most unusual way. Be wary though. I have no intention
of falling prey to your bewitching spells."

Abandoning her ear, his mouth worked a path down the
column of her neck, the silk of her dressing gown parting
willingly as he pushed it aside. Not sure how it happened
so quickly, Calypso was lost in the passion he kindled in
her body.

She was lost, revenge trampled beneath desire, as she
nuzzled into his chest, forgetting for a moment that she
was drugging the earl so as to have him at her mercy!

TRAITOR'S KISS

TERRI VALENTINE

ZEBRA BOOKS
KENSINGTON PUBLISHING CORP.

To my sister, Rae Harrell. Your spirit and perserverance is the epitome of what a heroine should be.

And to my editor, Pesha Finkelstein, for all your support and guidance and for giving me the opportunity to tell my stories to the reading public.

Chapter One

Long Island, Bahamas
January 13, 1784

"Egads, Clarissa, can't you see what a scoundrel Lovelace is?" Calypso Collingsworth hissed between her clenched teeth. Her eyes darted down the printed words, her breath coming in little wisps as her heart clackity-clacked in her chest. She flipped the page, the sound her movement made crackling sharp and defined, as clear as her frustration and inability to understand why any woman could fall for a man's honeyed words, especially ones that rang with such a false note.

"Oh, good lord, girl, have enough sense to run while you still have the chance," she muttered in exasperation, closing the leather-bound volume with a snap as her delicately shaped finger ran over the raised lettering on the cover, *Clarissa, or the History of a Young Lady.*

Pressing her head back against the sofa on which she curled, she brushed impatiently at one fiery red curl that looped down into her mouth and then swept the entire mass of hair from her neck in one smooth motion to twist it into a knot on top of her head. "Stupid girl," she whispered. "You'd never find me letting some man take advantage that way."

7

Her hand dropped to the finely woven damask of the settee, the book she held plopping on the seat beside her. Her fingers traced the tufted pattern there until they happened upon the silkiness of the calico cat's tail, which began to twitch and thump at her touch with the measured control only a feline could master.

"What do you think, Phoebe?" Her head lifted to observe the cat's tail weaving around her hand. "Some females are so stupid, especially those on the written page."

The animal began to purr.

"But I suppose you could care less, you lazy old cat." Calypso's head drifted back to rest against the sofa.

She had gone to so much trouble to find an opportunity to read Mr. Richardson's book—only to be disappointed. Having observed her mother weeping softly as she read the novel, she had expected so much more. At the ripe old age of eighteen Calypso was still forbidden to read the adult literature her mother seemed to thrive on, but she had to admit her father had been right. She had gleaned a satchel of information from the pages she had read; she had had no idea such things went on between men and women.

No man would do anything so disgusting to her! Her lashes fluttered down over her green eyes, the color of highly polished jade. Not *him*. She conjured up the familiar image: dark wavy hair, brown eyes that could melt diamonds, and a smile—oh those lips curling in that special way no real man could capture precisely. Him. The only name she had given this imaginery beau. Some day she would meet him, and when she did—her lips responded with a radiant smile—he would take her away from the humdrum life she lived on this island to places she had only dreamed about: Paris, Rome, London.

The click of boot heels outside the library door snapped her attention back to the present. Twisting, she gazed out over the back of the sofa to the door she had taken such care to shut, hoping no one would find her. The latch squeaked in protest as a hand turned it, and Calypso felt pulsating fear leap into her throat. Whoever approached was coming into the library. With a little girl squeal, she slouched down, grabbing Phoebe in one arm and the book in the other, until her knees reached the floor with her torso draped over the sofa seat, her bottom lip caught between her teeth to keep another telltale sound from escaping her throat.

"I tell you, Evan, I never thought the rebels would last this long. How could a motley assortment of colonials defeat the king's own army?" The sound of a fist slamming into a open hand reached her ears. Booted feet clicked across the wooden floor, then became muffled as they encountered the rug behind the sofa on which she crouched.

Panic trickled down her spine as beads of perspiration dampened her brow. Heaven help her, that was her father's voice, and her brother, Evan, wouldn't be far behind him.

"I know, Father, but the missive from England is quite clear." Fingers snapped against paper. "Clinton pulled out of New York on November twenty-fifth."

Calypso clutched the cat to her bosom and buried the offending book deep in the lime folds of her dress. If her father discovered her here . . . She swallowed so hard she thought for sure the two men would hear the sound. Phoebe wiggled, but she clung tightly to the cat though one sharp claw hooked into the skin of her arm. *Be still,* she mentally willed her pet. Phoebe responded by lifting her back legs and embedding those needlelike nails into her flesh as well.

The pain was too much. Calypso released her prisoner at the same moment it meowed its indignation at being clutched so tightly. With little regard for loyalty, Phoebe scrambled onto the sofa's overstuffed cushion.

"What was that?" She heard her father's quick intake of air. She was caught now. A groan of despair lodged in her throat.

With feline grace, Phoebe leaped onto the hump of the sofa's arm and again yowled a protest at the undignified way she had been treated.

"Why is that animal in my study? You damned cat. Get out of here," her father demanded.

Phoebe leaped to the floor with a thud. Calypso could imagine the way she strutted from the room, her tail raised high like a flag, her dainty paws moving deliberately so as to remove herself from Lord Collingsworth's way with dignity.

"Who allowed that beast in here?" her father roared.

Calypso's concern shot back to her own predicament. His anger at her cat was nothing compared to the ire he would direct at her if he discovered her crouched behind the sofa. *Please, Lord, don't let him find me, and I'll do anything you say,* she prayed. *I'll never read another book as long as I live.* She squeezed her eyes shut, waiting with resignation, doom lying heavy in her heart.

"You know how sly that animal is, Father," Evan said with a chuckle. "I'm sure it slipped by some unsuspecting servant without a sound."

Her father turned with a swoosh, the tap of his boot heels moving away to again clack against the bare wood of the parquet floor. The breath hissed like a leaky balloon from her near-bursting lungs. She was safe—for the moment, at least. *Thank you, Brother dear, though I'm sure you would never have said those words if you were aware you had helped me.*

Evan was a typical older brother, she supposed, always threatening to tattle on her every chance he had. If he got wind of what she was doing . . . she swallowed hard, imagining the revenge he would extract from her.

"I suppose you're right, my boy. 'Tis not what's important at the moment, anyway." Her father's voice rose with a catch. "We've lost it all, Evan. The land, the stables, and the house. Those uncouth colonials will never give it

10

back." His words hung with emotion, electrifying the air in the room.

A strange sense of loss clutched at Calypso's heart, the meaning of her father's words plucking at her soul like plectra upon a harpsichord. Childhood memories pressed against her mind, a nightmare measured in a ten year old's imagination. The torches as they blazed high above her head, her father being dragged from the house by angry men demanding he change his loyalties—from sovereign to mob. The proud baron had refused, again pledging his allegiance to the king of England in a loud, steady voice. A nauseating smell had permeated the air, and even now as she remembered, a knot lodged in her throat, and she placed her hand over her mouth. Hot tar, especially once it was swabbed on human flesh, was an odor never to be forgotten. A shiver swirled down her tense spine. How could her father wish to return to their confiscated lands in Maryland when such horrid memories waited there for them? He still carried scars on the backs of his hands and neck from the terrible experience of being tarred and feathered. She wouldn't go back to that heathen country—no matter what!

"It's not over yet, Father," Evan insisted. "Just because the military is pulling out, doesn't mean England has given up the battle. You've heard the rumors. The rebels bicker among themselves like jackals over a rotting carcass. Give them time to bring about their own destruction." He chuckled with confidence. "Where will they find a regent among them to rule? Most of their citizenry are commoners from the gutters of England. King George will sit and wait—until the right moment—then bring the colonial dogs to heel."

"If only it were so, my son. I would sacrifice most anything to see those common bastards returned to their lowly stations."

Calypso yearned to stretch her neck and watch the scenario taking place in the room. Her father's face would be bloated crimson with emotion, Evan's flushed with self-importance.

A hesitant knock sounded upon the library door. "My lord," called out a voice Calypso recognized as the butler's. The tap of footsteps recrossing the room and a mumble of indistinguishable words made her cock her head in order to hear better.

"By all means, show the gentleman in, Gerard," her father commanded.

An air of expectancy invaded the room.

"Who's here, Father?" Evan queried.

"Our man from the colonies. I'll be anxious to hear what he has to say."

Calypso strained forward, curiosity tilting her head. This must be her father and brother's contact from Philadelphia, but she had never seen the man. She heard a strangely gaited walk enter the library, the click of a heel followed by the tap of something much lighter than a man's foot, then the sound of something dragging. The pattern repeated itself over and over until the stranger reached the center of the room.

"Lord Collingsworth," the man acknowledged, his voice rough with gravel. "It's good to see you're doing so well. Many were not so fortunate as you."

"I care not for the misfortune of others. Tell us, sir, how goes it in the colonies?"

"No longer colonies, my lord, but the United States of America. King George has pulled out the royal troops."

"So we've heard," Evan interjected, the paper he held crackling loudly.

"What can you tell us we don't already know?"

The man's strange walk continued across the room. "I came to offer hope and to confirm allegiance from those of us like you who were forced to leave."

12

"Do you question my loyalties, sir?" her father demanded.

"Not at all. The king's Secret Society counts you and your family as one of our strongest members, but how far does your support extend? If called upon, how much will you do to see that the success of our mission is accomplished?"

"I will do whatever is necessary to assure our home in Maryland is returned to us."

The stranger cleared his throat in what almost sounded like amusement to Calypso. "I had hoped you would say as much. You will be hearing soon from the Society, so be prepared, Lord Collingsworth, to keep the pledge you've just given me. You *shall* be called upon. The rebel bastards will bring about their own destruction, but if they need help, we shall be there to supply it." The man made a shuffling turn and worked his way back toward the door.

"Sir," she heard her father say. "You are welcome to stay the night, if you wish."

"No need, my lord, there are many in the islands to visit, but you, sir, are our key person. Be prepared for the summons." As the man left the room, the rhythm of his walk ingrained itself into Calypso's mind. Though she had no idea what this messenger looked like, she knew she would recognize him by his distinctive walk and rough-hewn voice if she ever heard them again.

"You're right, Evan," her father's voice interjected into her thoughts. "Patience is the medicine called for to rid America of the vermin infesting it now. We will wait and watch, but so help me, if they find a leader of strength among them who is capable of keeping them severed from the motherland, I will do everything in my power to bring him down, even if I must shoot him in the streets myself, personally, to stop the rabid mongrels from carrying through with their clamor for freedom."

Evan snorted in disgust. "May God give them the free-

13

dom to bury themselves."

The smack of hands clasping reached Calypso.

"I'll support you always, Father. No matter what. If it comes to assassination, I demand the honor."

"You're a true son, Evan. More than any man could ask for. If such strong measures are needed, I'll consider your request." Emotion rang high in the baron's voice. "But for now, we must display patience and allow those traitors to bring about their own destruction."

A moment of silence passed, then the sound of boot heels clicking back toward the door sent a rush of relief coursing through Calypso's body. At last the two men were leaving, and she had not been discovered.

"Come, Evan, there's much to do in the meantime. This plantation will not run itself."

"I know, Father. I'll be along in a moment. There's one small detail I need to take care of first. I won't be but a minute."

Her father left the room and closed the door behind him.

Calypso sucked in her breath and held it tight. Not a sound came from the spot where her brother stood. Whatever was he doing? The urge to look overwhelmed her, and she fought to keep her curiosity in check.

Thump—thump. Thump—thump. Her heart sounded like a drumbeat in her chest. Could Evan hear it, too? Balanced on the balls of her feet, she eased up until her gaze crested the back of the couch. Her brother stared at her, a cocksure smile lifting one side of his thin-lipped mouth.

"Callie," he offered with a nod of his chin. "I wondered how long it would take before your inquisitiveness won out." He shook his head and clucked his tongue. "Eavesdropping. My, but we have sunk to new depths, haven't we?"

"I wasn't spying." The denial rushed from her lips before

she had a chance to consider her words. She bit down on her betraying tongue, knowing full well what her brother's next question would be.

"Then what are you doing here in Father's study?"

Her mind searched frantically for a way out of her predicament. The lies darted through her brain, each one quickly discarded. It would take a grand story, indeed, to fool Evan. He was a master of untruths. For the briefest of moments she considered the magnitude of the sin she was about to commit. God would strike her dead, most likely, but the thought of facing her Maker was not as frightening as imagining the punishment Evan would extract if he discovered the real reason she was in the study. She swallowed, her throat sticking with fear as she latched onto her only possible excuse. "My cat. I came to get Phoebe out of here before Father discovered her."

"Is that so?" His eyes bored into her as if trying to uncover the truth. He placed his hands behind his back, breaking the line of his somber brown jacket, and began to pace the room back and forth.

Calypso's gaze followed his every move, looking for a sign of what he was thinking. At twenty-one, Evan seemed much older to her. His brown hair, straight and slick, was pulled back and tied at the nape of his neck with a black ribbon. His jawline, severely square, worked back and forth. He mulled over her response, giving it serious consideration. Her shoulders eased as increasing confidence he would accept her excuse pulsed through her veins.

"Stand up, girl."

The command cracked with unexpected suddenness. Calypso scrambled from her crouch to a ramrod stance, without considering the consequences of her action. The book twisted from her nervous fingers and tumbled down the folds of her skirt to land with a dull thud on the carpet beneath her feet. Face up, the title glistened like burnished gold against the plain leather of its binding. Like magnets, her eyes were drawn downward. Evan's eyes followed her lead, the greenness of his irises a mirror reflection of her own, but where hers glistened with dread, his sparkled with triumph.

"Your cat, you say." He began to circle her, his gaze stinging like pinpricks wherever it touched.

Curse him. He would force her to repeat the lie. "I searched everywhere for her. This was the last place I looked." Her eyes never left the book.

Evan circled until he stood inches from the offending object. He knelt, falling into her line of vision, his long fingers reaching out to grasp the volume.

"And tell me, dear Sister, was the beast reading when you found her?"

One more lie wouldn't make any difference now. "I don't know what you're talking about, Brother dear." The word "dear" rang with sarcasm.

"And when the kindhearted Lovelace drugged Clarissa and seduced her, did you especially enjoy that part?"

"He's a scoundrel who deserves to be shot." Her hand darted up to cover her impulsive mouth. Why couldn't she think before she spoke? Evan always caught her that way with trickery. He unnerved her, stripping her emotions bare.

His laughter pressed against her, leaving her breathless and afraid. What would he demand from her this time? Always he forced her to do something she didn't want to do. *Blackmailer,* she accused him in her mind but didn't have the courage to say it aloud.

He rose, the book clutched in his fist. Flipping it open to the first page, he skimmed it, then thumbed through the volume.

"Devil, take you, Evan. You caught me." She paused, twisting her wayward tongue in her mouth. "Now, tell me. What do you plan to do about it?" she whispered.

"Do, Callie dear? What is there *I* can do . . ." Their

gazes locked. Enjoyment twinkled in his eyes so like hers.
". . . except lay the evidence before Father?"

"No, please. He'll lock me in my room for weeks. I'll do anything if you just don't tell Father." The plea spilled from her mouth, the words so familiar as she had said them a million times before to her brother. Her own weakness disgusted her. One day she would stand up to Evan. One day—but not today. The thought of being locked in her room for weeks on end with only bread and water was unbearable. No matter what Evan demanded, it couldn't be as bad as her father's punishment. Or could it?

The look he conjured up left her mouth dry. She closed her eyes and waited with the lost hope of a trapped mouse in the pantry.

"I imagine we could bargain."

She could see the grin splitting his lips without looking up. He had won and he knew it.

"You know the tavern in Collingsville?"

Her gaze darted up and locked with his, puzzlement contorting her features. "The King's Ransom?"

"That's the one. There's a girl there, Jenny. She could use an evening off. Time of her own to spend however she wished, without anyone knowing where she had gone."

"Jenny?" She had seen the girl he spoke of, pretty and dark. Whatever did she see in Evan? Money and title, she answered her own foolish question. "I don't understand. What can I do?"

"How hard can it be to slap ale before the conch and serve a meal or two?"

"Don't call the locals 'conch,' Evan. I don't like the term. They were here long before we were and deserve respect."

"Respect for being lazy and salvaging shipwrecks for a living?" He snorted in disgust. Placing one hand on his hip, he grinned. "Good try, little Sister. You aren't going to change the subject. Even someone as ignorant as you could wait tables for a few hours."

"Evan," she groaned, "Father will kill me if he finds out."

"Now, tell me. How is he going to find out? He never sets foot in that tavern. You know that. Besides most of the conch hardly know what you look like, except for your hair—that damn red flag. Do something with it, hide it under a cap. I don't care. But if you want to keep me silent, you'll agree to my terms."

Evan was right. How bad could it be? She was getting off easy this time. He had extracted far worse from her in the past.

"I don't know, Evan. What will Mr. Hatterly, the owner, say when I show up in Jenny's place?"

"Don't worry. I'll make the arrangements. He'll accept you as a cousin or something. I'll work out the details." He turned as if to leave, assuming the plan was settled.

Calypso grasped his arm. "If I do this, you won't tell Father?"

He nodded.

"And you won't demand anything else from me."

Evan chuckled. "You learn fast, don't you, Callie dear?"

"Is that a promise?" she demanded, ignoring his comment.

Nodding once, he pried her fingers from his jacket and straightened imaginary wrinkles from the sleeve. "Tonight. I'll supply you with clothes to wear as soon as I talk to Jenny." He angled the book in her direction and turned, placing it back on the shelf from which it came. "Next time, little Sister, take more care in your sneaking around. Until later." Spinning on his heels, he strode from the room.

Fear eased its way into her mind. The plan sounded so simple, too simple, in fact. *This is the last time, Evan Collingsworth, you'll trap me this way. I'll get even one day. Just you wait and see. You'll pay for all the times you used extortion on me, if I manage to survive this farce you*

18

have planned for me this evening.

Calypso tied her mount to a bush and glanced about the tiny glade, her breath easing from her lungs. Without a doubt this was the spot Evan had described—the place where the three conspirators were to meet. The wind moaned, whipping the leaves of a nearby palm tree into action, the sound it made reminding her of voices issuing a warning to return home and call a halt to the insane adventure on which she was about to embark.

"I would if I could," she responded to the ghostly whispers, wishing she could think of a way to circumvent her brother, but nothing came to mind.

"What would you do, little Sister?"

She whirled, confronting Evan. Beside him stood the tavern girl, Jenny, a sly-eyed wench if she had ever seen one. Yes, she could understand what the woman saw in Evan—they were two of a kind.

Jenny stretched out her arms, offering a bundle to Calypso. "These should fit you. We're about the same size."

About, she thought, *except you're wider in the hips and much smaller in the bosom.* Her left hand came to rest on the swell of her breasts concealed beneath the forest-green joseph she wore; her right reached out to accept the clothing. "Thank you," she uttered through tight, compressed lips.

She held the costume up for inspection. The simple, homespun skirt was serviceable, the separate bodice embellished with bowknots to hold the divided front together. Perhaps she could fit into the garment if she laced it loosely. The chemise was another story altogether. No longer white but a dingy gray, it was of a rough cotton. She wrapped it around her fist and shoved the balled material back at its owner. "No, thank you. I think I prefer my own."

19

"Silk under homespun?" Jenny questioned, one eyebrow lifting in amusement. "Some tavern wench you'll make."

Animosity sparked like lightning between the two women.

Evan snatched the undergarment from Calypso's hand and pressed it back into Jenny's fingers. "Silk or sackcloth. Does it matter what she wears underneath? No one will see it."

Jenny gave him that sly-eyed look of hers and shrugged. "It doesn't matter to me."

"Good," he said with finality, turning back to his sister. "Now, will you change your clothes, please?"

Calypso's bowed chin angled upward, her eyes wide with disbelief. "I'll not undress here in the middle of the woods."

"Would you prefer I told Father what you were up to this afternoon?" His smile was anything but pleasant.

"No," she answered in a small voice, angry bile rising high in her throat.

Evan placed his hand on his hip, waiting. Jenny's gaze bored into her, leaving her feeling already undressed. She turned her back and began unbuttoning the long coatdress, determined to keep her pride firmly intact as she exposed her limbs to the winter nip in the tropic air. The brown skirt and bodice appeared at her elbow unrequested. Without hesitating, she accepted them and slipped the garments on. Much too large in the hips, the skirt hung long and uneven, and the bodice—no matter how she tried, her bosom was mashed and pressed upwards against the neckline of the lacy exposure of chemise in a most unladylike fashion.

She reached out to locate the scarf she had worn around her neck on a nearby bush and attempted to stuff it in the exposed décolletage.

"I think not, sweetie," Jenny warned, jerking the silk from Calypso's fingers. "No girl from my station would

20

come by anything so fine legitimately." She shoved it into a pocket in her skirt.

Calypso scowled. That was her favorite scarf. Evan caught her by the upper arm and twisted her around to face him. "It's only a scarf, Callie. Listen to me. Don't you spoil this, you hear? You can leave the tavern at midnight."

"Midnight? But I thought . . ."

He shook her arm to silence her. "Come around to the plantation kitchens, and I'll let you in. In the meantime I'll cover for you. Annie will say you retired early since you were not feeling well."

"Nannette will never accept the word of a slave. You know how protective she is. She'll come to my room to check on me."

"Strangely enough, Nanna won't be feeling too good herself this evening."

"Evan, what did you do to her?"

"Just added a little something to her evening tea. She'll be back to normal in the morning. You'll have returned by then, too. No one will be the wiser."

She pulled her arm from his bruising grip. "You go too far, Brother. One day you'll pay for all the horrible things you've done."

"Perhaps, but right now you're the one who's paying, dear Sister. Get down to the tavern. You only have a half-hour."

Her nose inched high in the air as she turned, taking the reins of the mare she had ridden.

Evan issued an exasperated sigh. "No horse, Callie. Tavern girls don't ride, much less an expensive horse."

"Then how am I suppose to get there?"

"Walk." He swatted her on the behind. "You'd better get going if you don't want to be late. I understand ol' Hatterly can be a tyrant when he doesn't get his pound's worth from a servant."

Calypso crossed her arms defiantly over her chest, indecision ripping through her.

"Squeeze much tighter, sweetie, and your tits will pop right out." The other girl laughed a coarse, hard sound.

Face flaming as red as her hair, Calypso turned to leave the glade.

"Callie," her brother called, spasmodic giggles tripping from his lips.

She turned back, her arms rigid at her sides.

He tossed her a large chunk of coal. "Here. Rub this in your hair. No one will recognize you then."

She caught the sooty charcoal and squeezed it until it cut into the palm of her hand.

"Damn you, Evan. You'll never do this to me again as long as I live. I swear."

His head snapped back in hilarity. "That's it, Callie. Now you sound like a tavern wench. Keep up the cursing, and you might pull this charade off. I hope so for your sake. Father would strip your hide if he ever found out what you've done."

Calypso swirled and stalked away, too large tears of frustration staining her cheeks. Of all the demands Evan had ever placed on her, most assuredly this was the most degrading.

Chapter Two

Calypso cut around a cotton field, the tall perennial bushes green and alive but awaiting the faint winter chill to dissipate before presenting their pink blossoms that would eventually mature into the snowy balls of fiber toward the end of April. The anger that had propelled her forward from the glade weakened with each step she took, reshaping itself into emotions she found much harder to cope with—self-doubt and fear of the unknown.

Would she be able to successfully portray the part of a serving girl? Would someone recognize her and give her identity away? She reached into her pocket and pulled out the chunk of coal and again raked it through her burnt sienna tresses until it crumbled in her fist, no longer usable.

Dusting her hands as best she could, she inspected one long strand of hair, but in the waning sunset she couldn't be sure if the flaming color of her hair had been disguised at all. Her fingers reached about her head patting, touching, and when she pulled her hand back, it was sooty, evidence she had done all she could.

Following a turn row running between two fields, she proceeded down the rutted trail until she reached the edge of Collingsville. The first buildings, belonging to locals and free blacks, were built of little more than pieces of scrap wood and thatched roofs. The few people she passed paid her no mind, and she continued on her way toward the center of the wharfside village, her confidence growing stronger with each step she took.

Reaching the tavern, she glanced up at the sign flapping back and forth in the ocean breeze. The King's Ransom, the swinging board proclaimed, as if there was any doubt for the building was the only two-story one in town. She skirted down a side alley until she reached a back entrance, then drawing air into her lungs, she grasped the door handle and opened it, stepping into the confines of the kitchen, dark and dingy and smelling of cooked cabbage.

Her eyes darted about as she tried to get her bearings. A voice called out. "You Callie, girl?"

She whirled at the familiar nickname, one only her brother used and a name she found most distasteful.

"Jenny's cousin?" the little man nearly as wide as he was tall demanded.

She nodded, her voice caught somewhere between her throat and her tongue. Mr. Hatterly. She had seen him about town enough times to recognize him.

"Good," he replied, turning his back and signaling for her to follow. "You're late. You'll stay an extra half-hour tonight to make up the time. Understood?" He shot her a glower over his shoulder.

Calypso glanced down, not wanting the innkeeper to read the defiance in her eyes. She would not stay one minute after midnight. Let Jenny deal with his anger tomorrow for her disobedience. She smiled slightly at the thought of the other girl's wages suffering because of her.

He led her into the common room, which at the moment was quiet. One customer sat at a long trestle table, sipping from a mug of ale. She glanced around, eyeing the bar where wooden mugs hung from pegs on the walls and a

24

squat barrel housing the bitter stout occupied one end and another of rum crowded the other. At least that was what the carefully penned signs tacked to the staves proclaimed. She wrinkled her patrician nose in distaste.

"Ale, rum," Hatterly confirmed, pointing from one barrel to the next. "In case ya can't read."

Again she nodded, not uttering a sound.

"Quiet one, ain't ya, wench?" The rotund man eyed her up and down. For a moment she feared he recognized her. Then he grinned, a glint sparkling in his buttonlike eyes. "I believe the customers will like ya best that-a-way. Silent and docile. No trouble."

She studied his back as he spun about and circled behind the bar. *Silent and docile,* she fumed but maintained her dignity. He crooked a finger at her, and she stepped around to the counter.

"Wood," he said, pointing at the mugs suspended on the walls, "for most of the customers." He angled his finger down to a shelf, knee-high. "Use the good pewter if'n someone *very* important comes in like the honorable Evan Collingsworth."

She nearly choked as the man mentioned her brother. Little chance of Evan showing his face in the tavern tonight.

"Understand, girl?"

She nodded.

"What be the matter with ya? Are you deaf and dumb?" Exasperation edged his voice.

"No," she murmured.

"Good. I'd've docked Jenny's pay a whole week if'n she'd done somethin' like that."

Now she wished she had kept her mouth shut.

He reached into the pocket of his green vest and pulled out a watch. Snapping the lid up with his thumbnail, he studied the timepiece for a moment. "We'll be gettin' busy in a hour, so accustom yourself with the kitchens and talk

25

to Cook about what she's preparin' to eat."

Calypso hesitated, realization of what she was about to do rushing in. She would serve the local population as if she were no more than one of her father's slaves. The most she had ever done was occasionally offer Phoebe a plate of leftovers from the plantation kitchen. Her hand traveled up to press against her brow.

"Well, go on, wench," the innkeeper commanded, his beefy hand swinging down to slap her on the behind.

She startled, her eyes widening in disbelief as he waddled away. How dare the man touch her that way! Evan's crassness earlier in the woods had been bad enough. No one would get away with such a gesture again this night. No one. She would not stand for it. Not at all!

She rubbed her stinging buttock and turned to stalk into the kitchen, the laughter of the lone customer in the room nipping at her heels as she went.

"More soup at the far table," Hatterly bellowed, reaching out to pinch her on the arm. "And the four gentlemen by the hearth, refill their mugs." He slapped the meaty part of his palm against his forehead. "Girl, you're costin' me a fortune tonight because of your diddlin' ways."

Calypso caught her ragged breath and continued to move as quickly as she could on her aching feet. If Evan didn't have such a hold over her, she would walk out of this tavern. No, she would run and never look back. No nightmare she had ever dreamed was as awful as the reality of her present situation. But worse, it was hours before midnight arrived.

Stumbling through the kitchen doors, she slumped against the far wall. How would she survive the next three hours? *The devil take you, Evan Collingsworth, for making me suffer this way.*

"There ya are, ya lazy slut," the innkeeper shouted,

bringing Calypso straight up from her slouch. His hand descended, cuffing her on the shoulder. "Can't ya do anythin' right?"

Angry frustration built to a crescendo inside her. She bit her tongue to keep back the sharp words threatening to gush from her lips as she pictured her father's wrath if he discovered her whereabouts for the last few hours. She could only imagine her punishment, but it would make the normal confinement with nothing but bread and water seem mild by comparison. Tears crested in the corners of her eyes, threatening to spill down her cheeks.

"Leave her be, Hatterly," barked the cook from behind, her ladle thumping down against his pudgy back.

Hatterly twisted, his anger riveting on the woman who had not said a word all night except to inform Calypso when her orders were ready. Calypso blinked in surprise at the woman's sudden interest in her welfare.

"Ya can't tell me what to do in my own establishment."

"Can't I? You hit this child one more time, and I'll walk out never to come back. You'll not find a cook as good as me anywhere in the islands, at least not one willin' to work for the pittance you pay."

The innkeeper's eyes narrowed in defeat. He whirled about to face Calypso again. "Finish servin' those meals, Callie, then come back to the kitchen."

She nodded, thankful for the reprieve, and glancing up at the cook's face, she smiled her gratitude.

"Don't be thankin' me. Just remember this night." Cook shook her ladle in emphasis. "Don't be lettin' that Jenny talk you into takin' her place again." She grabbed Calypso's wrists. "Hands like these weren't never meant to serve. I've decided you're somebody, but I'm not sure who. I figure ya owe me a return favor."

Calypso's chin dipped in agreement.

"One thing more. No matter what Hatterly tells you, don't go upstairs with any of the customers."

"I won't," she whispered, sensing the urgency in the woman's voice but unsure of its meaning.

"Good girl. Be finishin' up, then go home." The woman wagged a finger in her face. "Don't you show up here again."

"Believe me, I have no intention of ever setting foot in The King's Ransom again as long as I live. I wouldn't be here now if I had a choice." She spun, gathering up the plates and bowls to carry into the common room.

"Oh, Callie, girl." Cook's hand stretched toward her. "Tell old Hatterly the captain in room nine sent this message down with his dinner tray. Would you be givin' it to him for me?"

"Of course." Calypso took the bit of folded paper. As if it were on fire, it burned her fingers, a little voice in the back of her mind nagging, *Read it. For your own good see what the note says.*

Instead she slipped it into her pocket and pushed her way through the kitchen doors and out into the dining room to take the cook's advice. Be done and leave as quick as she could and be thankful the night would eventually be over with nothing worse than a few bruises and sore feet as reminders.

Nearly midnight. Calypso sighed, relief flooding through her in tidal wave proportions. The crowd began to thin; the overnight guest, of which there was only one as far as she could tell, drifted up the stairs to his room, a thin man of indeterminate age and origin.

Calypso reached into her pockets, her tired, aching hands seeking a cradle of support. Her fingers brushed against the folded paper she had placed there. How long ago? Hours. The message she was supposed to pass on to Mr. Hatterly. The missive from "the captain in room nine." She had forgotten to hand it over to the innkeeper, her mind had been so busy trying to survive the ordeal of the evening.

Hatterly would be furious when she gave the paper to him this late. If she gave it to him. Her finger rubbed the doubled sheet in indecision. What did she care what some pompous ass who was too lazy to come downstairs demanded from Hatterly? She would never see him or this tavern again.

Her fingers stilled. But then there was Cook to consider. The little woman would more than likely be the one to suffer if the note never reached the old dog. Cook had rescued her from his wrath. She had no choice except to give the missive to him, but then she could leave. What could the innkeeper do to her now?

She marched to where Hatterly stood behind the bar and took the missive from her pocket and slapped it on the varnished counter.

"What's this?" the man growled, one eyebrow lifting in suspicion. "Your pay comes at the end of the week, just the same as Jenny's, though I don't see ya deserve any."

" 'Tis a message Cook gave me earlier."

"She can't read nor write, how could she give ya a message?" he grumbled, snatching the paper and opening it.

Again that little voice nagged. *You should've read it first*. Ignoring the bewildering warning, she angled about, heading toward the kitchen as she untied the apron from around her waist.

"Confound it, girl. Why didn't ya show me this earlier? It's from one of my guests. There's no time now to arrange for anyone, and it's too late to inform the captain I can't oblige his request."

You're right, it is too late. I'm leaving. I don't care what your customers want. She wadded the stained apron into a ball, preparing to toss it into a corner as soon as she reached the confines of the kitchen.

"Just where do ya think you're goin', missy?"

29

She whirled. "Home," she answered, planting her fists on her hips. She had had enough of the innkeeper, his establishment, and his demands.

"No, you're not. Jenny wouldn't like to hear that ya didn't do the job ya were sent here for."

Calypso pressed her lips into a thin line. Hang Jenny and Evan, too. She closed her eyes, determined to leave. The image of her father's face filled the darkness on the insides of her eyelids — scowling, condemning. She swallowed her anger and her pride, her eyes dipping down to stare at the floor in forced concession.

"Tell me, girl, do ya know how to warm a bed?" Hatterly's voice lowered to a conspiratorial whisper that made her feel uncomfortable, but she couldn't decide why. "So far ya haven't shown much aptitude for anythin', but even a dull-witted wench can accomplish that simple chore. Ya don't even have to think."

Her chin lifted in indignation. She had seen the servants run the copper bedwarmers over sheets enough times. How hard could the task be? "Of course," she retorted.

"Good, good." Hatterly patted her on the shoulder. "Just take care of the captain in room nine," he instructed with a grin, "then ya can be goin' home even if it's a little early." He winked. "Make 'im happy, girl, ya hear?"

She blinked in confusion at the innkeeper's change in attitude. All he had asked her to do was warm sheets, and it wasn't even that cold. Why did Hatterly place such importance on the job? She turned and headed back toward the kitchen.

The room was dark, the fires banked to glowing embers. Cook was nowhere to be seen. Most likely the little woman had headed home. She glanced around the hearth, looking for a warming pan. There wasn't one in sight. Perhaps in one of the cabinets. Opening cupboards and closets, she rummaged around, looking for something that would serve her purpose, anything. Finally in a broom closet she

30

discovered what she sought. The copper pan was tarnished as if it was never used, the long wooden handle not oiled.

Taking tongs, she gingerly lifted the squeaky lid and dropped three live coals into the yawning mouth, then allowed the lid to snap back in place. A set of back steps led to the rooms above, servant stairs. Calypso lifted her coarse, cotton skirt and proceeded up the dark incline.

Like gallows steps, she thought. Almost as if she were headed toward her doom. She paused halfway up the stairway. Why would she think that? The cook's warning words whispered in her mind. "Don't go upstairs with any of the customers." She wasn't going with anyone, she rationalized.

Lifting her shoulders, she shook off the ominous feeling and continued on her way. How long could it take to warm a bed? Five minutes at the most? The night was over, and she had survived the ordeal practically unscathed. She smiled with relief as she worked her way down the dimly lit hallway, looking for room number nine.

Rhys Winghurst paced his quarters in long, impatient strides, his large, powerful hands clasped behind his bare back making the heavy cords in his neck and shoulders stand out like new hemp on a ship's mast. His lean hips and powerful thighs strained against the fabric of his breeches, his stockingless calves and ankles covered with a fine pelt as dark as the hair on his well-muscled chest.

"Damn," he growled aloud, "what's taking the innkeeper so long to send up a wench?" He ran his fingers through his auburn mane, the other hand perching on his hip.

With a snort of self-disgust, he turned away from the door. He had been too long at sea, he decided, and was acting like a spring buck loose for the first time with a herd of does in season. The girl would arrive eventually; he just needed to display patience. But his problems pressed heavily on his shoulders, demanding his attention. He resumed his pacing. Damn it, he didn't want to think about the difficulties, not now. What he required was a few hours of diversion so he could tackle his dilemma with a fresh mind.

Throwing himself onto the lone chair in the room, he pressed his fingers into his eye sockets. Why was this happening to him now? After all the years of family turmoil, he had managed to create contentment for himself. Being the third son of the Earl of Flint had never been an easy existence, but he had made the best of his situation. His present life was of his own choosing.

A new country found him important, not because of his inherited name but for his ability, and friends respected him for himself and not as his father's son. His life was settled and secure; he brought in needed supplies for his fellow Americans, items they were desperate for: sugar, molasses, rum, and salt. He prided himself on the fact he was one of the few shippers not to charge the exorbitant prices the market would bear, but received a fair, honest profit for his labor.

His labor. He chuckled, the sound deep and rich in texture. The mighty Earl of Flint would be mortified in his grave to know his son had lowered himself to work for a living.

His full, sensual mouth sloped downward. Without a doubt, his circumstances had changed dramatically in the last three months. First Duncan, the heir, had died in a drunken brawl on the streets of London—without issue. Then Lloyd, the middle brother, had been killed by a band of Welsh coal miners, who had mistaken the carriage in which he traveled to Flint as that of the government official sent to squelch the riots, and had left a young wife pregnant and alone.

So many lives hinged on the birth of that child. A son would assume the title—a daughter . . .

He shook his head, sadness coursing through him. The

earldom would fall to him if the baby was a girl child, and after twenty-five years of coveting the title, and the lands and prestige that went with it, he no longer desired that inheritance. All he wanted was peace, now that the Revolution at last was at an end.

At twenty-nine he wasn't ready to turn his life topsy-turvy. He was happy as a commoner, yet a man of means, a citizen of the United States of America. There was self-satisfaction in running international cargo, even if it meant dealing with a Loyalist like John Collingsworth who owned an enormous saltworks and was willing to trade with "the rebellious colonials" as long as they paid in English pounds, not American scrip.

It was easy to understand the bitterness men like Collingsworth felt. They had been stripped of their lands and possessions, then banned from their homes. What had happened when the war began wasn't right, but there had been no other way of securing the country from possible traitors. A sad beginning for a land offering freedom for all, but nonetheless, a necessary evil.

Damn it! Here he was, doing it again. He wasn't ready to make such a monumental decision, not at this moment. A soft, willing woman to lose himself in and a hold filled with salt to take back to New York was all he wanted. If that damned innkeeper didn't hurry, he would demand his pudgy, bald head on a pewter serving dish as well.

The soft, hesitant knock brought Rhys to his feet.

"Who is it?" he challenged.

The person on the other side paused, almost unsure of what to say. " 'Tis Callie, the serving girl. Here to warm your bed, sir."

Did the "sir" sound derisive from the feminine voice on the other side of the door? More likely his imagination. He had paid Hatterly well for the girl's services. Any woman would be pleased to spend a few hours with the wealthy American captain.

33

With long strides, he crossed to the door and opened it to reveal as pretty a wench as he had ever seen. Her hips were slim, but the bosom—his eyes slid over her ripe figure—more than enough for one man, spilled generously from the confines of the tightly laced bodice.

He smiled, pleased. The old codger had done well. In fact, Rhys couldn't have been more satisfied.

Calypso blinked. The stranger's bare chest and his glistening eyes raking over her flesh left her speechless. She had never seen a male in such a state of undress. The warming pan dropped from her fingers and clattered to the floor.

"Oh," she blurted as one of the hot coals rolled from the open lid through the doorway into the man's room. She knelt, frustrated, wanting to grab the live ember, yet knowing the feat was impossible, as she had no way of protecting her bare fingers.

"I'll get it," the man said, reaching for one of his boots propped by the entrance, as he squatted down beside her.

Their eyes locked, his gaze radiating curiosity, his mouth lifting in a smile that left her heart flopping in her chest like a startled rabbit. That smile with even, white teeth and the left side a little higher than the right. This stranger mastered the special expression only her imaginary beau could accomplish. Her gaze moved back up to his eyes to discover what she knew couldn't possibly be. The chocolate brown of the orbs were familiar, too much so; she had seen them many nights staring back at her in a dream.

"You can't be," she murmured, her breath coming in short pants.

"I can't be what, sweeting?" The smile flashed again, and Calypso's soul melted like so much snow under the fire of the sun.

"This entire affair has only been a dream," she whispered incredulously.

"A pleasant one, then." His fingers clasped her chin and tilted her face upward. "I'm most pleased to be sharing it with you."

His face moved closer, his lips parting in anticipation. Fascinated, Calypso watched, not believing what she saw, and most assuredly not accepting as real what she felt as his warm breath caressed her cheek. The smell of something burning invaded her senses.

"The coals," she protested, twisting from his gentle grip, attempting to use the hem of her skirt to scoop the smoking ember back into the copper pan.

He pushed her hand away, and using the toe of the boot he held, he thumped the burning lump back into its proper place. "There," he offered, tossing the boot against its mate, "no harm done. Hatterly will never notice one more scar on the floor."

Calypso stood, the need to run so strong she turned to escape out the doorway.

"Wait, Callie. That is what you said your name was, wasn't it?"

Her chin dipped in acquiescense, her heart fluttering with butterfly wings.

"Callie," he repeated, and for some reason the nickname her brother had pinned on her no longer bothered her. "Where are you going? I thought you were to warm my bed."

"Yes, of course." She lifted the warming pan, using it as a barrier between them. Edging around his tall figure, she couldn't find the courage, or was it desire, to tear her eyes from him. As the back of her knees bumped against the bedstead, she turned, setting the warmer on the foot of the bed, freeing her hands to turn down the covers.

"I'm curious, wench," he whispered, so close behind her she nearly fell face forward on the mattress. His hands eased down the slope of her rump, coming to rest on the

35

fronts of her thighs, pulling her buttocks into the cradle of his groin which radiated a magnetic heat the likes of which she had never experienced. "Is this some new form of amusement I've not heard of before? What do you plan to do with that weapon of domesticity?" He removed one hand and pointed toward the warming pan.

Calypso scrambled onto the bed, her chest heaving in confusion and disbelief. This stranger had grabbed her intimately. And now he was asking her what a bedwarmer was. Was he some kind of lunatic? Her gaze flew to the door, still open the way they had left it moments before.

" 'Tis to warm your bed, sir," she breathed, slipping from the far side of the mattress and edging around the footboard.

The stranger's head flew back, laughter spilling from his lips. "You know, Callie, you're quite amusing."

His relaxed stance gave her confidence, and she scurried toward the gateway to freedom. With the speed of a lightning bolt, his hand whipped out, clamping on her elbow. He reeled her closer until she found herself a prisoner in the circle of his arms, the fine down on his chest tickling her cheek, the smell of sea and male musk strong in her nostrils. His lips touched her hair as his hand drifted down to fondle her backside as if he had ever right. Pressing forward, he eased them down on the bed.

"Oh—no," she gasped, struggling to escape, but managing only to dislodge his hand from her rump. She glanced up to read his mood. His mouth and chin were dusted with black from the charcoal she had used to disguise her hair.

How funny he looked, this stranger whom she felt as if she had known all her life. A giggle tripped over her lips, and she raised a hand to smother the sound.

"You are a odd one, wench," he offered with a shake of his head, "laughing at nothing at all. Where did Hatterly unearth you from, some madhouse?"

"Me, mad?" she demanded. "I'm not the one who

doesn't know what a bedwarmer is."

"Bedwarmer?" He crooked a brow at her. "Why you, woman. You're about the finest one I've ever seen." His mouth descended, snaring her open lips with a kiss that burned into her brain. His tongue slipped into her mouth, exploring, sending waves of bolting shock coursing through her.

What was this man talking about? She, a warming pan? What kind of lunatic held her in his arms, kissing her?

Kissing her? She tore her mouth from his, struggling to escape the confines of his mesmerizing essence, but his weight held her pinned to the mattress, that strange, stirring heat from his loins seeping through the rough fabric of her skirt. A sensation as pure and primeval as the need to survive rushed through her. She liked his power and dominance as surely as a child yielded to parental authority.

Her chest heaved with a mixture of bafflement and excitement. Again he smiled, almost as if he knew the power the gesture held over her, as if he understood the brink she stood upon, ready to accept his ascendancy. With nimble fingers he loosened the bowknots of her bodice, which willingly released the bunched swells of her breasts into his waiting palm.

"Nice," he murmured, as his fingers kneaded the tip of the globe he held until it peaked with straining need against the silk of her chemise. "Very nice, indeed." He twisted until his mouth touched the throbbing nodule with a sucking caress.

Calypso's mind spun as if captured by a hurricane. She should discourage him. Instead, her back arched to press closer to his face. She should tell him to stop. She opened her mouth to speak and found his lips covering hers. Her traitorous tongue did a minuet with his at the slow tempo he demanded. She must push him away. Her hands flattened against his chest, and like innocent children discovering a new forest, her fingers explored, tracing the muscular hills and valleys beckoning to them.

She had to escape or she would be lost. From deep inside she found a well of resistance. Dragging her face away from his, she took deep gulps of air. Each time her lungs rose, her bare nipples brushed against the fur of his chest, sending sparks of delight up and down her spine. "No, you must stop. I didn't understand what you wanted. I must —"

His mouth stifled the rest of her words. His spearing tongue doused the remaining flame of defense with tidal waves of sensations that inundated her. Drowning and subdued, she floated in a pool of wonderment, allowing him to take her down, down, deep into the vortex of his desires.

Him. The dreams of the budding woman of the last few years came rushing in. The imaginary beau who would take her away to a land of fulfillment had at last found her; yet the innocent caresses she had conjured in her mind couldn't compare with what was happening to her now. His silken fingers stroked the skin of her naked thighs in a melody her limbs comprehended. Open to me, his fingers crooned, and, as if her knees had minds of their own, they parted like dancers at the end of a gavotte, her body waiting for the music to begin again, willing to accept her partner's lead.

His hand set the tempo, exploring, questing, caressing her in places she had never even touched herself. A gasp of surprised delight, followed by a moan of desire, escaped her lips and urged him on.

"Yes, my sweeting," he whispered, "beg me, and I'll give you what you want."

How could he know what she wanted when she had no idea herself? Was he offering her love and escape from the doldrums of her life? If so, she would plead, if that was what was needed.

"Please," she purred, angling to give him better access to the core of her being, not caring that her skirt and shift bunched about her waist. "Please, I beg you."

His hand stilled, and she gasped in disappointed surprise. Yet when the weight of his hips pressed against the tenderness of her inner thighs, the soft doeskin of his breeches felt rough and wrong. She had wanted him naked as well. Then the probing warmth of his manhood pressed against her soft folds, and her mind came swirling to the surface.

Sweet heaven, what was she doing? She wiggled, trying to stop what was happening. "No, I—"

One thrust of his hips, and a pain so sharp she cried out brought her struggle to a halt. Each breath she drew seemed to drive him deeper, and the agony was already more than she could bear.

"Sweeting?" he whispered, uncertainty waxing his word. His hips stilled as he waited. "What's this? You couldn't possibly be a virgin." His short breaths echoed hers, and he pushed back on his elbows to observe her.

Brow arching, his serious expression melted to one of amusement. "Of course, I should have known. 'Tis a trick even the best courtesans in France would kill to master." He chuckled, his hips raised, and Calypso thought he would release her. Instead he plunged, burying himself deep inside her chasteness.

"You're hurting me," she gasped as his body lifted ready to plummet again.

He paused, watching her face as if trying to sear her brain. "There's no need to continue this charade." He pressed easily against her, and she tensed in anticipation of the pain. "You please me well."

He pushed on, and much to her surprise, a tightening intensity replaced the sharp stabs she had felt before. Without thinking she lifted her hips, meeting his halfway.

Again he laughed, the sound almost an erotic growl. "That's better, Callie, love." Taking an earlobe between his teeth, he set a rhythm she found easy to follow. His warm

39

breath sent her mind whirling back down into that place where nothing existed but her body and the need to reach something she couldn't imagine.

The peaks stretched like fingers toward the sky, then slithered back down into tingling hollows, only to rise again, coming closer and closer to the ultimate heights. As knowing as an eloquent orator, he steered them toward the finale, carrying her higher and higher.

Climactic release came in a rush so strong she cried out, clinging to this stranger she had known in her dreams since childhood. She trusted him. In her naivety, how could she not, as never once in her imaginary experiences with him had he ever betrayed her.

As the storm of desire gentled around them, Calypso discovered her arms still wound about his neck, and, opening her eyes, she knew the expression she would see shining in the familiar brown eyes. Love and loyalty. Undying devotion.

Her lashes lifted with a sigh, and her lips parted in a smile of response as their gazes locked. Her breath caught and hung in her throat. A stranger stared back at her. The sated look he gave her showed amused pleasure, nothing more. He placed a chaste smack of a kiss on the side of her nose and rolled to his back, leaving her exposed and feeling sick inside. What had happened? Why had the dream shattered so?

" 'Twas quite a tumble you gave me, wench," he complimented her, a lazy smile curling his lips.

Her belly roiled in fear and dread. She twisted to her stomach, grabbing the tangled, sweaty sheet as she moved.

He moved with her. "Are you all right, sweeting?" He tossed the love name at her as if it meant nothing now. His hand patted her rear with familiarity.

Calypso scrambled from the bed, shoving her skirts down as she stumbled across the room.

"Callie, girl. You needn't leave so soon, I'm willing to

pay for a little more time."

"Pay?" she mumbled, the sickening feeling turning a knife's edge deep in the pit of her stomach.

The stranger rolled to one hip and reached for some coins that had been tossed carelessly on a nightstand. He flipped one toward her, and her hand automatically reached out and caught it. "Enough?" he asked with concentrated sincerity.

"Enough?" she repeated. She glanced down at the silver crown in disbelief. He was offering to pay her. Compensate her as if she were no more than a . . .

Her gaze shot up and the open, honest look on his face confirmed her thought. A sob of humiliation ripped through her, and she spun, her free hand fumbling with the loosened bowknots of her bodice.

"No, no, never enough," she cried as she stumbled out the still open door and skittered across the hallway, tripping down the backstairs and out the kitchen exit.

"Nanna," she sobbed once, as she fled through Collingsville, the coin still clutched in her fingers. "Say this is only a nightmare."

When finally she reached the mansion kitchen entrance, she slumped against the wooden barrier. A nightmare, no doubt, she decided, but real nonetheless.

"Callie," hissed Evan. "You must be quieter if you don't wish to be caught."

Calypso glanced up, brushed by her brother without a word, and slunk up the darkened stairs to her room. Never as long as she lived would she forget the degradation of her experience at the hands of . . .

She paused in the doorway, her hand fluttering to rest on her breast. The worst part was she didn't have a name to curse at night as she wished the "captain in room nine" a life in Hell for what he had done to her.

With a soft click, she closed the door behind her back and leaned her weary shoulders against the solidness of the

41

oak slab. If ever she should see *him* again, even in her womanly dreams, she would plan her revenge well. She would extract justice, if only in her imagination.

Chapter Three

October 25, 1784

"The name, damn you, girl."

Through the haze of pain, Calypso heard her father's demand, the anger in his voice undeniable. She opened her mouth to speak, but the twisting agony inside her womb allowed nothing more than an animalistic puling to pass her dry, swollen lips.

"My lord," begged Nannette, her cool hand brushing back limp curls from Calypso's face, "can't ye see the lass is unable to answer? Please let me give her something to ease the pain."

"Don't challenge me, old woman," her father snapped. "Her suffering means nothing to me. It is God's punishment for the sin she's committed. If she'll give me the name of the bastard who planted his seed inside her, perhaps I'll reconsider."

"I don't know . . ." Calypso managed to force out, the rest of her statement squelched by the next wave of contraction. She had wanted to say, *I don't know his name,* but her jaws locked, biting off the remainder of her sentence.

She felt herself propelled skyward, then the earth seemed to be clutched in an earthquake. She lifted her lashes and found her father's face inches from hers as he shook her roughly.

"You don't know! Dear God in Heaven, what kind of whore are you that you can't decide which man fathered the bastard child you carry?" His voice carried a desperate note.

"I'm sorry," she mouthed, having no desire to hurt her father. But would it not anger him more to think she had been bedded by a man whose name she had never known? A man whose image she had cursed each night for the last nine months.

"Damn you, girl." Lord Collingsworth tossed her back against the bedding, disgust showing in his eyes. Their gazes locked one brief moment, then another contraction took control, and Calypso's mind centered on what was happening inside her.

As if from far away, she heard Nannette pleading with her father. "My lord, let me ease her pain. Please. She suffers so." The nursemaid's voice was a near sob.

"No. More than she is injured by her misconduct. My lady too suffers for the girl's betrayal. The child my wife carries is not due for another month, yet she begins her lying-in this night, also."

Nannette crossed herself and genuflected. "Dear God, not Lady Collingsworth. She's much too weak to begin her labor so soon. Perhaps, my lord, if we could move her in here with Calypso, I could tend them both."

"I think not. I have called for the doctor, and he has sent word he will attend her."

"Doctor, my lord?" the little woman questioned. "What does he know of childbirth? 'Tis a midwife ye need, not a man."

"Silence, woman," Lord Collingsworth thundered. "You deliver the devil's spawn my daughter carries, and let me know the moment the child arrives."

"What do ye plan to do, my lord?"

" 'Tis not your place to question me."

"Ye wouldna destroy the infant. Pray say ye wouldna," Nannette persisted.

"Desist in this line of badgering. I care little what happens to the brat, but my daughter, she is a valuable commodity to me. What good is an unmarried girl with a bastard at her breast?"

"And the child?"

"Notify me of its arrival, then I will decide."

Calypso's mind swam in a sea of pain, the conversation around her coming in bits and pieces. *My baby,* she worried. *Please protect my baby from his wrath.* Her hand reached out, clutching Nannette's arm. "Don't let him harm my little one," she whispered.

"Ye needn't be worryin', lassie," the Scottish woman promised as she patted Calypso's hand. "I will see the tyke is well cared for."

A crescendo of agony sent her mind spinning back into a glazed haze, an overwhelming desire to push the new little being from her body so strong she couldn't fight it.

"That's good, lassie, push. 'Tis almost over. Push, girl, push," Nannette urged.

Calypso released her fears and followed the nursemaid's directions. Soon a thin mewing reached her ears, and her head swelled with motherly pride. *My child,* she thought as her strength deserted her and her mind went whirling down into oblivion.

Nannette padded down the long hallway leading to the mistress's bedchamber, the tiny infant tucked securely in a blanket in her arms.

"Don't worry, wee one, Nanna will take care of you. I promised your mother I would. Your grandsire wouldna hurt you." She bunched the covering about the child's face. "Surely not." Drawing the babe closer in the protection of

45

her arms, she prayed, "Dear Lord, watch over us."

Reaching the door, she shifted the bundled weight and knocked softly, then waited, breath held, for permission to enter the lady's rooms.

"Come," answered the sharp voice of the master.

The nursemaid checked the child one last time, planted a kiss on the newborn-red face, and entered, taking in the scene before her. In one corner stood a slave girl, a tiny covered bundle gripped in her thin arms—the master's issue no doubt.

"Sir," Nannette said, dipping a respectful curtsy to the baron.

Lord Collingsworth rose from his station beside his wife, his arms stretched out, the nature of his command undeniable. The little Scottish woman hesitated only a moment, then placed the wiggling, wailing babe, Calypso's child, into his embrace.

" 'Tis a beautiful bairn, is he not, my lord?" She hoped her words would soften his face.

"I care not what he looks like, only that he's alive."

"And the lady's babe," Nannette questioned. "A lad or a lass?"

"Doesn't matter," Lord Collingsworth mumbled. "Stillborn."

The nursemaid sucked in her breath with a loud catch as the master's gaze bored into her. What did he plan to do? She stepped forward protectively toward her new ward. "You can't possibly mean to . . ."

"Dare you question me, woman? I could choose a burlap sack and a stone weight for the bastard." He stepped toward her menacingly. "One word of this to anyone, especially my daughter, and all three of you will suffer the full impact of my wrath. Understood?"

"Dear God, no," she whispered and eased backward, the knuckles of her hand pressed against her mouth. Nodding, she swallowed hard, knowing he meant what he

46

threatened.

Lord Collingsworth turned, kneeling beside the prone figure of his wife. "Cathleen," he whispered, "look, my love, our child." He folded back the blanket as the wan woman opened her eyes.

"My baby," the woman sighed, one bloodless hand reaching out to caress the small cheek. "He does live, just as you promised."

Lord Collingsworth laid the tiny bundle in the crook of his wife's arm. "See, my darling, you must try. He needs you, just as we all do."

"Tristan," she whispered, placing pale lips on the child's forehead, the same spot Nannette had touched only moments before. "My son," she sighed, her eyes closing, her hand falling limply on the pillow.

"Cathleen," the lord wailed in a thin, high voice.

From a corner the doctor stepped forward, placing a hand on John Collingsworth's shoulder. "She only rests, sir. 'Tis best. You have given her a reason to try now. All we can do is wait." The elderly man circled the bed, lifting the fragile wrist of his patient between thumb and forefinger. "It would be appropriate if I bled her of the possible poisons in her system."

The baron nodded gravely in agreement.

Nannette's gaze shot from master to physician. "Oh, no, my lord, don't let him. She's lost enough blood as it is."

"Begone, woman. What know you of modern-day medicine?"

"Perhaps nothing, my lord, but taking more precious life fluids from my lady can only harm her," she pleaded. As the baron pushed her from the room, she could see the doctor removing the leeches from his satchel. "No, my lord, please reconsider."

The door slammed unceremoniously in her face. Nannette wrung her hands. What could she do? Lord Collingsworth was so distraught he was making decisions and changing people's lives as easily as autumn leaves fell from the trees back home in Scotland. God in Heaven help him, but here would be long-felt repercussions from this day of devil's work.

The silence of the room baffled Calypso as she opened her eyes. Just what she expected, she wasn't sure, but her ears strained, listening. Her hand drifted down to the swell of her belly that had become a part of her hellish existence over the months, but what she discovered brought her memory whirling up to the present. Her stomach was flat and empty.

With eyes darting about the room, she lifted onto her elbows. The silence shouldn't be there. Her baby.

"Nanna?" she called in a weak voice. "Where are you?" The emptiness of the room unnerved her, as much as the hollowness of her womb.

The little Scottish woman entered from the hallway, her hands twisting about each other in a worried motion. With trusting eyes, Calypso sought the nursemaid's gaze and an explanation of what distressed her so.

"Nanna, what is it?"

A cool hand cupped her cheek, then moved up to her brow in a familiar motherly gesture. " 'Tis nothing, child. Just rest and regain your strength."

Calypso stretched out her arm and stilled the soothing fingers. "Where's my baby?" she queried in a soft voice.

Her jade-green eyes locked with the kindly gray ones, then several heartbeats later Nannette glanced away.

"Nanna, where's my . . ."

" 'Tis the will of the Lord." The woman crossed herself and turned away. "The babe was stillborn."

"No, Nanna, I'm sure I heard it cry!" she exclaimed, rising up from the bedding. She reached out and forced the woman to face her. "I'm sure," she insisted, "my baby lived at its birth."

Nannette stroked her clutching hand. "Only your imagination, girl. The poor, wee bairn has been taken to the sexton." She took a deep breath and knelt beside the bed. "I'm sorry, Calypso, truly I am, but 'twas the will of the Lord," she repeated, "and is probably best this way."

The will of the Lord. Calypso frowned and pierced the nursemaid with a penetrating stare. She trusted Nannette more than any other person in her life. "Tell me honestly, Nannette, which lord? The one above or my father?"

The Scottish woman never flinched, but tears filled her kindly eyes. "The one above most assuredly." She tore from Calypso's grasp and hurried across the room, busying herself with straightening a curtain at the window.

Calypso's heart swelled with sorrow for the child she had never wanted from the moment of its conception—until now. Why make her suffer those long months, only to take her baby away? Her flesh and blood, born of her body. Her heart ached with the emptiness.

So much had changed as a result of that night so long ago at The King's Ransom: her childhood smothered by the skillful kisses of a stranger, her romantic daydreams shattered as he had tossed a crown at her in compensation. Her hand traveled up to the chain about her neck, the same silver coin pressing against her collarbone, a reminder of how foolish she had been to believe anyone truly cared what happened to her.

There had been no one to support her, not her father who shunned her as unfit to carry the Collingsworth name, or her mother whose frail health rendered her unable to comfort, and especially not Evan who had chuckled at her predicament as he whispered she should have kept her knees clamped as tight as her mouth.

Only Nannette had stood by her and championed her cause. Calypso watched the little woman wring her hands again. Until now, she thought again. Her baby had been alive, she had heard it cry. Whatever her father had done with the child, Nanna must know the truth.

Calypso tore her eyes from the nursemaid. There was no one now. Bitterness swelled and brimmed over her lashes. No one. Not even a baby to fill the empty void. She clutched the silver crown to her heart and felt the pulsing organ harden beneath her fist. Only herself to rely upon. She bowed her chin in resignation.

The hallway door crashed against the wall across the room. Calypso's head jerked up to find her father, his hair disheveled, his eyes crazed with grief, holding himself upright by clinging to the framework.

"You killed her," he hissed. "You and your whoring ways."

"Father?" she answered, confused by what he was implying.

From the corner of her eyes she saw Nannette slip to her knees by the window, keening as she swayed. "Dear God, not my lady. Say it's not the mistress."

The bundle he clutched to his chest began to wiggle, and a high-pitched wail issued from the blankets in response to the Scotswoman's sounds of distress.

"You and this bantling." He shook the wrapped child at her.

"My baby," she cried, trying to push her weakened body from the bed.

"No, Daughter," he taunted, crushing the protesting infant back against his chest. "My child, you mother's and mine." His eyes narrowed. "Mine to do with as I please."

"Mama?" She blinked in confusion. "But she wasn't due for weeks. What do you mean?"

"Just as I said, wench. You killed her as surely as if you'd pressed a knife into her heart. The humiliation of your transgressions was too much for her."

"Mama?" she mouthed, fear and disbelief flooding to the surface like blood into an open wound. Falling back

50

against the bed, she felt the silent tears roll down her cheeks and disappear into her hairline.

"My lord, the baby." Nannette knelt before the baron, her arms uplifted in a plea. "I can care for him like all your issue before."

Lord Collingsworth's gaze drifted down to the serving woman. "Yes, I suppose so." His eyes shot back up at Calypso, then lowered to pierce the little woman. "You'll find the child a wet nurse."

"Aye, my lord. I know of just such a woman in the village."

"But, Father, there's no need. I can—"

"You," he cut Calypso off, his finger pinning her from across the room as if she were a butterfly, "will have nothing to do with this brat. I'll not have it."

The baby released an indignant wail, and Calypso felt her breasts respond with maternal need.

He dropped the child unceremoniously into the nurse's waiting arms. "Lady Collingsworth named him before she died. Tristan."

Nannette nodded and rocked the baby to calm him. " 'Tis a lovely name, my lord."

"The child's name means nothing to me. Care for him, but keep him out of my sight."

"Father, you can't mean that."

He whirled to face Calypso. "As for you, girl. Your betrayal is as heinous as the American dogs who forced us from our home. I'll have my revenge against them and you as well. Mark my words, you'll pay dearly for the destruction you've caused."

"But, Father."

He raked her with a hard look. "As soon as you heal, I shall find a husband who can control your wanton ways, and it matters little to me how he accomplishes the feat. At least, married, you're safe from this happening again."

"Father, no," she cried, swinging her feet from the bed

51

and rising to a tottering stance.

The baron ignored her plea, disappearing from the doorway. Her spirits flagging as quickly as her strength, Calypso sank down on the bed. "I'll fight him with my last breath. I'll be so unappealing no man will want me as a wife. Not even the most odious of cads will take on a sharp-tongued shrew."

"No, child, I'll not have you speak that way," Nannette scolded. She turned and settled Tristan in the cradle.

"But, Nanna. I mean it. I have no need of more men in my life. Between, Father and Evan, and—" She bit off her words. She had nearly said that damned American in the inn.

"There's one you need and who needs you." She nodded toward the sleeping child. "Tristan. Your . . . brother. The little lad will need all the love you can give him as I fear there will be none other."

"Tristan," Calypso whispered, liking the name immediately. "He's another reason, Nanna, I can't allow Father to send me away. I must fight his desire to be rid of me. You must help me. Please."

Nannette's gaze locked with hers. "Aye, child. 'Tis the least I can be doin' for ye." She glanced down at the sleeping infant. "And for him. Together. You must stay together."

The music played against her temples like talented hands upon a drum, its simplistic rhythm setting her toe to tapping and her mind to wandering back to a time when her life had not been so complicated. *Junkanoo*, the slaves and locals called it, a unique way known only to the islanders to celebrate the Christmas holidays.

Calypso smiled, for the first time in months, as she settled herself on the ground beside a young Negro girl who offered her a platter of native fruits: coconut, dates, pineapple, and bananas. The music built to a crashing crescendo as she sampled a slice of pineapple, the sweet juice running down her chin.

Using the palm of her free hand to catch the liquids before it stained her simple blue gown, she sighed, the sound deep and unfettered. Freedom was priceless, even if it was only a few stolen moments.

Her father had departed the day before, Christmas Eve, to join friends in Nassau and celebrate the holidays. She had not been invited, but the slight didn't distress her. Nanna and Tristan had remained behind as well, and to Calypso they were everything, the center of her world.

Her little brother fascinated her. His tiny hands and feet swiped at the air with staccato movements, and his big brown eyes were heart stoppers that seemed to speak volumes to her. She thought she could never love anyone as much as the infant, not even her own child, had it survived.

Her eyes traveled northward to where the faint outline of the plantation graveyard poked its fingerlike tombstones toward the evening sky. Her baby. Her heart had shattered a thousand times because she had never seen what it looked like, never known if it was a boy or a girl. She lifted her shoulders in sadness, the corners of her mouth angling down in response. After two months her loss was still a tight knot in a corner of her heart.

"Miss Calypso," intruded the soft query of the Negro child beside her on the ground.

She glanced up, and the girl offered another platter toward her, this one holding *accara,* little patties consisting of spiced black-eyed peas and okra, a native food Calypso found surprisingly delicious.

"Thank you," she murmured, taking a big bite. She chewed for a while, watching the crowd of blacks add fuel to the large bonfire that was burning brightly. Each time the flames flared, excitement rose with them. She turned to her companion. "What now, Lizzie?" she inquired of the girl.

Lizzie's glistening black eyes found hers. "The Fire Dance," she replied, excitement illuminating her words.

The crowd formed a large circle, the fire in the center. At Lizzie's urging, Calypso rose and joined hands with her father's slaves. Those around her smiled, welcoming her in their midst more so than her own family did.

The clapping began, sporadic and soft, and soon built to a thunderous unity as the circle shuffled and swayed, moving slowly clockwise. Calypso watched the girl beside her, picked up the rhythm, and soon found herself immersed in the anticipation of what would happen next.

A couple stepped from the circle, the man tall and chocolate in complexion, the woman, sleek and lithe and almost a golden color. Their movements were precise as if composed and arranged by a dance master, their bodies weaving together and around the fire in such a way that Calypso found her breath held deep in her lungs. Her body responded with long-suppressed urges as the dancers teased each other as well as the crowd with gestures and movements that could only be interpreted as sexual.

Calypso's palm traveled upward to press against her collarbone, the rising and falling of her breath pressing her bosom against the crook of her arm, the pulse in her throat pounding beneath her fingertips.

Flashing memories of the stranger who less than a year ago had brought these same feelings gushing through her body played tricks on her mind, and soon it was the tall American captain straining his body against hers in the erotic Fire Dance. She blinked her eyes and shook her head, trying to erase the image, but his magnetic gaze bored into her, demanding she give in to the need to experience this most wanton dream.

Why did she think of the cad this way? She should despise him, and she did, she reminded herself. He had degraded her and made her life an unbearable existence. She struggled to push his image away, but instead, found him even closer, his presence creating a whirlwind in the core of her being.

"I hate you," she groaned, squeezing her eyes closed and turning her face away from the dancers glistening in the firelight. She must punish him the only way available to her, in her mind, because what chance could there be she would ever see him again in real life.

"Enjoying John Canoe?"

The sound of her brother's smirking question, a slur on the *junkanoo* festival, brought the battle in her mind to a halt.

"Evan," she whispered, whirling to face the contempt she knew she would see on his countenance. "I thought you left with Father to go to Nassau?"

"Did you, Sister dear?"

Her heart plummeted. Without a doubt in her mind she knew where this conversation was leading. Blackmail. *I can't allow him. I won't cower before my brother or any man. Never again.*

"Your affinity to lewd forms of entertainment amazes me, Callie. I thought you would have learned your lesson by now."

How dare he call her lewd. Even she had heard the wild stories of Evan's lecherous ways. She turned on him, her dander high as a hissing cat's back. "Shut up, Evan," she spat.

He blinked at her, a look of shock registering on his face. "What did you say, Calypso?"

The drums and clapping increased in volume as the dancers, she could see in the corner of her eye, bantered back and forth. "You heard me, Brother. I don't care to hear what you have to say."

His eyebrow lifted. "Perhaps you don't care, but Father might feel differently."

55

Yes, she supposed her father would believe anything Evan told him. But did she care? He had done all he could to punish her. She had nothing to lose by standing up to her brother now.

"Do your worst, Evan. Your threats to run to Father don't frighten me anymore."

Evan blustered his indignation. "I'm going to tell him I caught you down here with the slaves, doing all kinds of obscene things. I saw you, Callie, your head thrown back in abandonment, your hips moving in a most provocative way. Tell me, Sister, which of the bucks did you plan to take to your bed?"

A red haze of fury colored her mind. Her hand whipped back with all the force she could muster, and she sent it flying to eradicate the foul words her brother had flung at her.

"No," she screamed at the top of her voice as her palm connected with his cheek.

The music came to an abrupt halt, her one word and the sound of the slap still ringing in the air. Dark, frightened eyes watched her, waiting, their owners unanimous in preparing to flee at the slightest provocation.

Her gaze flew back to Evan. How could one man evoke such feelings in others? He had done it to her for years, but no more. Dropping her hand, she straightened her shoulders and began walking way. "Go to hell, Evan. No man, not you, or Father, or . . . anyone will ever tell me what to do again."

"We'll see about that, Callie," he threatened her retreating back. "Father has plans for you. He'll find a husband to master your shrewish ways, a man who will bring you to your knees."

She spun, planting one fist on her hip. "Hollow threats, Evan. So far I've run off every so-called suitor who's come around."

"Small beer," he said with a confidence that left an uneasy feeling in the pit of her stomach. "Father has big plans, little Sister. They make take a while, a long while, but you'll be sorry you didn't listen to me when you had the chance."

"I can take care of myself. Not even Father can force me to marry."

"Can't he, Callie? Don't be so sure of yourself. When the proper time comes, you'll be no more than the lowliest understrapper in the stables to him to use any way he wishes, to the success of the cause."

Calypso eyed him warily. What was he ranting about? She twisted away and raced toward the manor. To Tristan. To protect the only person who meant anything to her. To the reason she continued to fight to keep her head above the sea of hatred threatening to suck her deep into its bowels.

Chapter Four

October 25, 1790

"Oh, Callie," Tristan shrieked with delight. "For me?" His small hands held up the tan doeskin breeches, white cotton shirt, green broadcloth jacket, and vest. Within minutes, without thought of modesty, he stripped off the dark, drop-seat pantaloons he was accustomed to wearing and tossed them on the floor.

Calypso laughed, enjoying the way her little brother gave her a quick hug before pulling on the new clothes. "You're six now, Tristan, a man of considerable age," she informed him with as much seriousness as she could muster. " 'Tis time you dressed like one."

Tristan's chest puffed like a rock pigeon's in springtime, his stocking feet lifting in a march that could only be described as a strut. "I'm a man, I'm a man," he shouted with glee.

"That's not all," Calypso informed him with a chuckle. She reached behind her back and pulled out another gaily wrapped package. "Happy birthday, Tristan."

The boy tore through the wrappings and lifted up a pair of leather knee-high boots. "See, Nanna," he said in a proud voice as the little nursemaid entered the room. He squatted in the middle of the floor to draw on the new boots. "See what Callie gave me." His hands caressed the

58

new clothes as if they were made of spun-gold threads.

Nannette knelt before him, straightening his collar and slipping his vest lapels over the jacket. " 'Tis the way of gentlemen, laddie," she informed the boy, brushing back the unruly brown curls from his face. "I suppose now, ye'll be wantin' to let your hair grow so ye can tie it back like the older boys."

Tristan reached behind him, gathering his short locks in his fist. "Would be seemly, Nanna," he said so seriously Calypso couldn't help the spurt of laughter that spilled from her lips. He shot her a squelching look that, had he been older, she would have found quite intimidating.

She opened her arms, and Tristan fell into them, his laughter and quick peck on her cheek announcing he forgave her.

"Callie," he said, stepping back and lifting his shoulders. "I would like to show Father how grown I am."

Calypso angled a look of fear at Nannette, then turned uncertain eyes on her little brother. "Are you sure, Tristan? Perhaps it would be better not . . ."

"I want to, Callie. Maybe Father will find me . . ." the boy searched for the right words, "more acceptable if he sees I'm not a baby anymore."

Calypso attempted to draw his head back against her shoulder. Over the years she had learned to love the nickname "Callie," especially when Tristan used it.

"No, Callie." Tristan stiffened his spine. "A man don't hug and show he's weak. A man—"

"Who told you that, Tristan?" She grasped him by his ramrod-straight shoulders.

Confusion clouded his big brown eyes. "Evan did," he replied.

"Listen to me, Tristan. Have I ever lied to you?"

The boy shook his head, his eyes widening.

"Then believe me now. Showing affection for those you love is never wrong, and it's *very* manly."

He stared at her as if making up his mind. Then he glanced up at Nannette, seeking her opinion.

" 'Tis true, laddie. The bravest man in the world is one who isn't afraid of lettin' people see what he feels."

The smile that unsealed his lips was like sunshine after a storm. He hugged Calypso and then Nannette. "I love you. Both. Very much." He spun about and headed toward the door, the heels of his new boots clicking with a bold air. "I love Father, too. I'm not afraid to tell him."

"Tristan, wait," Calypso called.

Nannette touched her shoulder. "Let it alone, lassie. Could be for the best. Even as hard as the lord's heart has grown, who could resist such an innocent soul?"

"I pray you're right, Nanna." Her arms drifted down to lie at her sides. "But Evan. That's a different story. I think I'll just tell him what I feel about his brotherly advice."

"Callie girl, are you sure?"

"If Tristan can face Father, surely I can handle Evan." She offered Nannette a confident smile.

"Then give 'im one for me." The nursemaid swung her fisted hand level with her stomach into the empty space before her.

"I'll save that punch for emphasis if he refuses to listen." Callie's mouth lifted in confidence.

Calypso left the nursery, making a mental note to see that Tristan was given another bedroom. He was too grown-up to remain surrounded with baby things. His own room. She smiled. Yes, that would please her little brother.

Grabbing a shawl from her bedroom, she hurried down the stairs and out the back door, which was the servants' exit to the kitchen in a small, separate building behind the manor house. A gravel path led to the left where the stables, housing the dozen or so pure breeds her father prided himself on, sat among a grove of sabicu trees. She pulled her wrapper about her shoulders; the early morning chill was only slight and would dissipate within the hour. The stable was the most likely place to find Evan as he spent the majority of his mornings there.

She sped along the pathway, wanting nothing more than to confront her older brother and be done with it. For the last six years there had been an unspoken truce between brother and sister; neither got in the other's way. But the idea of Evan turning Tristan into an insensitive boor like himself was not something Calypso would tolerate. Her father ignored the boy, and so, for the most part, did Evan. What right did he have to interfere?

Her hurried steps metamorphosed into a march. Tristan would be different from the other men she knew, not calloused or arrogant or self-centered like . . .

Damn, she was thinking about *him* again. She crossed her arms over her chest, the shawl weaved about her limbs. Why didn't the image of that long-ago stranger leave her alone?

In the cool confines of the stables, Calypso blinked her eyes, adjusting to the darkness. From the rear a horse nickered a greeting as she closed the door behind her. A stableboy appeared from the loft above, picking bits of straw from his kinky hair.

"Is my brother here?" she queried, not giving the boy a chance to speak first.

He dipped his head and pointed toward a back exit. "Yes'm. In the paddock outside."

Nodding her thanks, she continued down the alley between the stalls and out one of the double doors in the rear. What she saw stopped her dead in her tracks.

Another stableboy of Tristan's size was sitting in the saddle of a Hackney pony, as Evan adjusted the stirrups to the child's legs.

Calypso brushed the hair from her eyes. "Evan," she called in a low, steady voice, "what are you doing?"

He turned, a surprised look on his face at seeing her there. "Was to have been a surprise. Do you think he'll like

61

it?"

"Who?" she asked, but in her heart she knew.

"Why, Tristan, of course. It's time the boy had his own mount."

Dumbfounded, Calypso stepped toward the dapple gray steed. "You bought this pony especially for Tristan?"

"All the way from England," he stated proudly.

"But why?" She couldn't understand his reasoning, not the Evan she had known all her life.

"For his birthday, silly. I know you couldn't have forgotten today."

"No, of course not. But—"

"No buts. Help me surprise him. I'll lead the beast to the front; you bring him out on the veranda." There was no denying the excitement in his voice.

Evan cared. At least about Tristan. Her mouth hung open at the realization. As he walked past her, he raised his hand and lifted her chin, closing her jaws with a snap.

"I'm not the ogre you think I am, you know. I love him, too. He's a good little tyke."

When had Evan changed? Not so long ago she remembered him threatening to make her life miserable if she didn't do what he said. Not so long ago? More like several years. Almost six years, in fact, since that day she had refused to bend to his will. Had this soft spot for Tristan always been there? She could not remember his ever saying anything harsh to the boy. Always, she had assumed his cold-hearted airs extended to their baby brother, as well.

She studied his back as he led the little pony down a footpath. The pony. Tristan would be thrilled. Most important in her mind was her little brother. This was his day.

"I'll go through the back and get him," she announced.

Evan twisted toward her, lifted a hand in agreement, and continued around the side of the manor.

Calypso rushed through the kitchen entrance and up the stairs to the main level of the house. By now the boy would have had ample time to confront their father.

Father. Her forward motion came to a halt. She had no desire to confront the man as he never had a nice word to say to her; he only glared from hooded eyes.

Evan would be around front on the lawn, waiting for them to appear at the veranda railing. She couldn't disappoint him. Her arms stiff at her sides, she crossed through the dining room to the small L-shaped hallway leading to her father's office. The door was firmly shut, and she hesitated, remembering that day when she had been caught hiding by her brother. Taking a deep breath, she raised her fist and knocked.

"Come," commanded her father from the other side.

She shuddered in apprehension, then squared her shoulders, preparing to face the man in the room beyond who held no love in his heart for her.

The barrier of the door that had separated them soon was to her back. The baron sat behind a mahogany writing table, poring over ledger books. There was no sign of Tristan.

"Father," Calypso began, her voice breaking from uncertainty.

His brows furled in annoyance as he glanced up at her. "Why do you disturb me, girl?"

Calypso wondered the same thing. She should have checked the rest of the house before coming in here. "I was looking for Tristan. He was coming to see you."

"Tristan? The boy?" He glanced away from her, returning to his work. "Yes, he did disrupt me earlier, babbling something about being a man. I sent him away. Told him to go tell that nanny of his."

Calypso's heart fell to the pit of her stomach. *Oh, Father, how could you be so cruel?* Without commenting, she turned about to leave the room.

"Where do you think you're going? I haven't dismissed you yet." He tapped a finger against the ledger beneath his hand. Straightening in his seat, he studied her as if he had never noticed her before. "How old are you, girl?"

Calypso stiffened. How could her father not know the answer to that question? "Twenty-four," she replied, her chin jutting out with renewed strength of mind.

The annoyed tap of a single finger evolved into a five-finger drumming. "There have been no requests for your hand in marriage." His statement rang with unkindness and disgust. The tattoo stopped. "What does one do with a spinster daughter of questionable reputation?"

The barb pricked her flesh, piercing through the thick skin she had cultivated over the years. Perhaps he should drown her in a burlap sack like an unwanted puppy. "I have no wish to marry, Father."

"No wish. What do I care what you desire. 'Tis the way of civilized society. Daughters are to be used in marriage — advantageously." His eyes narrowed. "When possible." He glanced back down at his ledgers.

Her chin notched higher. She would not be used like horseflesh, sold to the highest bidder or traded for political favors. "No man will have me."

"Perhaps none that know you . . . and your past, but there are those who wish to curry favor with me."

Suspicion lurched in her chest, the threat Evan had made that Christmas so many years ago surfacing in her mind to haunt her. Over the years she had let down her guard, feeling comfortable in her obscurity. "What do you plan to do?" Her voice shook with dread.

"Why, give you a choice, Daughter, of several, in fact. I have prospective suitors on the way here now, from England. They are either titled or rich, but, more important, they see politically as I do. Choose one, wench, or I will select one for you." He dropped his head, once more becoming absorbed in the figures on the page before him.

Calypso blinked in disbelief. She was dismissed without thought of her feelings. Pick a husband from among a group of coddled fools? She twisted away from her father's ultimatum, her fiery nature accentuated by the flame of her hair. Not likely. She would be more inclined to pluck a mate from the cauldrons of Hell.

In the hallway, she pressed her shoulders against the wall above the oak wainscoting. Dear God, what was she to do?

"Callie?"

She glanced up to find her little brother's tear-streaked face seeking comfort from her. "Oh, Tristan," she cried, kneeling down to gather him in her arms.

"Did Father send you away, too?" he asked, his small hand clutching her neck.

"It's not important. I was looking for you anyway."

"Me? Why?" His eyes shone with a new wellspring of tears. Then he clung tighter. "You're not leaving me, are you, Callie?"

Like a contagious disease, the fear in the boy's heart traveled to hers. "No, no, Tristan, never." How could he be so perceptive? "I promise I'll never leave you here alone. I wanted to show you something very special." She took his trembling hand in hers and led him toward the front entry-way.

Never, Tristan, she vowed, the love she felt for him the strongest she had ever experienced. *No one will separate us.* She forced a smile to her lips as she led him onto the veranda. *Not Father, or God in Heaven. And especially not some fawning Englishman seeking Father's favor by marrying his wayward daughter.*

Her lips curled into a determined smile. She would have these so-called suitors on the run before they had a chance to unpack their bags.

The first arrivals docked with the mail packet from Nassau two days later. The three men were young, well dressed, and no doubt of aristocratic background. One was a

65

dandy. The excess lace at his throat and cuffs made Calypso shake her head in exasperation as he brought out a snuffbox from his satin vest pocket to sprinkle some of the vile substance on a crooked finger, bringing it to his nostrils with a loud sniff. From her vantage point, high atop a bluff, she snorted in disgust at the gesture. If these popinjays were her father's idea of men, he knew her not at all. Lifting her chin, she tossed back the burnt sienna tresses that were falling in her eyes. One hadn't tangled with a tigress until challenging Calypso Collingsworth! She would have no problem dealing with these three buffoons.

Beside the mail packet sat a medium-sized merchant ship, but Calypso ignored it, explaining in her mind its presence as a trader come to load salt from her father's saltworks and of little importance.

She turned her mare's head about, satisfied she had everything under control for the moment. What concerned her was how many of these suitors had her father invited and for how long. As she galloped down the lane, she envisioned a dozen or so constantly surrounding her, vying for attention, demanding time she would much rather spend elsewhere. She, Tristan, and Nannette, they were a family of their own; she needed no one else.

The fast pace the mare set whipped her problems from her mind as she concentrated on the path before them to avoid dips and stones that might make the mare stumble. As the lane smoothed out and the stables appeared, doubts returned to nag at her consciousness. If the situation became too trying during this ordeal, she could always resort to spending her days in the saddle as far away as possible from the odious task at hand. Pick one of these men as a husband? She smiled. They would be begging her father for permission to leave the island in no time. She would be the most obnoxious, outspoken shrew the cads had ever met.

Dismounting, she tossed the reins to the stablehand,

straightened her wine-colored riding habit, and started toward the plantation house. At the back door, she paused, and on impulse, ripped out the satin ribbon holding her hair at the nape of her neck, mischief glistening in her jade-green eyes. With a downward toss of her head, she sent her red curls flying over her brow. Taking her hands, she fluffed the tresses into dishevelment, so that when she straightened, her hair stood out like Medusa's of old, appearing to be alive with serpents to present the picture of a wild-eyed Fury set loose upon the land.

Her steps rang with determination as she crossed the main-floor foyer, heading to the stairway that led to the bedrooms above.

"Calypso." Her father's sharp voice reverberated across the expanse of marble.

She turned, tossing her wild mane, knowing full well he would be accompanied by the men she had seen earlier disembarking from the ship at the docks.

"Father," she replied, attempting to look as imperious as she could as she eyed the three guests with disdain.

The trio looked at her, their mouths flopping open in shock at her unorthodox appearance.

She let loose with an uncensored laugh as she planted her fist on her hip and cocked her head. "Are these your latest victims, Father?"

The courage to glance at her father deserted her. He would punish her most severely for her actions, but the first impression these men had of her would never fade. The results would be worth the consequences.

"Calypso Collingsworth, mind your manners," the baron bellowed, grabbing her by the shoulders and shaking her. "What have you been doing to look this way?"

"Just the usual, Father. I've been down at the stables." Her insides quaked with fear as his fury bored into her.

From over her father's left shoulder, an amused voice rang out. "Is this the intended bride?" The voice chuckled.

"I believe introductions are called for, Lord Collingsworth."

Callie glanced in the direction of the front parlor to see a fourth man leaning against the doorframe, a glass of brandy held casually in one hand in front of him, the other supporting him in the doorway, a cheroot clasped between long, masculine fingers.

Her mind reeled, her ruse forgotten, as her gaze smoldered at the derision flickering in the brown eyes. She swallowed, unable to believe what she saw. Those were familiar brown eyes. It was the American captain who had occupied room nine at the inn almost seven years before. Her hand reached up to touch the familiar coin hanging around her neck. The coin this man had tossed at her in payment.

"Your Lordship," her father hissed, "I know not what's gotten into the girl; most likely a fever." He released her and whirled to face her long-ago seducer, at the same time attempting to stuff his wayward daughter behind his back and out of view.

"Your Lordship?" Calypso mused aloud, confused by the events taking place. Why, this man was nothing more than a common colonial sailor.

"Perhaps later would be a more appropriate time for introduction when my daughter is herself. She's actually a quite comely wench."

"I'm sure." The guest pushed away from the support of the doorframe, the glass of brandy rising to his lips. As he took a swallow, his gaze smirked at her. " 'Tis best to see a woman at her worst when considering marriage, in my opinion. Do you not agree, sir? Husbands see much of that state over the years. Better to be prepared."

"I couldn't agree with you more, sir," Calypso interjected. "Give me a moment, and I'll be most happy to show you my worst. But then, sir, perhaps you could give us a sampling of your best, as I do believe I must be observing you at your most unbecoming state."

The gentleman lifted his snifter in salute, one eyebrow arching in hearty enjoyment of the banter. "Your daughter, sir, is most entertaining. Please introduce us."

"Your Lordship," the baron began with a loud swallow, "my daughter, the Honorable Calypso Collingsworth." He turned to Callie, his hand swinging in the stranger's direction, the other guests forgotten. "My dear, Rhys Winghurst, the Earl of Flint." His gaze dared her to be anything but polite.

An earl? Calypso's heart skipped three beats in shock as the gentleman took her still gloved hand in his and pressed the back to his lips. "Miss Collingsworth, 'tis a pleasure to make your acquaintance."

Calypso watched his face closely. Was this the same man she had met in tavern? Without a doubt, it was. She would know that smiling face anywhere, no matter how many years had passed.

Furling her brows, she stared harder. He didn't appear to recognize her. The realization sent a shot of relief laced with anger through her veins. Damn the bastard, how could he not remember that ill-fated meeting? She jerked her fingers from his, the heat of his magnetism searing her kid-covered flesh.

"I'm sure the pleasure is all mine," she mouthed the nicety without meaning a word of it.

"I imagine if you find pleasure desirable, it could be arranged," he replied as he dipped a bow to her.

She shot him a glare, recognizing the innuendo of his words. Had he meant to be so crass? His smile suggested he did.

Rhys glanced at her father, ignoring the fury in her gaze. "I think, sir, you neglect your duties. Have you forgotten your other guests?"

Her father flustered before this almighty earl, and had the situation been different, she would have enjoyed watching him squirm to rectify the lack of civility on his part.

Introductions were made, yet she didn't catch the other gentlemen's names. There was a silent communication between her and the earl, a probing of her mind by a stranger at a first meeting, seeking answers to age-old questions. Just what kind of woman was she?

Her hand swept up, pushing at the matted tangle of curls she had created in a fit of rebellion, and for the briefest of moments what this man must think of her wedged concern in her mind.

She snapped her hand back down to her side. She didn't care what this cad's opinion of her was. Instead she concentrated on the fact that her wildest dreams had come true. There was a chance to get even, to pay this man back for all he had done to her. And the fact he didn't seem to recognize her would be to her advantage.

It was time for strategy, an occasion to plan her attack with minute detail. She dimpled sweetly up at the well-remembered face, and he responded with a cautious smile of his own, obviously leery of her suddenly subdued manner.

"Until later, Your Lordship," she offered with a dip of a curtsy.

"Of course," the earl replied, his perplexity real as he bowed stiffly from the waist.

Calypso's mind churned with a plan of revenge that shocked even her sense of fair play. Justice wasn't what was called for at this moment. The earl, if in truth that was what he was, had much restitution to make before she would consider his debt paid.

She left the gathering, knowing in her heart he was smirking behind her back. *Laugh now, Your Lordship. Soon you won't think the situation so amusing.*

Chapter Five

Rhys Winghurst eyed the swaying figure of the woman as she fled the foyer, her wild hair bouncing with each step she took. He had never met a female with such a sharp tongue. He would bet money that the Honorable Calypso Collingsworth could let loose with a string of oaths that would redden even his ears. And as for the wench being a virgin, no matter how loudly the baron proclaimed that as fact, he knew in his heart she was no innocent, blushing girl. He had seen the knowledge in her eyes as he had made underhanded suggestions to her. No woman, unless she remained in a convent, lived to twenty-four and remained lily-white.

He frowned slightly as the baron droned on, making excuses for his daughter's impetuous nature. He cared little how she acted; he was here to accomplish certain goals, and nothing would stop him. Many lives, in fact the very health of a nation, depended on the outcome of his mission. No matter how distasteful the task, he would do what he had to do, including court a waspish-tongued wench who needed a good spanking.

An uneasy feeling invaded the depths of his soul. There was something uncomfortably familiar about Calypso Collingsworth. But how could that be? He had only had contact with one female on Long Island, a serving wench he had encountered many years ago at the local tavern. That girl had had dark, smutty hair—not flame-colored curls. Yet . . .

He glanced at Lord Collingsworth, acknowledging with a nod his plea not to judge the girl on one meeting. Perhaps that tavern maid had been a by-blow of the baron's. But then all the information he had on the Collingsworths stated they had resided in the Bahamas not more than ten years. If the servant he bedded so long ago was related, she had come in the influx of immigrants.

Loyalists were a funny breed. They stuck together like a pestilent swarm; so most likely the girl he had met years before had stayed close to her sire. He would have to remain alert and watchful for signs of recognition. It was necessary no one draw a connection between his two visits.

At least, if he did run into trouble, he had his own ship anchored at the docks. He had given the ship a new name and it carried an English flag to prevent anyone from recognizing the craft and becoming suspicious. At the first sign of a problem, he could depart with a moment's notice.

From the corner of his eye he inspected his fellow "suitors." Were the three men who had arrived on the island the same time as he here for the sole purpose of courting the baron's daughter? It could be possible, but highly unlikely. Only time would tell what Collingsworth was up to, and Rhys had all the time in the world at his disposal.

"You heard me, Nanna. A potion, something to put a man to sleep for a few hours. Nothing more."

"And who would ye want to be druggin', Calypso?" Nannette frowned, planted her fists on her hips, and held her ground.

" 'Tis no concern of yours."

"Ye don't go around puttin' a jasmine concoction in a person's drink for nothin'."

"Jasmine, is that what I need?" Calypso edged forward, excitement lacing her words. The lovely, vining flowers grew profusely in the mansion's gardens.

Nannette reddened. "I'll not be givin' to ye anythin' without an explanation."

"If you don't," Calypso threatened, "I'll go down to the Obeah Man in the quarters and get something from him."

"You wouldna, lassie. 'Tis not safe for ye to fool around with bush medicine."

"Nanna," Calypso spoke with a sigh, hoping the old woman would capitulate to her desire, "I would tell you more, but I can't." She circled the nursemaid's shoulders with her arms and hugged her. "Won't you trust me to know what I'm doing? I promise no one will be hurt." *Unless you count arrogant pride.* "Please, Nanna, help me."

"Oh, Callie girl. Each time ye get in trouble, I wish I had done somethin' to keep ye from hurtin' yourself."

"Just something mild, enough to make a body sleep without waking for an hour or two."

"I shouldna give in to ye. Somehow I know I'll be makin' a mistake."

"When can you have the potion ready?"

"When do ye need it?" Nannette's lips thinned as she glanced away, unable to meet her gaze.

"This evening. By dinnertime."

The nursemaid nodded and gave Calypso one more pleading look. "I'll place a small vial on your dressin' table. Use it wisely, my dear."

Calypso's hand lay curled in her pocket, the vial safely cradled in her palm, when the baron led the group into the spacious dining room. Pleased with the way she looked, she glanced in the long mirror of the foyer as they passed it, checking to make sure the pale blue tippet remained firmly anchored in the deep décolletage of the sky-blue gown she wore.

As the partakers settled around the huge table, she slipped into the Windsor chair that one of the suitors slid out for her. She smiled her thanks, embarrassment shrouding her. She couldn't remember the man's name.

The situation worsened as the gentleman sank into the seat beside here and turned to her expectantly. What would she converse with this person about?

The earl entered, immaculately dressed in the latest London fashion: fawn breeches, exquisite yellow vest beneath an earth-tone jacket of stylish cut, his pale blue shirt sporting no lawn or frills. The only touch of lace was his jabot filling the vee of his waistcoat with a casualness that accented his hair that was dressed with a studied neglect. He paused in the doorway as if expecting to enter grandly, his eyes touching briefly on each of the room's occupants. When they reached Calypso, his mouth lifted in a derisive smile that made her hand clutch the vial of liquid in her fist.

She ignored him and turned her attention to the gentleman beside her, who seemed quite taken aback at her sudden interest in him.

"Tell me, sir, all about yourself," she asked sweetly, yet unable to resist watching Rhys Winghurst from the corner of her eye as he sat in the chair directly across the table.

"There's not much to tell," he began, leaning back in his seat as if ready to embark on a long soliloquy.

"I imagine you're right, Sir Galloway," the earl interrupted. "Don't bore the lady with the details."

Sir Galloway twisted in his place and shot his adversary a glare of distaste.

"You're looking most lovely this evening, Miss Collingsworth," Rhys continued, conjuring up a flashing smile, the angle of his lips causing a tingling reaction in Calypso that she had no power to control.

Damn him, she smoldered, *why did something so common as a smile turn her insides into jelly?* The need to avenge herself against this man grew stronger. Her fingers caressed the bottled potion in her pocket as she batted her lashes in a coy manner. "You're most kind, Your Lordship. And may I say you look as decorative as a Christmas goose."

Rhys's brow angled upward as if trying to decide if her comment was a compliment or not.

She smile bonhomously, cursing herself for her impulsive tongue. She needed him to trust her, to be willing to follow her lead. Her plan depended on his cooperation.

Servants appeared, bringing in the first course, a seafood bisque, light and creamy. Calypso concentrated on her food, dipping her spoon in the thick soup and bringing samplings to her mouth. She was relieved to find the earl's attention directed toward the meal as well.

From the head of the table her father began an earnest accounting of the trials and tribulations the many Loyalists had suffered in the American colonies. Her brother, Evan, occupying the seat at the other end of the table, added tidbits to what the baron said. Under hooded lids, Calypso took the opportunity to sneak a peek at the man across the table from her, fully expecting his attention to be centered on the conversation the same as the rest of the diners. Instead she found the arrogant earl staring back at her.

She swallowed a gasp, and flipped her gaze toward her father, her insides quivering with confusion. Was the man not interested in what her father said? Her eyes darted around the table. All the rest of the men gave the baron their earnest attention, their heads nodding in agreement with his grievances, as if they had experienced, firsthand, the same indignations at the hands of the rebels as he had.

She angled another look at the earl. This time he was watching her father, his arms crossed over his powerful chest; yet she could detect a note of amusement in the set of his mouth.

Something was wrong here. Why would a man, who almost seven years ago was no more than an American sea captain, parade himself before her father as a peer of the realm . . . unless he was up to something? Was his plan to marry the baron's daughter under false pretense and thereby to gain substantial wealth? She wouldn't put it past the arrogant cad.

No. There was more to this man than a jackdaw in peacock feathers, more than dupery to convince her father he was a worthy suitor for his daughter. She cocked her head, trying to work the puzzle out in her mind. An American masquerading as an Englishman — her eyes widened with realization. There was only one possibility. He was a spy. A rebel agent sent here . . . for what?

Her heart pounded against her chest. She would need to be cautious around Rhys Winghurst. If the Americans were watching her father, they had to feel threatened by him. The long-ago conversation she had overheard in the library became full-blown in her mind. The king's Society, the need to halt the growth of the new nation, the United States, her father's declaration he would do what he must to aid resistance. Fear snowballed in the pit of her stomach. What was her family up to?

Her heart hardened for the moment. After the way her father had treated her all these years, did she really care what happened to him? Her gaze drifted to Evan, a brother who had tormented her youth, yet they shared a common bond — Tristan. Was Evan involved? Most likely. Calypso's loyalties pulled her back and forth. Though she felt nothing but contempt for her father, family was still family; there was no getting around the fact she felt an obligation to her blood ties.

Besides the personal revenge festering deep inside her, she must find out what Rhys Winghurst planned. Her eyes begged to snatch a glimpse of the earl, but she forced them to remain staring at her father's gesturing figure.

Servants reappeared, removed the soup bowls, and replaced them with small dishes of iced seafood from shrimp to lobster artfully arranged, Calypso's favorite, but tonight her mouth was so dry she could barely swallow the few bites she managed to chew.

Only hours ago her scheme had seemed so simple: lure the earl to her bedroom, drug him, then teach him how virgin-seducing cads were treated here in the islands. But now, watching him spear chunks of lobster across the table from her, she wasn't sure if she could handle such a devious man. Her gaze trailed down the line of his throat to the broad expanse of chest and shoulders and would have traveled lower if the table hadn't blocked her view.

She jumped, her fork clattering against the china, shocked by the way she had examined him in so unladylike a manner, as if she judged him on his masculine attributes, as if she found him attractive—this deceiving bounder, this . . .

"Miss Collingsworth? Is something wrong with your food?" The richness of the timbre in the earl's voice made her choke on the bit of shrimp in her mouth.

She shot him a watery glare as she sputtered, "'Tis nothing wrong with my meal." Mortified, she couldn't dislodge the food and covered her mouth with her hand in an attempt to cough it up. Dear God, she was making an utter fool of herself.

Sir Galloway leaned toward her, the glass of water in his hand approaching her face. "Perhaps fluid would help . . ."

She shook her head. She couldn't breathe, much less take a drink. She knew she must be turning blue in the face. Maybe she should flee the room. Pushing back her chair, she attempted to rise but found the task impossible to do.

Her tear-flecked gaze traveled upward, seeking assistance. Someone drew the chair from the back of her legs, and she willingly leaned back into the arms circling her rib cage.

Help me, someone help me, she pleaded silently as she caught sight of the empty chair across the table from her. Her knees weakened, and she feared she would pass out from lack of air. *Why did this have to happen to me now?*

The warmth of an arm around her pressed shockingly against her bosom. She should protest but didn't have the strength to do so. Then what little breath remained in her lungs whooshed out as the heel of a hand rapped sharply between her shoulder blades, forcing the obstruction out of her air passage.

Sanity returned, laced with chagrin, and she closed her eyes. She couldn't be sick here in the dining room with a crowd of onlookers. She forced the food rising in her throat down the proper way. Relieved to have saved a scrap of her dignity, she dropped her head against the shoulder attached to the supporting arm around her.

Gasps slowed to easy breathing, and she lifted her lashes to find the liquid brown of her rescuer's eyes staring down at her.

"Feeling better, Miss Collingsworth?" the mouth, inches from her forehead, asked. Her savior's hand, still pressed against the swell of the side of her bosom, stroked the curve of her breast in an intimate way that sent a wave of pleasure pulsing through her chest.

Her savior? She tensed beneath the blatant caress. More like her seducer. Struggling from the earl's grasp holding her chest, she felt mortification return full force. Rhys Winghurst had been the one to rescue her. Anger rose on a wave of frustration. She wanted to spit in his face and tell him just what she thought of him.

Calm yourself, Calypso Collingsworth. This might be just the opportunity you need. She swallowed her fury and sagged back against the hardness of his chest covered by the soft vest. "Oh, sir," she began, batting her lashes and biting her tongue to keep it in line. "Perhaps a bit of fresh air is what I need."

"Fresh air?" The earl lifted a brow in skepticism, his mouth pressed intimately against her ear "Or perhaps a moment of privacy to thank me properly."

Calypso shoved into her pocket the wayward hand itching to slap his insolent face. Her fingers curled around the vial of crushed jasmine petals, which soothed her ire to calculated vengeance. Her lips split into a seductive smile. "Your Lordship is most perceptive," she huskily whispered the lie.

"Then a breath of fresh air it will be," he said loudly, taking her arm and turning to her father. "With your permission, sir."

Lord Collingsworth beamed with pleasure. "By all means Your Lordship. You have my blessing. Perhaps a stroll about the gardens would be appropriate as well."

"By your leave, sir." The earl bowed from the waist in a courtly fashion; then he straightened and placed a hand on Calypso's back, propelling her toward the door.

The stiff formality between the baron and the earl sickened her. Couldn't her father read the falseness radiating from Rhys Winghurst? She took a peek over her shoulder as she and her escort cleared the room. If he did, he didn't care. She considered telling her father about her suspicions, but the gleam in his eyes told her he would never believe any derogatory remarks she might make about the great Earl of Flint.

Perhaps she should confide in Evan. She caught a fleeting glimpse of her brother sitting down to resume his meal. No, first she would extract her own revenge, then denounce Rhys Winghurst for the deceiver he was.

She flashed a dazzling smile over her shoulder at the enemy. " 'Twas most kind of you to come to my aid, Your Lordship." The honeyed falsehood soured her mouth. She led the way to the formal gardens, taking the path leading to the beds of jasmine located by the side of the house. How appropriate to lure the earl into a flower-scented trap with the evidence all about him, at his very fingertips. Again her hand found the sleeping potion in her pocket, and she derived a source of strength from its presence.

"It was *my* pleasure I assure you, Miss Collingsworth."

Yes I imagine it was, she thought, thinking of the way his hand had intimately explored her bosom. She walked on until they reached an arbor archway dripping with jasmine. Plucking a stem dotted with the tiny white blossoms, she brought the branch to her nose and took a deep breath. "Jasmine," she sighed, closing her eyes with delight. "I do believe it's my favorite flower."

Rhys took the flora from her fingers, and with a chuckle he broke off a spray and weaved it into her coiffured hair. Her eyes still shut, she could almost believe for a moment the romantic setting was real. A handsome man courting her, the whirling perfume of jasmine capturing her senses, her heart that had never known the throb of true love pounding in anticipation of what would transpire next.

Her eyes snapped open. She was not a flighty-headed young girl, but a knowledgeable woman of twenty-four in the presence of a man of considerable talent to lure the foolish-hearted down the path of transgression. She would not succumb to his smooth charm again.

Rhys leaned so close to her his face filled her scope of vision. "I believe I will claim payment for my heroics now."

Without asking permission, he pressed his mouth down against her surprised lips, molding the protest she was about to utter into a helpless moan. This man affected her, that she couldn't deny, but she was no weak-kneed wench to melt under the arrogant kiss of a cad. Yet for the briefest of moments she wished the situation were different. Oh, how she wished she could wrap herself in virginal innocence and allow herself to be wooed.

His tongue pressed against her softening lips, demanding entrance. She acquiesced to the intimate probing, telling herself she had to make him think she was open to his advances. Then she discovered her tongue entwining with his. Panicking, she realized control of the situation was slipping from her grasp. No, she couldn't allow that to happen.

Twisting her face from his, she gulped a deep breath of jasmine-scented air. "You assume too much, sir," she insisted, pressing her fists against his lapels in an attempt to put space between them.

He reached up, grabbed her hands in his much larger ones, and pinned them in the gentlest of grips behind her back; then he pressed her body from knees to shoulders tightly against his. "I think not, sweeting. Before this night is over, I plan to assume a lot more."

She squirmed to escape his clutch as his mouth swooped down to claim hers again in a searing kiss. With one hand he clasped her wrists behind her, and with the other he cupped her backside, pressing her lower body closer to his. Even through the heavy silk of her gown she could feel the contours of his masculine body straining against the confines of his breeches.

Her goal was accomplished; he was aroused, but damn him, she no longer had the upper hand. Realizing the wiggling of her hips as she struggled to break loose from his hold served only to inflame him further, she relented, reminding herself of the importance of her plans of revenge. He must think her willing. Yet as she returned his kiss, a little voice warned her she was enjoying the encounter too much. Then her mind spun around in a whirlpool of sensations, and she forgot all else except the feel of his mouth plundering hers and the silk of his fingers as they explored the contours of her body.

At some point he released her wrists, and her arms wound like ivy vines around his neck, her fingers combing through the thick, brown hair at the nape of his neck. His hand found its way to the wide-scooped décolletage, brushing aside the piece of gauze filling the opening, exposing her breasts to his skillful caress. Her nipples peaked in response, creating a network of sparks singing through her nerves. And as he lowered his head, taking one taut button in his mouth, she gasped in intense pleasure. A sensation well remembered from seven years before.

Before? Calypso's languid resolve rose to the surface, squelching her body's traitorous response. She jerked her arms from about his neck and wedged her palms between his face and her chest. She had to escape, to catch her breath; yet she didn't want to quell his interest, just bridle it. She had too much at stake.

"I beg you, sir, not here. Someone might see us."

The earl's eyes glistened with a conqueror's exultation. "Then where, my sweeting?"

"Later this evening when all have retired, come to my rooms. I'll be waiting." She stepped back, cramming the tippet into her neckline, praying she hadn't made a fatal mistake by allowing him access to her bedroom. No, everything would be fine. The moment he arrived she would offer him the drugged wine and wait for the potion to take effect. Confident she would be perfectly safe, she smiled, undisturbed by her devious intentions, as her fingers stroked the concealed vial in her pocket.

She turned and fled the gardens, her self-assuredness pumping through her cooling veins. *You will get all you deserve, Rhys Winghurst, and then some,* she vowed forcing her heart to return to a normal pace.

Rhys took a deep, cleansing breath as the hem of Calypso's skirt vanished around the flagstone corner. Damn, that woman was a siren true to her name. He had better be careful, or he would find himself in a situation out of his control. Carnal desires could not be allowed to interfere with his plans. He wanted the Honorable Calypso Collingsworth, but on his terms and at a time of his choosing.

He shrugged off his coat, the heat of passion having left him uncomfortably warm. There was something about the wench, something his well-honed caution warned him to be wary of. She was not simply a woman seeking pleasure in the bedroom, a mere romp in the sheets; she wanted more from him. Having known too many easy women in his lifetime, he had sensed the difference the moment she had swooned in his arms in the dining room.

Did she know of his mission? Was she the one he sought, a woman? It seemed highly unlikely, but he had met with stranger situations over the last few years.

Cocking his head, he ran his fingers through his hair, perplexed by his disturbing thoughts. "Calypso Collingsworth," he whispered, plucking a branch of jasmine flowers and lifting it to his nose. "If in truth you are the enemy, I have a feeling I'm in for one hell of a fight. Tonight, my sweeting, we shall see who has the stronger will— you or me."

Chapter Six

Calypso ran the brush through her fire-kissed hair for the thousandth time, pinched her cheeks to give them a touch of color, then pushed away from the dressing table. Unsure how a woman prepared for a clandestine meeting in her bedroom with a man, she hoped everything would look natural to her quarry. There was no doubt in her mind Rhys Winghurst had spent many hours in ladies' boudoirs. For some reason the thought rankled, and she chided herself for feeling anything close to jealousy toward a man who meant nothing to her. Absolutely nothing! Except for the satisfaction of seeing him put in his place.

She took a turn about the room, straightened the lime coverlet on the canopied bed, fluffed the down-filled pillows, made sure the taper wick was properly trimmed so the light wouldn't go out unexpectedly, then pushed open the window to allow the evening breezes access to the room that had grown stuffy over the last few moments.

The sharp cackle of a wild parrot drifted through the casement accompanied by the sweet smell of jasmine mixed with other tropical scents. Calypso took a deep, cleansing breath to clear her head.

The wine. Her eyes darted to the low table by the settee where a tray with a decanter and two glasses sat ready to set her plan in action. The vial of crushed jasmine petals with which Nanna had supplied her still rested in her pocket.

As a last-minute thought, she bent over the window ledge and plucked a fresh branch of jasmine from the lattice on the exterior of the mansion and crossed to the sofa. *The earl should be here any moment,* she thought, glancing at the clock on her dressing table. In minutes it would be midnight, and the house had been quiet for an hour.

Carefully she poured the wine, slipped the potion from her dressing gown pocket and dribbled some of its contents into one glass. Nannette had warned her earlier that evening to use caution, as it wouldn't take much of the concoction to put a man asleep. She hesitated, the vial suspended over the glass. Better too much than not enough. She dumped the contents into the pale pink liquid.

She stepped back. Now to remember which glass was which. Stripping one of the starlike flowers from the branch in her hand, she dropped it into the drink meant for her victim. Pleased with the results, she smiled.

Recrossing the room, she knelt before the nightstand and opened the door of the small cabinet where the chamber pot usually resided. In its place was a pitcher of molasses, the only thing sticky she could find in the kitchen. She grinned. The dark syrup would serve her purpose well.

She glanced nervously at the clock again. Ten after midnight. Damn! Where was Rhys Winghurst? Perhaps he had changed his mind. No. He would be here, she had no doubt. She couldn't imagine him passing up the opportunity to spend an evening with a willing woman.

Standing up, she dried her sweaty palm on the pale green silk of the negligee she wore, one of her mother's she had found in a trunk in the mistress's deserted rooms at the other end of the hall. The sheerness of the nightgown once the wrapper was removed appalled her as the rose of her nipples and the duskiness between her thighs were highlighted by the thin gauze; yet she supposed a man would find it most titillating. She had no intention of taking the wrap off. Her costume was only another ploy to make the scene seem authentic when Rhys entered the trap she had so painstakingly set.

A soft knock sounded, and she jumped, not sure if she was ready to face the coming events. As she crossed the room, she slowed her steps. Let him wait a few minutes. Stopping at the dressing table, she stooped, and grabbing up the branch of blossoms, she worked it into her hair. Rhys had liked it that way earlier. Hopefully he would find it appealing now.

At the door, she checked the lay of her bodice, decided to open the neckline a little more; then realizing she didn't want him to jump on her the moment he entered, she worked the vee closed to a more modest plunge.

As ready as she would ever be, she eased the door open. The moment the latch was released, she found the barrier taken from her control as Rhys's large hand pushed it out of his way. Draped in the doorway, his jacket, vest, and jabot removed and his shirt unbuttoned at the throat, he looked quite comfortable with the situation. His easy manner set her on edge. Why couldn't he appear more humble and appreciative of her hospitality? She swallowed hard. Why did she find his masculinity so unnerving?

"Your Lordship," she rasped, desperately wishing she could slam the door in his face to escape the way his eyes stripped the dressing gown from her body.

"Rhys," he corrected. "I don't think 'Your Lordship' is appropriate at this time, sweeting. You're not a serving girl sating the needs of the master, you know."

Calypso startled at his comment. The cad really didn't recognize her, or he would never have made such a statement. Or would he? Perhaps he found her past humiliation a source of amusement.

"Won't you come in, Rhys," she offered, stepping back

from the door, her eyes narrowing with suspicion.

Rhys strolled into the room as if he knew it intimately. Reaching the middle, he pivoted, his gaze again devouring her as if she were a plate of succulent prime rib, and waited for her to make the next move.

"Wine," she offered, covering up the abject fear turning her insides into mush. She tripped toward the settee, attempting to cut him off before he reached the waiting glasses ahead of her. She didn't make it.

Taking the two glasses, Rhys studied them, his eyebrow shooting up as he spied the blossom floating in the drink meant for him. "Is there something special about this one?"

Calypso wished the floor would open up and swallow her. If he figured out she was trying to drug him, she had no idea what his reaction would be. What should she do? If he suspected she had tampered with a glass, then he would automatically want whichever one she showed a preference for.

She smiled, hoping she looked at ease. "Of course not, silly. I would have put a flower in the other one if you hadn't arrived at that moment." She reached for the glass with the flower in it.

"Then all means continue." He pressed the unadorned stemware into her waiting hand.

Calypso sighed with silent relief. Praying her hand didn't shake, she reached up and pinched a flower from the branch intertwined in her hair and dropped it into her wine.

"To a most interesting evening," Rhys toasted, raising his glass and tapping hers.

"To the evening," she echoed, watching over the rim as she took a drink to see if he did the same.

He took a long swallow, that ever-active brow of his lifting again. "Very sweet and spicy."

"We like our wine that way in the islands." She prayed he

believed her.

With a decisive look she instantly understood, he bent to place his glass back on the table. Not yet. She wanted him to drink all of the potion.

"My turn," she began, lifting her glass in a salute.

He paused and straightened, waiting for her to speak.

"To . . . to . . .." Dear God, what was she going to say? Something to keep his interest. "To love," she blurted.

Rhys broke out in amused laughter. "To love? I don't think so, sweeting. To *making* love, I'll agree to."

What an insensitive cad, she fumed. She smiled, dipped her glass in acquiescence. *To revenge,* she vowed inwardly as she dashed the remainder of her drink down her throat. The earl followed suit, draining the last of his as well.

Now it was only a matter of time. But how long? She had forgotten to ask.

Placing his empty glass on the table, he reached out and removed the one from her hand. His intent was plain on his face as he drew her into the circle of his arms, his mouth capturing her earlobe when she turned her face from his.

What if the concoction took an hour to take effect? She would never be able to hold him off for that length of time.

Nibbling her ear, he whispered, "You stir me, woman, in a most unusual way. Be wary though. I have no intention of falling prey to your bewitching spells."

Her knees buckled with the warmth of his breath. If the drug didn't work soon, she would find herself not caring if it ever did. To keep from falling on the floor, she circled his neck with her arms.

Abandoning her ear, his mouth worked a path down the column of her neck, the silk of her dressing gown parting willingly as he pushed it aside. Not sure how it had happened so quickly, she knew she was lost in the passion he kindled in her body as he drew one aching nipple into his mouth, his tongue circling, caressing, molding the nodule to please himself. And her. The enjoyment racing through every nerve in her body couldn't be denied.

With one swift motion, he scooped her up into his arms and angled toward the bed. She was lost, revenge trampled beneath desire, as she nuzzled into his chest, her fingers slipping beneath his shirt to coil in the fur of his chest.

Rhys chuckled, his strides lengthening; then he paused, swayed, and Calypso's feet brushed the carpeting as he released her legs from an unsure arm. A muscle twitched in his chest beneath her palm. He glanced down, a look of amazement flicking in his eyes as his knees buckled, and she found herself supporting his massive weight.

"Rhys," she hissed, "you can't pass out like this. Help me get you to the bed."

Working an unsteady hand up her spine, he grabbed a fistful of her unbound hair, tugging her head back until they stood eye to eye. "You bitch," he rasped.

His clutch loosened, and he slumped against her, nearly throwing them both to the floor. Forcing her trembling arms to remain steady, she shoved him as hard as she could, and he fell backward on the waiting bed, oblivious to his surroundings, exactly as she had planned the evening to happen. Precisely, except she hadn't meant to succumb to the magnetism of his virile charm.

She glanced down at his face, relaxed in vulnerable repose, and wiped her mouth with the back of her hand in an attempt to eradicate the lingering taste of his lips on hers. She felt nothing for this arrogant man but spite and a need to teach him how it felt to have a mockery made out of one's life. Reaching down, she unbuttoned the front of his shirt, stopping only for a moment to appreciate the way his flat stomach hollowed at the base of his rib cage rising and falling with each shallow breath he took.

Forcing her brain to concentrate on the task at hand, she shoved the blue cambric from his shoulders and loosened the shirt's cuffs. Hiking up her skirt, she crawled onto the bed in order to manipulate his body at the best angles as she stripped the garment from his torso. By that time she had worked up a most unladylike sweat.

How could a man weigh so much? With an unconscious motion, she dabbed at her damp brow with his clothing. Jerking her hand down, she shook out the garment she had crumpled into a ball, but the once-crisp shirt was wrinkled beyond hope.

Illogical guilt sent her flying across the room to drape the garment over the back of a chair. She frowned at her action. Now, what had made her do something so silly? Her lips pressed tightly together. Misplaced priorities. Rhys Winghurst would care less about the state of his clothing once she was through with him.

Skirting the bed, she worked her way over to the nightstand, bent to open the small cabinet, and removed the pitcher of molasses and two short coils of rope. Beginning with his left wrist she secured his hands to the bedposts, then stepped back to admire her handiwork. The mighty Earl of Flint was trussed up like the Christmas goose she had compared him with earlier that evening. Staked out like weaver's wool ready to be carded and spun. Best of all, he was at her mercy. No matter what she did to him, he couldn't do anything to stop her. She smiled, her lips curving in impish delight.

Returning to the other side, she dragged one of the winged armchairs to the edge of the bed. There she settled, kicking off her slippers to wait, the pitcher of molasses resting in her lap, one of the down pillows from the bed under her arm. Rhys Winghurst would experience the humiliation of being tarred and feathered, well syruped and downed, just as her father had been so long ago. But she wanted him awake and aware so she could tell him precisely what kind of bastard he was.

* * *

Rhys's drugged mind lumbered to the surface like a bear emerging from hibernation. The first thing he became aware of was the smell of jasmine. The second, the cramp in his left shoulder that he was helpless to do anything about. For some crazy reason he couldn't move his arm. Moments before he forced his eyelids open, he heard the soft sound of someone breathing, easy and rhythmic as if asleep. Why did he have trouble recalling where he was?

His eyes fluttered open, his focus weaving in and out with maddening slowness until, at last, he discovered the woman curled in the wing chair, her flame-colored hair draped over a pillow-cushioned arm.

Then memory rushed in. Calypso Collingsworth. She had drugged him. Lured him into her black widow's web and slipped some unknown potion into his wine. Little brazen-faced tease. He should have been more cautious. Muscles tight with rage, the forgotten cramp twisted in his shoulder with sharp, shooting pains.

"Damn," he hissed in the dark when his arm refused to move. In fact, neither of his arms was mobile. He tugged and could feel the hemp about his wrists tighten. The bitch had tied him to the bed.

For one wild moment, the helplessness of his situation threatened to take control. The urge to struggle within his bonds almost overwhelmed him, but, taking a deep breath, he forced the unwise reaction down. He shot another look at the sleeping woman, his captor, slim and petite, yet she had managed to snare him. An odd sense of admiration took him by surprise. She had accomplished what no one before her ever had. Rhys Winghurst had been no man's prisoner, much less a woman's.

Confusion whirled in his brain. What did she have planned in that devious mind encased by such a lovely body? Somehow he sensed she had no intention of harming him, at least not physically. If she had wanted to murder him, she could have easily slit his throat while he slept.

He had no doubt he was in for a most unusual evening.

Tugging gently, he tested the knots holding him bound to the bedposts. Damn, but the wench had done a decent job. He angled his body until the fingers of his right hand could pick at the half hitches she'd woven in the rope. Given enough time, he could get loose.

Calypso sighed and shifted uncomfortably on her perch. Rhys snapped ramrod straight, closing his eyes in order to appear asleep. Perhaps he could use surprise to his advantage. He heard her rise and bend over him, her warm, sweet breath whooshing out to tickle his cheek as she leaned close. He nearly jumped from his bared skin as her small hand skimmed over his chest looking for a response. His nipples peaked and his groin tightened; he was helpless to stop the reaction to the most intimate of touch.

"You're awake," she announced. Apprehension rang in her voice, as if she was unsure of her plan of action.

He opened his lashes and met with the jade of her gaze. "If you fancy bondage so much, sweeting, you should have told me. I'm sure we could have worked something out without all this trouble." His words smacked with sarcasm. "I'm willing to try anything once, especially with such a lovely accomplice."

Her eyes narrowed in anger, a deep-seated rage instilled by more than his taunting words. What had he done to this woman that would cause her to go to the extent of making him a prisoner in her chambers?

He cocked his head, studying her. In the waning candle-light her illustrious hair lost its flame. The serving wench in the tavern those many years ago—could she possibly be the same girl? But why would a tavern whore masquerade as a rich planter's daughter? What was John Collingsworth up to? This entire affair made no sense to him. He angled ever so slightly until his fingers again reached the rope he had worked to release earlier. If he were careful, she would never notice the movement in the night-clad shadows.

"Now what, wench?" he demanded, his voice devoid of any pretenses.

"Why, sir," she answered, a sweet smile curving her lips, yet the innocence never overrode the vengeful spite in her eyes. " 'Tis time I gave you what I promised—payment for all you've done." She lifted the porcelain pitcher she had clutched in her lap and held it over his unprotected chest.

He twisted, unsure what would emerge from the tilted lip, but his struggle did no good. Like an artist squeezing paint onto a palette, she drew a circle on his chest with dark, sticky molasses.

"Damn it, woman. What in the hell do you think you're doing?"

Then she etched spirals in the middle of the arc, her tongue flicking out to moisten her lips in unconscious pleasure. There was no point in trying to avoid her childlike designs, so he steeled himself and concentrated on working loose the knots binding his right wrist. The first hitch released, but there were at least a half-dozen more.

The pitcher moved upward, molasses coating his neck, and as he turned his face to the side, Calypso giggled when the syrup blobbed on one of his cheeks. Feeling no better than a stack of pancakes, he ground his teeth as the stickiness oozed over his nose and into his hairline. The wench would pay for the humiliation she was heaping on him— pay, then pray for mercy. Rhys clamped his jaw tight as the sweetener trickled across his forehead.

Then the torture ceased. He stretched his neck to observe the madwoman from the corner of his eye as she took up the bed pillow from where she had dropped it on her seat of vigilance and ripped the sacking open. Duck down puffed out with the force of her movement, and he watched as one tiny feather weaved a path downward over his head to come to a final rest in the sticky molasses on his cheek.

His eyes widened in unsuppressed irritation as he fathomed what she was doing. The lump of feathers hit him square in the chest, then spewed like puffball spores about the room. She had made a fool of him with her childish antics. He had had enough, he vowed as he spit down from his mouth with a growl.

Like a little girl suddenly aware she had pressed authority too far, Calypso edged backward, her eyes darting about the room as if seeking a place to hide. Then she straightened, and her jaws tightened with resolution as she stepped forward, scooping up the candlestick from the nearby table.

"That, Your Lordship, is how we treat scoundrels like you." She lifted the taper high in order to see him more clearly. "Perhaps you don't remember seven years ago, the way you degraded me at the Collingsville inn, but I could never forget." She reached across him to a side table and picked up an object.

"You offered payment for my services, then. A silver crown." She tossed a chain with a coin dangling from it into the sticky mess on his chest. "You've entertained me well this evening. I feel it's only right to compensate you in return."

"Damn you, woman. I remember you well. You're as insane as I thought even then all those years ago." She was the same girl, but he had never insulted her. He had paid for a woman, and she had come willingly to his room that night. "Your little ruse with the warming pan never fooled me. What did you expect to do for a whore's wages?"

As if he had opened the gates of Hell and released the ancient Furies, she leaped on him, the candlestick tipping and pouring hot wax along his right shoulder and into the soft fold in front of his elbow. His arm jerked from the pain; the final knot binding his wrist released, freeing his hand.

The struggle couldn't have been worse if he had fought with an enraged hellcat; her fists, claws, and feet seemed

94

innumerable as he worked to subdue her beneath him. She sank her sharp teeth into his bound arm; yet he refused to hit her, though he seriously reconsidered when he pinned her wrists above her head and she spit at him, all her other forms of weaponry tamed beneath his superior strength.

"Let me go," she seethed, bucking against the crush of his body pressing her deep in the mattress beneath their collective weight.

"Why should I?" he taunted, the feel of her naked breasts exposed during the tussle accentuated by the molasses coating his chest. Sparks of desire ricocheted through his entire body. Between their stomachs pressed the silver crown, the payment that had passed between them. "I once paid for services well rendered. 'Tis my turn to service you."

His lips pressed down against her open lips, his intent to be brutal and punishing. But the moment his tongue slipped into the softness of her mouth, his anger melted into a strange need to please.

Seven years ago, he had callously taken her virginity, he had no doubt of that fact, though he had rationalized the obvious as whore's trickery at the time. She had been young, scared, and out of her element, and he had never stopped to consider her feelings. He had used her to escape his own troubling thoughts. He supposed he had deserved the tar and feathering she had given him.

"Calypso," he whispered, brushing his mouth against her ear. " 'Twas never my intent to hurt you. I don't want to harm you now." He kissed one of her eyes closed, then the other, nuzzled her chin, and moved lower to capture her pliant bottom lip between his teeth, tugging gently.

Something about this woman fascinated him, but most beautiful women did. What was it about her that piqued his interest beyond the usual? Her spunk, her drive, her fearless attempt to best him? Perhaps all those things wrapped in a vulnerability that was almost invisible unless one looked for it.

The warmth of her body spoke to him with an unpolished response. There had not been many men in her life; in fact he doubted there had been any other than himself. He could feel the undirected desire in the curve of her lips as she returned his kiss, in the touch of her hand as her fingers combed through his hair. She knew the ultimate outcome of their actions, but had no concept of all the wonderful things that could occur before. He would teach her and relish each moment of her awakening.

"Calypso," he whispered again, this time between the curve of her breasts, the sweetness of molasses mingling with the more luscious taste of womanly skin. The tiny pearls buttoning the wrapper she wore had long since been ripped from the satin during their struggle; the sheer negligee beneath hid nothing from his gaze—the gentle curve of her waist, the flare of her hip, the teasing glimpse of the dark, feminine triangle between her thighs—but only served to titillate his imagination.

Shifting his weight, intent on removing the thin layer of gauze covering her body, he found his left wrist still strapped to the bedpost. With a frustrated sigh, he released the grip on her hands to unbind himself.

Too late he cursed his unwise action. Would she spring to life and attempt to escape? He gazed into the passion-sheened jade of her eyes and found only desire mirrored there. Subdued, she was his to do with as he pleased.

At last free, his left wrist red and raw where the hemp had scraped his skin, he lowered his hand to inspect the wound in the flickering light of the candle he had managed to keep upright during their struggle and return to the side table.

Her small hands moved up, gathering his fist into their protective curl as she brought his wrist down to eye level to inspect the injury.

"I'm sorry," she began, "I never intended to hurt you,

either."

"My flesh will heal. I'm not so sure about my pride."

"Your arrogance was my victim, and I daresay it needed knocking down a notch or two." Her eyes lifted, challenging his with sparkling defiance.

"And what of yours, wench?" He rolled, pinning her beneath him.

Calypso's chin inched upward. "I have no problem seeing myself for what I am."

"Is that so? So tell me, sweeting, just what kind of woman are you?"

"I am simply determined to survive in a world meant only to serve the whims and amusements of men."

"Are you telling me you seek not your own gratification?" He shook his head with mock sorrow. "I sense you know little of how pleasurable it can be between a man and a woman—for both."

Her proud little chin jutted higher. "I know how it is," she answered with a twinge of distaste.

"No, I don't believe you do, but I'm willing to show you."

"Your arrogance is as offensive as ever." Her fists curled and pushed against his naked chest, her hand sticking to the syrup mixed in the pelt of hair. "I don't need you to teach me anything."

He captured her wrists and pinned them to the bed, her arms outstretched. "Then let's say I'm giving back what I got, a lesson in humiliation. Only I think you'll find my instruction to your liking."

"Never," she hurled at him.

He molded her unyielding lips into pliant receptacles with a kiss, deep and demanding. Like an ebb tide he felt her resistance receding as the seconds ticked by, washed away by waves of passion. Still holding her arms out wide, he lifted his weight to his knees, straddling her thighs. Her head thrown back, her breasts shivering with each ragged breath she took, she glistened with Olympian pride in her surrender. Sweet deity, he had wanted no woman as much as he desired this one. At the moment he cared little whether or not she was the enemy he had come so far to locate.

"Never," Calypso moaned, the cloying smell of molasses seasoned with the more erotic scent of virile male assaulting her senses. Like a gentle spring wind, his warm breath caressed her skin; then his mouth imprisoned one peaked breast, sucking, tugging at the ignited nerve endings signaling a network of showering sparks throughout her bewildered body.

Why did this man affect her so? His arrogance was undeniable, and she knew him to be a liar and a cheat, yet she sensed there was unshakable benevolence in him, an understanding for those who were weaker, less fortunate than he—a trait she had never seen in a man, not her father or her brother. A man capable of giving devotion and receiving it in return, he could supply her with what she needed most, unconditional love, without buckling to the winds of nature seeking to destroy even the strongest of fortresses. He truly embodied the man of her dreams if only she could find the key to release him.

"Never," she repeated, the denial no more than a whisper ruffling the soft, brown hair of his head inches from her mouth.

His imprisoning grip on her wrists relaxed, and his fingers blazed a trail of liquid fire down the insides of her arms, eradicating the last of her resistance. She didn't care who he was, or what he was, only that he offered escape from the misery in her life. And though she probably would regret her action later, she turned eager attention to his tutelage as he eased the ruined clothing from her body.

Remembering how it had been the first time they had

been together, she moved her fingers down to the waistband on his breeches, seeking to fathom the puzzle of unfamiliar fasteners holding them snugly to his hips.

"Worry not, sweet siren. All in good time," he assured her, taking her hand, sticky with molasses, and leading it to his mouth. Then he sucked each finger clean with a slow, calculated up-and-down motion that drove her wild with want.

Her hand dropped like molten liquid onto the coverlet, and she waited in breath-held anticipation for his next move.

"All in good time," he reconfirmed, his promise like searing tongues of fire against the arc of her ribs as he tasted each ridge and dip of her heart's cage.

Each place his chest touched her, a vestige of molasses lingered, and he lapped at the sweetness until no traces remained, only to move lower and repeat the process with a maddening slowness that left her whimpering for more.

As much as she hated to admit it, even to herself, she found his gentle instructions anything but humiliating; in fact, it was almost as if he worshiped her with each demanding caress he lavished upon her. And she obeyed his command, opening her soul and body to his exploration.

At first, it was as if she floated high above the bed, observing what he did, his dancing fingers, his fondling mouth, amazed at the way she writhed beneath him in response. But at some point he drew her down, until she participated, her senses alive and probing every aspect of his being, his manly smell, the soft sounds of lovemaking wafting about her, his moans of delight as he discovered each uncharted crag and crevice of her body.

He looked up, their eyes meeting over the swell of her stomach, and she read her destiny in his gaze. This was not a mere chance encounter, but a beginning of a lifelong path they would struggle to traverse together. As if he sensed the truth as well, his liquid brown eyes fogged with startled disbelief, his caresses stilling; yet his heart pounded a barrage where he lay against the softness of her inner thigh.

"Rhys, I . . ."

"No," he rasped, "don't say anything." He returned to his lovemaking with a zeal that snatched away her breath as well as her power to reason and tossed them to the jasmine-scented air. There was nothing now, but the electricity sizzling from his hands and mouth as he took her to a plane of sensations she had never known existed. There he left her bobbing helplessly as a bit of debris in a gale of emotion, breathless and floundering for release.

His mouth covered hers, the taste of molasses tingeing his tongue. His full length, naked and warm, pressed against her womanly curves, his hips cradled against hers, his manhood seeking the contours of her femininity with a gentle rocking. She welcomed him, her heart swelling with joy, knowing the completion of what she sought rested in this man who could control her body and mind with his masterful touch.

His hips set a pace she easily matched, each coming together, taking her to a higher pinnacle of wonderment, leaving her to anticipate the next rise. She ached to cry out to him, to plead for him to hurry, yet something stopped her, perhaps his look of denial she had witnessed at that naked moment when their eyes had met in mutual understanding.

Like the quaking of the earth at nature's moment of release, waves of fulfillment shuddered through her one after another until she lay spent and sated, in awe of what had taken place inside her.

Her eyes snapped open. What had happened to her? Above her the man she had labeled the enemy for so long trembled in the aftermath of sexual culmination. What she had felt, he had experienced as well; yet she knew in her heart it had been different for him. "A lesson in humiliation," he had told her only moments before. He had exploited her again, as he had seven years ago, and had used his well-honed skills to make her enjoy her degradation.

He was the enemy, and she was a milksop fool to have fallen so easily under his spell.

Her hands, still tingling with climactic afterglow, fisted and wedged their way between their symphonious hearts. "You cad, you seducer. Get off me."

"What's wrong, sweeting? You seemed to enjoy yourself well enough."

She wiggled out from beneath him, grabbing the remnants of her nightgown to cover her nudity. Molasses coated the clothing and the bed sheets, even the remaining pillow. Feathers drifted about the room, dusted the floor, a few even sticking to both Rhys and her. She had set out to punish him, and he had managed to turn the situation into a frolic to sate his male ego. She was the loser as he had gotten what he had come for, a night of entertainment. To judge from the shambles of her bedroom, it had been a most unusual sport.

"Get out of here," she demanded, her back pressed like a cornered feline against the headboard, her knees, on which she balanced, spread to keep her distance from the man sprawled on her bed in unabashed apathy at her attempt to avoid his touch.

He laughed, pushed up on his elbows, and with the flair she had come to associate with the arrogant Earl of Flint, he placed a kiss on each of her knees, his hair brushing against her inner thighs. Rising from the bed, he scooped up the silver crown, chain and all, which swung like a pendulum from his hand as he lifted her chin with a forefinger and thumb, unconcerned about his state of undress.

" 'Tis nothing worse than a sated woman with a vengeance." His brow lifted in mock distress as he turned to retrieve his breeches.

"Damn you, Rhys Winghurst," she cursed, closing her eyes to rid her mind of the vision of his muscled body.

101

"This business isn't finished between us."

He turned, buttoning up his pants, his gaze skipping over her nudity insufficiently covered by the bunched negligee. "Is that an invitation to visit you again, perhaps tomorrow night?" He bent, picked up the shirt she had draped over the back of the chair, giving it a disgruntled inspection. "Next time, I'll bring the wine."

"There won't be a next time. In fact, by tomorrow you'll find your disguise exposed. My father would be most interested in hearing about your past as an American sea captain."

His hands stilled on the third fastener of his shirt, his mouth quirking in disbelief. "You plan on informing him about our little meeting seven years ago?"

"I'll tell him whatever it takes to see you arrested as a spy. I find the thought of watching your execution as the hangman squeezes the life out of you most titillating."

He returned to the nonchalant buttoning of his shirt. "Yes, I suppose you would find that most stimulating. Then, perhaps, madam"—he bowed from the waist—"I should leave you to your schemes."

Straightening, he crossed the room in easy strides, then turned back to face her. "Until tomorrow. I think the day will prove most amusing." The door closed softly behind him.

Calypso blinked, still sitting in the middle of the disaster she called her bed, unable to believe the easy way he had accepted her threats. Did he think she joked about turning him in? Did he put such value on his prowess in the bedroom that he thought she would never inform her father he was an American spy? He had never denied the accusation, not once to her. In fact, he never said anything to her except to humiliate her.

Mortification burned like scalding tea at the back of her throat. He would not be smirking tomorrow when the governor's troops showed up to march him away. Before the week was out, the drums would roll as Rhys Winghurst was led to the gallows at Fort Charlotte. She doubted his arrogance would last long as they slipped the noose about his aristocratic neck. And maybe, if he begged her before the bloodthirsty crowd, she might recant her accusations. Yes, that would salve her injured pride — him pleading on his knees for her forgiveness. And an apology, a public confession for the way he had treated her, might gain him release.

No, on second thought, she would rather see him hang.

Chapter Seven

The sun peeked over the horizon, its warm, tropical rays illuminating the lone rider on the road from Collingsville. The long night had taken its toll on Rhys, but as he sped his way back to the Collingsworth plantation, satisfaction lifted the corners of his mouth. Calypso was in for a rude awakening this morning, and he hurried to return in order to set his plan in motion.

After leaving Calypso's room, he had gone to the stables, saddled a mount, and journeyed into the village to visit The King's Ransom. Enough money had bought him the responses he needed from the innkeeper and his serving wench to snare the baron's daughter in her own trap.

A twinge of regret nagged at him, but he had had no choice in his solution to the situation. Her threats to expose him as a spy had jolted him into action. Too much depended on his identity remaining hidden. She couldn't be allowed to carry through with her plans.

Only too well he knew what would happen if he were caught. Although the war was at an official end, he had no doubt his demise would be swift and brutal should the king's authorities discover his intent. He remembered well watching Nathan Hale's last moments on the gallows. In helpless frustration he had witnessed his friend's courageous ending, unable to stop the execution at direct orders from his superiors.

"Damn it, Nate," he mumbled as he uncinched the saddle from the gelding's heaving sides. "This one's for you. The little Loyalist minx can learn a lesson about deception in a British prison. They'll never hang her, not a woman."

Leading the mount into a stall, he allowed the sleepy-eyed stableboy to take over the animal's care. It mattered little who knew he had been out for an early morning ride; by this afternoon the entire island would know of Calypso Collingsworth's arrest as an American spy.

"Hurry, Nanna," Calypso pressed, her hands reaching behind her back in an attempt to aid the little Scotswoman in lacing her corset.

"What's your rush, lassie? Even the beasties have barely stirred this morning."

"I must speak with Father, right away, before . . ." Before what? Before Rhys Winghurst had a chance to escape? No, that wasn't what spurred her into action so early this morning. The man who had left her room last night had seemed unconcerned about her threat to turn him in. Uneasy about why, she knew it was important to reach her father as soon as possible. "Never mind, Nanna, just finish up as quickly as you can. I'm sure Tristan will be looking for you by now."

"Ach, that laddie can rise early, but this morning you beat him by an hour." She tied the final knotting, issuing a little grunt of satisfaction as she stepped back.

Calypso whirled, grabbed up her rust-colored gown, and slipped into it, allowing the nursemaid to button it up the back. Then she turned, stuffing a tippet into the low neckline, trying to hurry as fast as she could.

"Here, child," Nannette cautioned, "if you want to look your best, you'd better let me do this right." With expert fingers she lined the gaping neckline with the bit of gauze, straightening the edges as she went. She glanced up into Calypso's anxious eyes, her fingers stilling. "What is it, lass? Are you in trouble again?"

"No, Nanna, of course not." Perhaps her father would be angry to find out she had been to The King's Ransom so long ago, but the revelation about Rhys Winghurst would override his ire. She swallowed and reconsidered her course of action. Maybe it would be best to say nothing. No. It was her duty to reveal what she knew about the Earl of Flint. If in truth that was who he was.

She fled from the room and Nannette's insistent stare and hurried down the stairway toward her father's office. Though it was early, she knew without a doubt she would find him there as he spent most of his time closeted with his accounting books since the chenille bugs had destroyed most of the cotton crop two seasons back. If it hadn't been for the saltworks, chances were the plantation would have gone under like so many of the others, but her father hung on, fighting the hairy, little pests and refusing to give up.

She heard the scratching of his quill as she knocked on the door.

"Whoever is there, come back later," her father commanded.

She chewed her bottom lip. Later might be too late. "Father, it's important I talk with you right away."

A mumble of voices reached her ears. Someone was with the baron. She swallowed the lump in her throat. Perhaps she should have left as he had ordered.

The door was jerked from her hands. Evan faced her, a look of puzzlement twisting his features. "I hope you have a good explanation, little Sister," he hissed as he grabbed her arm and led her into the room.

Her father's glare sent a chill racing down her spine, the ominous feeling that she was on trial followed in its cold tracks. Her brother released her arm, and she rushed forward to grasp the chair on which the baron sat, her words gushing forward. "I must speak with you right away, Father. 'Tis very important. The Earl of Flint, Rhys Winghurst—"

"Most interesting, girl, you should mention the earl." He glanced up and angled a look at the other side of the room.

Calypso followed his stare and gasped. Impeccably dressed, Rhys stood by the fireplace, one foot propped on the hearth stones. Was this the same man who had come to her room the night before and taught her the ways of love? The cold-eyed stare he gave her suggested an aloofness belonging to a stranger.

Her gaze shot back to her father and brother. What had the cad said to make her family glare at her so? "Father, you mustn't listen to him. He's a spy. An American spy."

"How odd, little Sister, that's exactly what he said about you."

"Quiet, Evan," her father snapped. His mouth slashed into a grim line. "Tell me, Daughter. Where were you January thirteenth, almost seven years ago?"

In desperation, she glanced at Rhys. He met her terror with a slight lift of the left side of his mouth. "I win," the look boasted.

"That's why I'm here, Father, to tell you what I discovered that night at The King's Ransom." Evan knew the truth. She turned to him for confirmation. His look twisted as if with uncertainty; then he stared back as if he knew nothing about the event.

"Then you admit you were there, meeting with an American."

"There was an American, Father, but—"

He never allowed her to finish. His hand swung back and caught her full on the mouth. "You bitch, you whore, you little conniving traitor," he bellowed.

She stumbled backward and would have fallen if Rhys hadn't stepped in and caught her.

"I think, sir, it's unnecessary—"

107

"I care not what you think. She is my daughter, and no concern of yours."

Rhys's arm tightened about her as if he meant to protect her.

" 'Tis bad enough you accepted the devil's spawn that night but to learn you betrayed your family loyalties as well is too much." He stepped forward as if to strike her again.

The earl shoved her behind his back. "Consider your actions, sir. Beating her will not change what has happened."

"Stand aside. I want the truth from my daughter."

"You've seen the testimony of the innkeeper and his serving wench. What does it matter if she denies the truth or not?"

"Father," she pleaded from behind the protection of Rhys's body, "make him tell you the facts. Tell him, Rhys, whom I met there."

Somehow she had expected softness to dwell in his eyes. Instead, that soulless stranger stared down at her. "How would I know whom you met?" he lied. "Not even the innkeeper was aware of the American's name."

The sound of marching steps filled the hallway outside her father's study. At the sharp rap, the baron issued a "come." Red-coated troops filed through the entry in a lined column, an officer stepping forward.

"At your service, Lord Collingsworth," the major said with a snappy salute.

Her father pointed a finger at Calypso. "Take her. She's an American spy and has been for some time."

"Father, no," she cried, stepping away from her incriminator, who stood between her and the military escort.

Rhys turned, grasped her arm, and pulled her forward, offering her up to the major. In that brief moment of contact she gave him a look he had no trouble reading. *You've betrayed me,* it accused.

Perhaps, his look replied, *but you were willing to betray me as well.* His mouth lifted in a sneer. *I was quicker.*

"Father, please," she entreated, "let me explain."

"Take her away before I do something I regret."

She straightened, her chin lifting with pride. She wouldn't beg, not now, not ever, especially before Rhys Winghurst.

As the handcuffs snapped about her wrists, she felt as if someone had snipped the lifeline of her existence. What would happen to her? The troops formed a barrier about her, as they marched her down the hallway into the foyer toward the front door.

She glanced up at the staircase circling to the floor above. Nannette stared wide-eyed down at her, her small, age-spotted fist pressed to her mouth. Beside her stood Tristan, his elfin face a work of confusion.

"Callie," he cried, "don't leave me."

She halted and turned pleading eyes up at the officer. "Please, just a moment with the boy."

"Your son?"

His comment jarred her. "No, of course not. My brother."

The major nodded and made a path as Tristan stumbled down the stairway to where she knelt.

"Callie?" he asked, confused. "Where are you going?"

She glanced up over his trembling shoulders to find Rhys staring down at her, a perplexed look on his face. "I'll be back, Tristan. Don't you worry. Stay with Nanna, and do what she tells you." Her manacled wrist weighed tons as she lifted his chin to make eye contact. "Understand?"

The boy nodded, then buried his face in her collarbone. "Please, Callie, don't be gone long."

Dear God, she thought, forcing her tears to remain unshed, *what will happen to Tristan with me not here to protect him from Father's abuse?*

A well of accusation bubbled in her throat. This was Rhys Winghurst's doing. Her eyes narrowed as she glanced back up at him. *You'll pay,* she pledged. *Somehow, some way, some day soon, if anything happens to my brother.*

For a brief moment she witnessed regret in his brown eyes, but the major forced her to stand, ripping their gazes apart.

"I'm sorry, miss, but we've a long way to go to reach Fort Charlotte. It's time we leave."

"Yes, of course," she answered, her chin held high as the troops marched her down to the wharfside and aboard the waiting ship.

At last the tears she had held back for so long spilled over her lashes and tumbled down her cheeks. Her manacled hand clasped her convulsing throat as she imagined how it would feel to have the life squeezed from her body by the hangman's hemp. The picture of haughty contempt she had conjured up the night before reversed itself in her head. Now she pleaded with Rhys for mercy as he stood above her on the scaffold, her fate in his hands. With cold disregard he eyed her groveling form at his feet. Then the left side of his mouth worked upward into a smirk as he lifted his hand and signaled to the hangman to finish his task.

"No," she cried as she felt the burning jerk of the noose snapping her neck, cutting off the breath from her body.

"Are you sure, miss? The breeze can get chilly this time of year up here on deck. I think you'd be more comfortable below."

Confused, Calypso whirled to find the arresting officer beside her, his face registering genuine concern. "I'm sorry, I didn't hear your question."

He smiled, the expression lighting up his face in boyish delight. "I thought you'd want to go below. You were shivering. The captain has offered you the warmth of his cabin."

She pulled the thin shawl she wore tighter about her. What had made her shiver wasn't the temperature of the air, but the chill of the unknown racing through her veins. "Yes, please. Below would be much better."

The young officer took her arm to guide her across the littered deck. The manacles about her wrists jangled. "I'm sorry about those," he said, pointing at the chains, "but they're required in this instance." He glanced down at the tangle of rope at his feet. "I'm sorry," he repeated.

" 'Tis not your fault. I understand you're only doing your duty." She graciously accepted his hand and allowed him to assist her down the companionway stairs. Sensing the deep-rooted guilt within her escort, she offered up an angelic look. Perhaps she could learn something of her fate from this man. As they neared the cabin entrance, she frantically searched her mind for a way to persuade the major to stay with her.

Opening the door, he stepped to the side to allow her entry into the quarters.

In desperation, she turned, placing both of her hands up on his coat sleeve. "Sir," she faltered, hoping she sounded convincing. "I've never cared for ships." She pinned him with her jade-green eyes. "Please don't leave me alone. I cannot abide the silence with nothing but the creak of the timbers and the whine of the sea. I'm not much of a sailor."

He swayed in indecision.

She pressed him with the gentlest of gazes. "Please."

Removing his hat, he sighed. "Of course, miss. I wouldn't want you to be frightened."

A smile of gratitude parted her lips. Frightened? She was as scared as an abandoned kitten, but she would not let it get the best of her. She dipped her head in a gesture of meekness. "Your companionship is most appreciated, sir."

"James Farrington at your services, Miss Collingsworth."

"Major Farrington," she probed, "there's so much of what's happening to me I don't understand."

111

"Well, miss, there's not much to tell except that evidence has been provided indicating you've supplied information to the Americans, though, personally," he added, "I find that hard to believe."

She cast her eyes down demurely. "Thank you, sir. I find this whole affair hard to believe myself. One moment I'm merely the pampered daughter of the baron"—the simpering words were a chore to get out—"then the next thing I knew that awful Earl of Flint was flinging lies about me at my father." Burying her face in her hands, she staged a pitiful sob.

A comforting arm curled about her shoulders. "Please, don't cry, Miss Collingsworth. If there is no truth in the accusation, you'll be free eventually."

"Tell me, sir, how long will that take?" Her heart pounded in fear. Tristan would be alone, facing the wrath of their father every moment she was away.

"That I can't say. You'll be housed at Fort Charlotte until a military escort can be arranged to take you to trial."

"An escort to Nassau can't be that difficult to find."

"Not Nassau, but England."

"England?" Her mind reeled. This could mean months, not days, away from home. "But that's impossible, Major, I can't be away for that long."

"I'm sorry, Miss Collingsworth, but it can't be helped. Yours is a capital offense, not one for the governor's courts, but for the high courts of England."

"But, if I'm gone for months—"

"Years, Miss Collingsworth. I think you'll find, if you come back at all, it will be after several years."

Calypso's heart plummeted to the floor. At the snap of his fingers, Rhys Winghurst had rid himself of her pesty interference. Whatever devious plot he had formulated would go unchecked. Hope for salvation shattered like an ill-fated mirror, leaving nothing but bad luck in its wake.

"Tristan," she whispered, a fear worse than death grip-

112

ping her insides. She had promised to return to him and now . . .

Her little brother, who looked to her for protection, would most likely never see her again. She couldn't let him down, couldn't renege on her word. Somehow she must find a way to get back to the defenseless child who needed her.

Chapter Eight

Nannette twisted her plump, motherly hands into the folds of her woolen skirt. Her babies. Dear God, her beloved bairns. First, her darling Calypso had been dragged from the house under suspicion of espionage. The wrinkles between her eyes accentuated as she frowned. That man, the Earl of Flint, was somehow the source of the accusation. But why? What was between the lassie and the Welshman? She has witnessed the unsuppressed animosity between the two on more than one occasion. There was something unexplained there. Perplexed, she tapped a finger against her compressed lips.

Then her thumbnail replaced the contemplative gesture as she nibbled in worry, her concern turning to her younger ward. Tristan. The baron had called him to his chambers nearly an hour ago, and the laddie had not, as of yet, returned. The master would beat the bairn. Always it was the boy who received the brunt of the lord's anger whenever he was displeased. There was no doubt in her mind, Calypso had done something to upset her father. Why else would he have her marched away by the governor's troops? Dear God in Heaven, the nursemaid pleaded to some inner well of strength, what was she to do? She crossed herself and bowed her head, hoping for an answer. None came.

Instead, an image of Rhys Winghurst seeped into her

mind. Something about the man was familiar. But why? She had never laid eyes on him before his arrival at the plantation with the group of suitors the baron had invited to court his daughter. The earl was not like the others. The difference was obvious in the way he acted, the manner in which he treated Calypso. There was something between them, more than normal courtship, but what that something was, she wasn't sure.

Her anxious thoughts returned to Tristan. His situation was the one she felt she had control over. Somehow, she had to get him away from the plantation, away from his father's abusive ways. But how? A lone serving woman on an island, whom could she turn to for help?

Oddly enough, only one name came to mind—Rhys Winghurst. Yet she couldn't think of any reason to hope the aloof Earl of Flint would wish to help her with her plight.

Assassination. What an ugly word. Rhys crumpled the missive he had just finished reading as if the remarks on the paper were poison. In truth, they were. His first hunch had been right those many months ago as he had sat in the Secretary of State Thomas Jefferson's office, discussing the unconfirmed reports of a possible attempt to assassinate the president.

Now the rumors were fact, at least in his own mind. A secret society existed that would go to any extent to see the still floundering United States government reduced to chaos. What better way than eliminating the stabilizing force of the government, George Washington? Even Jefferson had admitted at the time there was no continuity in the cabinet; he and Hamilton were always at each other's throats, never in agreement about how the country should be run. What would happen if Washington wasn't there to mediate?

The answer was obvious—the United States would most likely crumble under British pressure to regain control. The only people who would wish to see that happen were those who had lost the most during the rebellion, men like John Collingsworth, who had been banned from the country after their lands were confiscated.

Damn. Tearing the message into innumerable pieces, he released the debris to the wind whipping the palm trees into a clattering frenzy and watched the bits of paper settle into the thundering surge. With unaccountable illogic he wished the baron was not involved in an attempt to destroy the American government, and he knew the reason why.

He slipped the silver crown affixed to a chain from his breast pocket. Calypso Collingsworth. Chances were, if her father was a participant, she was, too. The possibility upset him more than it should. The woman interested him, but not to the point of interfering with his duty. He couldn't allow that to happen, as his country was most important in his life. Nothing superseded his patriotism. Nothing. Especially not a conniving female. He dropped the silver coin symbolizing their contest of wills back into its resting place next to his heart.

Shaking off the disturbing images of her glistening skin as she had lain beneath him, he pressed his heels into the flanks of his steed to begin another round of thorough inspection of the island. For the fourth fruitless day in a row, he refused to give up looking for evidence to support his suspicions. Today he would comb the plantation grounds. What exactly he sought, he wasn't sure, but a group as widespread and organized as this assassins' society seemed to be would need a place to store arms and ammunition, and a considerable amount at that. It would take an army to overrun the American shores and threaten the president's life. What better place to establish a working base than this isolated island so close to their intended victim?

His ride took him down dusty, isolated roads, past the sprawling slave quarters, around the ever-active saltworks, through the salt ponds where black men in tattered clothing raked the crusted white crystals in several dried lagoons. He paused, his arms crossed in silent contemplation as he watched the slaves move in an endless rhythm as a white man behind the protection of a rude shelter directed their progress, his hands cupping a mug of steaming brew. It saddened him to think that free men felt the need to make vassals of their fellow human beings. What a waste of human souls in a world struggling to grasp the concept of democracy.

Reining his horse about to continue on his way, he saw in the corner of his eye a fast-paced movement that made him hold his ground. Another horse and rider thundered down the road on which he had traveled moments before. Was he being followed? He guided his mount behind a clump of bushes to watch.

The other horseman drew nearer; then several yards from where Rhys hid, the rider turned his roan sharply, taking the path down to the salt ponds. Evan Collingsworth. He would recognize the drab-clad figure anywhere.

The baron's son was a man he found most obnoxious. He had seen the way Calypso had turned to her brother during the confrontation four days before in their father's library. Obviously Evan knew the real reason she had been at the inn that night seven years ago, had known and said nothing in support of his sister. What kind of man refused to help his own flesh and blood in a time of need? Though the other man's silence had aided his plan, it irked him to think Evan had betrayed his own sister.

He hung his head. But then, what he had done had been just as cruel, accusing her wrongly and watching in triumph as she was led away. It had been for the cause, he reminded himself, for the safety of an entire nation. He wouldn't have done such a dastardly thing otherwise. It wasn't in his make-up, as he was a protector by nature. Not that a woman who could drug and hold him captive in her bed would need his patronage and support. A cool resentment welled within him, replacing the guilt clouding his heart.

With no reason to remain in hiding, he whipped his mount's head around and continued his inspection of the plantation. Past fields of dormant cotton bushes, his circle took him along the outer edge of the island toward the wharfs. He saw nothing out of the ordinary to arouse his interest. Damn. The evidence had to be somewhere, and he was running out of places to look.

Slowing his mount to a plodding walk, he started across a small, stone bridge arching over a brook tumbling on its way to the open beach. The water seemed to sob with sadness that its freshness would soon mingle with the salt-contaminated sea water only yards away. The sound echoed similar emotions in his own heart, and he brought his steed to a halt at the crest of the bridge.

The sobbing halted, and he cocked his head in curiosity. If what he had heard wasn't the water, then what was it? He dismounted and stepped toward the railing to glance over the side to the stream below.

What he saw snapped the strings of his heart. A boy, not more than five or six, squatted beside the water, crying, his hands reaching behind his back to pull the shirt away that kept sticking to his hunched back. Every now and then one small fist would swipe at his nose and eyes, both running unchecked.

Poor, little pup, Rhys thought, reaching back to unloop the reins from the horse's neck so he could lead the animal as he walked. *He looks so alone and forlorn.*

As he neared, the little head shot up, and he stared into soft brown eyes that reminded himself of how he must have looked at that age. Tears streaked trails down a familiar

118

dirty face. Now he recognized the boy. Tristan. The baron's youngest son. A spark of guilt ignited. Most likely the little tyke missed his big sister, and that was why he was crying.

"Tristan?" he asked, halting his approach a few feet away.

Using his knuckles, the boy dabbed at his nose and rose to his feet, the stray pebbles that had been in his lap dropping to the ground. His only reply was a watery stare.

"I heard you crying. Is there something I can do to help you,"

"Weren't cryin'." The boy sniffed with a telltale rattle.

"Not crying, perhaps," Rhys conceded, "but I heard you. You're rather far from the house, aren't you? Would you like a ride back?" Damn. What had made him offer to return the boy to the mansion? He had a few more places he wanted to check before ending his ride.

"I don't need no help," Tristan mumbled. "At least not yours." He turned his back, his hand snaking behind him to ease the shirt away from his skin as if it caused discomfort.

"If that's the way you want it." Rhys draped the reins down the horse's neck in order to mount. He placed one foot in a stirrup.

"Why'd you lie about Callie?"

Rhys twisted, his foot lowering to the ground. "Callie?" He thought for a moment. "Of course, Callie." The name Calypso had used that night at the inn. He smiled, remembering the wide-eyed girl she had been then. "Whyever would you think I lied?" Was it obvious to this small boy?

" 'Cause Callie's good. She don't lie. She loves me."

How simple. 'Twas a shame life couldn't remain so easily explained. He glanced back at the saddle and repositioned his footing. "Everyone lies now and then." He studied the boy. "Haven't you ever told one?"

Tristan ducked his head. "Suppose. But not about Callie like you did." Again he reached behind his back, picking at

119

the cotton shirt.

"What's wrong with you, boy?" Rhys's boot thudded against the ground as he gave up his attempt to mount his horse.

"Nuthin'. At leastwise, nuthin' to concern you."

He examined the face tight with pain. Wrapping the reins about a small bush, he stepped forward, wanting a better look at the boy's back.

Tristan moved to keep the distance separating them unchanged.

Rhys stilled. Proud boy. As determined as he had been at the same age. "All right, Tristan. If I tell you the truth, will you let me look at your back?"

The small hand twisted behind him in a defensive motion. "Maybe."

"The truth is your sister was seen that night at The King's Ransom, was seen meeting with an American." He shrugged his wide shoulders. He wasn't lying to the boy. "I felt it my duty to present the facts to your father."

Tristan's face screwed with indignation. "She wasn't spyin'. Callie's no traitor."

"If that's the case, the judge will decide that she is innocent." Something about the way this boy looked at him brought the waves of guilt tumbling back. He would see to it, personally, nothing happened to Calypso Collingsworth. "Now, turn around and let me see what's wrong with you."

The boy hesitated.

"Tristan," Rhys chided, "we made a bargain." He drew a circle in the air with a finger indicating his command. What was it about this child that made him care? Children had always seemed so alien to him before. He felt at ease with Calypso's little brother. Strange.

With a sigh, the boy turned about, presenting his posterior. Lifting the soft cotton of the shirt, Rhys felt his stomach churn in disbelief. Scars crisscrossed the small spine, then a layer of knitting wounds covered the healed whip marks. What disturbed him the most were the fresh, still bleeding lashes, at least a half-dozen, cutting through puckering scabs.

"Damn," he hissed, unable to believe anyone would do something so horrendous to a child, no matter what the crime. "Who did this to you, Tristan?" If this was the work of a servant he would see the bastard whipped in return.

Tristan whimpered and pulled out of Rhys's gentle grip. His eyes pleaded with Rhys to ask no further questions.

"Was it one of the servants? Your nanny?"

Adamantly, the lad shook his head.

"Then who? Evan?"

"No," he denied with a whoosh of air.

"Not your sister, those wounds are much too fresh." The words he said aloud had been meant only to be thought silently.

"Not Callie." Tristan rushed toward him, his little fists balled and flying, catching Rhys in the stomach. "Don't never say that about Callie."

Trying to avoid the boy's swings as well as his injured back, Rhys carefully enveloped the small body in the circle of his arms. Something in his heart lurched as the warm child first wiggled, then accepted his controlling hug, a pitiful sob gushing from the boy's convulsing throat.

"Did the baron do this, son?" He couldn't title the man as this boy's father if that was the truth of the matter.

Tristan's muffled face rubbed up and down against his cambric shirt, confirming his suspicions.

"Damn, the son of a bitch," he mumbled, remembering only too well his abuse at the hands of his own father, though nothing this severe.

He pushed the boy to arm's length, his hands gripping the frail shoulders, in order to look him in the eyes. "Tristan. You must trust me. Aboard my ship is a man who'll put a salve on your wounds and make them feel better. Will

121

you come with me now?" For unexplained reasons it was most important the boy comply.

Their eyes locked, equal in intensity. He could see the battle raging within the child. Trust the man who had betrayed his sister? Why should he? Rhys waited for his decision. Agreement came with a simple nod.

"Good boy," he said, reaching out with one hand to ruffle Tristan's hair.

The gelding stood quietly as he placed his newly acquired ward in the saddle, then mounted up behind the small body to grasp it in the circle of a protective arm. To his surprise Tristan sat his seat well even under the cramped circumstances, a born horseman much as he had been at the same age.

He was doing it again, comparing Tristan to himself as if the similarities were important. Why did he place such significance on this boy? Because he was a younger son like himself? Perhaps. Or was it because Calypso was his sister? None of his reasons made sense.

At the wharf, he dismounted and eased Tristan down beside him. Turning to a lounging sailor, he tossed the horse's reins to the unsuspecting man and started down the pier, one hand gently urging the boy ahead of him.

" 'Cuse me, Captain," the surprised sailor inquired, eyeing the steed with a doubtful glare. "What do I do with this beast?"

"Hold him till I return." He glanced back at the old salt who fingered the reins, his body dead in front of the fidgeting horse. "But my advice is to step to the side in case he decides he'll have none of your strange smells."

The old man jumped out of the way, nervously patting the now placid animal. "Whatever you say, Captain. Try not to be too long."

Tristan snickered. "Don't know nuthin' about horses, do he?"

"Most sailors don't," Rhys replied, smiling down in a

conspiratorial manner. "Give 'em canvas, and they can whip the wind into shape, but a lazy-eyed nag not nearly as dangerous as a ship's mast scares the living hell out of them." He winked.

Tristan smiled back, at ease.

"Come on," Rhys said, urging the boy down the gangplank and to the left toward the companionway stairs. Luther would know what to do and would have something soothing to coat the boy's wounds.

Entering the galley, Rhys guided the boy through an assortment of bolted-down tables to a exit in the rear.

"Luther," he called, pushing the door out of his way. "I have a patient out here for you.

Luther's size unnerved most people at the first meeting. Barely reaching four feet in height, the small man seemed unaffected by his stature.

Tristan eyed him once, then glanced up at Rhys. "He didn't grow up all the way," he commented.

"No, I suppose not, but you mind him all the same."

The boy nodded.

"It's his back. I thought you might be able to do something for him."

Luther's brows knotted between his eyes. "Go on, Captain. The boy and I can take care of this ourselves."

Reluctant to leave, Rhys retreated from the dwarf's private quarters, grabbing a mug and filling it with coffee, finally settling in one corner to wait.

Would the boy have scars for the rest of his life? The thought disturbed him. What would make a man beat his own child so cruelly? The urge to wrap his hands around the baron's neck and squeeze the answer out of him curled his mouth in an unpleasant smile.

He heard Tristan cry out once, and he was instantly on his feet, concern spearing through his chest. "Easy, Luther," he called out. "He's not one of these tough-hided, old sailors."

There was no response.

The minutes ticked by; the coffee grew cold. Rhys gave up his attempt to appear calm and took to pacing about the galley.

"Captain." Luther stuck his head around the corner, his small, black eyes glittering with concern. "I think this is somethin' you should see."

Dear God, the boy's injuries were worse than he thought. He slammed down the mug and skirted the benches and tables.

Rhys was forced to duck his head in order to enter the tiny room tucked under the ship's bow. The stub of a candle flickered in the windowless quarters, the small bed, though just right for the midget, dwarfed Tristan as he lay face down on the multicolored quilt.

"What is it, Luther? Is it worse than I thought?"

"No, Captain. The wounds are clean. They'll heal in time, if his back is given a rest. It's the mark, Captain. I thought you should see it."

Rhys glanced at the smaller man, confusion contorting his features. "Mark? What mark?"

Luther lifted the chamberstick and angled it over Tristan's prone body. The crisscrossing lashes arched down the boy's buttocks, a few even on the backs of his thighs, a greasy smear of the dwarf's infamous concoction coating those that were still red and raw.

"Dear God," Rhys hissed.

Luther dipped the candle until the shadows that had played along the boy's hips dissipated, leaving the unmarred skin clear to view.

Rhys blinked, unable to believe what he saw. Grabbing the light in order to see more clearly, he reached out with one finger to touch the dark mark on the creamy white skin, as if the physical contact would erase its presence.

A birthmark. A perfect fleur-de-lis. The Winghurst emblem that inevitably appeared on every male child on exactly the same spot on the left hip.

Impossible. This was John Collingsworth's son. How could Tristan end up with this marking?

He glanced at Luther, looking for signs of denial.

"Can't explain it myself, Your Lordship, but the mark's identical to yours. I'd stake my life on the fact this boy's related to you."

Rhys's brows met in a frown, his mind a whirl of confused thoughts. "How old are you, Tristan?"

"I was six in October."

October. The boy would have been born in '84. He had been here in January of the same year—exactly nine months before his birth.

Tristan turned his head, the shadows from the candle-light dancing across his small face. Brown hair, brown eyes, the Winghurst mark.

Rhys stepped away and returned the candlestick to Luther. As much as he found it hard to believe, there was no doubt Tristan was his son. The product of that fateful union with Calypso Collingsworth nearly seven years before.

His gaze misted with an emotion he had never experienced before—parental pride. A son. He had a son.

Then a frown marred the perfection of his features. Why had the bitch neglected to mention the fact?

Chapter Nine

A cold draft whipped up the dank stairs winding deep into the bowels of the earth. Shivering at the top of the stairs, Calypso pulled the thin, inadequate shawl tightly about her shoulders. Fort Charlotte was a horrible place, not fit to house a pig, much less a person.

From far below her she heard a scream, agonizingly human as it gave way to a gurgling moan. She paused, her hand pressed against the moss-slimed wall, her heart pounding so hard she couldn't swallow.

"Get along there, missy," the guard behind her ordered, his finger poking into her rib.

Stiff-kneed, she took the next step, the desire to turn and run so strong she considered trying. But how far would she get? She glanced back and up at the lank-haired guard and realized the answer. Not far enough. Better to meet her fate with dignity than be tossed over the man's shoulder like a sack of feed.

Lifting her chin, she forced her feet to continue the descent, down and around the curve of the stairwell leading to God knew what. The darkness that met her revealed nothing more than the next step, undermining her determination to remain calm. She prayed the winding stairs would end soon; then she appealed to a higher order that they wouldn't, that they could instead just go on and on, never reaching their destination.

The end came as her foot eased out, discovering solid ground.

"Keep going straight, wench," the guard commanded, gripping her arm and propelling her forward.

"Yes, of course," she choked, willing her feet to continue.

Again the scream pierced the air, this time closer. Calypso's knees began to shake uncontrollably as she feared her turn to be tortured would be next. She stuffed her fist against her mouth to squelch the scream of terror forming there. The guard forced her to move along.

A lone lantern lit the room, which was more like a long antechamber and which was lined with closed doors of massive size. Doors to dungeons, she guessed. Behind which one would they throw her? The recurring scream ripped through her cascading terror. Her courage threatened to take wing and fly away; only by closing her eyes and chanting in her mind, *I cannot break down,* was she able to maintain a semblance of calm.

"Sit," the guard ordered, indicating a small bench against one wall.

The roughness of the wood penetrated her clothing as she settled down, her back ramrod straight, on the hand-hewn plank. Taking her chains, the man snapped them into a ring on the wall, giving her barely enough slack to wipe her eyes if she needed to.

Without a word, the guard turned to retrace his steps.

"Please, sir," she croaked, "what is going to happen to me?"

He looked back, blinking like an owl in the yellow lantern light. "You're to be interrogated."

"Thank you," she whispered in a small voice. They would torture her, force her to say things that weren't true. She had read about the horrible ways jailers used to make prisoners confess to a crime. She wouldn't give in. Never would she give them the satisfaction of breaking her. She was innocent.

"Miss Collingsworth," snapped a voice to her right in a few moments.

She would have jumped from her seat except the chain prevented her. "Yes?" The word rushed from her body in fearful anticipation.

The inquisitor's face was shadowed, but the rustle of paper sounded crisp and clear. "It says here you're accused of spying against the Crown during a time of war."

"I am unjustly accused."

"So say all criminals." The paper shuffled again. " 'Twas a lord of the realm that brought the charge against you, a Rhys Winghurst, the Earl of Flint."

"He's a liar."

He glanced at her, his eyes shining like crystals in the semidarkness. "A common response."

"But it's true. I've done nothing but upset an arrogant man's ego and his poltroon plans to do—I'm not sure what, but I can assure you if anyone is an American spy, he is." Her voice shook with conviction.

"Are you saying he's your accomplice?"

"No. Yes. I mean—"

"Thank you, miss. 'Tis all the confession I need."

"No," she cried in frustration. "I've nothing to do with Rhys Winghurst's plans. You must believe me."

Silence greeted her. She was alone. Damn. Why hadn't she kept her mouth shut? She took what comfort she could from the possibility the earl might be joining her soon—if the inquisitor believed her statement.

"Come," issued the voice of the jailer.

She rose as he released her chains and guided her toward another exit. Panic began to drown her other emotions. He would take her deeper into this pit in the earth. Something snapped inside her.

"No," she screamed, pulling with all her might against

the restraints, attempting to turn and retrace her steps.

"Calm down, wench," he insisted, pulling on her chains as if she were a crazed mongrel. "I'm taking you to a small waiting chamber until the major decides where to house you."

"House me?" Her breath came in sharp, little gasps. "You mean decide what dungeon to throw me in and what torture to use on me." She ceased her senseless struggle.

He laughed, the sound not a pleasant one at all. "I think you'll find your quarters acceptable. Most of them overlook the bay."

As she walked, the ground below her feet began to rise and confirmed his words. "Then why take me through that horrible place? And that man, screaming in agony."

Again his ghoulish humor washed over her. "Was meant to give you a sample of where you could end up if you didn't cooperate."

The tunnel emerged into the sky-blue sunlight onto a rampart surrounded by a parapet wall. Behind her a medieval turret that really belonged on a castle surmounted the bridge she had crossed to enter the fort. Beneath her were the dungeons. Beyond was a mammoth arena looking for all the world as if Roman gladiators would step forward at any moment. Her first impression had been accurate. Fort Charlotte was a horrible place.

To think the governor, Lord Dunsmore, had built this structure only a year ago. Why? Unless to satisfy some ungodly whim to play lord of the land.

"This way."

Dead ahead stood twin buildings, each constructed of the same stone as the rest of the fort. As she crossed the inner bailey, a whipping wind captured her skirts, tugging and pulling them seaward, a friend trying to pick her up and carry her away to safety.

A friend. She laughed inwardly. She didn't have one in the whole world. With bowed head, she entered the austere

129

building and sat where indicated to await her fate. Perhaps if things became bad enough, she could throw herself from the parapet wall to the sea far below. The thought comforted her in a strange way.

Then she remembered her little brother. Dear God, what terrible punishment was he suffering at this moment because of her? She couldn't die; her brother needed her too much. She lifted her chin, determined to find a way to escape and return to the only thing of importance to her. Tristan.

Tristan. With a grim set of his jaws, Rhys watched the boy at play from a distance, the nursemaid sitting on a bench not far away. The little Scottish woman seemed to care for her ward, a source of relief to him. The hardest thing he had ever done was to return his son to the baron's household, when all he had wanted to do was to carry him away from the island and forget his mission and those at home depending upon him to succeed.

Somehow he must manage to take care of both. And he would, he vowed inwardly. He needed only to display patience. His ship, *The Oceanid,* had been gone over a week. The vessel's return was expected soon and with it came the papers he counted on and waited for, orders giving him, the Earl of Flint, the right to claim Calypso as his prisoner to take to England for trial. He could only hope his superiors in Philadelphia would agree with his plan to escort a supposed British informer for interrogation. How he would explain the presence of the boy, he hadn't figured out yet. Knee-deep in deception with the State Department already, what harm could one more lie do?

He sighed, not sure how he had reached such a state of dereliction in his duty, but if he could find proof of the baron's involvement, then who was to say the man's daughter could not shed more light on his assassination plans.

His attention riveted back to the playing child. The nursemaid stood, motioning to Tristan to join her. It was obvious the lad wanted to continue his game, and Rhys caught the sharpness in the woman's voice, though not the words, as she ordered him to cease his disobedience.

The woman glanced up as if sensing someone was watching them, her gaze connecting with Rhys's. Her hand lifted, shading her eyes from the afternoon sun as she studied his tall figure outlined in the golden rays of the sun.

A silent communication electrified the air between them. This woman possessed the answers to his questions, even if she wasn't aware of the fact herself. She held the key that could verify Tristan's lineage. He needed her and knew, without a doubt, she had a need for him as well. Perhaps, together, their combined desires could unify into a tightly sealed plan to get what he wanted—information and his son.

The house echoed with an empty stillness belying the presence of the many servants and slaves through the corridors. Rhys stood statue still at the door to the library, attune to any noise around him giving away the possibility he was being watched. The only sound he could detect was the unbroken thump-thump of his heart, as steady as a force pump under the most demanding of pressure.

This was the part he hated about his job, the need to invade another man's private domain in order to find the proof he needed. Papers. Documents. Something, anything to shed light on John Collingsworth's involvement in the assassination plot.

Surprisingly, the well-oiled door opened without a squeak, and he stepped into the room smelling of book print and fresh writing ink, an odor reminding him of his family estate back in Flintshire. Afternoon sun poured through the one large window, highlighting several stacks of papers edging the mahogany writing table the baron used as his desk. He shrugged his wide shoulders. As good a place as any to begin.

The papers revealed nothing. Estimates from the saltworks and the taxes due the governor on the shipping of the commodity out of the islands. A report showing the losses the plantation had suffered over the years from the chenille bug infestation. Rhys shook his head. Why did the man continue to grow cotton so unprofitably? If it wasn't for his revenue from raking salt, he would have gone under years ago as so many of his fellow Loyalists had. Fool. Stubborn fool.

He paused at the next report. A research on the progress made with a new strain of cotton plants suited for growth in Maryland, a handwritten note in the baron's scrawl to one side proclaiming, "We'll try this one when we return home."

Rhys set the paper to the side. Circumstantial, but not nearly enough to prove the man had plans to assassinate the president. He needed more. Much more.

He continued his search, warming to the task, as he carefully dug through ledgers and papers in one drawer after another. At last he unearthed what he sought, a personal journal belonging to the baron. Quickly he flipped to the last entry.

"The day comes soon, and my heart races with joy. At last, Cathleen, we will return, and I shall take what I have left of you, the sweetest of memories, back to where we belong. With the support of loved ones who will do whatever is necessary, we'll ride the steed of triumph through Maryland. The bastards will pay with their very lives for the pain they caused you for so many years." The account ended there.

The page was marked with a missive, its seal broken, and Rhys didn't hesitate to open it. Dated four days before from Wilmington, North Carolina, the ornate penmanship said, "The eagle nods unaware upon his aerie. The time to strike nears. You and yours be prepared." The note was unsigned.

Rhys closed the letter and studied the design pressed into the sealing wax, trying to etch the markings firmly in his mind. They could be important, a clue to who had written the preparatory lines from the United States. If the plot had reached the American shores, no wonder he found no evidence of plans for an invasion. This was worse, much worse, than he or his superiors had ever suspected. Infiltration was harder to defeat than outright aggression. God help them all if this plan for assassination was more solidified than expected.

"Who are you?" hissed a voice from the doorway.

Rhys stumbled away from the desk, the missive still clutched in his hand. The thought of his own safety didn't concern him as much as the possibility that what he had just discovered might go unrevealed to his superiors. His muscles tensed, ready to do battle.

"I knew you weren't what you appeared." Fear etched the soft Scottish brogue. Tristan's nursemaid stood in the doorway, her small hand pressed against her matronly bosom. Her gaze bored into him as if trying to read his thoughts, as if attempting to place him accurately in the pattern of her world, an existence centered about her custodial duties.

Carefully he replaced the letter into the diary, returned the book to its resting place, and shut the drawer with a soft thud. "Why does he beat the boy so?"

She seemed totally unprepared for the inquiry. "Tristan? Why this concern for the laddie?" Her eyes narrowed, then widened, realization striking her. "You're the one who tended his fresh wounds."

He nodded.

"But why?"

With a shrug of his shoulders, he turned so she didn't

133

witness the paternal softening in his eyes. "I have my reasons." Collecting himself, he whirled back to face her. "Nannette, isn't it?"

She dipped her head, her gaze never ceasing its attempt to probe his feelings.

"Then let's say we have a common interest. I wish to see the boy removed from this environment."

Her round body swayed forward in relief and approval. "Aye, 'tis what I wish for, too. But how?"

"Leave it to me, Nannette. I have a plan." Stepping toward where she stood in the entranceway, he deftly guided her out of the library, closing the door behind them. The papers were safe enough. He knew where they were and could retrieve them at a moment's notice. "Pack essentials for you and the boy, and be prepared to leave posthaste."

Without waiting for a response, he hurried up to his quarters to prepare to depart the moment *The Oceanid* appeared in the harbor.

"Please, Major, can't you understand?" Calypso stared up into the boyish face of the officer in charge of the fort, the same man who had arrested and escorted her here. He had been sympathetic to her plight aboard ship; perhaps she could convince him to see things her way now.

He patted her wrists, still tingling from the crush of the manacles he had removed moments before. "Truly, Miss Collingsworth, I know what you're feeling, but there is nothing I can do. If this cad, Winghurst, is in truth the one at fault, why has no one recognized him?" With a sigh, he lifted his shoulders in a fatalistic shrug. "I have my orders."

She looked away, seeing the staunchness of his resolve would not be compromised. *You have orders, I have responsibilities. Let's see whose will is the stronger.* She smiled, forcing an accepting, courageous tremble to work her mouth. "Of course, Major." The movement of her bottom lip accelerated as she allowed a small sob to escape. Let him believe she was soft and yielding.

"Please, Miss Collingsworth, don't cry," he said consolingly, the distress obvious in his voice. "Perhaps there is something I can do." He stood, placing his hands behind his back as he began to pace.

She eyed him stealthily from the cover of her hand.

"Was anyone there that night in question who could verify your story?"

There were plenty, she steamed within. *My brother, the serving girl, Rhys Winghurst himself, but none will vouch for me. None . . . except the kindly cook who gave me the note from Rhys. Perhaps . . .* Her eyes brightened, and her body leaned forward. "There was one, the cook."

Major Farrington lifted his hands in a dramatic gesture. "See, there is hope. I will personally return to Collingsville and interview this woman. What is her name?"

"Her name?" She swallowed, the lump hard and unyielding in her throat. "I'm not sure." She glanced up, pleading. "How hard can she be to find?"

For a moment he hesitated as if to withdraw his support. She released her bottom lip, forcing it to tremble again.

"Don't worry, Miss Collingsworth. I'll follow every lead. I won't permit the authorities to take you to England until all the facts are presented. If you say this Rhys Winghurst is a fraud, then I believe you. I won't leave Long Island until I find the truth. In the meantime, I'll give orders to allow you as much freedom as possible, the parade ground, the parapet walls. You need only ask, and an escort will release you from your quarters and take you wherever you wish within the fort boundaries." He swept to the door, his cape swaying behind him. With a gentlemanly bow he exited, leaving her alone.

At last someone believed her. From the barred window, she watched Major Farrington stride across the inner bailey, her lips that had seemed to quiver so easily only moments before a strong, thin line, her hopes for rescue riding on the flying tails of his cape. He would go to the inn and talk to the cook. She would tell him about the note sent down to the innkeeper demanding a companion for the evening. The woman would tell him that the girl substituting for the regular serving wench that night would have gone upstairs unknowingly. She would tell him . . .

Her heart stopped in midbeat, the wild exhilaration she had experienced moments before whooshed from her lungs like air from a bellows. The cook could tell him nothing. The little woman couldn't read. The note could have said anything. She had known Calypso didn't belong at the inn; she had said as much that night. She had told Calypso not to go upstairs.

Calypso's head sagged. Rhys Winghurst was no fool. Never would he have allowed a dangling end left unraveled. Most likely he would have paid the cook off or gotten rid of her some way. What poor wretch could resist the jingle of the earl's money? Major Farrington would find nothing.

The panic that had been soothed by his encouraging words rose again like a hellish demon. She must escape and find her way into Nassau. There she had friends who would believe her innocence and help her escape New Providence Island. But to Maryland? Never. To England? There was nothing for her there. The only place dear to her was where Tristan was, but her father would turn her back over to the authorities if she were to show up at home.

Perhaps if she confronted Rhys Winghurst, promised not to reveal what she knew about him, he would retract his accusation. She could tell Major Farrington she had made up the wild story about the earl's involvement in order to gain time.

Would Rhys be willing to bargain? Maybe, if she made the stakes high enough. There was only one thing about her that he seemed interested in. Her body. She would traffic with the devil if she needed to for the safety of herself and Tristan. One couldn't lose what one no longer had. Her reputation had been sacrificed a long time ago. Sin was sin, and if God had plans to send her to Hell for her wayward actions, whether she committed the crime once or thrice would not make any difference on her Judgment Day.

She squared her shoulders, set her chin at a determined angle, and called for the bailiff. She would escape at the first opportunity presented to her and return home in hopes of finding Rhys Winghurst before the authorities found her. Somehow, some way, she would convince the cad to listen.

Like icy fingers radiating the chill of malcontent, Fort Charlotte loomed upon its cliff, no welcome extended to visitors nearing its bleak walls. As *The Oceanid* entered the small harbor, Rhys felt anything but a visitor. An intruder at best. He could picture the spyglasses on the parapet wall level on them: focus, scrutinize, digest, and snap shut—curiosity and procedure satisfied his ship posed no immediate threat to the welfare of the island. He knew without a doubt he would be met by a military escort upon arrival.

Glancing down at the papers in his hand, he prayed they would pass close inspection as well. The forgery looked amazingly authentic to his trained eye, but even if Major Farrington accepted the orders of transportation as genuine, he might hesitate to release the prisoner into the hands of her accuser. Rhys's character would have to appear impeccable, and, hopefully, the letter of introduction from the Prince of Wales to Lord Dunsmore, the governor of the islands, would soothe any suspicions cast his way. The letter was his coign of vantage. He wouldn't use it unless forced to; then he would wave it about like a flag of honor, demanding he be treated with the respect accorded to his royal connections.

He chuckled, thinking about King George's oldest son. The heir spent most of his time whoring and gambling. Rhys had met him once when they had both been no more than boys; he doubted the prince would ever remember him. How his superiors had obtained the letter of introduction, he had never asked, but he was glad he had the document as it might come in handy.

Slipping the papers into his breast pocket, he turned his attention to matters at hand, anchoring *The Oceanid* and having one of the tenders launched so that he could go ashore. A few curt orders, the groan of the anchor chain, and the squeal of the rigging, and all was ready for him to disembark.

As he stepped toward the rope ladder dropping to the bobbing boat below, he glanced over his shoulder once, considering the foolishness of his action. Was Calypso Collingsworth worth all the trouble he was going to? He could easily be tossed in a cell beside her if she opened her mouth about his involvement in this affair. She was the mother of his child, he reminded himself, turning to begin his climb down. He owed it to his son to see her taken to safety, even if she resisted his efforts. And fight him she would, like an unleashed banshee with truth on her side. He grinned at the prospects of tossing her lush curves over his shoulder and toting her back to his ship, kicking and screaming.

He paused in mid-descent. What the hell was wrong with him? He wasn't a man who normally considered treating a woman like so much baggage. He enjoyed them, took pleasure in pampering them and watching them succumb to his magnetism. And though he had never been serious about any of the women in his life, he had never felt the need to force them to his will. He had never had to. They had always come willingly with a little encouragement. Why was this woman different?

He shook his head to eradicate the disturbing thoughts.

Responsibility to the mother of his child, he repeated to himself. That was the explanation for his odd behavior.

"Take care, Captain."

Rhys shot his gaze upward to find Luther straddling the brass railing of the ship, his short legs dangling on either side. A mischievous glint sparkled in the little man's eyes as if he shared the turmoil that was racing through Rhys's brain.

Damn. He couldn't hide anything from Luther. Ever since he could remember, the little man had known his every introspection. They had shared painful experiences and exuberant moments alike since they were boys growing up on the Welsh highlands.

He returned the impish grin with one of his own. "I'll be back before you know it."

"I don't doubt you," Luther replied, jumping down from his perch and disappearing out of Rhys's line of vision.

Skimming across the surf, Rhys watched the welcome committee—if one could call the line of well-armed troops by such a gentle name—form a barrier across the beach. He jumped from the craft, taking the last few yards of surging water on foot, allowing the rowers to secure the boat on shore.

"Lieutenant," he said, acknowledging the young officer who stepped forward to confront him.

"Sir," the officer replied, taking a quick survey of Rhys's long, lean figure. "To what do we owe the honor?"

"Rhys Winghurst, the Earl of Flint," he offered, extending the orders of transportation. He wondered where Farrington was. Perhaps he was in luck and wouldn't have to deal with that aspect of the problem of getting Calypso away from the fort. Relief settled in.

The young man's face turned scarlet. "You're here for the prisoner, Miss Collingsworth?"

"That's right."

The lieutenant handed him the papers back. "I'm sorry,

sir, but she's no longer here."

It took Rhys a few moments to digest the meaning of the man's words. "What are you saying? Has another escort been arranged for her?" Damn it, he should have gotten here sooner.

"No, sir." He shuffled his feet in a most unmilitary manner. "She disappeared this morning, and we can't seem to locate her. We're afraid she went over the walls and fell into the tangle of briars below. The fall probably killed her."

Rhys's heart hammered with painful guilt. Calypso dead? Damn it to hell, he should have known she would try something stupid like attempting to escape on her own.

Chapter Ten

She was free. Calypso giggled to herself, a seed of hysteria leaving her feeling giddy and light-headed. It had been easy, too easy in fact. She had sneaked right past the sleeping guard at the front entrance and down the winding road leading toward Nassau without once being stopped.

If she had figured right, she was less than a mile from Vendue House, the centralized marketplace on Bay Street. Once there, she could get her bearing and find her way to the family town house just a few blocks up the hill on George Street.

It wouldn't be hard to convince the servants her father left to care for the house when unoccupied that she had every right to be there. She could contact some of her friends who owned light sailing vessels and find one willing to take her home. If that proved impossible, she could always hire one of the local fishermen to return her to Long Island. Her determination to carry through with her plan to confront Rhys Winghurst would not be daunted by the mere lack of transportation.

The dusty road soon widened and traffic grew steadier. Lifting her shawl, she covered the flame of her hair and tried to appear unobtrusive to the people she passed. A mixture of white and black, most ignored her as there was plenty of foot traffic moving both ways.

She kept glancing over her shoulder, looking for signs of pursuit from the fort. Nothing. It was almost as if they were unaware of her escape or didn't care. Her lips curled in a mocking smile. Her good fortune.

The road curved, and suddenly she arrived at her destination, Vendue House. The tall stone structure buzzed with excitement, the voice of an auctioneer ringing loudly over the crowd. A sale, most likely of slaves, was taking place inside. Carts loaded with local produce lined the streets, and an old woman sat humped before a low table heaped high with *accara,* selling them as fast as she could wrap them in bits of tissue paper.

Calypso's stomach growled as the spicy smell reached her, but with no money she couldn't buy one of the tasty patties. She focused on the pavement heading up the incline to the family residence, ignoring the hunger pains spearing through her stomach. She would eat later, once she was safe inside the house.

George Street wound its way up the side of the hill, the silence of the empty avenue making the sound of her racing heart roar in her ears, the only external noise the click of her heels against the pavement. Why was she so nervous? No one pursued her; there was no reason for alarm. Yet she couldn't eradicate the feeling all was not right.

The white picket fence edging the small landscaped yard in front of the town house came into view. At last she began to run, ignoring the steepness of the grade as she neared the gate. She hesitated at the walkway up to the front steps, feeling as if disaster awaited her behind the closed door.

She shook herself. Ridiculous. No one knew where she was. Yet, as her fingers grasped the door knocker, she again felt an impulse to turn and run away.

Foolish girl. She must use the town house as a base of

142

operation. She had nowhere else to go. Her fingers lifted the heavy brass knocker and pounded with assumed confidence.

A few moments passed before her summons was answered. Dark irises peered at her from the partially opened door. "Miss Calypso?" inquired their owner, the eyes widening until the pupils appeared like chunks of coal against the surrounding whites. "What are you doing here?"

"Don't stand there gawking, Molly." She pushed against the barrier, wanting to slip behind the protection of its solidness. Her earlier momentary fears had been foolish. She was safe on the other side of the closed door.

"Yes'm." The slave girl let her pass.

"I'm hungry, Molly," she informed the servant, not giving her a chance to question her arrival further. "See that something simple is fixed for me to eat."

"Yes'm."

"And visiting cards." She rushed through the foyer and into the sitting room. Rifling through the drawers of the writing table in one corner, she came up empty-handed. "Where are they?" she demanded, glancing up at the open-mouthed girl.

Molly hurried to the mantel and picked up the small mother-of-pearl dish holding the cards and envelopes. "Here, Miss Calypso."

Accepting the offering, she sat herself at the writing table and began filling out messages: "The Honorable Calypso Collingsworth requests a social visit at your earliest convenience." Then she filled out envelopes to every potential sympathizer owning a home in Nassau. At least a few should be in residence, though the holidays were over. All she needed was one willing to take her back to Long Island.

"Molly, please see to a bath for me and dress yourself to deliver my missives right away."

The girl dipped a curtsy and scurried from the room, mumbling unintelligible words of frustration at the unannounced upset in her life.

After sealing over a dozen messages, Calypso sat back in the chair. What if all her friends refused to assist her? "Impossible," she answered herself aloud.

Yes, but what if? Then she would hire a boat to take her back. Hire a boat? With what? She hadn't a farthing to her name. Her eyes began scanning the room, looking for objects of worth that one of the locals might be willing to accept in trade. There was enough silver in the room to buy a boat, much less hire one. She would have no problem with that aspect, but the idea of taking items from the house and fencing them just didn't set well with her.

Molly entered, a dark, shapeless cape about her shoulders. "I'm ready, Miss Calypso."

She glanced up. "Good." Handing the messages to the girl, she instructed, "Deliver them all and wait for answers if possible." Carefully she went over each recipient's name and address until the girl could repeat each one without hesitation.

"Yes'm." The servant tucked the envelopes into her dress pocket and headed toward the front door.

Calypso watched her go. It would be at least an hour or two before the girl returned, enough time to bathe and find something decent in her closet to wear. She turned and fled up the staircase, feeling the curious stares of the other servants follow her movements.

By tomorrow she would be on her way back to the plantation. There she would confront Rhys Winghurst. He would listen; she would make him. She slammed her fist against her thigh as she walked. Her entire life depended on his cooperation.

* * *

"This was the only reply?"

Molly nodded. " 'Twas the only one I could deliver. None of the others was at home, as they've returned to their plantations."

Calypso tapped the letter against the blue satinet of her gown. Though pretty in a young-girl way, the dress was unflattering and out of style, but it was the best she could find in the wardrobe in her room. Now it wouldn't matter whether what she wore was fashionable or not. Old Mister Hanson who had answered her letter wouldn't know the difference. She had sent the letter to his granddaughter, Beatrice, but he had replied, stating the rest of the family were no longer in residence.

Damn! How could this be happening to her? What chance would she have of Mr. Hanson helping her? She chewed her bottom lip, her eyes skimming over the dress she wore in distaste. Perhaps she could make this situation work to her favor. Looking young and vulnerable in his eyes might be to her advantage. How much easier it would be to make up a story about why she was in Nassau needing a way home to a senile old man than to an inquisitive female her own age.

Rising, she pushed at the wrinkles in her skirt, a smile taking control of her lips. Yes, this could work in her favor. She would visit with Mr. Hanson this afternoon and be on a boat to Long Island by this evening.

Putting her thoughts aside, she rose and crossed over to the mirror above the mantel to inspect her appearance. The dress made her look younger than her twenty-four years, and if she allowed her hair to fall in simple curls about her shoulders and face, he would probably think her no more than seventeen.

She paused, several hairpins gripped in her hand. If only it were that easy to regain her youth. If only she could take back all those years and return to a time before Rhys Winghurst had entered her life. If only, if only.

She lifted her chin and continued working the pins from her hair until the burnished tresses lay smooth and silky against her neck.

"Come, Molly, we have a visit to make."

Wordlessly, the girl followed behind her as she retrieved her wrap and headed toward the front door.

The afternoon sun caressed her cheek as they crossed the street and worked their way down an intersecting thoroughfare leading to Market Street running parallel to George Street. Within a matter of minutes they reached the Hansons' house, a tall, three-story structure with a two-story veranda running its width. She climbed the outside staircase to the second story, the main floor of the house, and, squaring her shoulders, knocked. Mr. Hanson would help her; he must.

The servant who greeted them led them through the foyer. Then whisking Molly toward the servant quarters downstairs, she left Calypso at the entrance to the study.

Mr. Hanson's stooped figure sat in a wing chair near the fire, comforters draped about his knees and shoulders.

Calypso's heart plummeted, realizing just how old he was. Dear lord, she hoped him coherent enough to carry on a conversation.

"Mr. Hanson?"

He swiveled in his chair, his eyes lighting with delight upon discovering her. "Why, Miss Collingsworth, I'm pleased, yet a bit surprised at your presence." He pointed a shaky finger toward a twin chair opposite him. "Join me. My old bones have trouble keeping the chill away."

Sitting, she arranged her gown about her, her mind trying to decide the best way to bring up her need without sounding forward. "I was happy to find you still in residence. Beatrice, how is she?" She hadn't seen Beatrice Hanson for years.

"She's as spunky as ever, even after three babies."

"Three?" Oh dear, she had not known her friend had married, much less had children. Embarrassment flushed her face. Her father had kept her so isolated since . . . her mother's death. "How the time does fly."

"Tell me, Miss Collingsworth," he asked, reaching out a gnarled hand and placing it over one of hers, "why are you here? Since the death of Lady Collingsworth . . ." he paused, his hand gently patting hers, "we haven't seen much of you." A look of understanding crossed his wizened face.

Her head dipped in defeat. "Please, Mr. Hanson, I need your help. I must return to the plantation right away, tonight if possible."

"There's no boat at the docks for you?" Puzzlement crinkled his eyes. His next question registered in the faded blue irises. Then how had she gotten to Nassau?

She shook her head, willing him to ignore the obvious and offer her assistance without question.

His hand returned to his own lap. "So you need a sloop and an old man to keep his inquiries to himself."

Her shoulders eased forward, feeling there was a chance he would help her.

"I remember once being young myself, not so very long ago." His head angled back against the chair.

Calypso's heart began to race. *Oh, please, Mr. Hanson, don't launch into a long reminiscence of the past.*

"I had a need then to get somewhere without anyone knowing. In fact," he said, turning to look at his audience. "Ah, but you don't want to hear the ramblings of an old man, now, do you?"

She smiled, her eyes pleading. "Will you help me?"

"I'm most willing, Miss Collingsworth."

She leaped from her chair and knelt before him taking his icy hands in hers. "However can I thank you?"

"But what you don't understand, child, is I've nothing to offer. The children took the sloop back to Exuma. I

147

have no boat."

Calypso wanted to sob. Instead she rose, collecting her dignity as she stared down into the kindly eyes of Mr. Hanson. What could she say? "I appreciate your listening to me."

"Perhaps you could hire transportation."

"I've thought of that, but I have no money."

"Left without funds, were you? I hope the cad who deserted you this way left you with nothing else."

She tilted her head. What was the old man rambling about? What cad? Her eyes widened with realization. *Of course, he thinks I've eloped with a lover.* If he knew the truth of her situation, he might not be so understanding. She was a fugitive from the authorities, an accused spy. She twisted her hands about each other. "The situation never got that far, Mr. Hanson."

"Good girl," he replied with a decisive nod. He tapped a finger against the chair's varnished arm. "Money. Now, I might be able to help you there. I've a few pounds about the house." He stood on shaky legs. With slow, shuffling steps he crossed the room to a game table against the far wall. Opening a drawer, he removed a small pouch of silver crowns. "Here," he offered, stretching his arm toward her.

Should she take the money? How much easier it would be to hire a boat with cash. She stepped forward, accepting the coins. "Thank you, Mr. Hanson. I will repay you one day."

"No need, young lady. Next time be wiser about your lovers."

"I will, sir." He had no idea how much to heart she took his advice. If it hadn't been for Rhys Winghurst, she would not be in this predicament, taking money from an old man.

Rising, she crossed the room. A servant met her in the foyer and retrieved her shawl and Molly. Once out the door, she turned to the girl. "Go on to the house. I'll be home in a bit. I'll bring something back for dinner."

"You're goin' to the market alone?"

Molly's surprise irritated her. Who was she to question what her mistress did? "Go, Molly." With a swish of her skirts, she started down Market Street toward Bay Street and the docks. If she found transportation, she would not return to the town house at all but board the craft and leave right away.

Within minutes she reached her destination. The docks were crowded with fishermen, the piers lined with men cleaning conch shells of their delicate meat. The shells they set to the side. They would be sold later to jewelry manufacturers who used the polished inner shell for cameos, the likes of which were prized by women everywhere in the New World.

She glanced about, looking for prospects. Fishermen with an abundance of catch might turn her offer down. She paced the wharf searching for just the right boat.

What a slovenly lot these men were. Their clothes were ragged and dirty, their beards and hair unkempt. She reconsidered her options. She had no choice. She must choose one of these fisherman.

At the end of the pier, a small boat bobbed in the wake of the sea traffic. A man, middle-aged and relatively clean, worked his catch, a few conch and lobsters, a disgruntled mumbling issuing from his mouth. Calypso paused, watching him as he labored.

"A poor catch?"

The man glanced up at her, surprise etching his features. He turned away, moving about some rope, then swung back around. "Aye. I've had better days. Better months in fact."

She fingered the money pouch deep in a pocket. "Perhaps you might try something more lucrative."

Winding the hemp about his arm, he paused. "What

did you have in mind, miss?"

She breathed a sigh of relief. "Perhaps you would be willing to ferry a passenger to Long Island."

He secured the line with a sailor's knot and hooked it on a cleat. "Perhaps, if the pay was right — and up front."

"How much would you need?" She edged closer to the boat.

"Depends on who the passenger is." He eyed her up and down.

"Me."

A grin split his face. "Well, little lady, you must be desperate to approach a stranger. How much can you pay?"

Calypso glanced around. Several of the other fishermen paused in their work to listen to their conversation. She reached out her empty hand. "Help me aboard so we can discuss our business in private."

The fisherman cocked his head. "In private the lady says." Fingering her wrist as if it were coated with some despicable substance, he guided her toward the gunwale of the boat.

The coins clutched in her hidden hand, she stepped forward, her smooth-bottomed shoe slipping on the slick planks. The deck seemed to fall away, leaving her suspended on a tightrope. Her arms flew up flaying the air for balance, then swung like windmill blades from her shoulder sockets. *The money. I can't let go of the money,* she thought as she lost her equilibrium and tumbled backward.

She hit the water with a splash, a shower of little pings dotting around her. The heaviness of her skirts dragged her down in a whirlpool of fear, her hands clawing at the liquid world surrounding her, keeping her from catching her breath. The only thing she could think of was her aching lungs, and she flung her arms skyward, struggling to break the surface of the water.

As if appendages from heaven scooped her up, she felt her head reach the air, the chill sending a jolting thunderbolt shuddering down her spine. Her teeth chattering, she grasped the sinewy arms of the fisherman as he hauled her to safety as if she were no more important than his daily catch.

Her hand flew up to push from her eyes the seaweedlike mat her hair had become. From her fingers dangled the money pouch strings, the bag and the coins gone.

"My money," she sputtered, taking in a mouthful of salty water. She coughed, sobbed her frustration, then struggled to take another breath of precious air.

"Strewn across the bottom of the bay," the fisherman answered, heaving her up and over the side of his boat.

With blue-nipped fingers and lips quivering with cold, she turned to the man, grasping him by the shirt. "You must take me to Long Island." Wet circles spread across the front of his garment like blotting paper soaking up ink.

"I'm sorry, miss. I can't see takin' a half-drowned little pup aboard my boat and risk being caught by a disgruntled father or husband all for nothin'. I could lose my boat or, worse, my life because some pretty little wench decided to run away from home." He pried her fingers from his clothing.

"But I can pay you. A pair of silver candlesticks worth far more than the money I lost." She waited, breath held as he considered her offer.

"All right." The man rose from his squat and stepped back. "I'll accept your payment, but if you're not back in a hour, I'll not be here."

Calypso scrambled to her feet. "I'll return, don't worry." She stuck her hand out to seal their bargain.

The fisherman looked at the outstretched fingers but didn't lift his hand to meet hers. "One hour. After that

I'll be too damn drunk to sail soapsuds in a barrel."

On all fours she crawled from the boat back onto the pier. As she ran down the planking, her ruined shoes squished and gurgled with each step she took. An hour. She would be back in half that time if she hurried.

Dodging the light traffic she crossed Bay Street and cut down to George Street. She puffed up the hill, moving as fast as she could, her speed increasing when she caught sight of the familiar picket fence. Pausing long enough to remove her sodden shoes and drop them on the portico, she pushed open the front door, hopping as she gathered up her wet skirts.

With the unabated energy of a child she rushed up the stairs while deciding in her mind which gown to change into, which would best suit her needs.

"Molly," she called, limping down the hallway, her frozen feet at last awakening to discover themselves vulnerable to every stone she had stumbled over on her way back from the docks. "Some towels, Molly. And hurry."

The girl's button eyes cut around a corner as she sped to do her mistress's bidding. "Wait, Miss Calypso," the servant cried as she started to enter the room. "I think you should know—"

"Not now, Molly. I'm in a hurry."

The strange feeling she had experienced when she entered the house the first time that morning rushed in like a rising tide, then ebbed out just as quickly. She must hurry. She couldn't miss that boat. Pushing open the door to her room, she entered, blinking in the darkness. The curtains were pulled shut. She didn't remember leaving them that way.

"Ouch," she mumbled, stumbling over a shoe she had casually tossed on the floor earlier in her frantic search for something to wear. Reaching the bedside table, she reached into the drawer for a phosphoric candle to light the taper beside the headboard. She fumbled with the glass tube, at last snapping it in half catching the wick on fire.

A hand reached out, circling her wrist like a band of steel.

"Oh," she choked, unprepared for an intruder in the room, her heart vaulting to her throat. The authorities had found her.

No. Not now. She was so close to escaping. Concentrating on the curled fingers clamped about her wrist, she bared her teeth, willing to use the only form of defense she could think of, ladylike or not. She must get away.

As her teeth sank into the fleshy ball of the restraining thumb, its owner issued a painful grunt. Then the mate to her captor pushed against her nose and eyes, forcing her face away from her victim.

"Damn it, wench, you're as untamed as a badger and just as vicious." A restricting arm crossed her chest, dragging her back against the solidity of a male body, hard and lean and ungiving. "It's a damn good thing I'm a man of peace. Otherwise, you would find yourself senseless on the floor. It's what you deserve." The sound of her assailant sucking the wounded flesh of his hand filled the darkness.

She fought to escape the clutch, but the arm tightened, squeezing the breath from her lungs.

"Don't try me further, Calypso." He spun her about, crushing her hard against his chest, and she saw Rhys Winghurst staring down at her, molten anger tightening the muscles of his face.

"What are you doing here?" she hissed. "Come to watch the spy shot at dawn?"

His mouth quirked up on one side in amusement. "The prospect could be entertaining." He jerked his gaze away with a sigh, his brown eyes settling on her mouth. "No, sweeting, nothing so sinister. The fort seems to think you threw yourself from the parapet walls. They're searching

153

the brambles for your broken body at this moment."

"And you decided I wasn't worth looking for?"

"On the contrary. I know the workings of your devious mind well. You might be foolish enough to try and escape, but suicide—it's just not your style." He pushed her wet body back to study her. "Though I must say you look as if you tried to drown yourself. What happened?"

Embarrassment at her bumbling stupidity flamed across her face. "My actions don't concern you."

His face set with an inner frustration. Why was he looking at her as if she had lied to him? As if she owed him an explanation?

"You *are* my responsibility."

She wrenched from his unyielding grip. "I don't understand you, Rhys Winghurst. First, you see me dragged away as a spy; now you tell me you feel responsible for me. Do you really expect me to believe you?" Her gaze darted to the doorway.

His eyes followed, and he crossed the room with a casualness that set her nerves on edge as he leaned against the framework, cutting off her route of escape.

"Where would you go, Calypso?" he whispered softly. "Back home? You know your father would only return you to Fort Charlotte. Probably he would escort you personally and toss you in one of the cells."

The truth hurt bad enough, but coming from Rhys Winghurst it stung deep and hard. "Why would it matter to you what happened to me?"

He studied her, his arms crossed over his chest. "I have my reasons and believe me they are selfish ones."

She spun away. "I should have suspected as much. Plan to use me further in your despicable plot?" She swung back around, remembering her vow to do whatever she had to to make this man release her. "Please, Rhys, let me go and clear my name. I'll keep quiet about what you're up to. I don't care whom you spy for, just allow me to return home—to Tristan. He needs me. I must protect him from—"

"Tristan?" Rhys straightened and crossed the room to grasp her shoulders in his strong, demanding hands. "What about the boy?"

The intensity of his glare bored through her. What did Rhys Winghurst know about her little brother? Why was there such genuine concern etched on his face? She debated her response to his question. His reasons didn't matter. Whatever they were, she would use them to her advantage.

She lifted her chin. "I'll do whatever I must, whatever you want, if you'll help me."

His eyes flicked over her rising and falling breast and down the curve of her hips outlined by the wet gown. "My, we are the martyr today, aren't we?"

Lips pressed in a taut line, she swallowed the sharp retort that popped into her head. "If I must be—if you force me."

He released her as if her touch scalded him, and he presented his back, his hands clasped behind him. "I have only one request of you."

"Request?" Her breath sucked in and out with indignation laced with fear. "Call your demands by their proper title, sir," she sneered. "Where do you want me?" Her hand lifted, ready to remove her clothing at his nod. Without a doubt she knew how it would be this time with him. Cold, calculated, impersonal—a man with a woman bought and paid for. And though it had been that way the first time—this was different. This time she knew the circumstances; she was no longer naive and innocent of his intentions.

Completely still, his linked hands white with tension, he never looked back at her. "How little you know me, Calypso. I'm not near the cad you think." He spun so fast, she startled, the intensity of his glare like burning

155

coals against her skin. "Change your clothes, and be ready to leave within the hour." Crossing the room, he opened the door.

"Rhys?" she asked, dogging his footsteps, anxiety forcing her feet to move. "Where are we going?"

"To get Tristan, of course."

Her eyes widened. Unable to believe how easily he had agreed to help her, she asked. "And then?"

"And then we'll seal our bargain. You're going back with me to Philadelphia."

Chapter Eleven

The silver reflection of the moon streaking across the undulating bay reminded Rhys of a satin ribbon trailing through a woman's carefully coiffured hair, long and unbroken until a man ran his fingers through the tresses destroying the perfection, yet leaving something eminently more desirable in its wake. Something irresistible and exciting. Like the woman he had left aboard his ship. The ghostly image of Calypso, her gown blowing about her ankles, standing at the railing watching the small boat dart toward the shore, refused to give him peace. Her eyes had glistened with conflicting emotions—first softening in gratitude, then clouding with suspicion.

How could she not understand a man's need to rescue his son from the abuse of others? Did she think him so calloused that he required "payment" for saving the boy?

Payment. Unconsciously, he fingered the silver crown tucked in his vest pocket, an object he had been unable to rid himself of—a symbol of Calypso and her unpredictable ways. He frowned, pulling his hand away. Why did she persist with this story that Tristan was her brother?

The oars of the rowboat descended, cutting the watery imagery in half and stirring him from his musing. Angling his chin, he studied the empty docks of the Collingsworths' plantation. Had anyone seen the unlit ilhouette of *The Oceanid* as she had slipped into the harbor? Hopefully not. And if his luck held, he should be able to sneak in and out this late at night with no one the wiser, at least not until morning when the household discovered Tristan and his nursemaid's absence. Would they be pursued? Not likely; there was no reason to suspect the departed Earl of Flint of kidnapping the baron's "son," as if the old bastard cared one iota about the boy in the first place.

That was—not until Collingsworth discovered the loss of the condemning missive and diary from his desk. Rhys's need to present the physical evidence to his superiors, especially the seal pressed into the wax on the back of the letter, battled with his desire to slip away unnoticed with his son. By the time the theft was found, he consoled his restless fears, the ship should be too far away to be overtaken—if his luck held.

He glanced back to where the vessel rested at silent anchor. No more than a blotting of a few stars betrayed its presence. Again the restless image of the woman staring down at him from the railing above pricked at his conscience, igniting the guilt that refused to be squelched.

His eyes narrowed in condemnation as he denied the rebuke he heaped upon himself. She had given in too easily to his request that she accompany him and had followed meekly behind as he had led her to his ship. If she trusted him so little, why did she place herself in jeopardy without resistance? He had fully expected the necessity of dragging her aboard, fighting tooth and nail. What was the wench up to?

Tapping his finger against his thigh, he mulled over the possibilities. What if Collingsworth did suspect him and had arranged for his daughter to spy on him? Was he walking into a well-set trap by coming ashore? He had no alternative; he had to take that chance. His son was too important to him. No matter what deception the baron might have planned, Tristan was his flesh and blood. He must take the boy to a safe haven.

"Shore, Captain," the head rower announced, the small boat wedging into the soft sand of the beach, its stern angling in the gentle surge.

Rhys stepped out, glanced back one final time at *The Oceanid*, then signaled his men to wait there on the beach for him.

"Are you sure, Captain, you don't want help?" the man inquired.

He shook his head. "Give me an hour. Then if I don't show up, return to the ship and sail. Luther has instructions. Follow them."

The sailor nodded.

He turned and started up the path leading to the mansion. If he didn't return, Luther would follow his orders without question, and Calypso Collingsworth would find herself in deeper trouble than she knew existed. Her life wouldn't be worth living, and hell wouldn't want her once the little man finished with her.

"Where are we going, Nanna?" Tristan rubbed his sleepy eyes with his fists as Nannette led him down the hallway, a small satchel tucked under her free arm.

"Shh, laddie. We don't want to wake anyone." Her heart pattered like a cornered hare's with fear and uncertainty. Was she doing the right thing by going with this intense, unreadable stranger? She gripped the boy's shoulder, seeking an answer. She didn't know. Dear God in Heaven, she wasn't sure whom to trust in a world gone lopsided.

All she knew for certain was that she and Tristan must escape. This chance was one she must take—an opportunity to get Tristan away from the insane vengeance of the master. One day the baron would go too far, and the boy would suffer permanent injury or worse—death. She couldn't allow that to happen. She just couldn't. Crossing herself piously, she mumbled a prayer for saintly guidance.

On silent feet she led her ward down the corridor, once more placing a finger to her lips as he turned, his mouth opening to question their strange, nocturnal behavior. His liquid brown eyes studied her so trustingly. Her heart lurched in genuine love. If she failed Tristan, her very existence was for naught.

She hesitated, unsure what she should do. Rhys Winghurst unnerved her, he was so brooding and mysterious, yet she couldn't forget the fleeting look in his eyes as they had lit upon the boy. He cared. Her instincts told her Tristan meant more to him than anyone knew.

With that encouraging thought, she pushed forward, taking the boy's small hand in hers as she eased them down the staircase to the main-floor foyer. The earl had said he would be waiting there for them.

Halfway down, she brought them to a halt as she analyzed the tall, uncompromising figure braced at the bottom of the stairs. The moon poured in through a large, octagonal window to his left, its silver light reflecting on his hair and shoulders as he turned to confront them.

"Rhys," Tristan squealed in pure delight as he pushed past the barrier of her body.

"No, Tristan," she whispered, reaching out to stop him unsuccessfully. The boy and the man clung for a brief moment; then the earl released the small body and stared up at her.

What was it about this man that bothered her so? A small frown furled between her brows. The eyes. She know them, trusted them, could read them as if printed words emerged from their darkness, manufactured deep inside his soul. She glanced down at Tristan and found the boy staring up at her also, the same concentration radiating from his gaze as the man's who stood beside him.

Her eyes shot to the earl and back to Tristan in a zigzag pattern until she could no longer doubt. They were identical in color and intensity. And the jawline—the same, as well as the hair and nose.

How could that be? Her breath caught with a jagged hitch deep in her chest. Rhys Winghurst couldn't possibly be the laddie's sire? Or could he? Calypso had never revealed the name of her seducer, not even to her trusted Nanna.

She glanced back at the man, his hand lifting in impatience as he urged her to hurry. How many times had Tristan gestured to her in the same manner? Her heart thundered, and her hand reached out, seeking assurance.

Rhys grabbed her wrist and pulled her along through the foyer and down the long hallway leading to the narrow staircase that went below to the servants' quarters on the ground floor. *Tristan's father,* she thought with amazement.

Once they reached the outside exit, the full impact of what her last thought implied struck her. She pulled back, dragging Tristan, who had trouble keeping his eyes open, into the circle of her arms. The boy's head pillowed against her shoulder. "You," she hissed in a whispered threat. "You are the one."

Rhys turned, perplexed at her sudden outburst. His brow lifted as he gripped her arm and forced her into the concealment of some shrubbery.

"What are you babbling about, woman?"

"You. You sired the bairn."

"Yes," he replied in the silence of the night enveloping them, his lips compressed determination, his eyes never flinching. "And if you resist me, I'll take the boy without you. He'll not stay here another day. I'll not have it."

"Why didn't you come back for them long ago?"

He stared, then glanced away. "I never knew or suspected my son existed. Not until the other day when I cared for Tristan's wounds and I saw the birthmark."

There, he had admitted to the truth. Turning so the sleeping boy was enveloped by the bulk of her body, she demanded. "You knew then, yet you allowed them to take my lassie? How could you?"

"I'll not stand here arguing with you, old woman." He reached behind her and pulled Tristan's sagging body from her arms. "Stay or follow; the choice is yours, but my son's coming with me."

The time stretched endlessly. Standing idly at the ship's rail, Calypso could feel every nerve in her body drawn taut, strained with apprehension. Would Rhys, in truth, bring Tristan with him, or had his agreement to help her get her brother to safety only been a ploy to get her aboard his ship without resistance? She sighed, fidgeted, shifting from foot to foot with a restlessness that refused to be disciplined, then turned away from the railing. What was the point in scanning the darkness? She couldn't see a blessed thing anyway.

"Come with me, miss." The voice spoke from the gloom to her right.

She spun about, her eyes probing the night. Her gaze settled on a shadowy silhouette, no taller than a boy. Yet the voice had been definitely manly. "I would much rather wait here until Rhys returns."

"I appreciate that, miss, but I've my orders. You're to go below until the captain comes back."

"Your captain's orders I imagine," she replied, a grim determination molding her lips into an angry slash against her face. She had been right. Rhys had tricked her.

"Aye, miss. The captain's doing." The small figure

stepped forward, his large head and broad shoulders out of place on the short, stumpy legs.

She stared. She couldn't help it. Many times she had read about people like this, dwarfs, but never had she met one. Had his size been normal, he would have been most handsome. Tearing her eyes away, she blushed from her rudeness. "I'm sorry." What an inane thing to say.

" 'Tis no blame of yours." He eyed her back just as boldly.

Again Calypso blushed, this time in discomfort at the rakish way the dwarf assessed her. "I didn't mean to imply I was at fault. I was only—" Only what?

"Ah, yes, sympathy. I suppose I'm to be grateful for your kindheartedness."

"Not at all." Her chin lifted, and she turned away, annoyed by his sarcasm. "You caught me by surprise, that's all."

"Well, if you've accustomed yourself to my abnormalities now, I would appreciate your following me."

She whipped back around. "I think I'll stay here, if you don't mind." Their eyes locked, unflinching. What was he going to do? She was bigger than he was. He hadn't the strength to force her to do anything she didn't want to do. Her mouth curled into a challenging smile.

"Luther." A burly sailor approached the stalemated pair.

"Aye, Kraemer, what do you want?" Luther refused to look away, and so did she.

"It's been over an hour since the captain left. What do you think?" There was uncertainty in the man's voice.

"I think we follow the captain's orders." Luther pulled his eyes away, glancing toward Kraemer. "Escort the lady to quarters." He pinned Calypso with a triumphant stare and pivoted.

"What orders?" she demanded, jerking her arm away as the sailor reached out to take charge of her. At last she

163

would know the truth of Rhys Winghurst's deception. "He can't do this to me. I'm not your captain's prisoner."

Luther spun back around, contempt and distrust twisting his face. "You're right, miss, you're not the captain's prisoner, but if he doesn't return, you'll be mine, and believe me, you'll be in a much worse predicament. Rhys seems to have a soft spot for you." He eyed her with distaste. "I don't."

"What are you saying?" Unexpected fear snowballed in her stomach.

With a nod from Luther, Kraemer took a firm grip on her arm. "I'm saying, miss, you better hope Rhys returns. If he doesn't, I'm to assume you are at fault. If that's the case, you'll find yourself at the bottom of the bay before the day breaks."

She sucked in a thin breath of air. "You would murder me?"

He smiled without warmth. "Like I said, I've my orders, and I will follow through with them."

Kraemer gave her a shove and forced her toward the companionway stairs. Without a doubt, the dwarf would do what he had threatened to do, and the worst part was that no one would miss her or care if she was sacrificed to the sea. The thought that Rhys Winghurst didn't trust her rankled. She had never deceived him or lied, not the way he had once and twice again. What right did he have to fault her if he failed to return?

Within minutes she found herself in a darkened cabin, not much bigger than a pantry, one that was rarely used. There was a small crate against one wall, some place to sit, and a pile of blankets in a corner smelling of seaweed. She wrinkled her nose in distaste; then she shuddered in fear as a key was turned, locking the door. A small candle flickered in a sconce above her head.

She sat down, brushing away the panic creeping up her spine. Rhys would return at any moment. Why wouldn't he? She knew the routine of the household at the mansion. All slept soundly, especially the servants. It would be simple to slip in and out unless . . .

Nannette. What if the nursemaid refused to cooperate? There was a good possibility she might. The little woman knew of her dislike for the earl. Calypso wrung her hands. Why hadn't she thought of that possibility earlier and warned Rhys of the fact?

The rising panic inched higher, twining itself about her heart. The minutes marched by, measured only by the shortening of the candle above her head. At one point, she stood and paced, four steps one way, four steps back, until a feeling that the walls were closing about her and she couldn't breathe possessed her, overwhelming any rational thought.

She flung herself against the door, pounding, her voice rising with the flood of fear choking her sanity.

"Let me out," she demanded in rhythm to her hammering. By the dozenth time the words came out as a plea, her fists raw and sore, unable to beat anymore against the hard wood.

Her cheek pressed against the door, she stilled. She had heard sounds from the other side. "Rhys," she sobbed. "Thank God you're back."

The key worked in the lock, and she stepped away fully intending to throw herself into his arms with relief. The door opened and light from a lantern poured in, momentarily blinding her. She threw her arm up to shade her eyes.

"Take her," demanded a familiar voice.

A multitude of hands grabbed her, pulling her out of the cabin.

"No," she cried, realizing her fate was at the mercy of the ship's crew. They would drown her without hesitation. Surrounded by the angry mob, she was pushed and shoved down the corridor and up the stairway, Luther in the lead.

To the east the first tinge of sunrise painted the horizon with golden fingers of light, outlining the curve of Long Island. The dwarf had sworn she would die before daybreak. Her time was limited; the end near. She must find a way to stop this insanity.

Struggling to escape her captors, she managed only to lose a shoe and the ribbon controlling her flaming hair. The long tresses fell into her face as someone grabbed her arms behind her back and bound them with a length of rope.

Picked up like a bundle of sticks, she was draped over the railing by strong arms. She glanced down once at the churning water and wondered how long it would take to die—seconds, minutes? God help her, would she feel pain? She closed her eyes and waited for the inevitable moment when she would fall through the air and be swallowed up by the watery demons below.

"Stop," cried a voice.

Her eyes snapped open and followed the stares of the mob. In the light of early dawn, the dark, bobbing shape of the rowboat could be seen nearing the ship. A deep sob of relief bubbled from her throat as a roar of pleasure ripped through the crowd.

She was returned to the deck and settled on her feet, her arms released from their bondage. She found herself forgotten and pushed to the background by the sailors, who edged to the railing, laughing and calling to those approaching in the skiff. She glanced at the eager faces, amazed to find such loyalty toward a man she utterly distrusted. Obviously there was a side to Rhys Winghurst she knew nothing about. A facet of his personality that evoked allegiance, a willingness to commit murder if ordered.

She turned in silence to watch the boarders as they climbed the rope ladder dangling over the side of the ship, but it wasn't until they reached the last few rungs that she could make out their features as their faces were shadowed by the yellow light of a lantern, the morning sun still too low to give much assistance.

One sailor, two. Strangers. Had she been correct in her assumption that Rhys wouldn't bring Tristan? Then why had he returned to the mansion? As a spy he could have had a number of reasons.

A small, familiar face popped into view, the brown eyes shining with adventurous delight.

"Tristan," she called, trying to push her way through the crowd to reach her brother.

"Callie," he trilled, his body jerking with excitement. She could almost see his hidden feet scrambling on the ropes in order to hurry.

"Careful, Tristan," she warned, elbowing her way toward the one person who meant everything to her.

The boy grunted, and his face slipped from view, the last glimpse she had of him his eyes were wide with fear.

"Oh, God, no," she blurted as the thud of a tumbling body reached her ears. He had fallen, and she wasn't there to help him.

The crowd parted in concern as if they sensed her distress as she struggled to reach the side of the ship. What would she find far below? Her brother's twisted body or, worse, nothing? Had the sea swallowed him up?

Panting, she angled into a position to make the descent down the ladder as quickly as possible, not once considering she would most likely trip over her gown and fall as well.

Her dress hem caught in the breeze billowing full circle as one foot touched and clung to the rung of the ladder, her mind a swirl of foreboding thoughts. Tristan. Tristan. She must reach Tristan.

"What are you trying to do, wench, suffocate us with your skirts?" The contemptuous growl brought her frantic action to a halt.

She glanced back and down from her perch at the top of the ladder to find Rhys staring up at her, Tristan safe and sound in the circle of one arm. Her gown flapped like an untied sail, then ballooned with the wind interrupting the sparks sizzling between their gazes. Mortified, she felt the heat of a flush spread across her face. No doubt he had full view of her legs and underclothing beneath her dress.

Without thinking, she reached down with one hand to seize the wayward yards of cloth and pulled them snugly about her body. Realizing her mistake too late, her other hand lost its grip, and she would have gone tumbling backward if the press of a solid chest against her back hadn't caught her.

Rhys. He had saved her from her own foolishness. His mouth inches from her ear, she could distinguish the suppressed humor rumbling in his chest. Damn him. It was bad enough he had ordered her thrown overboard, then had had a full view of her bare legs as she had stumbled down the rope; now he was laughing at her. The humiliation was too much. Her fist balled and swung behind her, catching him on the shoulder.

"Let me go, you wretched person."

"Be still, woman, or we'll all three take a cold dunking in the bay." His mocking laughter ended, and his other arm grasped her about the waist as Tristan worked his way over her and up to the railing. "Go on, boy," Rhys urged, "Callie and I will be right behind you." His arm tightened about her middle. "If she behaves."

"I'll not go anywhere with you, Rhys Winghurst," she hissed as the full contour of his rock-solid body pressed against her back.

"Just what do you plan to do?" he taunted.

The wind plucked at the rope ladder, causing it to sway to and fro. Her clutch tightened on the rung in front of her. At the moment she was glad the sure-footed sea captain held her in place. But why did it have to be Rhys Winghurst, the man who had destroyed her life?

His warm breath tickled her ear. "Come on, Calypso. You're shivering with cold. Let's go aboard and discuss this rationally, not dangling from the side of a ship."

Her anger gave way to her fear, though she willed it not to, and she nodded, guilt nagging at her conscience; yet she was glad as her foot discovered the next rung higher. His body moved with hers, never letting up the pressure as if he expected her to change her mind. Perhaps he was right; she might have if given the room to consider the possibility.

Seconds later they were on the deck. Tristan pressed his compact body against her legs, his arms wrapping about her waist. "Oh, Callie," he sobbed, "you've not gone away and left me."

She knelt, bringing them face to face. "Of course not, Tristan. I promised, remember?"

His head bobbed, and he buried his face into the warmth of her neck. The love she felt for no one but this child expanded in her chest, leaving her breathless and in tears. "I love you, Tristan," she whispered so only he could hear.

"Lower the harness." At the sound of Rhys's crisp command, Calypso's gaze shifted back to the railing.

"Whatever is going on?" She straightened and curled an arm about her brother, keeping him close.

"It's Nanna," Tristan bubbled. "She came too, but she's afraid to climb the ladder."

Minutes later, the little Scotswoman, squawking like a ruffled hen, ascended over the side, a makeshift harness draped about her middle, her skirt-enclosed legs kicking like kittens caught in a burlap sack.

" 'Tis no way for a lady to travel," the woman grumbled as strong arms directed the pulleys that lowered her

169

to the deck.

Laughter built in Calypso's throat, and she covered her mouth to suppress the giggles attempting to escape.

"Is she always such a pain in the neck?" Rhys moved toward her, shaking his head. "I've never met a woman who could complain so much."

"Always," Calypso confirmed. "She hates boats, and, as long as I can remember, she never set foot in one." She gave him a suspicious look. "What did you threaten her with to get her to come along?"

"Only with being left behind." His mouth lifted with pained perplexity.

His comical face made her laugh, her eyes shining as they met his. Then she sobered, appalled at how quickly she forgot to whom she spoke. Rhys Winghurst didn't deserve her good-fellowship. She stepped back, refusing to look at him. Nanna needed her comforting, not this callous cad.

Yet as she moved away, she could hear Tristan speaking to him, comfortable and at ease with the man she thought of as her enemy.

"Thank you, Rhys," the boy piped. "I knew I could trust you. I just knew it."

She couldn't resist a peek at the man and boy, and a spear of unexpected jealousy pierced her wounded pride as Tristan hugged the earl with heartfelt gratitude, a gesture he had always reserved for her alone.

She glanced away. Why should she feel jealous? Just because this man had accomplished in a few short days what she had been trying to do for as long as she could remember—protect Tristan from the cold, cruel environment of her family—that was no reason to feel resentment. But Rhys Winghurst was a stranger. He meant nothing in the boy's life. Why should Tristan give him affection he didn't deserve?

Little fool, she chided herself. *I'm acting immature and spoiled.* She sighed with frustration. *But why does it have to be Rhys Winghurst? I could accept a display of loyalty toward anyone else.*

Reaching Nannette, she offered to help her companion from the straps and bindings of the harness. The two women fell into each other's arms, tears flowing freely down their cheeks.

"Thank god, my lassie, you're safe."

"I'm fine, Nanna. I'm so relieved you're here." She would talk to the nursemaid and tell her everything. Maybe the little woman could make her understand the twisting emotions ripping her apart.

Arm in arm, they started toward the companionway stairs. Passing Rhys, Calypso refused to look at him, but Nannette paused, taking his hand in her much smaller one.

"Thank ye kindly, sir." The woman's soft burr sliced through her.

" 'Twas nothing, Nannette. As you know, I have my reasons." Rhys shuffled his feet in what appeared to be almost a boyish way. This was not the man she knew, always cocksure and confident that whatever he did was the best.

He caught her eye, but the smile she anticipated never appeared on his lips. Instead he tried to tear away the thin patina of control keeping her from shouting accusations at him.

"We are very tired and would like to rest." She lifted her chin to ward off his prying glare.

The smile he reluctantly offered was anything but consoling. "A long night for all of us. I suppose our discussion can wait a few hours."

She had no idea what he was speaking about, but she kept her face blank and her eyes piercing.

"Cabins have been prepared for you." He nodded to someone behind her. "Show our guests to their quarters."

He glanced down at Tristan. "I'll come see you later, boy. We'll share some time."

Without a word, she urged Nannette to follow the sailor across the deck.

"Whatever is the matter with you, lassie? Couldn't you have thanked the earl for his assistance?" the nursemaid scolded as they moved away.

"No, Nanna." She gave the woman a pleading look. "His reasons are selfish. I'm sure of that." Glancing away, she balled her fist and thudded it against the side of her leg to confirm her beliefs about the man. "You couldn't possibly understand."

"Nay, lassie." Nannette patted her hand in a familiar gesture. "I understand more than you could imagine. Perhaps more than you do."

"Oh, Nanna," she whispered, dipping her head to rest it on the proffered shoulder, one she had cried on many times in her life. A peace she had not known since Rhys Winghurst had entered her life settled about her. Nanna would know and explain her jumbled feelings.

Reaching the stairs, they found their way blocked by the short body of Luther. His eyes narrowed and gleamed with malice.

"You've escaped this time, miss," the dwarf hissed, "but there will be others. You'll make a mistake, and Rhys will see things my way." He shook one stubby finger under her nose. "And don't think the blood tie you share with the boy will save you. It won't, I promise you."

Calypso sucked in her breath. In wary silence, she led Nannette past his formidable presence, his smallness no longer something she found to her advantage. 'Twas said demons stood no taller than children. Fear shivered down her spine.

"Tell me, lassie," Nannette asked. "Whatever did you do to that strange little man to make him despise you so?"

"I don't know, Nanna. Truly, I'm not sure." But one thing she was positive about was that she would tread carefully around Luther. Many secrets abounded she knew nothing about, and though she didn't understand the reasons why those around her did what they did, she was certain of one conclusion. Men, always men, made life hell for a woman.

Chapter Twelve

"But, Callie, I want to wait for Rhys. He said he'd come see me." Tristan's face screwed with resistance as Nannette's insistent hand urged him down the corridor to the cabin designated for her use.

"I know what the earl said, laddie," interceded the nursemaid, taking control of the situation, "but this mornin' I think the earl will need a time of rest, not an inquisitive little boy with an endless satchel of questions. Besides you could do with a nap as well, young man."

"I won't sleep, Nanna. I'm not tired." Tristan rubbed his eyes with a small fist, contradicting his words. "Only babies take naps."

"Ah, laddie, I would find an hour of quiet to my liking. Surely ye aren't calling your Nanna a bairn, now are ye?"

The door clicked softly behind the woman's back, leaving Calypso standing in the passageway alone. How would she ever manage without Nannette? Though she loved Tristan dearly, she didn't do well as a disciplinarian, but then sisters weren't supposed to be stern and demanding. That was for mothers and nannies.

Motherhood. She frowned slightly, her thoughts drifting back to six years before. Had her baby lived, what kind of parent would she have been? A terrible one, no doubt. Then a more startling thought flashed through her head. What kind of father would Rhys have been?

Like everything else he did, perfect. Her face contorted with disgust. Why was she thinking these ludicrous thoughts about babies and parenthood, especially where Rhys Winghurst was concerned?

She turned and entered the doorway to the cabin the sailor had indicated was hers and placed her hands on her hips. Quite a difference from the tiny closet she had been thrown into last night. A smile of triumph bowed her lips.

Though sparsely furnished, the cabin exuded a warmth and charm she had not expected aboard a ship. There was a desk bolted down in one corner, its work surface freshly polished and cleared; the chair, worn with use, was pushed tightly beneath the top. A small night table graced an alcove on the far side of the chamber, its top just as unused as the desk's. Next to the table stood a closed sea chest.

But it was the bed that caught her attention and held her spellbound. Large and wide with four short oak corner posts, it took up the major part of the cabin, its counterpane coverlet fresh and inviting with not a wrinkle breaking the perfection of its handsewn squares. Almost as if it was unused except for rare occasions.

Exhausted from the ordeal of the long night, she stepped closer, drawn to the down-filled mattress as if a magnet pulled her forward, so soft and inviting it looked. Lifting her hand to her mouth, she yawned and kicked off her shoes.

After a moment's hesitation, she unfastened her gown and drew the garment off. Glancing at its disheveled state, she lifted a brow in exasperation. The dress was ruined with stains and rips. How could she repair it? She would have no choice except to try, as it was the only item of clothing she had to her name now.

Too exhausted to battle with making even a simple

175

decision, she tossed the gown across the night table, and for one brief moment she felt a stab of guilt for disrupting the military tidiness of the room. Then she shrugged her shoulders. This was now her quarters and would be for days. She would make the facilities home, the way she liked it.

Dressed only in her chemise, she lowered her weight and sighed in anticipation of the ticking enfolding her in its comfortable depths. Sleep. Hours of unencumbered rest would be a dream come true.

As if the ship itself dipped into a deep trough, her legs flew out from beneath her when she dropped onto the bed. Rocking back and forth as if in a cradle, her bare feet kicking at the empty air, she squeaked her surprise as her fingers grasped the bedstead for balance.

Finally the bed stilled, her heart slowing as well. One toe crabbed to the edge of the coverlet, then dropped to the floor. She swayed with the slight movement. What kind of contraption was she on?

Easing from the swinging bed, she turned to inspect it. Her fingers grazed the frame, and it seesawed under the pressure. She snapped her hand away. Better yet, what kind of strange person designed such an oddity?

"I tell you, Rhys, you better watch your step," she suddenly heard a voice in the corridor outside. The tone brought her whirling about. She knew that voice and dreaded the sound of it. Luther. Taking a deep breath, she crept closer to the door.

"Drop it, Luther. You're wrong." The earl's deep timbre overshadowed the dwarf's higher-pitched one. "We'll discuss this later. Right now I'm tired."

The dwarf snorted. "We'd all be better off if I'd completed what I started."

Rhys sighed, the sound deep with exasperation. "Perhaps you're right, but we'll never know, will we? I'm back and we're headed home."

"Home? I don't call that colonial mud hole home. Let's really return home to the manor, where we rightly belong."

"Ah, Luther." Rhys's voice lowered with gentle understanding. "Give it up. I won't return to Flint. When will you accept that fact?"

"Never, my lord. Not as long as I live and breathe."

"I suppose not. You wouldn't be you otherwise."

The little man grunted, a sound of consent and acceptance. "I'll not disturb you, my lord, unless it is necessary."

"Thank you. I imagine I'll have my hands full for the next few hours, unless I'm lucky and she's already asleep."

She? Calypso caught her breath and took a step backward. Was he discussing her? Why was Rhys and that strange little man standing outside her quarters talking in the first place? As she scuttled away from the door, the back of her knees brushed against the bed, and she dropped like a wounded shore bird, its support shot out from beneath it, and again landed on the giant-sized cradle.

With her legs sprawled, the bed swinging as it issued squeals of protest, the door opened, revealing the surprised faces of the two men.

"Jesus Christ," Rhys muttered, stepping into the room and slamming the door on Luther's smirking countenance. "What in the world are you doing, wench?"

Always he caught her making an utter fool of herself. Fighting to still the bed and rise, she managed to set it swinging harder.

"What are you doing in here?" she demanded, flipping to her stomach and dropping backward to the floor on her knees. Her torso still draped over the bed, the sway-

177

ing stopped the moment she made contact with the rug below.

"This, sweeting, is my cabin." His stare dropped from her face to the roundness of her posterior peeking from the edge of her chemise.

"Your cabin?" She stood, then glanced down at her state of undress. With a gasp, she crouched in place, her knees nearly meeting her neck. "Then what am I doing here?"

His gaze traveled the short distance from her feet to her face. "Looks to me like you were getting ready to go to bed."

"I was." Again she sucked in a great gulp of air. "No, I wasn't," she sputtered in confusion. "Please leave this instant."

Rhys crossed the room, picked up her discarded gown, and assessed it, one eyebrow raised. "You must learn to be more tidy, if you plan on sharing quarters with me."

"With you?" She shot straight up from her squat. "I don't plan on sharing anything with you." Three steps brought her near enough to snatch the garment from his grasp. She tugged it on, her shaking fingers attempting to fasten it up her stomach and over her bosom. Until now she hadn't realized how damn many buttons the dress possessed. "This room is as austere as a convent cloister. I had no idea anyone occupied it. Otherwise I wouldn't have gotten . . ." Her face reddened in embarrassment.

". . . So comfortable?" He glanced around the cabin. "A cloister, huh?" He cocked his head to one side. "Honestly, wench, knowing your nature as I do, I doubt you've ever seen the inside of a convent." His mouth twisted with a grin. "Nun's accommodations are no more than a cot and a blanket—not really your style. You seemed more at home on my bed. Besides, the Mother

178

Superior would most likely have died of a heart attack if she had walked in and caught you the way I did. Most unsaintly." He clucked his tongue. "But very stirring from my point of view."

Arrogant cad! How could he talk to her that way? She grabbed the first thing her hand found, one of her discarded shoes. Tossing it, she felt a surge of glee as it glanced off his right shoulder and he flinched, a flicker of anger darkening his eyes before he regained his control. "How would you know what a convent looks like on the inside? Men aren't allowed." She offered a smirk of victory.

"You'd be surprised where I've been." He bent, picked up the slipper, and stretched out his arm, offering it back to her. "I'll not remind you again about keeping the cabin tidy."

"Oww," she uttered in frustration, wanting to say something that would silence his quick tongue as well as wipe the gloating look from his face. Her fists clenched at her sides, her nails biting sharply into her palms. Then she snatched the still offered shoe from his hand and dropped it beside its mate.

Rhys took a deep breath and let it out slowly, his eyes lingering on the curve of her breasts outlined in the hastily buttoned dress. She crossed her arms over her chest and presented her back.

"Look, Calypso," Rhys began, issuing a deep sigh. "Let's call a truce. I'm tired and so are you. Later, we'll have all the time in the world to spat and play childish word games to see who can outdo the other."

Childish? He dared call her childish. In her heart she recognized the truth of his words, but it was his fault she reacted in that manner. Oh, why couldn't she control her emotions around this man? One more minute with him and God only knew what she would do.

"I'd like another cabin," she requested. The silence was as crisp as a newly starched ruffle.

"The ship is crowded to capacity. I've no space available." He turned and began unbuttoning his jacket, dismissing her and her needs as if she were no more than a child.

"Then why don't you go elsewhere?" she asked, determined to be rid of him. "Go hang a hammock from some rafter. Isn't that what you sailors normally do?"

His back tensed with an unnamed emotion. "I suppose I could." He reached up and began undoing his jabot from his cravat. "But I won't. Personally, I like the present arrangement." He spun to face her as he untied his neckcloth. "You give my quarters a certain air." He lifted his wide shoulders with a shrug. "Rather—non-monastic, wouldn't you say?" His fingers found the buttons of his shirt.

Her eyes followed his every move. What was he doing? Did he plan to undress right here in front of her? At last his true nature shone through. He would finally demand his "payment" for rescuing Tristan. "Then put me back into that pantry-sized room I was in last night," she insisted in sheer desperation. She didn't wish to keep her end of the bargain. Now that Tristan was safe, she didn't feel the necessity. "I'll manage just fine with a blanket."

His shirt unbuttoned to the waist, yet still tucked into his breeches, he stilled, a frown denting the space between his brows. "What room?"

Her gaze traveled the length of the open vee of his shirt, then shot back up to his face. "You know darn well what room. I was put there on your orders. It was smelly and barely large enough to turn around in."

His hands snaked out and gripped her upper arms. "Who put you there?"

She paused, shaken by his supposed ignorance of the

180

way she had been treated. "Luther," she hissed. "Then at dawn when you didn't return, he had me dragged up top and ordered me thrown overboard." Her chin inched upward in indignation.

His ever-active brow lifted. "Luther did all that?"

Her head dipped once in affirmation.

"Damn, but his loyalty could strangle an elephant. What stopped him?"

"Your return."

His fingers relaxed and released her and returned to his shirt. "He wouldn't have done it, you know."

Calypso choked on the surprise clogging her throat. "Wouldn't have! He nearly did! I was hanging over the side of the ship when—"

"He was only trying to scare you."

"Well, he succeeded. Quite well, I might add."

Rhys turned his back and untucked his shirt.

Mouth opened, she skirted around him, confronting him. "Aren't you going to *do* anything about the way he treated me?"

He stripped the garment off, folding it neatly and placing it on the sea chest next to the jabot and cravat. "No. I probably would have done the same thing in his place."

"Damn you, Rhys Winghurst!" Her fists balled and crashed against his bare chest. "What do you want from me?"

He grabbed her wrists, crushing them in his strong clutch with a force that surprised her. His stare gripped, probed, and demanded. "The truth, woman. For once in your life, the truth."

A wisp of fear traveling down her back, her breath rasped in her lungs as she eyed his cold features. "I don't know what you're talking about. You're the one who's lied and schemed and seen that I have no home or family to return to. Since the first time I ran into you"—she struggled to escape his unrelenting grasp—"you've destroyed everything precious and important to me."

"Not everything, Calypso." He jerked her hard against his heaving chest until their noses nearly brushed. "Have you so easily forgotten Tristan?"

"Tristan?" The boy's name was the last thing she expected him to say. "What is my brother to you?"

His eyes narrowed, and for a moment she thought he would strike her. Instead, after seconds that seemed like years, he released her, pivoting toward the door. "You're right. It would be best if I left and went someplace else."

The angry crash of the door left her stunned. What was he talking about? Then, with crystal clarity she glimpsed a second of truth. Her brother was the reason Rhys Winghurst had taken the trouble to rescue her, not the other way around. Her eyes narrowed. Why in God's name did Tristan mean so much to him? She was determined to find out.

Damn her! Damn the way the wench looked at him as if she spoke the undying truth. Tristan was his, the old nursemaid had confirmed that fact. No woman could bear a child and not be aware of what had happened to her. Why did Calypso insist on pretending the boy was her brother?

As he entered the seamen's quarters, a cramped, irregular-shaped room in the forecastle, he wished he had never met her. No, that wasn't true. He wouldn't have Tristan otherwise. And Calypso Collingsworth, for all her stubborn pride and inadequacies, intrigued him. She was a fighter—just as he was—a rare quality to find in a woman.

"Captain," the lone occupant of the room sputtered to

a stance at Rhys's bare-chested entrance, surprised to discover his captain in the entryway. He rarely set foot in this part of his ship, and only under dire conditions. "What be the matter, sir?"

"Nothing, Kraemer. I'm in need of a berth, that's all."

The sailor said nothing; he didn't dare. "Aye, Captain, there be a hammock in the far corner no one's claimed."

Rhys turned to the indicated bed.

"Unless you want this one, sir." The man pointed to his own accommodations.

"Not necessary, Kraemer, this one will be fine. I have no intention of spending more than a few hours here." With the agility of one who had spent many hours hanging in canvas from a beam, Rhys rolled into the hammock and turned his face to the wall.

His active mind refused to give in to sleep and churned like bilge water. Calypso Collingsworth had been on his ship only a few hours, and, like a woman, she had already forced her will on all aboard, including him—the captain. He shifted angrily, the abrupt movement setting the hammock swinging. She was probably lying in *his* bed at this very moment, as comfortable as she could be, snickering at the way she had managed to send him packing out the door like a whipped mongrel. When he had had the chance, he should have shaken the truth out of her. Flipping in the bedding, he grunted in frustration.

"Captain, is there somethin' I can get ya?" Kraemer's query pierced the shell of mental recrimination engulfing him.

"Nothing," he grumbled. "Unless you know of some magical way of keeping a woman in her place."

"Cain't help you none there, sir. Some women are headstrong, and some just seem to mind their manners. My remedy is to stay away from them unless they're the kind you hand a few coins to at the end of the night. If you know what I mean."

"I understand what you're saying, sailor. That's damn good advice." Had Calypso Collingsworth been what he thought she was all those years ago when he had offered her payment he wouldn't be in this situation now.

The creaking of the ropes seemed to mock him. *You let a woman get the best of you. You're twice her size, and you let her push you around like a gelded beast.* The accusations refused to relent even when he forced the hammock to hang perfectly still.

The whispering gods of self-reproof didn't give up. *Are you going to lie down like a whipped mongrel and let her get away with such behavior?*

"No!" Rhys sat up and swung his feet to the floor.

" 'Cuse me, Captain?"

"Nothing, Kraemer. Go back to sleep." By damn, it was time the wench learned how to act around a man. He crashed through the door into the corridor and didn't halt until he reached the entrance to his cabin. Without considering the privacy of the room's unsurping occupant, he twisted the handle with the intention of letting the barrier slam against the far wall. The catch turned, but the door didn't budge as he pushed on it. What in the hell had she wedged against the oak slab?

"Open the door, Calypso," he demanded.

"Never. Go away, you brute."

Placing his broad shoulder against the door, he strained. Still it didn't open. Frustration steamed like a ripe volcano deep inside him. "I'll not ask you again, woman. Let me in."

"Don't you threaten me, Rhys Winghurst. I don't have to take orders from you." There was a note of uncertainty in her voice. "Why don't you go back to wherever you came from?"

He smiled, an image of her sitting up in the bed, her chemise dripping from her shoulders to reveal the soft globes of flesh rising and falling with each heart-pounding breath she took. The vision stirred the primitive male ego dwelling deep in his soul. Drawing back, he slammed his weight against the barrier.

The muffled splintering of wood urged him on, and within seconds, the door flew open revealing the shattered remains of the desk chair. Damn, that chair had been a favorite of his.

He glanced toward the bed, expecting to find her huddled with fear in one corner. The covers were in disarray, but empty. Where in the dickens was she?

He pivoted, his gaze skimming around the cabin in shock. The once-tidy quarters were a shambles. His sea chest was open and clothes were strewn about; the desk was in no better condition with papers and charts tossed on the floor, his sextant, an expensive, delicate instrument, used as a paperweight on top.

Calypso stood behind the desk, his spyglass lifted in a defensive action, as if she were ready to throw it at him. Her bare legs poked from a pair of his breeches. He could only imagine how she kept them up over her slim hips as she also wore one of his favorite shirts which hung to her knees.

"What in the hell are you doing?"

"Get out of here, Rhys Winghurst, or I swear I'll throw it." Her arm inched higher, the spyglass held like a club. The uncertainty he had heard earlier still rang clearly in her voice, but . . .

The erotic vision he had conjured up moments before disappeared like an image in a rippling pond. She looked anything but vulnerable and delicate, more like an Amazon ready to do battle, her wild, red hair emphasizing her proud determination.

185

He smiled, a gesture he knew appeared most wicked. "Then throw the damn thing. I'll dodge it, and you'll have no defense at all."

Her hand drew back, and for a moment he thought she would take his challenge. Then her wrist began to tremble in indecision, and finally she lowered her arm, the instrument held in front of her body like a barrier to protect her from his retaliation.

Taking one quick glance about the cabin, his privacy violated, the tidiness he required since his youthful exposure to the military a shambles, he turned to pin her with a glare that demanded an explanation.

She took a step backward. "I needed something to wear. My gown was in shreds."

His gaze darted to the open trunk, then flicked over her body, shapeless from his bulky clothing covering her feminine curves.

Her face reddened, and he could picture the wheels in her brain spinning hard to come up with a reason why she was looking through his desk. Brushing the wayward curls from her face, she clamped her mouth tight. "I was looking for a piece of paper and a quill, something to write a note on."

"To whom?" She had lied and he knew it. What was she looking for? Didn't the woman know how to tell the truth about anything?

She swallowed hard, those cogwheels clicking again at top speed. Her tongue eased out, moistening her lips. "To a friend of mine in Nassau. I wanted her to know I was all right."

His glare never lessened.

"I thought to post it once we reached . . . wherever it is we're going." Her eyes sparkled with wild desperation.

"Philadelphia," he supplied.

"Of course, Philadelphia." The words came out in a

whisper as she clutched the spyglass to her chest as if it was a buoy to keep her afloat.

The anger that had propelled him through the early morning dissipated like smoke on the wind at the sight of her standing there. The clothing hanging on her body made her seem like a young girl, not a full-blown woman—the girl she had been almost seven years before when he had first taken her to his bed.

He cocked his head as he studied her. Her eyes wide with doubt, she considered him as well. Had he been gentle with her that night in the inn, or had he used her without consideration? He couldn't remember much about her that evening except for the way she had looked at him—like now, afraid yet refusing to buckle under to the fear.

Lifting one palm, he took a step forward. Calypso edged back, one hand reaching behind her to brace against the wall which prevented her from moving further.

The accusation she had flung at him earlier returned to haunt him. Had he ruined her life? What had she suffered, young and unmarried, bearing the child of a stranger she had met one night at an inn? Could he truly blame her for covering up the truth?

Guilt-plagued, he turned away, busying his hands with straightening the clothing she had dragged from his sea chest. In truth, she was correct. She had nothing, not even a decent dress to call her own.

"Calypso," he began, spinning to face her. She was kneeling on the floor, straightening the papers and charts from his desk and putting them back in the drawers. Glancing up, the emotions she had been experiencing flashed across her face, mirror reflections to the ones he had felt. She brushed at her face with her knuckles. Had she been crying? The possibility sent a rush of concern

187

spearing through him.

"Please, Rhys, no more. I haven't the strength to battle with you." She paused in her sorting, one shaking hand ascending to press her brow.

Crossing to where she knelt, he squatted down beside her, gathering her up in his arms. How fragile she felt, crushed against his chest, the fleeting image of her rose-tipped breasts flashing in his brain. He wanted her, and the thought didn't surprise him, yet the desire was different than any he had ever felt before. The unfamiliar emotions set him off balance, leaving him wondering what madness had suddenly possessed him. A few tears and he turned to mush.

He struggled to grasp an explanation for his unexpected turn of feelings. This was not a selfish urge to satisfy a biological function, nor was it a need to prove he could dominate her and make her want him too. The desire was there already staring back at him. This was something much more vital, a yearning to reach an ethereal plane of joining as man and woman, to experience something special—something only this woman could offer. He drew her closer, as if her nearness would somehow make the feelings assaulting him seem familiar as they left a residue of unsureness lingering in his heart as well as a determination to make everything perfect between them. Overwhelmed, he wasn't sure how to begin.

Her chin lifted; her eyes softened; her lips parted in invitation. Angling and rising to her knees, she kissed him as if it was the most natural thing for her to do. The pressure of her mouth against his sent a surge rushing through his veins. Desire swept over him with tidal-wave proportions. How could one woman affect him so?

Rising to his feet, he lifted her up with him. Her resistance nil, she pressed against the solidness of his chest, her arms curling about his neck. As he swung her

188

up and carried her across the cabin, the fleeting ghosts of rivalry that had accompanied them this far in their relationship melted away—at least for the moment. They were man and woman now, bound only by their hearts and their need to acquaint themselves with the pureness of each other's soul.

Gently he laid her on the bed, which rocked like a giant cradle. Dropping to one knee on the floor beside her, he traced the curve of her jaw with the side of a finger, and a brilliant smile lifted the corners of his mouth as she responded, trapping the appendage between a lifted shoulder and her cheek.

"I think at last, my sweeting, I shall make love to you—honestly, completely—without reserve."

She blushed in understanding, her hands reaching out to capture his face and draw it down to hers. "Teach me, my love, as I have much to learn." Her voice was low and seductive, striking the chord of desire he had held in check for so long.

With silken ease he released the buttons of the shirt she wore and pushed it from her shoulders. Soft as quivering mounds of satin, her breasts beckoned, begging to be caressed. He complied, covering the swells with the cup of his hands, massaging until they peaked against his palms.

Then his fingers moved down to discover the ribbon she had tied about the waistband of the breeches to keep them up.

"They kept falling down, and I kept hitching them up until I thought I would scream." She giggled, the sound nervous and unsure. "The ribbon was the only cinch I could find."

He released one fastener, then slipped the pants from her slim body without troubling to undo the rest. His fingers danced up the sides of her legs to mold around

189

her small waist, fashioning a belt of flesh and bone about her slenderness. Dear God, she was lovely, more beautiful than any woman he had ever known.

With quick, decisive movements he stripped off the remainder of his own clothing, uncaring that he tossed them in a pile on the floor. Her gaze lingered, appraising, approving of what she saw as he stood above her.

Impish delight lit her gaze. Grinning, she lifted her hand, shaking a finger at him in an authoritative manner. "You dare scold me for being untidy, sir. Look at the mess you've made."

"Take a care, woman, or you'll pay dearly for your insolence." He stretched out his full length over her, trapping her beneath him, heart to heart, thigh to thigh.

"Pay, sir? Just what did you have planned in that devious mind of yours?" Her palms flattened against the mat of fur on his chest.

"Something that would make you plead and beg for mercy." Lowering his head, he captured the tip of her chin in his teeth and gave it a playful nip.

With a twist of one finger, she knotted a tuft of chest hair about the crook and tugged.

"Unruly wench," he growled, biting a little harder.

"Unprincipled cad," she retaliated, yanking again.

He released her chin, sliding his lips along her jawline until he reached her earlobe. Trustingly, she turned her head, a small sigh of pleasure accompanying the movement. Using the tip of his tongue, he traced the curves of her ear, then followed the column of her throat, stopping at the racing pulse to plant a kiss.

Her fingers brushed his chest, feathering over his nipples, and moved up across his collarbone, coming to final rest at the nape of his neck where his hair was pulled back and tied. The way her hands caressed him, encouraging him to continue his explorations, sent sparks coursing down his spine. So simple and innocent was her touch, yet it excited him more than the most experienced caresses of any woman he had known.

Siren and witch, he decided, lifting his head and staring down at her face, eyes closed and mouth slightly parted, but he wouldn't change her at this moment, even if he could. Then her hands pressed urgently against the back of his head, insisting he take up where he had left off. It was a command he was most willing to obey. He would teach her every delight, every nuance of love, and bind her to him with bonds she would be helpless to resist. And though he was aware he would most likely be snared in a trap of his own making, it somehow seemed the right move to make.

Angling himself to gain access to every inch of her body, he worked his way down, blazing a brand of ownership on each hill and valley—her breasts, her belly, her intimate recess of femininity—until she cried out with helpless rapture, totally open and uninhibited as he caressed her. Still he didn't give in to the almost unbearable need to consummate their lovemaking. He would give more pleasure and take more control until he could sense her mind succumbing as completely as her body to his desires.

With all the skill of a maestro, he composed an exquisite melody she followed note for note. She accepted when he offered, reached out when he withdrew, and vocalized her ecstasy whenever the music so demanded. As if he knew just how high her range was before the shattering crescendo would engulf her, he led her up the scale of love and knowingly left her hovering on the brink for several breath-held moments.

"Please, Rhys, I cannot wait any longer."

The rasp of her longing could not be denied. He rose above her, easing his hips into the cradle of her thighs, savoring the silkiness of her flesh as she opened to receive him. Stilling, he sucked in his breath. How easy it would be to give in to the demands his body screamed to have fulfilled. But not before it was perfect—the ultimate of finales—would he surrender to his desires.

Her hands reached around, grasping his buttocks, and with a soft feminine moan of pleasure she urged him to begin the rhythmic chorus familiar between them.

"We'll get there, sweeting," he promised, yet his hips remained stationary even when she tried to set a tempo though his weight pinned her down. Finally when she lay still and whimpering beneath him, he began a slow, easy pulsation that set the unique bed to swaying. Soon the rocking took over, dictating an even beat that orchestrated the harmonic close to the duet of love he had so painstakingly created.

The coda came in a rush, so strongly he was nearly lost in the maelstrom of emotions that swept through him—feelings he had never experienced in all his thirty-five years.

Opening his eyes, he found her staring up at him with a look of wonderment mirrored in her eyes. She had experienced the same as he had.

A dazzling smile curled his lips, and she melted, surrendering completely to his charm. What was it about the particular way he smiled that seemed to control her so easily?

He kissed the tip of her nose, the corner of her mouth, pleased with her response. She was his, completely—body and soul. And though the knowledge elated him, it frightened him as well. Was he truly man enough to deserve such mastery over another? Dear God, he prayed he was.

Chapter Thirteen

The noon sun rippled through the porthole above the bed, revealing dancing dust particles as they did a minuet across the room and sparkled in the nut brown of Tristan's hair as he wiggled impatiently on the stool that fit his bottom as if it were designed for him.

"Don't fidget so, Tristan," Calypso scolded. "Nanna will be here soon." Her fingers stilled, the sewing needle she held in one hand poised to stab into the yards of teal-blue silk bunched on her lap.

"I don't want Nanna. I want Rhys," the child demanded, his little bottom squirming with renewed vigor.

"Well, you'll just have to settle for Nanna, at least for the afternoon." *We'll both have to be content with the nursemaid's company,* she thought with a sigh. Then she jabbed the threaded needle into the fabric and continued her sewing, taking minute stitches along the designated seam Nannette had basted earlier that morning.

"But why, Callie?"

"Because I said so." She paused in her work a second time. There, she was doing it again—reprimanding Tristan—something she had never done until the last few days. What had gotten into her? Even she found it hard to sit and wait. How much more difficult the task must be for the boy. She glanced over the mound of silk and

193

graced her pouting brother with an affectionate smile. "It won't be long, and Rhys will be back."

"Promise?" he asked, his shoulders sagging in resignation.

"Promise," she pledged. Holding up the silk, she scrutinized the finished seam. Some of the most accomplished work she had ever done, and she was known for her ability to make fine, even stitches. But she had a worthwhile reason. Rhys had put the fabric at her disposal and encouraged her to make whatever she wanted. A gown, she had decided and designed with Nannette's help. A dress to please her lover.

"My lover." Dropping the creation in her lap, she whispered those two words over and over, amazed at how innocent they sounded, not sordid and evil as she had been led all her life to believe. If only she had known years before how love could be, how differently things might have been for her.

She hugged the unfinished garment to her breasts and rubbed her face against the soft texture. This was love, wasn't it? When Rhys had stormed from the room that morning three days ago accusing her of lying, she had doubted his reasons for bringing her with him on this voyage. But what else could his gentle nights of lovemaking indicate? She had misinterpreted the reasons for his anger. She had, she assured herself. He did love her . . . didn't he?

Rising from the chair, she dropped her sewing on the bed. She stooped and ran her hand over the patchwork coverlet, the blanket they wrapped in each night together, naked and warm. A rush of anticipation flooded her veins. He must love her. No other explanation made sense.

Even the time she had spent digging through his personal papers had turned up nothing to suggest otherwise. There was not one word about why he would want to abduct Tristan unless it had something to do with her father's personal journal she had found tucked in a secret drawer on the side of the desk.

She bit her lip, no longer sure of her reasoning. Did he plan to use her brother as ransom? Surely not. He must be aware of how little the baron cared for his youngest son.

She stretched out on the bed, burying her face in the pillow, and took a deep breath. The spicy, masculine scent she had come to equate with the man she now considered an essential part of her stirred her senses, but she fought to keep a clear head. She must. No matter how she felt about him, Rhys Winghurst was a spy, and though she had no idea whom he worked for or why, she must never forget that fact. Did he label her the enemy?

A decisive rap on the door brought her flying to her feet, pushing the disturbing thoughts down deep into the alcoves of her mind. My, but Nanna must be in a pother. Normally the little Scottish woman treaded softly, fearing to wake the sleeping demons that she insisted inhabited all ships. Something must be wrong.

Calypso rushed to the door and opened it. Prepared to chide Nannette for her recklessness, she wasn't ready for the person whom she discovered on the other side.

Luther. The desire to slam the barrier in his face overwhelmed her, but she stuffed the wild urge back where it came from, some deep recess of fear in her heart.

"What do you want?" Her voice sounded steady and in charge. Amazing.

"I've come for the boy."

The statement couldn't have rung more ominous, coming from the devil himself.

"Why?" She clutched the door, seeking the strength necessary to hold her ground.

Luther's gaze raked and penetrated. "Seems the nurse-maid isn't feeling well and won't be relieving you of your duties. Rhys thought the boy might be happier above deck."

She would not turn her brother over to this demon. "I don't think—"

"Luther," the boy squealed and rushed past her, eager to escape the confines of the cramped cabin. With a look that said more than spoken words, the dwarf turned and led Tristan away.

Luther despised her, of that she was sure. But why? What had she ever done to him?

And Tristan. The jumbled maze her thoughts traveled always returned to him. How did her little brother figure into Rhys's plans? She squeezed her lashes closed in confused frustration and dropped her head back against the door. That was one question that had plagued her for days, and she couldn't begin to fathom a proper answer.

Her eyelids popped wide. Maybe she should ask Rhys. But would he answer her truthfully? Love and trust. Did the two go hand in hand? Her shoulders stiffened against the door as she stared back into the cabin. She didn't know.

Angered by her inexperience when it came to understanding men, yet unsure she wanted to learn the answers to her many questions, especially if they weren't to her liking, she forced herself to remain calm and watchful. She would wait and learn as much as she could in the next few days about the intimate stranger who had captured her affections. Then, somehow, she would make everything right between them, even if it meant taking up his cause—could it be that diverse from her own beliefs?—and making it hers as well.

* * *

196

His cause. The people's right to free choice. Wasn't that what the American Revolution had been fought for? A bitter laugh echoed in the deepest caverns of his soul. In theory, the idea seemed so ideal and pure; yet in practice, it wasn't so simple. Life wasn't painted in black and white but was a picture revealed in various shades of gray.

He was a free man—free to make a decision, but in truth, he had only one path open to him. Tristan was his son, Calypso was the boy's mother. In order for his heir to take his rightful place, she would have to be his wife.

His heir. He gripped his hands behind his back as he paced the quarterdeck of *The Oceanid*. Trapped with a title—the Earl of Flint—he had no desire to retain the position, yet wasn't Tristan entitled to make the same choices as he? Did he, as a father, have the right to take a secure future away from the boy? Raised under the peerage system by an elder who desired nothing more than to lay claim to a lineage as old as time, perhaps Tristan would want the earldom passed on to him. It was the boy's right. So at what point did his desires to be a man of his own making override the freedom of choice belonging to his son? The answer wasn't clear to him.

He paused in his pacing, glancing out over the wide expanse of sea lying between him and the point when the decision would have to be made. Twenty-four hours at the most. Dear God, if only he could remain in this state of limbo: loving Calypso, watching his son in joyous amazement. But it wasn't to be. By this evening he must choose his path, and he must explain to Calypso the reasons for his actions.

It wasn't that he didn't want Calypso for a wife—he did. If their situation were different, he wouldn't hesitate to marry her. He would make that choice willingly. But now, would she accept his feelings and believe his reasons justified? Or would she doubt him for a whole lifetime, hating him and possibly the boy because she had rated second in his mind when making his decision? Having deceived her in the past, but for reasons of national security, he refused to lie to her for personal gain. That option was not one he would consider, not even to save the seedling of love sprouting between them.

Yes, love, he admitted. The feeling that gripped him by the throat and refused to release him was none other. From his pocket he slipped out the silver crown she had thrown at him in her bedroom and watched it swing from its chain. The coin began to take on a new meaning to him, a representation of her unflagging spirit. Her strength of will and character were traits he admired above all others. Her willingness to mold and bend to his gentle shaping a drug that held him addicted to her charms—a slave to the need to make her an irrevocable part of his life.

Crushing the coin within his palm, he cursed its very existence. His feelings had nothing to do with his decision. The reasons he would demand marriage from her now were not because he loved her, but because Tristan must be deemed legitimate. He could have it no other way when it came to his son. No child of his would be called a bastard. Calypso would have to understand and accept courtship after the marriage vows were spoken between them.

That was his choice to make and hers to concede. It could be no other way. Then, with time, Tristan could be guided down the path of his decision with a gentle, fatherly hand. But he, Rhys, would accept the boy's preference and work his life around the child's requirements. Even if it meant maintaining the earldom until his son matured enough to take the reins from him.

Dear God, that could possibly mean years. Rhys

bowed his head. Time wasted preserving a code of living he adamantly abhorred. But he would do it—for his son. And Calypso would have to make the same commitment—their son's future over their own.

Spinning about, he forced his thoughts to concentrate on other responsibilities. He would inform Calypso of his decision, tonight, and he wouldn't take no for an answer.

The iciness of the Atlantic winter swept over the deck, bone chilling to a thin-blooded islander who hadn't experienced cold since childhood. Calypso, huddled in the thick cape, the collar turned up under her chin, wished she could go below. But the fires of romantic idyll kept her stationary. Rhys's messenger had said to meet him here; he had something important to tell her, as did she him. Was he going to at last verbalize his love? Her heart raced at the notion. How perfect if he did, as she had decided to confess to him as well. She would tell him of her young-girl fantasies and how perfectly he fulfilled them. Most likely he would be flattered and laughingly take her in his arms to promise her the wonderful dreams were only beginning.

Yes, only the beginning. They had a lifetime to make every aspect of her musing become reality. Just she and Rhys—

No, that wasn't true. There would be Tristan as well. She frowned slightly, then gathered up her momentarily flagged courage. Rhys was fond of her brother—the affection between them was obvious even to a blind man. But would he be willing to accept her brother as a part of their everyday lives?

In time they would marry and there would be children, but Tristan would be with them from the beginning. Would Rhys find him a burden he didn't want to be responsible for? She prayed not, as there could be nothing between them if he was unwilling to accept the presence of her brother as well.

Decisive boot steps sounded behind her, their rhythm as familiar as a voice. She spun, her pulse racing with the wind. "Rhys," she whispered, one hand shaking with excitement fluttered to press against her throat.

He was dressed with the flair of a buccaneer, his fawn-colored breeches snug on his hips, his white shirt unbuttoned to the waist, its saillike sleeves billowing with the breeze. A short form-fitting vest of deep wine red completed his ensemble. He appeared unaffected by the cold; in fact it seemed a part of him.

"Rhys," she rasped again, as a chill slithered down her spine in spite of the warm, woolen cape she wore. "Did you wish to see me?"

How oddly he stood there, assessing her. She glanced down at the tightly fastened cape—his cape—and wondered if he was angry because she was wearing it.

Surely not. Days ago he had given her permission to use the garment. Plus he had been most generous. From some hidden recess of the ship he had produced the lovely bolt of French silk of which she and Nanna had spent hours fashioning her a gown.

His gaze traveled up and down, unrelenting, and she followed suit. From the hem of the cape the blue silk peeked out. Of course, he was only curious about what she wore.

Flashing a radiant smile, she unbuttoned the wrap, and ignoring the frigid air, she let it fall open to reveal the dress underneath. "Do you like it?"

He startled, as if his concentration was directed by some inner eye seeking answers to unspoken needs. "What?"

Stepping forward, she curtsied, as if a loyal subject before the lord, and indicated the dress with a sweep of her hand. "What do you think of the gown?"

His gaze flicked over her form. " 'Tis pretty enough. I'm glad you could make use of the fabric."

Calypso straightened. What was wrong with him? Of late he had been so warm and open with her. But now, it was almost as if he waited for her to shout in angry condemnation. The need to cover her vulnerability gripped her anxious heart. Whipping the edges of the cape together, she held them tightly against her throat as she turned away from him.

She could feel his warmth approach, and how she ached to arch against his protective presence. Instead she held herself in check, even when his breath brushed at the tendrils of hair curving about her neck and ear.

"Calypso, there's something we need to talk about."

Her knees began to tremble as a wild feeling took charge. He was going to say the affair was over; he no longer desired her. A fear so strong she wanted to collapse sucked the air from her lungs. What were his intentions? Would he desert her in some strange city without friends and go on his merry way? Or worse. Perhaps he was going to reveal the real reason he had brought her along on this trip. She closed her eyes, trapping the twin tears threatening to leak from her eyes.

"I know our situation has been anything but normal." His hands grasped her shoulders and squeezed.

She swayed, her head dropping back. No, perhaps not normal, but she had been happy for a few brief moments. More than she could say about the rest of her life, both past and future. She prayed he wouldn't say what she knew was coming.

"And if I had my choice, I would spend the time wooing you, letting you experience every nuance of courtship."

Yes, she was right. He was about to tell her, he was sorry, but his duty must come first. He had no time for her and their love.

"I'm sorry, Calypso . . ."

Her heart twisted painfully at the expected words.

". . . I would have preferred a moonlit night in a fragrant garden, but it's not to be."

A tiny sob lodged in her throat, and she trapped it there by sheer strength of will. She wouldn't make a fool of herself before this man.

"As soon as we reach Philadelphia . . ."

What would she do? Where would she go?

". . . you will marry me."

How could he be so callous with her when she had given so freely to him? She spun about to confront him and demand an explanation. "No, Rhys, you can't do this to me."

"Can't I?" He forced her to stand still in the vise his hands created. "Though you won't admit it, sometimes I think not even to yourself, you know this is the only solution. I won't accept no for an answer."

"No, Rhys, no. Don't forsake me."

A silence so complete she could hear both their hearts beating consumed the moments. "Forsake you?" His brow lifted in disbelief. "Didn't you listen to what I just said?"

She stared back, wide-eyed.

"I said we were getting married as soon as we reach land."

"Married?" Her confused mind whirled in a jumble of thoughts. "You asked me to marry you?" Dear God, he had proposed to her, and she hadn't even heard the words. An all-embracing joy swept through her. Rhys did love her and wanted her for a wife. "Oh, Rhys." She

202

melted against his strong frame, her arms flinging about his neck. "Of course I'll marry you."

He disengaged himself from her grasp and forced her to look at him. " 'Tis not for the reasons you think, Calypso. I will not lie to you."

"Oh, Rhys, of course it is." She giggled in uncertain relief and attempted to hug him again. "You love me. Why else would you wed me?"

His gaze hardened like cooling lava as he set her to one side. "What I feel for you, Calypso, will remain locked deep inside me, until you admit the truth—not only to me, but to yourself. 'Tis the best medicine for all of us."

Stunned by his declaration, she watched him stride away. What was he saying? What horrible crime did he unjustly accuse her of? What truth?

"Rhys, please," she called.

He turned, facing her, a sadness radiating from his eyes.

"I don't understand what you're saying."

"That's most unlikely, Calypso. Do you take me for a fool? Don't make the situation worse than it already is."

"Then I confess to whatever it is you think I've done," she offered in desperation.

His eyes narrowed. "A universal apology? Is that what you think I want?"

She didn't know what he wanted, but she knew she was losing him the same moment she was being bound to him, simply because she didn't understand his demands.

He shrugged his wide shoulders. "Then I forgive you . . . for whatever it is you think you've done. But that doesn't change the facts. I want what is rightfully mine, and I want you to acknowledge my claim."

Her heart plummeted, the pain so strong she couldn't

speak. There was nothing she had she would keep from him—her body, her soul, her very life, everything, except her loyalty to Tristan. She paused, her essence shattering about her feet. Was that what he was demanding of her? Must she choose between him and Tristan?

"Oh, Rhys, is it Tristan?"

"Of course, woman. What do you expect from me?"

"Then I can't give you what you want. I can't destroy my brother that way." Did she ask so much of him? She had room in her heart for both of them.

He threw his head back and curled his lip in disgust. "Then the lie lives on, doesn't it?" The antipathy dwelling in his eyes brought the suppressed tears to the surface. "So be it, Calypso. If that's the way you want it. But it doesn't change a thing. We *will* wed the moment we reach Philadelphia."

Calypso lifted her chin. More than anything in the world, she wanted to marry Rhys Winghurst, but she wouldn't give up Tristan. Never, not even if it broke her heart.

"No, Rhys, you're wrong. I'll see you in hell first."

Nanna watched Calypso, her heart constricting with each step the younger woman took. There was sadness in the hollow, unseeing eyes of her ward, a sorrow she had the power to eliminate, but she didn't dare.

Though they were hundreds of miles from the girl's father, she couldn't be sure how far the baron's influence reached. What if he found them and forced them to return to Long Island? Would he follow through with his long-ago threat to destroy Tristan if she told Calypso the truth about the child's birth. It was a possibility, and even if a slim one, she couldn't take a chance with the bairn's life.

Perhaps she should tell the earl the truth of the matter, that Calypso knew nothing about the true parentage of the boy. But would he believe her, or would he think she only covered for the lass?

Worse still. Rhys Winghurst was a man of deep passion and commitment. If he should discover the baron's deception, he might wish to turn about and confront the other man with his crime. She knew without a doubt the old master wouldn't hesitate to kill his adversary, leaving Calypso and Tristan to his mercilessness.

She bowed her head, pressing her fingertips into her temples. Dear God of the Saints, she wished she could pluck the horrible secrets she had carried for so long from her brain and forget what she knew about the boy's birth. She prayed for guidance, pleaded for forgiveness, and received nothing for her efforts except the stab of guilt ripping though her middle.

" 'Tis not as bad as it seems, lassie." Her eyes followed the pacing figure. "The earl will come to see things your way. I'm as sure as I know the sun will rise in the morn. He cares for Tristan."

"No, Nannette. Not enough. You don't understand." Calypso's soft, youthful shoulders lifted with a sigh. "He will force the issue, and until I succumb, he will make my life miserable, but what will become of you and Tristan if I don't resist him? He will not accept my brother as part of our lives." She whirled, pacing harder. "I can't be such a coward to think only of myself." She stilled, her chin jutting skyward as she pressed her pale lips together. "Oh, God, Nanna. I could have loved him so much. Why must it end this way?"

"Be patient, lassie; have faith. The end isn't final until it occurs." She cursed the inadequate comfort she offered the girl. Let them marry; then nature would decide the best course of action. The baron would have no power over his daughter once she became Rhys Winghurst's wife. But Tristan. Would the master be able to take the boy away? She wrung her hands, no closer to a solution than before.

Calypso paused, offering her a perplexed frown. "What is it, Nanna? If there is something you should tell me . . ." There was such heart-wrenching longing in the girl's voice.

"Tell you? Whatever do you mean, lassie?" The lie clogged her throat like dry bread. She was no better than Peter denying his Lord. She fully expected to hear the crowing of a cock.

Settled on the footstool at her feet, Calypso looked so young and vulnerable. "Oh, Nanna, what would I do without you? So wise and supportive. I cannot allow my troubles to consume you."

Patting the girl's flaming hair draped across her lap, she cursed her own weakness. "If I were truly wise, child, I would make your life much happier, but I don't know how." God forgive her for being so inadequate.

"Let it drop, Luther." Rhys turned away from the dwarf's insistent stare. "I will not change my plans."

"But to marry her. Good God, Rhys. Why not take the devil himself into your domain? You would be a lot safer."

"Watch your tongue, my friend. She'll be your mistress soon enough."

"My mistress, but your downfall. So much the worse for you."

Rhys formed fists with his rigidly held hands. His brows met on the battlefield between his eyes, angry ridges rippling the surface. Why did Luther feel so threatened by Calypso? "We've been over this ground before. The boy will be acknowledged as mine."

"So be it, then," Luther reasoned. "In this day and age and in a new country like the United States, no one cares. The child will be accepted. The birthmark is there as proof. What has the woman to do with it?"

Rhys turned away, refusing to meet his companion's questioning gaze. "What is it, Luther? Why do you oppose her so?" He spun about, piercing his childhood friend with a relentless glare.

"It's not her, per se, but what she represents. Common, colonial refuse. Not nearly good enough for the Winghurst name."

"Then what does that make us, my friend? I find the colonial life to my taste."

"For now, perhaps, but with time you'll come to your senses. We will go home one day, and you'll want to make a proper alliance. The daughter of some forgotten country squire banished to faraway islands . . ." Luther voice drifted off, leaving the rest to the imagination.

"Jesus, Luther, for a stable master's son you speak more like a blue blood than my own father. When will you accept me for what I am?"

"What you are? You're the Earl of Flint, that's what you are. It's only a matter of time before you return to your place."

"My place?" Anger rumbled deep inside him like faraway thunder. " 'My place,' as you call it, is not for you to decide. Leave Calypso alone—quit threatening her—and don't stare at her as if you're attempting to cast some Gypsy curse. Do you understand?"

"Yes, my lord," the dwarf conceded, but Rhys could see the determination still lingering in his eyes. "I only do what I think is best for you and your future."

"Let me worry about my future. Trust me. I'm not some schoolboy in the throes of first love. Calypso Collingsworth has no ring in this bull's nose. I can handle the wench."

"I pray you're right, my lord. I pray it's not too late."

With a shake of his head, Rhys turned away. Sometimes Luther took life too damn seriously. He would marry the woman, even if it was against her will, as there were ways to make her change her stubborn mind. Then, if she still persisted in her lies, he would set her up comfortably and leave her to her own devices. He wanted her, but on his terms only.

Tristan was a different story. He would take the boy with him and raise his son the way a man should be brought up.

Chapter Fourteen

Philadelphia, Pennsylvania
November 15, 1790

Calypso stepped from the gangplank to the pier, her foot hesitating in midair for one downstroke of a heartbeat. When her family had fled this land, then a turbulent group of colonies all those years ago, she had never wished to return—the agony and pain had run too deep. Now a country in its own right, would this new America accept her or take to snapping at her heels like an angry mongrel, she the daughter of a Tory traitor who had refused to accept change? How deep did embittered memories run here? As deep as the childhood nightmares scarring her heart? An uncertain chill wafted up her spine as she touched the ground that had harbored such rebellion, the land of her father's crushed dreams.

"Hurry up, you poke-alongs." Tristan was already at the end of the pier, his feet dancing a back-and-forth jig of anticipation.

"Tristan, stop," she called, her hand lifting in objection as she hurried toward where he nearly tumbled into the carriage-filled street, her personal fears forgotten.

"Let him be, Calypso. The boy's been pent up for a long time on an overcrowded ship. Allow him to regain his land legs." Rhys gripped her by the shoulders to stop her mad dash after him. "He's smart enough not to run in front of a moving vehicle."

She watched her brother with a concerned eye. Rhys was right, but she wouldn't admit it, at least not aloud to him. "My," she offered sarcastically, "we are sounding paternal today, aren't we? I didn't know you cared about his welfare."

Rhys's brow crooked up in a familiar gesture suggesting amused perplexity. "And you, my sweeting, sounded most maternal. You must be more careful next time. Someone might misinterpret."

Her mouth flopped open in surprise. His gibe didn't make sense, yet it was meant as ridicule, she had no doubt. Was he suggesting she showed too much attention to her younger sibling?

Lifting her chin in haughty disgust, she pulled from his grasp. "I don't have to answer to you, sir. Think what you will." She rushed down the planking and grabbed her brother by the arm.

"You must be more careful," she scolded, pulling him back on the pier. She did sound like a mother, and it rankled her to realize Rhys was right. But someone had to take charge of a six year old. Lord knew, Rhys had no intention of being responsible, and Nanna was getting too old to chase a fleet-footed child down the street. Who was left but her?

Within minutes, Rhys had her by the arm in a clutch much the same as the one she had administered to Tristan. With a jerk, she regained her freedom. "No need to treat me so roughly, Rhys Winghurst. I have no intention of running into the street. Give me as much credit as you give a six year old."

"With you I'm never sure what to expect." He resumed his grip but in a much more civil manner, and she allowed him to guide her down the street.

"Where are we going?"

"To my lodgings."

She kept pace in silence, and even Tristan seemed to sense the importance of staying close. What kind of home would Rhys Winghurst own? Would it be large and pretentious as befitting an earl? But was he really a titled peer or just a spy pretending to be one? All of her original doubts and fears regarding this elusive man rushed in with the force of a tidal wave. How little she knew about him. Her eyes slashed in his direction, a strange uncertainty plaguing her.

They followed the road edging the wharfs until they reached Walnut Street, the eight blocks or so they had traveled seeming miles to Calypso. The delicate, heelless shoes she wore were never meant to trod rough cobblestones.

"Is it much farther?" She winced when her toe stubbed against the sharp corner of a stone.

"Not much?" he offered.

His statement was maddeningly uninformative. She simmered, having hoped he would open up and tell her about his home. No, she thought, reflecting on his words, he had called his place of residence lodgings. Just what did that indicate? Glancing up at him, hoping to discover a clue to the mystery hidden behind his closed face, she stumbled, mumbling a mild oath. It would be better if she concentrated on where she placed her feet as she would have the answers soon enough.

Reaching Second Street, they paused at the intersection to allow the carriage traffic to clear. The extraordinary busyness on the dissecting thoroughfares piqued her curiosity. It was as if this corner was the core of activity in Philadelphia.

She darted looks between the rolling carriages and snorting horses. Were they near the presidential home or perhaps before the halls of Congress? What other explanation could there be?

She groaned, wondering why he would drag them somewhere so public. Tired and grimy, all she wanted was to remove her shoes and rest her feet. "Please, Rhys, can't we just go home?"

He lifted his brow in that smirking way she was beginning to despise. "Home?"

She bit her lip. How could she have made such a slip, calling his residence her home?

"Ah, but we are home, sweeting," he continued. With a sweep of his hand, he indicated the building across the street and down one. "Home, sweet home, my love."

She cocked her head in curiosity, studying the three-story structure he indicated. Canvas awning stretched across the front of the building, flapping and bucking in the light breeze. The front door was like an overactive mouth opening and closing constantly, laughing companions entering and exiting as if, indeed, it belonged to them.

Flooded with confusion, she blinked her eyes. What kind of person was this man who had control over her life? His hand pressed in the small of her back, urging her forward, and her concentration centered on placing her feet carefully on the cobblestones.

"Is this where you live, Rhys?" Tristan demanded, his mouth wide open with excitement.

"This is home." He shot Calypso a mischievous look from the corner of his eye.

"You sure have a big family," the boy concluded as he watched the people go in and out.

"You might say that," he replied with a chuckle. "All the boarders here have much in common."

"Boarders?" Calypso interjected. She paused in the middle of the street and planted her fists on her hips. "What kind of place are you taking us to?"

" 'Tis the City Tavern, sweeting, a most congenial

212

place where men of action and patriotism meet." His mouth curled in sarcasm.

"A tavern?" She sucked air indignantly into her body. "You expect me to live in a public house?" She shivered, remembering their first meeting at The King's Ransom. Feeling his gaze rest on her, she knew he was remembering the event as well.

"Aw, come on, Callie," Tristan trilled, pulling on her hand. "Don't be so strait-laced. Could be fun, if you give it half a chance."

Glancing down at her brother, she found him staring up at her, those big brown eyes of his sparkling with a look she found impossible to resist. That look, she surmised with a lift of her brow, was exactly like the one Rhys used whenever he wanted to persuade her to see things his way—the one that always made her melt. The boy spent too much time with the silver-tongued scoundrel and was beginning to look and act just like him. She must clamp down on her brother. The last thing she needed was to have Tristan turn out like Rhys.

"Very well, young man. I'll give it a try." She swung her gaze and pinned Rhys with a stern stare. "But if anything happens or anyone tries anything . . ."

"Most likely you'll hit them over the head with a bed-warmer," Rhys finished.

The heat of embarrassment rushed to her face. He was remembering their first encounter no doubt in every sordid detail. "Perhaps if I had done just that seven years ago, I wouldn't be concerned about it now."

He dipped his chin, conceding the issue, but the sparkle never deserted his eyes. "Point well taken."

"See that it is." Her nose lifted skyward as she marched across the remainder of the street, but she could hear snickers of amusement and well imagine the glances of shared masculine camaraderie passing between the boy and the man. She would have liked to box both

213

their ears, but she didn't give them the satisfaction of looking back.

Once inside, Rhys and Tristan close behind her, she came to a halt in the long room and took a moment to absorb her surroundings. She had to admit that, for a tavern, the establishment was exceedingly clean and airy. And though the smell of tobacco and ale filled her nose, the odors weren't stale and offensive; in fact, they suggested warmth and companionship. But still, she concluded, this was a public house, and she couldn't look too satisfied or Rhys would be sure to note it. Crossing her arms under her breasts, she moved to the side, exuding an air of impatience.

"Wait here, sweeting," Rhys whispered in her ear, placing Tristan's hand in hers. "I'll only be a moment."

She ignored the comment, turning her attention to brushing the boy's wind-blown hair from his eyes.

"Yer Lordship," called a pleasantly rotund man from the far side of the room. " 'Tis good to have ya home. Yer room is awaitin' for ya. Shall I have your bath sent up right away?"

"That will be fine, Master Hamer. However, I'm in need of an adjoining room." He turned and indicated Calypso and Tristan.

"That's no problem. Would the lady be caring for a bath, as well?"

"Yes," Calypso replied, pleased with the prospect of washing the smell of the sea from her skin.

"No," Rhys interceded. "The lady can share mine."

Heads turned to stare at her, then bowed together whispering as she flushed red to the tips of her ears. How she wished the floor would open up and devour her. Damn him! Damn him for making a spectacle of her. She squeezed Tristan's hand so tight, the boy squirmed in protest.

"You're hurtin' me, Callie," he complained.

Calmly, she released him and gathered up her shattered thoughts. She skewered Rhys with an angry glare. "I'll share nothing with you, sir. Especially not a bath." A smile tilting her lips, she faced the innkeeper. "If you don't mind, Mr. Hamer, a tub in the second room would be most welcome." There, she had put Rhys Winghurst in his place and in front of his friends. Turning, she started up the stairway.

"Why all this fuss now, wench?" Rhys's voice reverberated about the room. "Having shared a bed, a bath is nothing."

Calypso gasped out loud at his bold declaration, and so did half the other occupants of the room. Why was he doing this to her? Had he no sense of common decency? She spun about and stared down at him from her perch on the third step. He returned calculated determination from the bottom of the staircase without a flinch.

"I don't care what you think, Rhys Winghurst." In a huff that was closer to tears than bravery, she flew blindly up the stairs. *He'll pay, and dearly, for embarrassing me so.*

On the second floor, she waited for the innkeeper to catch up with her so he could show her to her room. Wiping her watery eyes on the back of one hand, she refused to let anyone see her cry. She would hold it until she was alone. No way would she give that unscrupulous cad the satisfaction of seeing her break down.

"Wait up, Calypso." Rhys was beside her, forcing her to slow her unchecked pace as she attempted to tear down the hallway without a destination in mind.

"You're the scum of the earth, Rhys Winghurst," she hissed. "Why would you compromise me that way?" She swallowed the sob threatening to burst from her throat.

He paused in the corridor and turned to face her with a gallant bow from the waist. "Devil take me, my lady. Have I compromised you? Then we've no choice except

215

to marry. 'Tis the gentlemanly thing for me to offer."

"Take your gentlemanly offer and shove it up—"

"That's not very ladylike, Miss Collingsworth. Whatever will the innkeeper think?"

"I'll not marry you," she mouthed with slow deliberation.

"Ah, but you will." He gripped her arm so tightly her hand began to tingle from the lack of circulation. "Don't doubt my strength of mind, sweeting. I'll do what I have to to get my way."

She clamped her teeth tight. *Don't give him the satisfaction of an answer. Let him think what he will. I'll die before I'll marry him.*

At the door of his room, he turned and inserted the key, but before he opened the barrier, he forced her up against it, her back pinned to the oak slab, his arms forming a barricade about her. "I'll leave you now, my love, and sacrifice my personal hygiene to your sense of pride. But I warn you, don't try to make a scene or to run away." His arms relaxed and his lip curled in a knowing sneer. "I've arranged for a seamstress to be here within the hour. Buy what you need to befit your station."

"What is my station, Rhys? Am I your high-class whore?"

"Don't try me, woman." His arms tightened beside her head. "You'll be my wife by tomorrow evening. I expect you to look the part of a countess."

"I'll not do it." Her lips pressed together in determination.

"Oh, yes, you will." He bent his head and kissed her hard on the mouth. Then the door swung open behind her, and she stumbled backward into the room. "I'll return in a couple of hours." He started to close the door, then reconsidered as he spun to face her. "Oh, yes, in case you're wondering, Tristan's with me. If you run away, you go without him." His eyes flicked over her once. "I honestly don't think you'd do that, or I wouldn't leave you to your own devices." His mouth lifted in a smile of triumph. "Until later." He slammed the door with such force it shook the sturdy hinges.

Flopping down on the bed, she slammed her fist into the coverlet. He knew her far too well. Never would she desert Tristan.

The tears she had held back for so long gushed forth in angry frustration, blinding her reason. She fought Rhys Winghurst with all the strength she possessed, and still it wasn't enough. The cad would win—he had proved he would go to any length to obtain his selfish desires—and she was powerless to stop him from making a mockery of her simple dreams of love and happiness. Somehow she had imagined marriage would rescue her from life's miseries, not destroy her last vestige of hope.

Thomas Jefferson thumbed through the pages of John Collingsworth's journal one at a time. His hazel-flecked gray eyes lifted as he snapped the book closed. Then he leaned back in his chair, one hand skimming through his sandy-colored hair, as he sized up Rhys and the situation. "You know, this information is not enough to convict the man—circumstantial, at best."

Rhys studied his superior, wishing he could fathom the inner workings of the other man's well-known genius. "I'm aware of that fact. However, my deepest instincts tell me we're on the right track."

Jefferson drummed his long, aristocratic fingers on the polished cherrywood desk. "Deepest instincts, you say." His mouth lifted in amusement. "I can understand that, being a man of passion myself." He turned in his seat, contemplating the other occupant of the room. "What about you, Jeremy? What do you think?"

Sitting in the high-backed wing chair opposite Rhys, the other man narrowed his light blue eyes. "I think it means nothing. The babbling of a grief-crazed Tory doesn't indicate an uprising. We're sniffing along the wrong path, Thomas. John Collingsworth, from the little I know about the man, is incapable of organizing a plot against the President of the United States. I say we look elsewhere."

Rhys considered his companion, a man he had worked with for years. He trusted Jeremy Stickback, with his very life if need be, but his friend was wrong. Dead wrong. "What about the missive from Wilmington? Doesn't that tell you something is amiss?" He reached across the desk and took the note from Jefferson's hand. " 'The eagle nods unaware upon his aerie,' " he read. " 'The time to strike nears. You and yours be prepared.' Damn it, man, the eagle is Washington. Can't you see that?"

Jeremy's eyes flashed with fire. "I see nothing of the sort, my friend. You're reaching, trying to make something out of nothing." With a snort, he rose, taking the cane beside his chair, and began a slow, uneven pacing across the room.

A frown brought Rhys's brows together over the bridge of his nose. He wasn't wrong, and though Jeremy's opinion mattered to him, what was important was to convince Thomas Jefferson there was merit in his conclusions. "What's at stake here is our president's life. Don't you think the situation deserves further investigation?"

Jefferson glanced from Rhys's intense face to Stickback's doubtful one, his already ruddy complexion reddening with indecision. At last, his gaze dropped, and he took up the diary and placed it on the corner of his desk. "All right, Rhys, if you feel this strongly, we'll follow through and have the Collingsworths watched."

Jeremy snorted again. "A waste of effort and government funds in my opinion."

Settling back in his chair with relief, Rhys volunteered, "I'll be glad to offer my services. I know that island inside and out."

"I'm sure you do, my friend," Jefferson reassured, "but a fresh face might obtain better results. Besides," he said, a slight grin on his face, "I hear you have your hands full at this time. Sounds as though you've become too close to the subject."

"Nothing I can't handle." He shifted in his chair uneasily. "News travels fast."

"Very." Jefferson chuckled. "One of my secretaries was at the tavern, eating lunch, when you arrived earlier this afternoon. A woman, a boy, and a nursemaid. I won't ask what you're doing housing a possible suspect. She is Collingsworth's daughter, isn't she?"

"It's not what you think."

Jefferson shook his head in amusement. "My secretary seems to think otherwise. Your domestic squabble with the lady in question is the talk of the town. Take all the time you need to straighten out your personal life, Rhys; you deserve a break."

Uncertainty wedged like a bad seed in a corner of his brain. What if Jefferson didn't take the information regarding Collingsworth seriously enough? If something were to happen to the president . . .

"Relax, Rhys. I'll see that every fact is checked out. Collingsworth won't be able to make a move without our knowing about it." He turned to Stickback. "Jeremy, I want you to handle this personally."

Rhys relaxed, his shoulders easing forward. He trusted Jeremy to do the best job possible, even if the man didn't agree. His friend had always been open-minded and willing to check out every detail of an assignment, regardless of his personal opinion. He turned to the other man. "Good luck, old friend. I hope you prove me wrong."

Jeremy grinned back. "I will. Then we'll be even after you solved that last case in New York. Emotional involvement always makes a man's judgment faulty."

"Perhaps you're right, Jeremy. I'd like to think I'm wrong about John Collingsworth. My life would be much less complicated if I were."

An onslaught of guilt tinged his consciousness. Never once had he mentioned to Calypso her father's possible involvement in an assassination plot. Somehow the timing had never been right. Their floundering relationship was much too fragile as it was and would never bear up to unproven accusations. She would never believe him and would think her father the reason he had brought her to Philadelphia. If he kept the truth from her, it was for a good purpose. Tristan. He deserved a chance to know his son better.

With Jeremy handling the possible problem with John Collingsworth, he could relax and work out the jumbled mess of his life. He would marry Calypso, then acknowledge Tristan as his own. But first, he would be smart to return to the lodging house and check on his bride-to-be.

Leaving the small, inconspicuous building on the northwest corner of Eighth and High that served as the State Department, he found Tristan sitting on the carriage seat beside the driver. From the boy's mouth spilled an unending procession of questions, which the coachman answered with extraordinary patience. Rhys was grateful to the man for keeping his son entertained.

Approaching the vehicle he called up. "Tristan, 'tis time we return home."

With the grace of a fawn, the boy slid down and joined Rhys inside the carriage. His eyes wide, he stared at Rhys in open amazement. "Saunders said you were

220

talkin' to the president. Is that true?"

Rhys shook his head in denial. "No, but to one of his cabinet members."

"President?" Tristan mulled the word in his mouth like mush. "Is that like being a king?"

"Not at all, boy." Rhys settled back in the seat and took the child into the crook of his arm. What better time to explain the working of democracy? He would teach Tristan to respect the freedom of all men, and would make him an American in no time. Tristan would be a son he would be proud of in every way.

Calypso sighed in angry relief as the door closed behind the dressmaker. True to his word, the woman had appeared within the hour, just as Rhys had said she would, bolts of cloth and measuring tape in hand. Moving the entire entourage to Nannette's adjoining room, Calypso had refused to stay one minute more in his quarters. His orders be damned. She would take the clothing, as she had none but the blue silk she wore. But she would not give him the satisfaction of remaining in his rooms like a paid mistress.

For the first time in her adult life she had total carte blanche to have what she wanted, and she had found the task a labor she wanted to be done with as quickly as possible.

She whirled to face Nannette, planted ramrod stiff in one of the chairs placed before the hearth. "What should I do, Nanna?"

The little Scottish woman followed her pacing figure with contrite eyes. "Marry him, lassie. 'Twould be the best thing for ye. For all of us."

"How can you say that, Nanna? He refuses to accept responsibility for the boy." Her hands flew up in emphasis.

221

Their gazes touched, clung for a moment; then the nursemaid glanced away, her hands coming together in that familiar wringing motion. Always Nanna acted like that whenever she made mention of Rhys or Tristan, especially in the same breath.

She scowled, opened her mouth to question the other woman further, then changed her mind as Nannette looked up, her face lined with worry. How old the dear woman appeared, as if she had aged eons over the last few weeks. The devotion shining in her familiar gray eyes couldn't be denied. Nanna would never do anything to hurt her. The older woman was concerned—just as she was—about their future.

Calypso turned with a resigned sigh and dropped down on the bed as if she were a child banished to her rooms by an angry parent. How could she circumvent the neat trap Rhys had set for her? Under different circumstances she would have willingly married him— blindly gone to the altar, oblivious to his real reason for wedding her if only he had mouthed the words of love. That stone-cold realization was what frustrated her most, his utter honesty, his admission that his feelings had nothing to do with his determination to bring her to heel. It was obvious he had come to the Bahamas not to court the baron's wayward daughter, but for reasons about which she still wasn't sure. A spy, a scoundrel come to harass her family. Hadn't they suffered enough? Her father had lost everything including his grasp on sanity, yet Rhys Winghurst was determined to prove . . .

To prove what? She pushed up from the coverlet and swung her slipperless feet to the floor. What dark secret about her family did he possess and wish to reveal to the world? He had stolen her father's personal diary—she had seen it with her own eyes hidden in Rhys's desk aboard his ship—seeking what? Was this ruse a personal vendetta, a need to seek revenge against her father?

Her gaze shot to Nannette. Nanna was aware of the truth. What horrible fact did Rhys Winghurst possess to frighten the nursemaid so thoroughly? The Scottish woman would have never boarded his ship or allowed Tristan to come so easily unless he had threatened her with something worse than death. Her heart contracted in pity for the woman who had devoted her lifetime to protecting her and Tristan.

The urge to question the older woman took root again, and Calypso stood and crossed the room to where the nursemaid sat, her hands twisting endlessly in her lap.

"He can't hurt you, you know." Her words were a stated plea.

Nannette's expression registered uncertainty as her tearful gaze connected with hers. "Ah, lassie, I canna be sure. He swore we all would suffer if I didna do what he ordered." Liver-spotted hands covered the lined face Calypso loved so well as the old woman dissolved into uncontrollable tears.

"He said that to you?" Blind anger choked her throat as she knelt and gathered the woman to her heart. How dare Rhys Winghurst threaten Nanna so.

Her mind raced with vengeful rage as she considered her options. Rhys had something to gain by marrying her, and though she couldn't fathom what that something could be, maybe she could use the tidbit of knowledge to her advantage. Marriage might be her best recourse against his dastardly plans. If vengeance was what he wanted, then vengeance it would be.

She stood, setting Nannette aside as she slipped on her shoes. "Rhys Winghurst, you'll be sorry the day our paths crossed. I'll see you in hell for what you've done."

"Calypso," Nannette gasped, sobering surprise catching her voice, "what do you mean to do?"

"I'll not have him threatening you or Tristan."

"But, lassie, you don't understand, it's your father I meant . . ."

"My father has nothing to do with the problem. This is between me and Rhys." She crossed the room and jerked open the door.

"No, Calypso, you mustn't. What you're doing is wrong."

She closed the barrier between them, cutting Nannette off. The nursemaid meant well, but she, Calypso, knew best how to handle a cad like Rhys Winghurst. One didn't face him head on, but took him by surprise by feigning surrender.

She smiled to herself as she entered his rooms, a freshly poured bath sending curls of steam toward the ceiling. Unabashed she stripped the clothing from her body and settled into the water. Then laying her head back against the rim, she closed her eyes and waited for her husband-to-be to return to his jackal's lair.

Chapter Fifteen

"Go on to your room, Son. Your Nanna is most likely waiting for you."

"But, Rhys, I wanna stay with you."

Rhys's large hand lifted and ruffled Tristan's hair. "We've a lifetime, boy. Besides, I'd like to see your . . . Callie alone for a few moments." His heart twisted. He had nearly said "mother."

"Will we talk some more later about dem—dem-oc-ra-cy?"

Rhys chuckled. "All you want."

"And will I meet the president like you told me?" the child persisted.

"Yes, yes. I promised, didn't I?"

The boy grinned in delight. "Promises are for keeps."

"For keeps," Rhys agreed, as he stooped and swatted Tristan on the behind. "Now go on and do what I say."

Tristan scooted ahead, then turned, his eyes radiating the emotions filling his little boy's heart. "I love you, Rhys," he said, then turned to dart like an elf down the hallway.

"I love you, too, my son," Rhys whispered to the flee-ing figure. "God knows, more than I should."

Once Tristan was safely behind the closed door, Rhys

revolved, facing the entrance to his own quarters. For the briefest of moments he hesitated, listening. Was Calypso inside waiting for him? Perhaps ready to pounce on him, claws unsheathed, that sharp tongue of hers, precision honed, prepared to meet him on the war-torn battleground their relationship had become?

Over the days he had grown to regret his own damned honesty. He should have lied, professed love for her that night he had demanded marriage from her. But he had refused to treat her as she treated him. If only she would admit the truth about their son, everything would be different.

With a resolute set to his jaw, he pressed the door open, his body tense and prepared for the red-headed Fury inside to fly across the room.

The scenario greeting him unhinged his gritted teeth. Wisping whorls of steam wavered about Calypso's head, which was resting peacefully against the rim of the tub. One long, lean leg was lifted from the water, her hands running sensuously down the calf as she washed soap bubbles from her golden flesh.

A lump of shooting desire clogged his throat, leaving him speechless and unable to turn away.

Then the leg lowered, and she arched her back, bringing the rosy tips of her bare bosom peeking from the water, thin circles of suds accenting the ripeness of her nipples.

He swallowed, numbed by the sight, until the heat of need tightened his loins with rock solidness. In response he squeezed the door latch to keep himself from rushing into the room.

A courtesan couldn't have staged it better, he decided, as she lifted her arms and wiggled in the water, causing splashes to ripple over the side onto the floor. At that moment he would have willingly changed places with the bath water that caressed every inch of her lush body.

Twisting, she rose from the tub, presenting the long line of one side, the small waist, the flared hip, the creamy curve of her thigh and buttock. She hummed, a light, lyrical bit of nonsense that beat against his temples like a fife and drum.

"Calypso," he rasped, his voice sounding like a young boy's cracking with puberty, "what in the hell are you doing?"

She turned, presenting a full view of her ripe, womanly body, water dripping from the tips of her breasts to puddle on the floor as she stepped out of the tub.

"Rhys, darling," she cooed, a radiant smile creasing her face. "I was waiting for you to return." She offered a wily pout. "You were gone much too long."

"Too long?" he repeated with a loud swallow. "I think, perhaps, you're right." His gaze skimmed over her flaunted nudity as she glided toward him, her arms outstretched, her feet leaving wet prints in their wake. What was the wench up to? He steeled himself and slammed the door behind his back, determined to stop her in her devious tracks. He could play games as well as she.

His hands pressed against his thighs as she sidled up against him, her fingers reaching down to cup the undeniable evidence of his desire. The point of her chin angled upward, and for the briefest of moments, he considered taking her up on her blatant offering without further questioning. His masculinity could find no objection; his pride was another matter.

With splayed fingers, his hand traveled up her spine to a point between her shoulder blades. The mass of red hair spilling down her back grazed his knuckles, and he grasped a handful, jerking her head back so far the column of her neck bowed like willow wood as he pressed her hard against his chest.

"What the hell do you think you're doing?" he repeated, this time his voice sounding confident and sure.

Her throat convulsed. Was it with fear or regret? He couldn't be sure as he sensed the brazenness washing from her when he slid his free hand down her belly to reciprocate the intimate way she caressed him. As if one could call what they did to each other a caress.

Body tense, she tried to pull away, but he refused to release her, his hand gliding skillfully over her nudity—touching, probing, demanding she accept his strength of will.

"Rhys, please," she whispered, her fists wedging between their compressed bodies, attempting to push him away.

"Gladly, my love." Yet he grasped her tighter, forcing her to accept and respond to his exploration. "You shouldn't begin something you have no intention of completing."

Her green eyes flashed with the fire of indignation. "You're a brute and don't deserve a willing woman."

"Maybe, but perhaps willing isn't what I want, but honest."

She sucked in a deep breath of surprise, then bucked like a tethered yearly forced to accept a bit. "Honesty?" she hissed. "Then by damn that's exactly what I'll give you."

At last the Fury emerged, talons gleaming, as she struggled to escape. Releasing her from the steel circle of his arm, he snared her hands in his larger ones, forcing them behind her back. Then he kissed her with such a strength, there was no way she could deny him.

At first, she refused to yield, her teeth clamped tightly together, but his lips stroked hers, his tongue wedging in one corner of her mouth like a silken serpent of passion. He might not understand her way of thinking, but her

228

body he knew like his own. She would surrender, given time and attention.

Her lips parted with a groan of capitulation, and her knees buckled like pillars of sand before the waves of desire emanating from the heat of his body. He scooped her up, the backs of her knees pressed against his forearm, her hair trailing like fragrant vines over his shoulder. Her eyes were closed, the lashes fanning against her cheeks, her mouth parted, the tips of her teeth gleaming whitely, seductively, against the rose of her lips.

A temporary truce had been called between warriors on the battlefield, as Rhys carried her to the bed and draped her across the coverlet. Her eyes fluttered open, watching as he removed his coat and vest, stripped the lace jabot from his throat with unconcern, and divested himself of his shirt, several buttons pinging to the floor in his haste.

Without bothering to remove his boots or breeches, he lowered his weight beside her, concentrating on the rise and fall of her quivering breasts.

"No, Rhys, please." Her hand curled about his arm, halting him. "Take off everything."

He paused, glanced down at this state of partial undress, then turned to kick off his boots. A hiss of a curse between his teeth when the shoes gave him trouble, it took him several minutes—precious moments—to complete the task, yet when he lay down beside the only woman who could manage to rouse him into such a state of no self-control, he was glad he had complied. How silky was the skin of her thighs feathering against his groin as he angled to face her.

The fear or regret, whichever he had seen earlier, was gone from her expression as she met his gaze head on. Without asking, he began to explore, his fingers trailing down the soft curves of her being, rediscovering the

229

places that sent shivers of delight coursing through her: the hollow behind her ear, the curve of her jaw, the valley between her breasts. Without answering, she eagerly offered up her body to his experimentation. If only they could trust each other with their outer lives as easily as they shared the intimacies of passion, how well suited they would be.

Rhys sighed, resigning himself to reality. There could be no permanent armistice without honesty, at least not for him. Pushing himself up, he covered her warm, sweet body with his own, seeking to join them in the only form of veracity that existed between them. Their desire was equal, unabashed, and without falseness of any sort. Her soft inner thighs pressed against his hips with urgency as he joined them in universal truth, his thrusts creating a whirling vortex that left them clinging together like small bits of flotsam in a raging sea.

The protective storm calmed about them, leaving them naked and vulnerable. He glanced down, brushing the damp tendrils from her reposed face, and touched the corner of her mouth with his.

"Tomorrow, you'll marry me."

"Tomorrow," she echoed tenaciously, her lashes never lifting.

"And you'll give me your solemn pledge you'll not create a scene."

"I'll not defy you, Rhys." Tiny tears formed in the corners of her eyes like miniature pearls refusing to run the gauntlet down her face. Was it remorse that created them? He had no way of knowing for sure.

"You'll be a countess, then, and I'll expect you to dignify that part." How he had wanted to say *his* countess, but he dared not.

Wordlessly she nodded.

At moments like this he deplored his only recourse of

action, but she left him no alternative. He had made love to her one last, sweet time. Tomorrow he would marry her. Then before the week was out, he would take his son and leave her to sort through her mistakes, making the best out of her life that she could. He would support her, provide for her, but he couldn't live with her, knowing she denied Tristan his rightful place as the child of their union that long-ago night.

Rolling to his back, he left her sleeping peacefully, the burnished filigree of her hair spread like a net across the pillows. He would not be caught in her web of deceit. Neither would his son.

Calypso glanced about Christ Church, a sea of unfamiliar faces staring back from the endless rows of pews. She knew none of them except for Nannette and Tristan. All strangers, watching, speculating, as the Earl of Flint married his Tory mistress. That was what they all were thinking, she knew for sure. Enemies, each and every one. No one cared that she was there against her will, a victim of circumstances she had no control over. She clutched the ivory netting covering the satin of her gown with lace-gloved fingers.

Now she was Rhys Winghurst's bride—a subject of every salon in the city. Why had he married her, a woman with a nanny and younger brother to care for, a woman of questionable reputation and loyalties?

Brushing away the expensive Belgian lace of her veil, Rhys graced her with a perfunctory kiss at the corner of her mouth. It was so impersonal, and yet all she could think of was the way he had kissed her the night before, eliciting a response she had never intended to give. Now she would do anything for the tiniest spark of emotion from him, but he denied her even that one concession.

231

Rhys took her arm and led her forward, a congratulatory line forming at the front door of the church. She glanced at his profile as they stepped down the aisle, man and wife, wondering to herself just why he had wed her. Not so long ago he had adamantly refused to accept Tristan, now the two went everywhere together, closer than father and son. What terrible fate did he have planned for her and her brother? She couldn't bear to think of the possibilities, couldn't stand to imagine the man beside her, the lover who had taken her to such heights the night before, might betray her.

She glanced back at the altar they had just departed, the arched, paned window allowing wisps of sunlight to dot the ambulatory and chancel rail before which they had stood. Not once had Rhys looked at her as he had said his vows, but had gazed at some point over her head, and she, in turn, had stared at the base of his throat, not wanting to see the total disinterest with which he played his part.

Turning away from the desolate memory, she greeted the tall stranger who stood before her, unwilling to confront the terrible truth. Her life and dreams were a shattered ruin, and there was nothing she could do to change that fact.

"My lady," the gentleman addressed her, lifting her lace-covered fingers to his lips. His strong, square-cut jaw brushed the back of her hand, and his kindly blue eyes touched hers with acknowledged respect as he waited for a response.

"Sir, I'm sorry. I didn't catch your name."

The regal man glanced at Rhys, one edge of his mouth lifting in amusement. "Quite refreshing, this bride of yours. It's not often I'm met with such innocent honesty."

Rhys's glare bore down her. "I'm sorry, Mr. President.

My wife is overcome with whatever sickness affects blushing brides."

Calypso's face crimsoned. This simple, comely man was the president? What did one do? Curtsy as before a king? She positioned her leg to drop down before him, but Rhys caught her arm, forcing her to stand. His glancing stare told her she was making a fool of herself. "Sir, Your Highness, I'm most pleased to be honored with your presence."

Washington's chin angled upward as he laughed wholeheartedly. "Please, no pretentious titles. The papers will have a field day if they hear you. They try to crown me constantly as it is. Don't give them fodder for their vicious fires. Please, dear lady, call me George. I'm just a simple farmer, not royalty. If anyone should be bending low, it should be me to you, Countess." His kindly smile spoke of his sincerity as he bent with a formal bow.

"By all means, sir, but you mustn't." Her hand fluttered out to tap his broad shoulder. "I will accept your conditions, for one small concession from you."

"Which is?" Washington stood to his full height, his noble bearing undeniable.

"That you call me Calypso in return."

"Calypso. A spirited name for a spirited lass. I would be most honored." The president guided her small hand into the crook of his arm and turned to Rhys. "I think, sir, I'll take full advantage of my position and claim your lady as my companion for a moment or two."

Rhys nodded his consent, but she could tell by the way he narrowed his eyes he didn't like it. Was he jealous? Not likely, just concerned that she wouldn't handle herself as he felt she should.

Flashing him a coy smile as Washington led her away, she fought down the urge to thumb her nose at him. His return glare seared her back as the president directed her to the entrance of the church.

Washington guided her about the vestibule, making introductions to the many guests who had come to watch the spectacle. She nodded and smiled, the names too many and offered too quickly for her to remember them. What surprised her was the friendly openness of her reception. It was as if these people judged her not by what they had heard, but by what they saw of her at the moment. Their lack of pretension was astounding. These were the same people who had criticized her family for remaining loyal to their king all those many years ago.

She glanced about as Washington steered her from group to group, their sincere welcome undeniable. Were her colonial memories inaccurate? Where were the condemning mobs who had destroyed her father and taken their family possessions? Confusion set in, doubt following closely on its heels.

Her escort directed her toward a final couple, the man dressed with stately dignity, the woman the epitome of fashion and grace, her blond hair swept up in the latest style, her blue eyes twinkling with a kindred spiritedness with which Calypso could identify. In her heart she knew she would like this woman immediately.

"Eliza, my dear," George Washington began, "I would like to introduce you and Samuel to America's latest acquisition, Calypso Winghurst, the Countess of Flint." He turned to her, angling his hand to indicate the couple. "My dearest of friends, Samuel and Eliza Powel."

Eliza dipped a small curtsy, her fan angling with the precision of a Castilian dancer.

"I think, Eliza, you will find Calypso most interesting, a welcome addition to your weekly salons."

Calypso looked up, startled at his total acceptance of her, and saw him wink at Eliza as if something personal had passed between them.

"And tell me, Mr. President," Eliza demanded, "do you find my parties boring now?" Her fan swished as if annoyed, but her smile suggested that the banter between the two was light-hearted and commonplace.

"Never, dear friend. I wouldn't keep returning if they were." He turned to Samuel. "But I must imagine that you find them most tedious at times. Half of Philadelphia traipses in and out of your drawing room on a regular basis."

Samuel laughed. "Not at all. Eliza would most likely shrivel up and die if I deprived her of her social gatherings. Besides, Philadelphia society would probably crumble without them. 'Tis the least I can do for my country."

Washington chuckled. "The least? I daresay you keep this government coherent with your generosity."

The gentlemen bowed respectfully to each other. Eliza dimpled and placed her hand possessively on her husband's arm, but offered Washington a knowing smile. Calypso watched in amazement. There was something very special between this woman and the president, and her husband didn't seem offended. Was she his mistress?

At that moment Rhys appeared behind her, one arm slipping about her waist. "You've had her long enough, Mr. President. I claim the right to share my wedding day with my bride."

Washington stepped back. "Of course. Seems only fair to me." Facing Calypso, he lifted her hand again in his and gave her a military bow. "This evening has been most pleasant, Calypso. Until later." His smile charmed her. "And you, sir," he commanded, indicating Rhys, "I shall see later tomorrow, but not too early. Spend a leisurely morning with your bride."

"Thank you, sir. I shall try." His grip tightened about

her, and he began leading her away.

Eliza tapped her shoulder, and she pivoted her head to look at the other woman.

"I hope we can meet also. Perhaps tomorrow when your husband is occupied with business. Two-forty-four South Third Street. Please come whenever you can."

Calypso's lonely heart swelled. It had been so long since she had had a friend, someone to share confidences with, someone to compare dreams. "As soon as I can, Eliza. Thank you."

They squeezed hands as if they had been close all of their lives.

Rhys urged her out of the church door and down the steps. She glanced back once, taking in the tall steeple and the crowd pressing through the door to throw rice at them.

"Come, wife," Rhys insisted, urging her toward the waiting carriage. "We've a long night before us."

A long night and an even longer life, she thought with a silent sigh as she followed his bidding.

She could not place him, the average-looking gentleman who stood before their table, yet there was something about him—a feeling she should know him.

Rhys stood, pushing back the pewterware that held his partially eaten breakfast. "Jeremy. It's good to see you, my friend. What brings you 'round to City Tavern so early this morning?"

The gentleman shifted his weight, leaning heavily on the horsehead cane in his right hand. "To see you and say good-bye before I leave."

Rhys signaled to the innkeeper to bring another chair, and within seconds a sturdy ladder back was added to the table. "Sit, Jeremy. Can you say when you're departing?"

Heavily he dropped into the offered seat and shot Calypso a curious stare. "I'm not sure. Can I?"

Rhys glanced down at her as if he just now remembered her presence. His eyes narrowed for a split second, then he resumed his place at the table. "My wife, Calypso. Jeremy Stickback, a good friend."

There was more warmth when he spoke Jeremy's name than when he said hers. At least it seemed that way to her.

"Mr. Stickback," she offered with a stiff nod. " 'Tis a pleasure to meet you."

"Madam." His gaze lingered as if trying to pierce her thoughts.

"So you're off to parts unknown," Rhys interjected, ending the staring contest between her and Stickback.

The man concentrated on Rhys. "For the most part unfamiliar to me, at least, but I'll manage. Most likely I'll be back in a fortnight, time wasted, suspicions unfounded." Jeremy grinned. "You can't always be right, you know."

Rhys lifted one brow. "Can't I?"

Stickback shook his head. "You arrogant silk-stocking, you don't know how to be wrong, do you?"

Rhys laughed. Calypso stared from man to man. What was going on here? What were they talking about? An uneasy feeling that the secrecy was for her sake brought her poised fork slicing through the air to clatter against her plate. "Just say you wish me to leave, if that is what you want."

Rhys caught her shoulder and kept her from rising. "No need. Finish your meal. I have a meeting to attend, and Jeremy can drop me off on his way. The carriage is at your disposal, dear wife. Nannette has instructions to take Tristan down to my tailor and have him fitted for

237

proper clothing, so your day is free to do what you will."

"What's wrong with Tristan's present attire?" she demanded, irritated at the way he took charge of everyone's life, especially hers.

"Nothing. But he's growing up, and it's time he dressed with a flair for style."

She was the one who saw to his clothing. She had style. Dropping back down in her seat, she seethed at his suggestion that she had not done her job well enough. "Do what you will." Her fork in hand, she tackled the remains of her eggs and refused to look at the man who was her husband.

For the briefest of moments Rhys hesitated beside the table. "Good-bye, Calypso."

She refused to look up at him. "Good-bye."

His hand reached down and lifted her chin, forcing her to meet his gaze. Saying nothing further, he released her and spun about, walking toward the tavern door, his friend, Jeremy Stickback, limping along beside him.

She blinked, swallowed the morsel of food in her mouth, and dropped her fork, no longer hungry. How strange he acted. For a minute she swore there had been a look of longing and regret in his eyes before he left. Was he sorry for the way he had treated her last night?

Their wedding night. What a farce. Though she had fully intended to reject his conjugal advances, he had not even bothered to try. Instead he had ignored her, turning his back, and quickly fallen asleep. For an eternity she had lain there, refusing to believe he would be so damnable. He had had no right to treat her so.

She clenched her fists and rose from the table, determined to forget his very existence, at least until this evening when she would be forced to share their room. She lifted her chin. The day would be a pleasant one.

Eliza Powel expected her. Her goal would be to make a friend, to find someone with whom she could share her life.

She didn't need Rhys Winghurst. Who gave a damn if he ever returned!

Chapter Sixteen

Giving the address to the driver, Calypso settled back against the seat and arranged her skirts, watching the scenery glide past her window as the carriage moved down Walnut Street. Nervously she plucked at the wine-colored pleats of her high-waisted muslin gown, hoping she would be well received by Eliza Powel. What if she had misinterpreted the other woman's offer, and Eliza had only meant to be polite in inviting her to visit? No, she assured herself, she wasn't wrong about the genuine interest the belle of Philadelphia society had bestowed upon her.

As the vehicle paused in the street, she sat forward, renewing her interests in the city sights. The heavy traffic had necessitated the halt before the driver turned left on Third Street. Several blocks later and up a drive, the carriage again stopped, and this time the coachman dropped down from his seat and opened her door.

The four-story brick structure was enormous. She blinked in the dazzling sunlight, her hand perched on the window ledge of the conveyance as she paused, indecisive. But the iron balustrade of the front stairs beckoned, and she stepped down, determined not to be denied, as she signaled for the driver to ring the front bell.

Minutes later a servant answered, and soon she was escorted in through the breathtaking foyer to the front parlor to await her hostess.

Eliza Powel's entrance was drama at its best. Dressed in the latest of styles, the shimmering canary of her morning dress dazzling, she swept in, her arms open in welcome. "I thought you'd never arrive," she announced, embracing Calypso as if they had been friends for life.

"Eliza," she returned, feeling completely at home with her hostess.

The pause was very short as Eliza eyed her carefully. "What shall it be, tea?" Her gaze lifted with a sparkle. "Or shall we be deliciously wicked and have chocolate?"

Calypso hadn't tasted the addictive brew since she had been a small girl on the Maryland farm. She smiled back. "I haven't had cocoa in years."

"Good. A lady of my own adventurousness. I knew we had much in common."

In the morning light, Calypso was surprised to discover Eliza was much older than she had thought last night in the dimness of the chapel, but her beauty was undeniable.

Eliza settled back on the settee. "How exciting it must be to be married to the dashing Earl of Flint."

Exciting? If one thought being keelhauled exciting, then Eliza was correct. "I must admit there's never a dull moment when Rhys is around."

"And have you known each other long?"

Her hostess was fishing—very properly and with the utmost of style, but fishing nonetheless. "For many years."

"Really." She seemed genuinely surprised. "Mr. Powel and I had known each other many years as well. He'd had business dealings with my father. It was one of those marriages just meant to be."

Calypso cocked her head. A marriage of convenience? Perhaps her suspicions of last night were correct. She was George Washington's mistress. "I imagine you could say the same about Rhys and myself. It was destined." Oh, how she wished to open up to Eliza and tell her the whole sordid truth, but did she dare?

The servant arrived with a pot of chocolate and two Nanking china cups and saucers. The pattern was ornate and spoke of being expensive.

"How lovely," Calypso complimented.

"They are, aren't they? The set was a gift from George and Martha." The blonde accepted a cup from the servant. "The president is a most generous man."

"He appeared most kind last night." She held her saucer balanced in her palm as she took a sip, savoring the flavor.

Eliza set her cup down on a side table. Again she studied Calypso as if trying to decide just how much to say. "You know, Calypso, George is quite taken with you."

"I am flattered by the president's attention." What was Eliza trying to suggest to her? She sat forward, determined to find out what was between George Washington and this woman. "You and the president seem quite close." There she had said it.

The blonde's tinkling laughter filled the parlor. "Why, of course, we're the best of companions. I daresay, I'm the closest female friend he has."

Calypso colored, assuming she was correct in her earlier observation.

Then Eliza's amusement stilled, and she placed her hand over her mouth. "Oh my, not you too. I do believe you've totally misunderstood. George and I are *just* friends. Really."

"Then you're not his mistress?" Calypso released her breath with relief, then stuck her hand to her mouth, wishing she hadn't spoken so bluntly. Damn, would she never learn to think before she verbalized?

"I can't say I haven't fantasized about it, but George is a man with strong continence. Never would he go against his wedding vows. We spoke of this subject once, in vague terms"—her hand fluttered in the air—"and he is more concerned about betraying the confidence of a lady than being caught in adultery. Besides, I love Samuel. Truly I do. It's just that George fulfills my dreams of the dashing cavalier. How lucky you are to have it all in your husband."

"Lucky?" she murmured. She didn't consider herself the fortunate one. "Oh, no. You're the one to envy, not me. Your social status, the stability of your life, your influence on a man as great as the president. What more could one want?"

"Oh, Calypso, how foolish you are." She reached out, taking the drink from her hands, and hugged her shoulders. "I would trade all of it for what every woman wants: the romance, the excitement of belonging to a man of power and passion who is willing to share it all with me. Rhys Winghurst loves you, silly girl."

"No, he doesn't." Her lips thinned and tightened.

"But he does." Eliza's mouth popped open as she released her hold. "It's there in his eyes when he thinks you're not looking. He's only holding back for your commitment. I know that with all my romantic soul."

Calypso stilled, her heart rattling in its empty cage. Was there truth in what her friend said? *Did* Rhys care for her? He constantly badgered her about honesty as if he felt there were secrets she kept from him. Were those secrets as simple as undeclared love?

"Besides, it's there when he looks at your . . ." Eliza stopped abruptly. "I'm not wrong to think we can be honest with each other, am I? I've shared my confi-

243

dences with you. You will do the same, won't you?"

"Eliza, of course." She returned a trusting smile of sincerity. "It's as if we've known each other all our lives. There's nothing I would keep from you."

"Then, how can you not realize how much he cares for you and his child?"

"His child? What child?" Rhys had a child? Why had she never been made aware of the fact?

Eliza's lips thinned. "I thought we were going to be truthful."

"I am, Eliza. What child?" she repeated.

"The boy. I've seen them together. Tristan is the spitting image of Rhys. And now that I've met you, there's no denying you're his mother."

"Tristan?" She barked a nervous, bewildered laugh. "No. You're mistaken. Tristan is my little brother."

The blonde rose and crossed to the hearth. "Of course, your brother. I didn't mean to pry."

Tristan's image filled her mind, then Rhys's face popped in beside him. She licked her dry lips as her heart came to a thunderous halt. Eliza was right. They did look alike. But that was impossible. Tristan was her brother!

A pain like needles stabbed at her middle until she thought she couldn't breathe. Dear God, Tristan *was* her brother, wasn't he?

Cool fingers grasped her sweating palms that were clutching her gown. "Calypso, I didn't mean to upset you. I never meant to insinuate something that wasn't—"

"No, Eliza," she broke in, the muddled puzzle of her life coming together in one simplistic stroke. A well deep inside her gushed forward, and the story of her youthful mistake bubbled to the surface—the tale of how her brother had coerced her, the mistaken meeting in the inn with Rhys, the terrible night her child was born, her

244

mother's death, her father's rage and hate, her baby that had been declared dead, and Tristan—her infant brother.

Her very soul leaked from the tear ducts of her eyes, as she crumbled before the deceitful truth. No wonder Rhys despised her so. He thought she denied their child. The truth. He had come to Long Island looking for his son. That was why he had stolen her father's diary, why he played his coy games, why he had had her arrested and dragged away; he was seeking evidence to attest to Tristan's parentage as well as revenge against those who had tried to keep his son from him, including herself. Tristan was *her* child. How could she have been so blind over the years?

"Dear Holy Father," Eliza whispered, holding Calypso to her heart as if she were a little girl clinging to a doll. "And there's no one now to confirm our suspicions."

Calypso's breath hitched. There was one. Nannette. The old woman knew the truth and had kept it from her all this time.

As if she had no power to think, only to act, Calypso rose, quiet but shaking. "I must go home, Eliza. I must know the truth."

"Would you like me to go with you?" The sincere concern radiating from the blue eyes captured the sane side of her mind for a moment.

She paused, contemplating the offer. "No, I'll be fine. I just need to go home."

"Of course. I'll order your carriage brought around." Eliza sped away, calling for a servant in a voice quivering with distress.

At the moment Calypso could only think about confronting Nannette and demanding the facts from the Scottish woman. Then she would find Rhys and tell him the whole sordid story from the beginning. He would understand and believe her. Until this minute she had never acknowledged how important he was to her. There was still time to save the remnants of their love. He would believe her tale of being deceived. Nanna would support her. And Tristan . . .

She paused in the parlor doorway. By all that was sacred, how was she going to explain the truth to a six-year-old child? He would be so confused and lost. Would he be able to cope with the monumental changes that would occur in his young life?

Rhys would help her make the transition smooth for the boy, she reassured herself. How could she have not recognized the love he felt for her brother all this time?

No, she thought, pressing her fingers to her temples. Her son. Her heart swelled with that special pride of a parent. Her very own child. Hers and Rhys's.

Eliza rushed back in and gently took her hand, leading her toward the front door. "Are you sure, Calypso, you don't want my company?"

"I must do this alone," she insisted, still attempting to cope with the shock of the revelation. "I'm fine." She glanced up with a fleeting smile. "Really, I'll be just fine."

As she glided down the front steps toward the waiting vehicle, Eliza called one more time. "Calypso, remember I'm here if you need me. Anytime, day or night. For anything."

She turned back and sensed the pain of blunder the other woman was feeling. "Thank you, Eliza. For everything you've done." She meant those words. If her new friend had never told her, she might have never figured the truth out.

Accepting the driver's assistance into the carriage, she demanded, "Hurry, Saunders. I need to get back to the tavern as quickly as possible."

"As you wish, madam."

The ride was torture, the few blocks seeming to go on endlessly. In that short expanse of time her mind screamed for answers. Instead of returning to the City Tavern, maybe she should seek out Rhys. But where would she find him? All she knew what that he was with the president, but she had no idea where Washington held his offices. The driver would know. She shifted in her seat to rap on the ceiling to gain Saunders' attention.

Just before knocking, she paused. She couldn't go running off prematurely, looking for Rhys. She could well imagine his anger if she showed up at the government offices demanding they locate her husband. First, she must confront Nannette and confirm the truth of Tristan's parentage. Sitting back, she fought down the urge to leap from the carriage and run the rest of the way in order to get back to the tavern as quickly as possible.

"Nannette. Come right away," she called as she raced down the corridor past the nursemaid's room on the way to her own. Somewhere between Eliza's house and the tavern, her shock had solidified into anger. Not so much at the Scottish woman, but at the circumstances of the deceit.

As she removed her cape and gloves, Nannette rushed into the room, her hands wringing as she cried. "Oh, thank the saints above you're back. What are we going to do, lassie? Whatever will we do?"

Spinning about, she grabbed the woman by the shoulders and shook her with frustration and sorrow. "Why have you lied to me all these years? Why didn't you tell me Tristan was my son?"

Nannette's babble ceased, her mouth popping open in fear as Calypso's anger sliced through her. "The baron

247

gave me no choice." A squeaking sob erupted from her chest. "I didna know what else to do."

"Then it is true? Tristan is my son?" From the well of scattered emotions rose a small whimper of disbelief. She had known it was fact, but somehow the confirmation hit her with the force of a bullet. Releasing the hold on the nursemaid, she dropped into the chair near the hearth. "Rhys. He's known all along, too, hasn't he?"

"He knew when he showed up to take us from Long Island. I don't know how, but he knew."

"Nanna, you should have told me," she cried, slapping her palm against the chair's arm. "My father can't do anything to us. He's hundreds of miles away." She looked up, sadness swelling like a festering wound. "Rhys will never believe I was unaware of the facts."

Nannette dropped down before her. "What Rhys believes doesn't matter now."

"How can you say that, Nanna. Rhys—"

"—is gone, and he took Tristan with him," Nannette wailed, burying her face in Calypso's lap.

"He's gone? Gone where?" Her mouth went instantly dry.

"I don't know. He wouldna tell me. He said to inform you he'd taken the boy where he can show him his true heritage."

Fear lurched in her heart. "Did he say when they'd be back?"

"Oh, lassie. I don't think they will. He made me pack all the laddie's clothes, and he left with several chests of his own."

Her eyes darted about the room, noting the absence of Rhys's presence. Rushing to the wardrobe, she tore the door open to find only her gowns hanging there. She stumbled to the dresser. His drawers were empty. "Rhys," she whispered with frightened clarity. "No, Rhys. You can't have left me."

She whirled back around, closing the drawer with the weight of her body that sagged with defeat. "Not now. Not when I can make it all right between us."

With dawning fatalism, she realized she had gained a family and lost it all in the span of an hour.

Chapter Seventeen

Two weeks later, Calypso was no closer to solving the mystery of her husband's whereabouts. The only fact she had gleaned was that *The Oceanid* was gone as well. But even that bit of information did her little good as Rhys had left no destination with the harbor master. The records indicated "no passengers, no cargo, personal," and the return date was left blank.

She slammed the book closed, pressing her lips tight to keep from verbalizing a curse in front of the official. Where had Rhys taken Tristan? It was as if the heavens had swallowed them up, erasing every clue. To her it was obvious. Rhys didn't intend to be found. He had abandoned her without a second thought—uncaring that the loss of Tristan would destroy her.

Her meeting with Thomas Jefferson earlier this morning confirmed the evidence. As kind as the secretary of state had been, he had listened to her story and her entreaty for assistance, folding his long, tapered fingers on his desktop.

"I'm sorry, Countess," he had stated, his eyes never wavering for an instant. "There's nothing I can tell you."

Her lashes slit, remembering the way Jefferson had watched her. "Can't or won't," she mumbled under her breath as she stepped out of the harbor master's wharfside office, accepting the carriage driver's assistance into the coach.

She settled back against the seat, avoiding Nannette's anxious stare.

"Did you learn anything, lassie?" the older woman asked.

"Nothing."

"Oh, my. What are we going to do now?"

Calypso knew exactly what she must do. But, damn, she didn't want to take the only avenue open to her. George Washington had befriended her once. He might not wish to lend his support again, especially to a woman deserted by her husband the day after their nuptials.

"What if we don't find him, Calypso?" Nannette's voicing of her own inner fears brought her chin up sharply.

"That won't happen."

The carriage bumped over the cobblestones as she reached out to gather the nursemaid in her arms. "We'll find them, Nanna," she assured her. "I haven't played my last card yet." Though her last card would be a trump, she wouldn't use it unless she had no other choices, but in the final moments, finding Tristan and Rhys was much more important than her pride.

Perhaps the thing to do was not to approach the president directly, but through Eliza. Recalling their last parting, the blonde's final words echoed. "Anytime, day or night, for anything." Perhaps her influential friend could find out what she could not.

She straightened, Nannette still slumped across her, and rapped on the carriage ceiling. Within moments the vehicle halted, and the driver's face appeared in the window.

"Two-forty-four South Third Street," she commanded.

In no time the coachman had the conveyance turned about and speeding down the avenue.

"Where are we going, Calypso?"

"Hopefully to where we can get assistance."

Nanna relaxed, accepting her authority. Cocking her head, Calypso tried to remember the precise moment when she and the nursemaid had exchanged roles. The night Nannette had confessed her part in the baby switching. Guilt released, the Scottish woman saw her former ward in a different light. A woman with a child, whose care they shared equally.

The familiar lines of the Powel house filled the window frame, and Calypso pushed forward before the driver had time to completely stop the carriage. She no longer cared about propriety, only in getting answers to her unresolved questions.

She burst upon the servant who responded to her summons with curt demands. "Your mistress. I must see her right away."

"Mistress Powel is in the conservatory now. 'Tis most unseemly. She's not expecting visitors." The maid curtsied as she protested.

"Just show me the way. I'm sure she'll be most pleased to see me." She prayed she was right.

"Please, ma'am. Your name. I must at least announce you before—"

"The Countess of Flint, Calypso Winghurst."

The girl dipped with unsteadiness, then rushed ahead of her to do her job.

"Mistress Powel," she called, racing down a flagstone path to the greenhouse at the rear of the house.

Eliza appeared in the doorway, wearing a simple muslin gown, her hand encased in a sturdy work glove holding down a straw hat to her head. "Maggie," she uttered in consternation.

As the girl dipped before her, her words of explanation catching in the breeze and whirling away, Calypso captured Eliza's eye.

" 'Tis fine, Maggie," the blonde announced. "You've done nothing wrong."

Tearing off her gloves and dropping her serviceable hat on a workbench, Eliza moved forward, ushering Calypso into the humid warmth of the conservatory. Taking in the disheveled red hair, concern edged her words. "Whatever is it, my dear?"

"Oh, Eliza. The very worst." Her earlier resolve to remain calm dissolved as her friend seated her on a marble bench along an arrangement of potted rosebushes. "He's gone, and I don't know where he is."

"Gone? Do you mean your husband?"

She nodded.

"That's to be expected in his line of work."

"No. You don't understand. He has Tristan with him. No one will tell me where's he taken him."

"You must be wrong, Calypso. Just the other night, Mr. Jefferson was saying he had his best men working on a top-priority assignment. He regretted taking your husband from you so soon after your marriage, but—"

"His top men?" She caught her breath, soaking in Eliza's words. What was she saying about her husband? He was a spy working for the American government. Was every bombshell she discovered about her life to come from Eliza Powel?

Straightening, she brushed her hair from her eyes. "I don't care what Rhys does for a living. And I care even less about what Thomas Jefferson might have insinuated. He's gone and taken my son with him. I don't think he's coming back."

Eliza lifted her chin a notch, her brows crinkling with concentration. "Then we'll find out, won't we? It seems

Mr. Jefferson thought to use me as a decoy—someone to lead you off the track. I don't like that." She smiled. "I have my contacts. I'll find out the truth." She patted Calypso's clasped hands. "Just give me a little time."

Calypso eased forward. "Thank you, Eliza. I knew you would help me."

The woman smiled. "What are friends for if not to help?" She urged her to stand and led her toward the garden house exit. "Go back to your lodgings and wait to hear from me. In a few days I'll have your answer."

Calypso struggled to maintain a semblance of calm. Days? Could she find the strength to remain inactive much longer? Maybe she should go directly to the president. Again that feeling of being relatively unimportant to someone of George Washington's stature gave her second thoughts.

Catching the determination in Eliza's gaze, she knew she must give her friend the time she asked for. But oh, waiting would take all her strength of mind as the need to find Tristan and hold him to her, knowing he was her son, was the most important thing in her life. Even the desire to face Rhys and demand the truth of his feelings for her and to explain her innocence in this entire affair gnawed at her insides like bitter brew.

Taking a deep breath, she squared her shoulders, determined to confront the idle time with the strength of a soldier marching to battle. "Please, Eliza," she whispered. "As fast as you can. I must find my husband and son."

"Stay put and wait for me. I shall not let you down. I'll call on you the moment I know anything."

She followed the servant girl back into the house, glancing over her shoulder once to see Eliza briskly completing her instructions to the gardeners as she left the warm, safe haven of the conservatory. With a fanning

254

motion of her hand she sent Calypso on her way.

Back in the carriage, she again faced Nannette's questioning concern.

"We wait. If anyone can discover Rhys's whereabouts, Eliza Powel can," she responded to the ever-repeated question of what she had learned.

Satisfied, Nannette folded her hands in her lap, a rock of patience. Calypso studied her lifelong companion with envy. If only she could be so accepting that fate would soothe the waves battering her existence. With a sigh, she drew her warm cape about her and pressed her aching head against the leather of the seat, accepting she had done all she could for the moment.

Eyes closed, Calypso listened to the serving girl recite the day's menu by rote. Nothing new she hadn't tried before. She had resided so long at the City Tavern that she had tasted the cook's entire repertoire of recipes. Nothing sounded exciting or stimulating. Like her life. A stalemate. An all-encompassing circle of checks keeping her from making a move.

Ordering the roast beef and Yorkshire pudding, she took up a folded issue of *The Pennsylvania Packet,* and spread it out to glance over the headlines, not really interested, yet bored with the idea of staring out over the growing number of diners, a lone woman in a crowd of hungry men who wanted nothing more than to discuss their politics and the happenings of their day.

Even Nannette had deserted her, requesting a tray sent up to the room for her. Of late, the little woman was so silent—brooding Calypso categorized the way the nursemaid remained in the comfortable old rocker by the hearth, pumping, pumping until she thought the repetitive squeaking would drive her insane.

Two days had passed and not a word from Eliza. Frowning she glanced down at the printed words, reading yet not comprehending what she saw. There was an account of an American sailor claiming to have been forced to serve on an English ship. "Now was not the best of times to be on the seas," the article announced. "The British Tyrants run amuck, and no American is safe on English turf."

She flashed on Rhys and Tristan somewhere in that vast watery world, concerned that something might happen to them. If it did, how would she ever find out? Would anyone contact her? The thought that those she loved could disappear without her ever knowing set her heart to knocking with an uneven rhythm. Such horrid thoughts were unacceptable. She would find them. She would.

Pushing the morbid images from her mind, she focused on the newspaper. A report that English shippers were refusing to accept American ships in port due to the large debts accumulated since the beginning of the war caught her attention and just as quickly lost it. Sighing, she tossed the paper aside, wishing the meal would arrive so she could eat and return to the solitude of her room as the noise level in the dining room was beginning to get on her nerves.

"Mistress Winghurst."

Her gaze slid sideways, taking in the man standing before her, Jeremy Stickback. Frowning, she sat up straight, and wished for all the world she wasn't alone. His tall figure leaned heavily against the horsehead cane clutched in his right hand. "Mr. Stickback, if I remember correctly."

He flashed her a smile. "I'm honored you remember me." Glancing about the room, he continued. " 'Tis a shame such a lovely lady must dine alone. By chance,

256

I'm by myself as well. Would it be too forward if I asked to join you?"

Yes, her mind screamed, but she bit her lip and indicated the empty seat across from her. "If you wish."

The uncomfortable silence between them pulsated, causing her head to throb. What was it about this man that made her so uncomfortable? She could feel him studying her as if forming exactly the right words to say.

Her eyes shot up. That was it. He was here to tell her something.

"I was most distressed to learn Rhys departed so soon after your marriage. The bride and groom had little time to be together." He clucked his tongue and shook his head. "You have my sincere sympathy."

"Do I?" Her mouth lifted in an unemotional smile. "I don't need it." *Say what you wish to tell me, then leave me alone.*

"I was even more surprised to hear he left without taking you."

She sat up straight. Without a doubt this man knew where Rhys had gone. He was playing a game with her, a feline batting a captured rodent between his paws, and most likely enjoying every moment.

"If you knew Rhys as well as I do, you'd know he's capable of anything."

"Ah, yes, the mighty earl who answers to no one." He shrugged. "I've discovered over the many years we've worked together, he always has his reasons. Usually good ones." Waiting for her cutting remark, he lifted his mouth on one side.

"I couldn't say."

At that moment her meal arrived, and Stickback took a dramatic sniff of the wafting scent of her food. "Looks good, I think I'll have the same. An end cut, wench," he demanded from the serving girl. Again, he

257

smiled that pat, insincere expression as he folded his hands, giving the impression he had all the patience of a stalking cat.

Realization struck her. He had no intention of revealing Rhys's whereabouts unless she asked him.

Frustration bubbled. She would kill for that knowledge, but could she humble herself before this man who seemed so determined to belittle her? But what if Eliza never came through? Whom else could she turn to?

The information she needed was there for the asking—no, Jeremy Stickback would make her plead. Or would he want something more? His gaze touched upon her breasts for the swiftest of moments—chilling her like the congealed drippings enveloped her untouched meal. If he asked "favors" of her, she wouldn't give them.

She gave up the pretense of eating, and, setting down her utensils, she stared him in the eye. "So, tell me, Mr. Stickback, since the two of you work so closely together, of course Rhys confided in you as to his final destination?" She prayed beyond hope he might reveal the facts, unaware of her ignorance regarding her husband's location.

"Of course." He offered nothing more.

"Mr. Stickback, what is the point of our avoiding the issue? You have the information I want and need, and I must—surely—have something you're willing to accept in exchange."

"Madam," he said, pushing back his chair in what only could be mock horror. "Are you attempting to bribe me in an official capacity?"

She hesitated. Was that what she was trying to do? "No, Mr. Stickback. I only wish to find my husband and child. No government would be unsympathetic to such a simple request."

He looked surprised, and for a moment she could

have sworn the expression genuine. "You don't know where he is? Why, that scoundrel. I can solve your problem quite easily. Flintshire, my lady. Rhys went home to settle a family matter."

"Flintshire," she mouthed, completely taken back at the ease with which Jeremy Stickback had given her the location as well as the implication of the revelation.

The news she had scanned in the morning paper only moments before settled like a lump of burning coal in the pit of her stomach. Rhys had returned to English soil, and if what the paper had said was true, she would find getting to Wales a task near impossible to accomplish.

Chapter Eighteen

Winghurst Castle
Flintshire, Wales
December 20, 1790

Tristan ran down the long corridor on the second floor of the mansion, screaming and waving his arms with the carefree delight known only to children. From his vantage point at the top of the stairs, Rhys watched his son with tolerant amusement. All his youth he had done the same thing, only there had been schoolmasters or spinsterly governesses who had stopped his playful antics. Not so for Tristan. What harm could a little noise do this drafty, old house? It might draw some warmth into its crusty existence.

"I wish Callie was here, Rhys," the boy shouted from the other end of the hall. "She would think this so much fun."

Rhys smiled strictly for Tristan's sake and nodded his head. Calypso. He thought about her relentlessly. There was a lonely corner of his heart she had managed to capture, and he couldn't deny he missed her. If only the circumstances between them had been different. She should be with them at the moment their son was told the truth. As all mothers did, she would know best how to comfort his youthful bewilderment as his life was turned topsy-turvy.

Setting his mouth in a hard angle, he pushed her image from his mind. Calypso had selected her path with her persistent lies. He wouldn't attempt to alter her choice. Only she could bring about such a change.

Unfortunately, their last few hours together had given no indication she had any intention of correcting her misguided attitude. He had lost her, but he consoled himself with the fact he had gained Tristan.

"Rhys, why do you always look so angry when I talk about my sister?"

The warmth of Tristan's smaller hand seeking reassurance in the protection of his own startled him.

"Since we left Father's"—the boy hesitated as if unsure—"I thought you liked her. I hoped, maybe, we could be like a real family." The innocence of his wish drifted away on the uncertainty of his whispered words.

Rhys's gaze darted down, taking in the expectation glistening in Tristan's eyes. He couldn't keep the truth from his son any longer. The boy had a right to know who his parents were. And though the timing felt wrong to him, he realized it would never be "right." The revelation would hurt and confuse the lad, no matter how long he waited.

"Tristan." He bent down until one knee brushed the carpeting of the hallway and he was eye level with the one person who meant everything to him. Reaching out, he grasped the child's shoulders and could feel his frailty beneath the smaller version of the maroon jacket identical to the one he wore himself. "I do like her, in fact, very much, but she has disappointed me."

The boy studied him, confused. No doubt in his eyes Callie could do no wrong. "But why?" he demanded with an intensity that matched Rhys's own.

261

"She hasn't told the truth about something very important to me."

"Callie don't lie!" Tristan stood to his full height and pulled from Rhys's grasp. "She would never tell a fib."

With a deep sigh, Rhys rose to his feet and crossed to a settee pushed against the hallway wall. "Come here, Son. There are some things I haven't been truthful with you about either." He pointed to the space beside him.

Tristan hesitated. "You lied, too?" Bewildered, he darted his innocent eyes about as if considering sprinting away.

"Please, Tristan. Give me a chance. Hear what I have to say. Then, together, we'll decide what to do."

The boy settled down beside him. Rhys made no attempt to touch him, though in his heart he wanted to press the child tight against his chest. "All my life, I've discovered there are two things that are important," he began, looking at the boy in earnestness. "Truth and the freedom to give others the right to make their own choices." He sighed, pulling his gaze away to stare at the ceiling.

"Callie made some decisions a long time ago, and perhaps what she did was for the best then, but now she refuses to acknowledge the truth." Glancing at Tristan's open face, he wondered if the boy understood at all what he was talking about. Was he only making matters worse by avoiding the issue?

"What I'm attempting to tell you, Son, is that Calypso and I . . ." No, he couldn't blurt the truth out like this. Tristan wouldn't understand. "We love you."

Pausing, he mulled over how to present the facts. Was it right to put the blame totally on Calypso? He didn't want Tristan to despise her. All children should love their mothers. He stared back down at his companion. "We . . . we tried to protect you, and in our concern for you,

262

we both told a lie. You see, Tristan, Callie and I are your parents." Taking a deep breath, he waited to see the boy's reaction.

Tristan blinked and glanced about the hallway, his eyes resting on one pastoral picture after another. Had the boy understood what he had told him? Was it too much for his young mind to accept? Rhys bunched his muscles in preparation to gather the boy to his heart when the tears of confusion gushed forward.

"Do you mean it, Rhys? You're my papa?" Tears welled in the innocent brown eyes, and Rhys reached out, ready to comfort him.

Instead of falling into his arms, Tristan jumped up and did a little jig down the hallway, the tears evidence of his relief and joy. "That means Father can't—" He spun about to face Rhys, his confusion real. "But if he's not my father, what do I call him?"

"Do you mean the baron?"

Tristan nodded.

The old fool didn't deserve being called anything polite. "He's your grandfather, Son."

Before Rhys could finish, the boy danced his way down the other end of the hall. "He can't touch me anymore. He can't make me—" His small body jerked to a halt. "Rhys," he questioned, "are you sure? Callie's my sister."

"That's the lie I was telling you about, Tristan. I think she meant well by leading you to believe that, but—"

"No, Rhys. I remember her telling me about her baby she had the same day I was born. But it died; she showed me the grave once, and she cried when she told me about how she'd never seen what it looked like, didn't even know if it was a boy or a girl."

Rhys rose from the settee. What an elaborate story to weave all for the benefit of a small child. Why had Calypso done so? He frowned, then shook himself mentally. What was important at the moment was proving to Tristan he was his son. There was physical testimony—the Winghurst birthmark.

Grabbing the boy's hand, he led him into his bedroom.

"Where are we going, Rhys?"

"To prove to you you're my son."

In front of the fretwork looking glass, he paused, bringing Tristan to stand by his side. "Look at us, Son. The same hair, the same eyes, you're Winghurst through and through."

"Lots of people have brown hair and eyes." The boy's sober reply tore at his heart. How like himself he was. Proof—always needing tangible evidence before accepting what others told him.

"Maybe, but I have another reason for asserting that you're my son. Have you ever noticed the birthmark on your left hip?"

Tristan looked up at him, as if amazed he knew about the disfigurement. "You mean the mark the devil branded me with?"

Rhys's mouth crooked with irony. "Whoever told you that hit nearer to the truth than they probably knew. 'Tis the mark of Winghurst men."

The boy's hand reached behind his body, grazing the spot where the fleur-de-lis stained his skin. "Do you have it, too?"

Rhys nodded.

"Let me see."

"Don't you believe me, Tristan?"

The boy hesitated several strokes of time. "You said you lied once. Who's to say you're not lyin' again."

Rhys ruffled his shaggy head. "No Winghurst accepts a man on his word alone. 'Tis nothing wrong in wanting

264

proof." Releasing the top fastener of his breeches, he flipped the waistband out of the way, easing the material down until the regal crest he had borne all his life was exposed to the boy's perusal.

"It's true. It's just like mine," Tristan chirped in amazement. Turning, he gripped Rhys's leg with all his strength and clung. "What does this mean, Rhys?" His voice caught with the sob of confusion Rhys had expected from the beginning. "Papa."

Squatting down with his son, Rhys wrapped his arms about the fragile shoulders. "A great deal. But we've plenty of time to talk about it. Go ahead and cry, boy." His own eyes misted as he clung to Tristan. "We've a whole lifetime to learn what it means to be father and son. A whole lifetime, and we won't waste a single moment."

"But, lassie, Wales is a world away. I canna allow you to go like this." Nannette wrung her hands.

"I'm going and that's final." Calypso stuffed the last of her gowns into the trunk and signaled to the Scottish woman to sit on the bulging lid so she could secure the latches.

"Besides," she continued as she struggled to force the catches in place and lock them, "there's nothing wrong with what I'm doing. I'm a married woman going to join her husband and son."

"But, Callie girl, what proof do you have that Rhys is truly there? The word of a stranger?"

"I know, Nannette," she agreed, plopping down on the trunk lid beside the older woman, the task of packing at last completed. "But for reasons I can't explain to you, I believe what Jeremy Stickback told me. I must go. I must find them."

265

"Aye, lassie, I understand. But take me with ye. I've never been without my wards—all alone." Her aging voice cracked with emotion. "I've lost Tristan. I canna lose you, too."

"Oh, Nanna. Please try to understand. I must do this by myself. I need you to stay in Philadelphia in case I'm wrong and Rhys returns. I need you here to explain for me. Can't you see?"

"Aye, lassie, I see far too well. I'll be staying if ye want me to, but I shall worry day and night until ye come back."

"I'll return. Don't you worry. I'll have Tristan with me."

As she hugged the older woman to her, she kept her worst fears to herself. *Pray God, with the world as unsettled as it is, I hope I reach Wales at all.* There had been only one ship she could find in all the Philadelphia harbor willing to take her into English waters. The brooding captain had been anything but friendly, but the weight of her purse—money Rhys had so "generously" left for her—had captured his consent to risk dangerous territory to take her to Flintshire. She had no doubt Captain Langley would plot some devious way of avoiding disaster, otherwise he would never have agreed. But what did she care how he did it, as long as he took her to her destination?

Taking a deep breath, she released the woman who had been more like a parent to her than anyone else in her life. "Take care, Nannette. I must leave now, or I'll miss my ship. And if Rhys returns before I do"—she gathered the aging face in the curve of her palms—"make him understand."

"I will, Calypso. I promise." Nannette covered her hands with her liver-spotted ones. "I'll not fail you again."

266

Sweeping from the room, Calypso didn't look back as she feared she would not have the courage to go on. *I'll find you, Rhys Winghurst, and I'll make you see the mistakes you've made judging me. Then I'll turn the tables on you and get even. I'll take your son away from you. Then you'll know how much I have been hurt.*

As the carriage neared the two-masted brig, *The Pilgrim*, Calypso doubted the wisdom of her decision. In the bright morning light the ship looked seedier, more derelict, a pirate ship from a childhood nightmare. Had it not been flying the Stars and Stripes, she most likely would never have considered boarding. But if she was going to Wales, this was her only means. Her momentary indecision solidified into a need to prove to the husband who had dared to desert her she could give as good as she got.

Dismissing Rhys's carriage several docks from *The Pilgrim*'s berth, she snagged a shoeless waif and paid him handsomely—enough to buy footwear to replace the rags binding his feet—to watch her luggage. For some crazy reason that she was yet to comprehend she had used her maiden name of Collingsworth when making her arrangements with Captain Langley. She wanted no one who knew her as Rhys's wife to see her board and no one on the ship to associate her with the earl's carriage. Let Captain Langley think what he would about why her baggage was dropped so far from the ship.

As she neared the gangplank, the man in question stepped from a knot of sailors to greet her. Relief trickled from her lungs, for though the captain was as large as she remembered, at least two hundred and fifty pounds, he was not as frightening to look upon as he had seemed yesterday evening. Visibly she relaxed, sure everything would be all right. Most likely she would have an uneventful voyage across the Atlantic.

She smiled, trying to appear genuinely pleased to see her escort, but as he neared, the smell of stale tobacco and ale mixed with the stench associated with seawater-logged canvas and hemp overpowered her. She had to force herself to accept his hand in assistance as she crossed over to the deck.

"Captain Langley," she acknowledged as he led her around equipment and sails. "My luggage is sitting several docks down. Could you arrange for it to be brought aboard?" The difference between this ship and Rhys's struck her immediately. *The Oceanid* had been spotless and orderly, almost military in nature. And the captains. She swiveled a peek at Langley. No comparison.

"Miss Collingsworth," he addressed her as he led her down the companionway after signaling to three men to go after her trunk. The ocean odors were even stronger in the lower confines, and she fought down the urge to cover her nose and mouth.

"I hope you find your accommodations satisfactory." With a knowing smile, he pushed open the cabin door.

The room was an abomination, and the thought of spending several weeks in it flipped her stomach. The bed was no more than a straw-stuffed mattress of indeterminate cleanliness on a wooden frame attached to the wall. From the broken, pieced-together nightstand came a smell that made the rest of the ship seem like a bed of spring blossoms. No longer able to keep the bile from rising in her throat, she lifted her hand, capturing her mouth and nose.

"Please, Captain, you must have other arrangements."

His laughter chilled her to the bones. "Figured you for more spine than that. A little lye soap and a mop, you'll have these quarters fresher than a breeze after a gale storm. Take 'em or leave 'em, the decision is yours."

Did she have much choice? It was Captain Langley's ship or none. She pushed up her sleeves. "If that's the case, sir, have soap and water—lots of soap—delivered right away."

He paused, and for one fearful moment she thought he was going to tell her to get the supplies herself. "Aye, miss," he conceded. "Would most likely be to my benefit to oblige."

Her shoulders lowered in relief as he strolled away. Closing the door to the cabin, she leaned against the companionway wall, wondering how long it would take to get her request. As she waited, several loud thuds overhead made her stand up straight. Then she settled back down. Most likely just the crew struggling with her overstuffed trunk.

The magnitude of her situation filled the emptiness of the companionway. Here she was, a lone woman on a ship filled with men of questionable reputation, trying to make her way across the Atlantic to an unfriendly port. How ironic it was to her that England was the enemy now, when not so long ago on Long Island with her family, the thought of Americans had conjured up images of ogres and demons. How had her life changed so drastically over the matter of a few months? Rhys Winghurst, she reminded herself. That pompous, overbearing jackanapes she had had the misfortune of marrying.

The clanking of buckets brought her back to the present as a small boy not much older than Tristan struggled from the depths of the ship, toting pails of water, a mop and scrub brush, as well as several wadded rags.

"Yer soap suds, mum," he muttered as he insolently dropped the supplies in the middle of the passageway and turned to retrace his steps.

"Wait, boy," she called. "Where do I dump the dirty water after I'm finished?"

He looked up blinking, his face as unsanitary as everything else around her. "Most likely the port'ole would be best. That's where all yer waste's to go."

"Of course, the porthole," she mumbled, gathering up the supplies, and, using the crook of one elbow, she struggled to open the cabin door. The smell was worse than she had remembered.

The porthole. A tiny round window directly above the bed and nearly out of her reach. If the wind was just right, probably what she attempted to dump would come flying back in her face. No wonder the quarters stunk like the sewers of Paris. Not that she had ever been to France, but she had read about the stench.

Arms akimbo, she assessed the work to be done. The mattress would be her first victim. Tugging with all of her strength, she managed to dislodge it from the framework and drag it across the deck and out the door. In the companionway, she was able to prop it on one end, and using the dry mop she pounded it until the narrow airspace was alive with dust particles.

Coughing, she paused long enough to catch her breath and dab her forehead with the back of her hand as a sailor passed by her, a look of pure amazement plastered on his face.

"Ma'am," he offered, sneezing from the flying dust as he touched the edge of his knit cap with dirty fingers and wiped his nose on his sleeve in one smooth notion.

Her lips thinned as he squeezed past her. It was all Rhys Winghurst's fault that she was forced to accept such humiliation. If he had had the sense of a goose, he would have never deserted her, forcing her to take such drastic action. Damn him for the fool he was.

270

Snatching up a bucket of sudsy water and the scrub brush, she reentered the room. The deck lurched beneath her, and she caught herself against the wall as the ship began to sway like a drunken sailor released from jail. The journey had begun; they had set sail, and a fear deep-rooted in the pit of her belly ignited like a flash fire. Was she doing the right thing by chasing off after Rhys? Her son, she reminded herself. She only wanted Tristan. Rhys Winghurst could drown in the depths of hell for all she cared.

Working her frustration out with the scrub brush, she started in the farthermost corner of the room, missing nothing, furniture, walls, and deck. Within a few hours the stronger smell of lye doused the rancid odors that had dominated the cabin earlier.

A sigh whistling from her lips, she sat back on her haunches to survey her work. The cabin was clean, the bed as fresh as possible. Then she glanced down at herself. It seemed that every bit of dirt had been drawn to her like iron to a magnet. Standing, she placed her hand in the small of her aching back and limped to the door. She would search the ship and find someone to bring her a bath. And she wouldn't accept no for an answer.

With stiff fingers she grasped the door handle and pushed it down. The catch didn't move. Irritated that nothing worked properly on this bucket of a ship, she pressed her full weight against the latch. Nothing. It had to be stuck.

She stood back and contemplated her newest dilemma. Damn Langley for keeping such an untidy vessel. Brushing the red tresses from her eyes, she tackled the door from a different angle and tried to force it open. Frustration balled in her throat as she jiggled the handle back and forth a dozen times. Why wouldn't the door open?

Had she mistakenly locked it? She glanced about, looking for a key, but there was nothing that even remotely resembled what she sought.

A strange sensation mantled her shoulders. The door was locked, but she had not done it. That meant someone had fastened the latch on the other side.

Only one name came to mind. Langley. She squeezed her lashes tight, forcing the panic to remain buried deep inside her. What sinister plot did the horrid Captain Langley have planned for her? She would have known he had accepted her offering much too easily not to have bigger game in mind.

Her fists rat-a-tatted against the door, hoping that her fertile imagination had run away with her and her fears were for naught. Why would Langley lock her in her cabin? He had her money. She had paid him well. He couldn't possibly think to get more from her. The silence from the other side of the door told her nothing.

She dropped her hands to her sides. She would not panic, but would maintain her head. There was a logical explanation for what was happening.

Several hours later, footsteps outside the door brought her rushing back to press her ear against the wooden slab. The lock creaked as a key was inserted and turned. Whom would she find on the other side? Captain Langley, of course, she reassured herself as she stepped back. Eyeing the bed, she moved to the other side. Only too well she remembered the last time a man had stormed into a cabin and found her too close to the bed. But that had been Rhys Winghurst, a man she should have never trusted from the beginning. On the safe side, she edged as far from the bed as she could.

Captain Langley was just as unsavory as she remembered. The grin he directed toward her was anything but friendly as he swung the ring of keys he held in his hand about one finger.

"Quite a little miracle worker, aren't we?" he commented, glancing around the scrubbed cabin. "But I can't say much for the likes of ye." He clucked his tongue as he took in her disheveled appearance.

Her chin angled upward in pride. Dirty she might be, but what right did this uncouth sailor have to make fun of her? "Nothing that a little fresh water and soap won't solve." She wanted to demand a tubful, but thought better of it.

"Soap and water. Is your brain addled, wench? Do you think of nothing but cleanin'?"

"I can think of worse things to consider."

"Can ya? Well, think about this. In a week or two you'll be entertainin' the dey of Algiers. My suggestion to you is to come up with somethin' more interestin' to discuss than housecleanin'."

"The dey of Algiers? Whatever are you talking about?" A pinprick of fear needled her spine.

"Did you really think me fool enough to sail into English waters? The piddling sum you paid me isn't worth risking my neck for. But the dey, he'll pay me royally for a prime specimen like you. 'Tis said he has a special itch for red-haired women. I would be thinkin' about how I was going to please him. 'Tis rumored he drowns females that don't."

Calypso stepped back, her palms pressed against the paneling of the wall. She had read horror stories of women kidnapped and sold into harems. This couldn't be happening to her. Not now, before she had a chance to tell Tristan how important he was to her.

Chapter Nineteen

Rhys loosened his grip on the quill and let the pen drop into its holder. Sprinkling sand on the balanced ledger, he sat back in the desk chair, his arms folded over his chest, waiting for the ink to dry. He was trapped. Snared in a country he no longer felt a loyalty to and in a life he despised with his entire being. But he would remain where he was for the rest of his life if necessary. Tristan's welfare meant more than his own contentment.

He had never seen the boy so carefree and happy. The once-troubled tyke was now all a child of six should be. Not once had he asked to return to America. Then, just yesterday he had referred to the Winghurst mansion as "home."

Even Luther had settled in like a brooding hen, taking over his position in the stable as if he had never left it, as if he were here to stay.

Here to stay. Rhys swallowed the impulse to groan and buried his face in his hands. He supposed that was exactly what would happen. Until Tristan was old enough to take over the responsibilities that came with the title, he would remain in Flint a prisoner of his heritage. Unfortunately, he would be well past his prime by then, so what would be the point in leaving?

Brushing the sand from the dried pages of the accounting book back into the container, he closed the ledger and slipped it into the open drawer to his left. If only Tristan would show an interest in something other than his pony he rode like a demon across the moors or the falcon Luther was training for him.

He paused in the process of slamming the drawer closed. Maybe the fault lay not in the boy, but in himself. He glanced out the window to catch a glimpse of his son racing from the stable to the house. Having told Tristan the estate and title were his if he wanted them, he had never made it clear what his other options were. Perhaps he had expected the boy to be the model son and know what his father's wishes were.

Standing, Rhys crossed the room and made his way to the door. It was time to take Tristan in hand and express his own personal desires to the lad, who had every right to know how his father felt. Tristan was a good boy, a sensitive person, all a man could ask for in a child. Together they would find a solution that was right for both of them.

Rhys admitted to himself there were times he had trouble thinking of more than self—he had been on his own for as long as he could remember with no one else to consider. Now he had Tristan, and there was a special joy in sacrificing for someone who looked up to him as if he was the most wonderful man in the world.

Crossing the foyer to take the hallway under the stairs leading to the kitchens, he knew without a doubt he would find Tristan sitting before the hearth, stuffing his face with whatever new confection Cook had conjured up especially for the boy. His eyes brightened the moment he spied his son. Yes, fatherhood agreed with him.

Tristan turned, his hand gesturing in such a way he was the living image of his mother. The happiness Rhys experienced shifted like desert sands before a wind, leaving the bleakness of failure in its path.

Why hadn't marriage agreed with him as easily? He remembered the silver crown he had placed in the drawer in the night table beside his bed—the token of all that had passed between him and Calypso—the only thing besides Tristan she had given him he didn't have the heart to get rid of. Why had they been unable to find that special something that could make their relationship cohesive? Perhaps it was his fault. Had he been too uncompromising?

He mulled the facts carefully. No, he could honestly reply to himself. He had tried to make her face reality, to accept the veracity of their situation. The existence of a child could not be denied forever, no matter how much the thought upset her.

Though he heeled his self-doubt with rationalization, responsibility refused to unleash him from its grip. Maybe he should have tried harder. Had he taken the easy way out by leaving her? Most likely he would never know as their lives were now worlds apart.

Oddly enough, the thought saddened him. Calypso was a woman he had found easy to love. He caught his breath deep in his lungs. The realization stunned him, making it impossible to swallow.

"Papa, is something wrong?"

His attention snapped downward to find Tristan standing before him, concern etching his tart-smeared face. If the situation hadn't been so serious, he might have laughed, something he hadn't done for so long he had forgotten how it felt. "Nothing's wrong, but we need to talk."

With a solemn nod, Tristan took him by the hand and led him toward the small sitting room that was no more than an alcove at the rear of the first floor. Tristan's room, he called it now though it hadn't changed [in] generations. Once it had been his mother's, a[nd] grandmother's before that, a warm, welcome sp[ot] tranquility he remembered well from his childhood. Ca-lypso would have liked it.

He came up short, the jarring thought as unexpected as the sharp twinge plaguing his heart. Why couldn't he forget the woman who had made such a fiasco of his entire life? Staring into the face of his son, he knew without a doubt she would haunt him for the rest of his existence; there was too much of her in the boy to ig-nore.

Tristan's small hand cupped his wrist. "Are we gonna talk about why you're so unhappy?"

The boy's perception was uncanny. He dropped onto the window-ledge seat, a spot where he had spent many hours as a lad, and waited for Tristan to join him. "Is it that obvious?"

"Do you miss Callie—Mama—too?"

"It's not just your mama I miss," he explained, at last admitting the truth out loud, "but many things I left behind in Philadelphia." Then the fact the boy had said "too" rammed home. "Do you miss her?"

"All the time," Tristan confessed, his chin so like hers, a knob of pride when lifted, drifted toward his chest. "I so want to call her mama, but then maybe she'd be mad at me if I did."

"No, Son," he instantly consoled. "Does she ever get angry with you for speaking the way you feel?"

Tristan shook his head. "Rhys, I know she lied about things, and lyin's wrong. But I forgave you, and you said you lied. Can't we forgive her, too?" His eyes pleaded for approval.

How unimportant his reasons for leaving Calypso seemed when expressed in the child's simplistic way.

uld forgiving her be so wrong? Doing so wouldn't cause a permanent blight on his male ego. "What do you suggest we do, Son?"

Tristan's eyes shone with hope. "Can't we go back and find her? Tell her we're sorry?"

Crawl back and admit he was wrong? The idea rankled, yet wasn't that what she deserved? "What about our responsibilities here, to Flintshire?"

The boy slumped his shoulders and squirmed his bottom against the cushion beneath him. "I know it's important to you that I like living here, Papa. Really, I've tried, but it's no fun. The stable boys are afraid of me and call me Lord Tristan. And the groundskeeper's sons won't even look me in the eye."

" 'Tis the way of British society, Son. They know one day you'll be their master. If they slight you now, you might remember when you become an earl." Was the boy's disillusionment real? He tried to avoid building up his hopes. "On Long Island you were thought of as the baron's son. Wasn't it the same there for you?"

Tristan shook his head in denial.

"Are you saying you want to give up your claim to the earldom?"

"Can I do that?" he chirped in such an expectant voice there was no longer any doubt in Rhys's mind.

"That's your right, but once you make such a decision you can't reverse it." Why was he playing devil's advocate? Tristan wanted exactly what he wished for. But it was important that the boy be sure, absolutely certain, in his choice.

The child grabbed him about the neck with a desperate clutch. "I don't want you to be mad at me, Rhys, but I want to go back to Callie, to America."

Rhys held him tight in response. "Lord, Son, I won't be angry. Would you be mad at me if you became the offspring of a less than wealthy commoner?"

Tristan glanced up blinking, questioning with his eyes. "As long as you're still my papa."

"Do you think your mama will want us?" Would she, indeed, desire a man who must work for a living, no longer the mighty Earl of Flint with all the money and power that came with the title?

"We could ask her," Tristan offered.

Ask? Not easy for a man used to demanding. "You're right, Son, we can ask."

Tristan wiggled from his arms and sat up straight. "When can we leave?"

"Well, there are solicitors to contact, my cousin William to locate and notify of his windfall." He ruffled Tristan's hair. "As soon as possible, which will be at least a couple of weeks."

"Hurry, Papa. It's time we return home."

Rhys smiled. Home. They couldn't get back quick enough to Philadelphia to suit him though it wouldn't be in time for Christmas. Would Calypso still be there? Of course, he assured himself. Where else would she go?

Fear oozed through Calypso's veins like an infection, seeking to destroy the facade of calm she had cultivated on a minute-by-minute basis. For nearly a week she had been locked in her cabin, a prisoner of her own stupidity. What a horrid way to have spent Christmas. How could she have trusted someone like Captain Langley and blithely gone aboard his ship alone and unprotected? She was in a barrel of pickle brine with no imaginable way of escaping. All she could do was wait for Fate to deal the cards.

She couldn't just sit there and maintain her sanity. Rising from the lone chair, she began pacing, trying to

279

think of some aspect of her dilemma she had not considered before, but nothing new came to mind. There were only two ways out of the cabin—the door which was locked from the other side and the porthole above the bed. That particular route she had tried within hours of discovering her predicament. She had attempted to wiggle through, but her shoulders were too broad. And though escaping would have meant plunging into the sea, she would have most likely done it, would do it now if she could, to escape a doom worse than death.

A harem girl. She shivered, remembering the times she had read stories about young women disappearing into the clutches of Arabian sheiks, their innocence stolen against their wills. When she had been a girl, the thought of being carried away and dominated by an exciting man had seemed so thrilling, but she had lived long enough to realize kidnapping and rape was not something to fantasize about. Knowing Rhys Winghurst had cooled her ardor for adventure—at least of that nature.

Her chin inched upward. She would resist, fight with all her might against some man in silken robes and turban making her a slave to his body. Her fingers drifted up and caressed the column of her neck. How would it feel to have one's head chopped off? It couldn't be very pleasant.

She sank back down in her chair. How many times in the last days had her mind taken this same carousel of thought only to come to the same conclusion? Dear lord, her life was over. Whether by death or degradation, what did it matter?

The door handle rattled, and a key turned in the lock. Calypso didn't look up. Why bother? It was only the cook bringing her another meal. Scooting the chair until her back was to the door, she waited, head bowed until the intruder came and left.

"Miss Collingsworth, how are we today?"

She spun about at the cheerful query from none other than Captain Langley, who sounded more like a concerned physician than a kidnapper. Her mouth thinned as she pressed her lips tightly together, refusing to answer.

Circling her, he eyed her up and down. "Appears to me, we're gettin' thin." He clucked his tongue. "That won't do, won't do at all. The dey likes his women with meat on their bones."

"I could care less what the dey likes or you think."

"And that tongue of yours. Ya best learn to curb it. 'Tis said he cut one woman's out to shut her up."

Calypso drew the proscribed organ deep into her mouth, clamping her jaws down. No one would dare cut out her tongue.

"That's better, much better." Langley rubbed his greedy hands together. "But it doesn't matter much. Your beauty and innocence will carry ya through." From the corner of her eyes she saw his eyes narrow. "You are innocent, aren't ya, wench?"

Calypso paused in indecision. What answer would best serve her. "What does it matter? If I am, I won't be once your 'friend' gets his slimy clutches on me."

Langley gripped her by the shoulders and lifted her bodily from the chair. "Answer my question. Now. You are innocent? You are *Miss* Collingsworth?"

Her insides quaked. What would this madman do if he discovered she wasn't? Slit her throat and throw her into the sea? Or would telling him the truth of who she was make him have second thoughts about selling her to some desert pervert?

"No," she hissed through her teeth. "It's not *Miss* Anything, but the Countess of Flintshire, Calypso

Winghurst."

Hilarity burst from his lips. "What is this, some joke ya think will save ya? Are ya tellin' me you're a married woman?"

Her head waggled on her neck. "Married with a child."

He dropped her as if she were scalding hot. "Damnation," he whined. "Don't nuthin' ever go right for me?"

Calypso gathered her feet beneath her, pushing upward to face him. "Take me on to Wales. My husband will pay you handsomely once we reach Flintshire—as much as any dey would pay." The lie grated on her ears. Rhys Winghurst, if he would even acknowledge her as his wife, would most likely laugh in her face rather than pay for her release.

"If he thinks so highly of ya, woman, what are ya doing on my ship all alone?"

Her brain scrambled for an answer. "Unfortunately we were separated by unforeseen circumstances." That wasn't a lie. *Think, Calypso, you've read enough to come up with a heart-wrenching story.* "He was told I perished in a terrible fire. Instead I lost my memory and stayed with a farm family deep in the woods." Samuel Richardson couldn't have done better. Clamping her fingers about his arm, she gazed up at him, a pitiful look emanating from her eyes. "I'm on my way home to find him. We love each other so much." The last outrageous statement nearly made her gag.

"Flintshire, ya say. Your husband's an . . ."

". . . earl," she supplied. "Rhys Winghurst, Earl of Flintshire." Holy heavens, the man appeared to be accepting her story.

His eyes narrowed.

She flinched. What had she said wrong?

"Rhys Winghurst, ya say. I knew a sea captain by that

name, but he weren't no earl. What kind of story are ya tellin' me?"

" 'Tis not a story." This was her only hope; she wouldn't give up, but would worry about the consequences once they reached Wales. "Rhys has his own vessel; in fact he ships salt from my father's works in the Bahamas to the United States."

He lifted one brow. She had struck a chord in his memory. "Aye, the Rhys Winghurst I know runs salt occasionally. He's still no high-and-mighty earl."

"He is. I promise you. Rhys never spoke about it much during the Revolution." She gripped his arm tighter. "You must believe me."

He removed her grasping fingers from his sleeve and rubbed his arm. "Let me think about what you've said."

Before she could continue with her charade, he slipped out the door, locking it behind him. Her fate rested in his fertile mind. He had to believe her. He just had to.

Rhys ran an appreciative hand over the rump of the high spirited horse as the dwarf supervised the stable boy leading the stallion into its stall. "Are you sure, Luther? I won't be back, you know."

Luther signaled to his underling, and the boy hefted a large crate and placed it beside the tethered animal.

"I'm sure, Rhys." He grinned as he stepped up on the box, a currycomb in one hand that he applied to the barrel of the horse with an expertise few men possessed. "I imagine 'my lord' is inappropriate these days. Didn't ever think a man would want to be a commoner." The instrument stilled in his hand for a quick moment, then he continued his task. "This is my place—my loyalty is to my lord," the dwarf said solemnly.

A twinge of jealousy pierced Rhys's heart. "I understand." And he did, but he wished his lifelong companion felt the compulsion to stay with him. He would miss the little man, in spite of their differences of opinion.

"Don't take that wrong, Rhys." Luther shot him a look from the corner of his eye. "I said loyalty, not friendship." He continued working his magic along the side of the horse up over its withers. " 'Twas never right our relationship—stable boy and master being more like brothers. 'Tis better this way. Lord William will never take my gruff. He'll keep me in my place."

"Ah, damn, Luther, I'll miss your interference."

The dwarf turned on his raised platform, placing his knuckles on his hips. "Then you forgive me for all the times I overstepped my bounds?"

"Forgive you?" Rhys gripped him with affection, which the dwarf's short arms returned. "Hell, man. I'll not know how to make a decision. You won't be there to tell me I'm wrong when I am. How else will I know when I make the right choice?"

"You'll muddle through, you pigheaded bastard." Luther turned, but not before Rhys caught a glimpse of the tears in his eyes. He returned to his task of brushing the horse. "So you're going back to the wench."

"I am, if she'll have me. I know you don't approve, but for the life of me, I can't understand why she rankles you so. None of the other women in my life bothered you."

The scrape, scrape, scrape of the metal comb was the only sound audible. Then Luther began. "Your mother, Rhys. God help me, but the chit is just like your mother. And you, my friend, are exactly like your father—uncompromising. Lady Anne made the earl's life a living hell—uncontrollable hellion that she was." He turned and dropped the grooming tool into the stable boy's outstretched hand. "Calypso Collingsworth will do the same

284

by you. Give her five years, and you'll be as bitter as your sire."

"You're wrong, Luther." He didn't bother to explain. There was a certain magic between Calypso and himself, something he had never experienced with any other woman. As much as he hated to admit it, he liked her resistance, her independence, her need to prove how capable of taking care of herself she was. "But only time will tell," he conceded.

"Ah, hell, Rhys, perhaps it's fate. For generations the Winghurst men have dared to be different, to wend their own way, to marry their mule-headed women. Perhaps that's what kept the line strong and vital, the breeders they chose." Luther shrugged his shoulders. "You make your own mistakes. I won't be around to witness them."

"Take care, Luther," Rhys offered as he placed his hand on the smaller man's shoulder.

Not looking back, the dwarf reached around and squeezed Rhys's fingers. "Same to ya." Then he jumped down from the crate and signaled to the boy to take it around to the other side of the horse.

Without further word, Rhys spun about and left the stables, his hands clutched behind his back. Luther was wrong. He and Calypso would make a good life together. He would allow it to be no other way.

"What proof have ya that what ya say is true?" Captain Langley crimped his brows and waited for Calypso to answer. For the last few hours she had waited in her cabin, waited for this unscrupulous man to make a decision, waited until he had had her brought up top.

She swallowed, her mind racing. What evidence had she? Nothing that proved she was Rhys Winghurst's wife. Bravely, she replied. "What choice do you have except to believe me?"

"I have plenty of options. I could take ya on to Algiers and sell ya to a whoremaster, or drown ya here and now." He took a step toward her, and she recoiled, her chin lifted, her pride, though wrapped in fear, intact.

"You're a feisty little thing. Just the kind of woman the Rhys Winghurst I know would find irresistible. Maybe I should take your word. How would ya figure I'd be acquainted with the man before ya spoke his name?"

"He'll pay you well," she reinforced the blatant lie.

"No money required." His mouth lifted in an unpleasant smile that made her almost regret her words. "If in truth Rhys Winghurst is waiting in Wales, my efforts will be payment of an old debt standin' between us. If not"—he edged toward her, his hand rising in a threat—"you'll pay dearly and not only in money."

"You'll take me to Wales?" She held her ground, hope sprouting like a seedling in her heart.

"Can't do that, but I'll take ya to Liverpool which is less than a day's ride away over land."

Then the expectation burst like a fragile bubble pricked by a pin. "You intend to go with me all the way to Flintshire?"

His eyes narrowed. "Do you have an objection?"

She had plenty, but didn't dare voice them. What would Rhys think when she appeared with this horrible man in tow? He would definitely turn his back on her.

"Very well. Then to Liverpool it shall be," she agreed. Her mind whirled in search of a plan. Somehow, some way she would lose Captain Langley when they reached port.

With the last of the luggage tossed in the carriage

286

boot, Rhys turned to absorb his surroundings one last time. Winghurst Castle. The looming monster, once a living part of his existence, now was of no more importance than a pared fingernail. He would miss the echoing halls, no doubt, but life would go on as usual without it.

"Ready, Papa," Tristan voiced as he swung up into the passenger compartment with the agility of a young monkey to wait for Rhys to join him.

"I'm coming, Son," he answered; yet some unfounded reason compelled him to linger, almost as if an important occurrence was about to happen. He pivoted, taking in the western horizon where the setting sun would soon dip into the mouth of the Dee River only a few leagues away. If they didn't hurry, they would miss the evening tide and would have to wait until the morning before setting sail. Yet knowing that, he angled to face the north where the craggy Welsh mountains eventually melted into the rolling English moors as if he expected something important — but what it could be he couldn't fathom.

Rhys shook himself emotionally and physically, chiding himself for his wild imagination. West was the way to watch, not north. Calypso waited for them across the watery expanse of ocean. What an idiot he had been to leave her. What a bigger fool not to hurry and make the rising tide. Yet his feet dragged in the dust of the drive as if trying to hold him back.

Grabbing the door, he leaped into the vehicle and tapped on the roof to signal to the driver to proceed. There was nothing in Flintshire for him or Tristan anymore — not one sane reason to stay another moment.

With a lurch the carriage began to roll forward under the arch of the trees lining the drive. Yet, as they moved down the frontage road, he found himself moving to the other side of the carriage in order to again scrutinize the northern horizon bordering England. Why this compulsion to hold his breath deep in his lungs in expectation?

"Papa, are you sorry we're leavin'?"

He swung about to face his son sitting on the opposite seat. "Of course not, Tristan. We're going home to your mama. What possible reason would there be to stay here?"

Sliding off his cushion, the boy joined his father, and they sat arm in arm as the coach swayed with the rhythm of the horses, taking them to the coastline and to *The Oceanid* waiting at anchor at the Flintshire wharfs.

The smell of the Liverpool docks was one Calypso would never forget. How could so much refuse collect in one spot? The odor was so obnoxious it made *The Pilgrim* seem the essence of cleanliness, and made her appreciate the confines of the cabin that had housed her over the weeks.

Sliding her eyes sideways, taking in the man who held her by the arm, she contemplated her chances of ridding herself of Captain Langley's presence. He clung to her arm like a snapping turtle, and, short of chopping off his fingers, she doubted he would release his claim.

"Captain," she complained, seeking any excuse she could conjure up to slow down his maddening pace. "I fear I've not regained my land legs. Going this fast will surely make me swoon." Her free hand swept up and touched her forehead in a dramatic display she hoped he would believe.

"You're about as likely to faint as a pit viper, Countess. May I suggest you hurry along? I don't want the harbor master questioning us too closely. Could be he'll delay us." He glanced down and gave her arm a jerk. "We wouldn't want that now, would we? Can't keep the lonesome earl waiting too long."

"Why would the harbor master show interest in us?"

"Don't ask questions. Just walk. There's a stable close by where *you* can hire a carriage."

Without a doubt Langley had no intention of spending his money. She prayed she had enough left of her dwindling funds to complete the transaction. But first she had to get rid of the troublesome captain.

So Langley wanted to slip by the authorities unnoticed, did he? More than likely his action had something to do with the newspaper articles she had read that day when Jeremy Stickback had approached her. Americans were not welcome in English ports. Her lips curled in a delicious smile. But wouldn't the Countess of Flintshire be welcomed by her fellow countrymen, even if Langley was detained? Of course she would.

Taking a peek at her escort, she felt a twinge of guilt for what she planned to do. Then she remembered. Why should she feel badly? Langley had been more than willing to sell her to some fat old toad without any compunction over his action. There was no reason for her to show concern over his fate. Let the port authorities do what they would.

She turned, pressing a hand to the crown of the seagreen, muslin and lace hat she wore to keep the breeze from whipping it from her head. Then she studied the docks and the people milling about. The tall man with the large black book had to be the harbor master. Again that mischievous smile of determination bowed her lips. As soon as the moment was right . . .

Langley began to steer her away from her target. She couldn't allow him to do that. Easing her foot from her slipper, she stumbled and collapsed to her knees with a loud shriek.

"Damn you, wench, what are you doing? Not now," Langley croaked, pulling on her arm until she thought she couldn't ignore the pain a second more.

The wharf official looked up from his conversation, his face scrunching into a frown as the crowd gathered about her. She continued to resist the captain's efforts to lift her up, praying the tall man would investigate. Would he never stop talking? She couldn't last much longer with Langley twisting her arm so.

At last the official sidestepped the crowd and crossed over the pier in her direction. When he was close enough to hear her words, she allowed Langley to pull her up. Then she turned sly eyes on the captain.

"I don't understand, sir. Since we left Philadelphia, I've not been myself."

"Shut up, wench. You're drawing attention. We don't want the authorities to know we're American," he hissed in her ear.

"Not let them know you're an American? Whatever for?"

Langley's mouth dropped open. "What the hell are you doing, you bitch?" he demanded under his breath as he grabbed her arm, pinching the tender inner skin.

Ignoring him, she turned and pointed a finger at *The Pilgrim*. "What does it matter what I say? The mast head flag will identify your nationality." She gasped in mock surprise as she took in the Dutch banner whipping in the breeze. "Captain Langley," she inquired, looking at him with eyes wide, "what happened to the American flag you were flying earlier?"

"American, you say, miss?" interceded the harbor master as he reached out and hooked Langley by an arm.

"Not miss," she offered, supplying the man with a flashing smile. "Calypso Winghurst, the Countess of

Flint."

The official instantly dipped her a bow. "Your Ladyship," he said in a deferential voice.

"Tell me, sir. Have I said something wrong?" She looked at Langley, tilting her head in a most innocent way.

The captain glared. Without a doubt he knew what she was about, but there was nothing he could do to stop her.

The harbor master pushed Langley into the hands of several of his men who stood about gawking. "Absolutely not, my lady," he answered her question, taking her gently by the elbow. At the nod of his head, his men began to converge on *The Pilgrim*. "But it is most important you tell me all you know and tell me accurately."

"Of course, sir." She slid her gaze to Langley. What had his false docking report said? Most likely, since he was flying a Dutch flag, he would have stated he had come from the Netherlands, not the American shores. She prayed her reasoning was sound. "I was stranded in Philadelphia, and Captain Langley, for a hefty sum, agreed to take me home. He assured me Liverpool was the closest port. 'Tis only a day's travel overland to Flintshire, you know." She smiled up, beaming with innocence.

"Unscrupulous cad, taking advantage of a fine lady like yourself." The official patted her hand consolingly.

Langley snarled and attempted to pull away from his captors.

"Have you arranged for transportation?" the wharf master asked, ignoring the scuffle.

"Not yet. The captain was escorting me to a hostler to hire a vehicle." The thought of continuing in this strange city alone did not appeal to her, and she hoped the harbor master would supply her with a guide.

291

With a flick of the official's wrist, his men began to drag Langley toward a small building set off to one side. Then he indicated with his other hand that she should follow him away from the docks. "I'll take you myself, my lady."

Langley began to fight in earnest, and that twinge of guilt she had hidden deep inside began rebounding in her heart. "Tell me, sir," she asked the harbor master as she watched the captain forced into the building and his ship overrun with officials. "What will happen to Captain Langley and his crew?"

"Not for you to worry. We'll check out your story, and if in truth they're Americans as you say, they'll be impressed and the ship impounded."

"Impressed?"

"They'll serve in His Majesty's Navy for a few years." "Then they'll remain sailors and not be thrown in jail."

She took a deep sigh of relief as she had not wanted Langley punished too severely. He had delivered her to England safe and sound, even though that hadn't been his original intention.

Within minutes they reached the public stables, and the harbor master proceeded to arrange a carriage and driver for her.

She glanced about as the team of sleek horses were harnessed and the vehicle prepared for her. *Interesting,* she thought. *It's nice being treated as a special person. Maybe being a countess isn't so bad. I could grow used to this station in no time.*

The coachman stepped toward her. "If you're ready, my lady, we can depart."

She lifted her chin, trying to appear as haughty as possible. Wasn't that how the peerage acted? Perhaps she would enjoy her time in the British Isles. She stepped into the carriage, and with a jerk it began to roll forward. And maybe once she joined Rhys at Winghurst Castle . . .

What was she thinking? Dropping back against the seat, she closed her eyes. She had no intention of joining Rhys Winghurst anywhere but was here only to confront him with the truth and take Tristan back.

Subtle images of his smile, his eyes, his fingers caressing the curve of her hip, his hands, so powerful yet gentle, touching, exploring, igniting her senses fingered their way into her thoughts. The very image of them sent a chill tumbling down her spine.

She shook her head to eradicate the disturbing feelings attempting to befuddle her clear-cut goal. He had deserted her, taken away her child. How could she think of him with such tenderness?

But what if once she found Rhys and Tristan, the boy didn't want to leave? Could she depart without him? Never. But would she be willing to stay with Rhys?

She forced her eyes open and pressed the heels of her hands against her temples. Rejection of the righteous indignation stemming from her treatment at his hands seeped in, diluting her determination to make him suffer as she had. She would be more than willing; eager would better describe her true feelings.

How could she be so weak? Is that what love did, turn one into a spineless creature?

Sitting up straight, she gripped the fabric of the seat. Love? Since when had those feelings entered the picture? She didn't love Rhys Winghurst. Or did she?

Whom was she trying to deceive? Like snapping jaws of a hound, that ethereal emotion had a clutch on her heart that she could never shake loose, no matter how hard she denied its existence.

Wearily she slumped back down on the upholstery in

uncharacteristic acceptance. What now? Did she crawl to Rhys and ask forgiveness? Her face lifted slightly. Forgiveness for what? For not knowing the truth, for not understanding what he wanted?

Her chin notched higher. Never. She loved him, she had admitted that, but never would she accept his superiority—his arrogance. There had to be a reference point where they could come together on mutual grounds. She would find Rhys, confront him, and pray he was willing to meet her halfway. Otherwise, they would find themselves exactly where they had started, on opposite sides, each determined to come out the winner in a war where no quarter was shown between combatants.

Chapter Twenty

"We'll have to wait till morning to cast off, Captain."

Rhys eyed the young sailor, then gave a curt nod of acceptance. Damn it, he had known this would happen. Why had he lingered so long at Winghurst Castle? If they had left even an hour earlier, they would have been out to sea now, returning home to Calypso.

Whirling about, he approached the brass railing of *The Oceanid* to study the surf and confirm the sailor's report. No doubt about it, they had missed the evening tide.

"Very well, Ferguson. All hands remain aboard this evening. We're setting sail the moment the morning tide is right."

"Aye, sir," the sailor answered. "If all calculations are accurate, that should be two hours before sunrise."

"So be it, sailor. See that the men retire early. This will be our last good night's sleep for a while. And Ferguson." He turned and gave the man a glare that couldn't be ignored. "No women aboard. Understood? Not for any reason. I want the crew sharp in the morning."

"Aye, sir," Ferguson repeated, turning to carry out his captain's orders.

"Papa?" Tristan ran up, his eyes questioning as he

pulled on the sleeve of Rhys's dark blue frock coat. "Why aren't we leaving?"

"The tide, Son. We'll have to wait till morning."

Disappointment shone in the boy's gaze. "Another day. 'Tisn't fair." His bottom lip poked out in defiance.

"Don't worry, Tristan. A few hours won't make any difference. Your mama will be there in Philadelphia waiting for us. I can assure you."

Winghurst Manor. The big house stood solemn and dark, almost as if it held its breath — waiting — anticipating her approach and its ultimate rejection of her. Calypso glanced up at the moon, a misty circle surrounding the silvery globe with ominous reality. The morning light would be here soon, three or four hours at the most. What would Rhys think when she appeared at his front door in the middle of the night? Would he be surprised and glad, or, more than likely, angry at her inconsiderate intrusion back into his life.

She should have spent the night in the local inn as the driver had suggested. But she wouldn't have slept and couldn't have waited that long. Tristan was here, somewhere in that gloomy, old mansion, and she would hold him in her arms before the sun rose. That she promised herself.

As the coachman opened the carriage door, she stepped out and took a long, deep breath. Digging into her reticule, she paid the driver with the last of her funds. She would not be refused entrance, she decided with a determined lift of her chin. She would pound against the ancient oak door until Rhys knew she was there, and she wouldn't give up until he let her in to have her say.

And Tristan. She paused one brief second before announcing her arrival. Did he know she was his mother? Had Rhys told the boy, or had he covered up the truth with his own lies? What would she say to the child so that he would suffer no shock from the news? *Caution,* she told herself. *Don't do anything that might upset Tristan.*

She lifted the heavy knocker, the emblem of a fleur-de-lis impressed on the head, and banged it against the door several times; then crossing her arms, she prepared to wait. But only for so long.

Standing there as the hired coach departed down the drive, she cut her eyes across the grounds and took in the extensive stables, the dairies, and the acres of dormant yet landscaped gardens highlighted in the bright moonlight. Rhys Winghurst was wealthy beyond what she had ever imagined. Why did he align himself with Americans when he had so much? And why had he wed her, an outcast baron's daughter with a holding small in comparison to the Winghurst lands? He could have married so much better than she.

Her hand lifted again, the staccato of the knocker ringing in her ears as she used it. Finally, the door opened, revealing a chamberstick illuminating a long, lean face that eyed her with curiosity.

"I'm sorry, madam," the butler stated. "Whatever it is could have surely waited until morning."

"If it could have waited, I wouldn't be here now. Please inform the earl his wife has arrived and demands his presence." She smiled, her lips barely curving. Demands. Isn't that what Rhys would say? Serves him right.

"His wife?" The butler stepped back, allowing her entrance. "But His Lordship never informed me . . ."

"I'm sure he didn't. But nonetheless I'm here. And I don't wish to be kept waiting."

297

"My lady." The man thrust the door open, and she stepped in.

How easily he accepted her story. Was Rhys so unpredictable that even his servants found him hard to fathom? It was almost as if the butler hardly knew his master.

She followed him into a large sitting room, taking in the opulent richness of the furnishings: the velvet curtains, the silver-threaded damask of the overstuffed couches, the handwoven wool of the Oriental carpets, the expensive silver and china accenting it all. How dowdy and dirty she felt in comparison. Her hand pushed at the wrinkles of her gown. Would Rhys notice how out of place she appeared?

From far away a voice boomed. "What do you mean, you fool, my wife?" The deep resonance rattled her, yet Rhys didn't sound like himself. How quickly she had forgotten his manner of speech.

"I'm sorry, Your Lordship, but the woman insisted," the servant whined.

The door to the sitting room crashed open, and in the few seconds before she turned to confront the anger she knew would be contorting Rhys's face, she took a deep, cleansing breath to calm her nerves.

"Rhys, I shan't forgive you," she announced, standing and spinning in one motion, determined to hold her ground.

She took a step back. The man standing before her had a familiar look—a relative to her husband no doubt—but he was not Rhys.

"Madam," he said with a nod of his sleep-tousled head, "when my cousin conceded the earldom to me, he forgot to tell me a wife came with the title as well."

"Conceded the earldom? Sir, what do you mean?" Something solid and painful thumped against the pit of

298

her stomach. Rhys wasn't here, she knew without asking. "Tell me, please, where is Rhys Winghurst?"

"Can't say where he was going, but I know he's not coming back. Though I can't comprehend his desire to leave all this behind." His hand swept the air in a vague motion. "But who am I to question his sanity? I've profited immensely from what I consider an irrational decision on his part."

"And Tristan, my son?" She swallowed hard, afraid to hear the answer.

"Took the boy with him, of course."

"Of course." Her heart sank like a weighted sack of kittens tossed into the depths of the ocean. How would she find them? But worse, what was she to do? In her haste to confront Rhys, she had dismissed her carriage and used the last of her money. Her desire to press on in her pursuit took wing, leaving her empty and defeated.

"I'll have your coachman informed to prepare to depart."

Her head flew up. This man was not going to even offer her shelter for the rest of the night. Cad. Conceited scoundrel. A Winghurst through and through. Her jaws tightened in anger. "No need, sir. I won't be going anywhere. I've already dismissed the carriage, and it's on its way back to Liverpool."

"You presume too much, madam."

"I assumed my husband would be here." An intense glare rebounded between them.

"Then if it's transportation you need, I'll see that one of the Winghurst carriages is provided to return you from whence you came." He rose, mumbling, and signaled to the butler to carry out his orders. "Two in one day. If this keeps up, I won't have a single horse left in the mews for my pleasure." He looked back at her, his lips thinning. "You can remain here until the team is harnessed."

Pride brought her to her feet. "I'll wait in the stables." She sailed past him toward the front door, confronting him at the entryway. "I will use your carriage, sir, only because I have no choice and because you owe Rhys that much."

Marching down the front drive, the panic she had been fighting took hold, clutching her about the throat as if it were alive and growing. Back to whence she had come. What good would it do her to return to Liverpool? Perhaps the harbor master would help. Not likely. But what choice did she have?

The odors of the barnyard humus reached out like fingers as she neared. Up ahead she could see the lantern the butler held as he conveyed the earl's orders to the stablehands. A figure turned, small and stout, and a voice she would recognize even in the dead of night shouted for the bays to be harnessed.

Luther. Dear God. Didn't she have enough problems? She didn't need to confront the horrid little man as well. The urge to race back to the mansion and offer the odious earl anything he wanted if he would only help her grew to enormous dimensions within her mind.

"Miss Collingsworth."

The calling of her maiden name brought her head around. Luther stood in the stable doorway, his eyes as dangerous as she recalled.

"Mistress Winghurst, if you remember. Your precious captain married me." She had almost said Countess, but if what she had heard was true, the title no longer applied to her. She pressed her lips tightly together. Nobility gained and lost at the flick of an eyelid.

"I remember only too well. The serpent in the garden of Eden."

Calypso sucked in a loud, rasping breath. The man's

uncalled-for hatred could not be denied. "Tell me, Luther," she demanded, "if all is so perfect without me around, why aren't you with Rhys now?" Surprised at her own boldness considering how frightened of the dwarf she was, she waited for an answer.

His glare penetrated to her very soul, stripping her of what little bravery she still possessed. Then he wheeled about, ignoring her, to check the leather on the team.

At that moment she realized Luther knew where Rhys had gone. Knew but did not plan to tell her. Somehow she must make him speak.

"Luther," she began, willing to plead, beg, or grovel in order to get the information she so desperately needed. "I don't understand why you despise me so, but, please, can't you see I must find Rhys—and Tristan?" she added.

"Must you?" He still refused to look at her. "Then find them. No one will stop you."

"But no one will help, either." She spoke softly, undemandingly.

He continued to shun her. "There, tighten that breast strap." The sleepy-eyed stableboy jumped to do his bidding.

She stared at his back, rigid and uncompromising, and prayed he would discover he had a heart after all, even if it was small and unused. She sank down on a bale of hay. "Luther, please tell me where Rhys has gone."

The muscles of his neck tightened in reaction to her request. Would he answer? She waited, breath held, for what seemed an eternity.

He turned so unexpectedly, with such intensity, she scooted back on the hay bale until she was pressed against the rough, wooden wall of the building.

"Why is it," he asked as if he were speaking to the heavens and not her, "that history repeats itself over and

301

over, generation to generation, father to son? It's as if the need to be destroyed is inherited with that damn, blasted birthmark."

She blinked up at him, confused and frightened, yet curiosity urged her to question him further. "What do you mean, Luther? Who wishes to harm Rhys?"

"You and every woman the Winghurst men align themselves with."

"I want nothing from Rhys except my son. Be damned with what happens to him." She would not stand there and allow Luther to misjudge her so.

"Just as I thought. You're no different. Take that boy from him, and you'll destroy him as surely as if you placed a bullet in his brain. You don't love him, just what he has."

"Oh, but I do." The confession popped out of her mouth before she could stop it. Her hand flew up to try to squash the words back down her throat. Admitting to herself she cared for Rhys was one thing, telling others was something else all together.

"How easily you say that, woman. What do you know of love? Neither you nor Rhys for a fact know the first thing about caring or committing to others." His lip curled in disgust. "Lust, perhaps. I seen that element between you, but little else. Lust eventually destroys those possessed by it."

"No, you're wrong—at least about me." She pushed up on her knees, bringing her eye level to the little man. Thinking back on the storminess of their relationship, perhaps Luther was right about Rhys. Had lust been his only motivation? Had that heartless passion driven him away?

Luther barked a derisive laugh. "I should let you go your merry way, and maybe God, in all his wisdom, would keep you from Rhys, but somehow I doubt that.

302

You think he cares so little for you?" He pressed one stubby finger into her shoulder. "He gave this all up." Swinging his arms about, he indicated an elusive vastness. "Damn it, wench, he gave it up for you. He's headed back to Philadelphia now to ask for your forgiveness. Ask, mind you, I said. Damn it, Rhys Winghurst never asked anybody for anything before he met you."

Completely taken aback, she returned to her nest in the hay. An elation so wonderful and dizzy whirled in the vestibule of her mind until she thought she would die from joy. Rhys cared. He was willing to sacrifice for her. Her eyes misted with wonderment as she stared up at Luther. "Oh, Luther, is what you tell me true?"

The little man settled on the hay bale beside her. She could sense the battle raging within him. "It's true, but what good will it do you? He's already gone."

"Is there no time to catch him?" Unexplained hope unfolded with each breath she took.

"Not if he left with the evening tide."

Her shoulders sagged. She was sure that flash of compassion she had witnessed in Luther's eyes was fading.

"But he was rushing at the end, concerned he might not make it."

She glanced up, joy leaping into her throat. Was he offering his help to her? "How far away is the harbor?"

"An hour, perhaps two. If you hurry, maybe . . ."

Jumping to her feet, she raced to the carriage standing in the drive. Luther followed as fast as he could.

Without waiting she flung open the door, and, gathering up her skirts, she scrambled aboard. Luther caught the door and slammed it, then stepped back so they could see each other.

"Good luck, Countess. May God speed you."

She nodded, smiling, recognizing his attempt to show

303

his acceptance by calling her Countess. "Thank you, Luther. Whatever your reasons for your change of heart — I'm grateful."

"Fate, my lady." He sighed, the sound of resignation. "You and Rhys are inevitable. Don't disappoint me." He tore his eyes from hers, turning his attention to the driver. "Begone, coachman," he shouted up to him. "To the Dee River harbor. Make that team give you all it has. 'Tis a matter of life and death."

The whip cracked; the carriage lurched. Calypso watched the dust swirl about the dwarf's small body until she could no longer see him. Would she reach the docks in time? God pray she would.

The stillness of the predawn hour, though cold and misty as now, would always be his favorite. Rhys continued his final round, checking lines and chains, looking for frays or weak links that might cause future problems on the long voyage before them. The lantern in his left hand created a circle of light, making him feel alone, though the shouts and replies of his crew seeped into his fantasy of solitude with regularity.

Running his hand down the bobstay, checking for tautness, the jingle of harness and the creak of a fast-moving carriage brought to a halt invaded the familiarity of nautical sounds. He ignored the commotion until he heard one of the deck hands arguing with someone.

"I'm sorry, but you can't come aboard."

Swinging the lantern high, he growled in pessimistic disgust. Now what? Couldn't his cousin William figure out where the chamber pot was kept? All he needed was another damned delay.

"But you don't understand, I must see my husband." The shrill feminine voice pierced the darkness.

"I'm sorry, ma'am, but Captain said no women aboard."

"Dockside doxies," Rhys mumbled under his breath. "Don't they ever give up?" Which poor bastard in his crew had up and married some whore while on a drunk.

Rounding the staysail boom, he worked his way to starboard with the intention of ending the argument on the gangplank, which was growing higher pitched by the second. A few coins and most likely the "bride" would accept a divorce then and there.

The red hair spilling down over the woman's shoulder was uncomfortably familiar. Impossible! Why did every female he saw remind him of Calypso in one way or another?

"Enough, mister," he growled, moving forward to step between the persistent female and his crewman to grip one fragile wrist between his strong fingers. All he needed now was a defiant whore unwilling to listen to reason.

The woman's head whipped up, the red hair flying, slashing him across the face, a well-remembered fragrance sending his head spinning. In the lantern light, her green eyes flashed with a fire he recognized only too well.

"Calypso?" he blurted, still unable to believe that what he saw was not an optical illusion.

The angry retort she had been about to issue turned into an incoherent babble as she fell limply against his chest. "I found you! You didn't go!" Tears washed away the rest of what she said.

Her wrist still clasped between his fingers pressed against his shirt front, the pulse against his thumb fluttering like a moth caught in a spiderweb. "Good heavens, Calypso," he asked incredulously, "what the hell are you doing here?" He reached out his arm to reel her closer, but her elbows stiffened.

Her weeper's hiccups stilled as she threw back her head. Indecision swam in those warm jade pools inches from his mouth. He wanted to kiss the eyelids closed, to eradicate the uncertainty that seemed to hold her in its grasp. But something in the way she looked at him stilled the impulse.

"I should have known Luther was lying," she said so softly he wasn't sure he heard her correctly.

His arm flexed and moved back down to his side. "What are you doing here?" he repeated, surprised at how sharp the question sounded to his own ears.

She must have heard the acrimony too, for her gaze crystalized into harsh, unforgiving stone. "Tristan," she declared. "I've come for my son."

His grip about her wrist tightened. By the way she tensed he knew he was hurting her, but he didn't let up the pressure, the release valve through which he vented his frustration. "Your *son,* madam? It seems the last time we discussed Tristan he was only your brother."

They parted with the force of a whirlwind ripping through tall grass. Her breast rose and fell, the power of her anger visually pumping the blood through the vein standing out on her neck. "You insensitive cad. What do you know of my past and what I suffered?"

"I know you bore me a son and refused to acknowledge the fact." His mouth clamped tight as he glanced about, taking in the curious faces of his crew that stood just outside the glow of the lantern at their feet. He bent, retrieved the light, and reclaimed her wrist with a speed she had no time to resist.

"Where are you taking me?" she asked, her legs stiffening as he pulled her along behind him.

"Captain, tide's right to lift anchor."

"Captain, Kraemer fell from the mainmast. I think his

306

leg is broken, sir."

Bombarded from all sides with responsibility, he thrust Calypso's arm into one of his men's hands. "See she's settled below." He eyed her one brief moment. "We'll discuss this later, Calypso."

"Discuss?" she quipped. "Most likely you'll bark your demands at me."

He ignored her barb, wheeling about to command his waiting crew. The squeal of rising sail raked his eardrums as he crossed the deck to where the injured sailor sat propped against a lifeboat. Why he was hurrying now to set sail, he had no idea. The reason to rush back to Philadelphia was pacing his cabin right now, probably plotting his demise. Maybe Luther had been right. Calypso would be his downfall, but was he not powerless to stop her?

He grunted under his breath as he bent down to inspect Kraemer's unnaturally crooked leg. The mighty Captain Winghurst, ex-Earl of Flint, bested by a woman half his size. But with a strength of mind to match his own, he reminded himself.

Gripping Kraemer's shoulder, he stood. "Not to worry, man, the break should mend properly. It's clean." He signaled to his men. "Take him below to the medic."

"Wish Luther was here," Kraemer managed to say as they lifted him.

"Aye, man, I agree. We both could use a little of his ministrations, couldn't we?" Rhys's mouth lifted in irony.

Kraemer grinned in spite of the pain. "To be honest, Captain, I'd not change places with ya. Before this voyage is over, most likely you'll suffer more than me."

Rhys's jaw tightened. "You're probably right. One woman is a bigger pain in the butt than an entire body of broken bones."

"You should've listened to your own orders, Captain.

307

No women aboard, remember?"

"I remember." He stepped back as Kraemer was carried down the companionway stairs; then he cursed himself for a fool of the biggest kind.

Calypso paced, her hands moving from their perch on her hips to cross over her chest. What had gone wrong? What had happened between her and Rhys in those few moments of reunion? The seesaw of her emotions, the back and forth of their relationship, left her bewildered. Why had she so easily accepted Luther's word that Rhys wanted her? She covered her face with her hands. Because she so needed to believe he loved her, only if a little.

She dropped her arms, and her face angled upward. What a fool—a silly, little, simpering fool—she had become, no different than she had been all those years ago when she had idled away her time daydreaming of romance. Love was not what poets wrote of—flowers and sighs and fluttering hearts, though she had to admit her heart did race uncontrollably each time she saw Rhys—but was an all-consuming emotion that left one spineless and at the mercy of another human being.

Her head returned to the cradle of protection her hands offered. No, that wasn't necessarily true. She cared for Tristan with all her heart, and that love made her strong. The problem wasn't what she felt, but for whom she felt it. Rhys Winghurst was not an easy man to have a weakness for.

Tristan. Her shoulders straightened, and her chin snapped high. Where was her son? He must be somewhere aboard this ship. He was her first priority.

Gliding across the confines of the cabin, she tested the door to see if it would open. She wouldn't put it past

Rhys to lock her in. The oak slab eased wide with a squeal.

Working her way down the companionway, she headed toward the cabin Tristan and Nannette had occupied on the first trip to Philadelphia. She pushed the door ajar, a stream of yellow light from the lantern hanging in the narrow corridor spilling into the tiny room to highlight Tristan's sleeping face.

Her mouth lifted in wonderment. Her son. God, how beautiful he was. Tiptoeing, she crossed the short expanse of planking, desperately wanting to touch the boy, but fearing the contact would wake him.

She paused a foot away, staring down into his untroubled features, confirming his parentage in the curve of his mouth, the angle of his chin, the sweep of his brown hair exactly like his father's. Why had she been so blind not to see the similarities before now?

Tristan moved, one hand coming across his face to scratch his cheek as he wiggled his nose. Then his eyes, as rich as fine Dutch chocolate, opened and focused on her.

"Callie?" he rasped in a sleep-ladened voice. Joy blossomed like an unfolding rosebud in his gaze, and with the exuberance of a child he scrambled to his knees and wrapped his arms about her waist.

"Tristan," she whispered, feeling her throat convulse and sting with the unshed tears of relief. "Oh, Tristan, how I've missed you so."

"Mama?" The precious name rang with uncertainty.

Dropping to the edge of the bed in order to take him in the circle of her arms, she issued a noise somewhere between a laugh and a sob. "My son. My darling, precious boy."

Cheek to cheek, their tears intermingled, they held each other as if they feared letting go.

"You're not mad at us, are you, Mama?"

She dragged her fingers through his down-soft hair, pulling his face to her chest. "Oh, no. How could you think I could blame you?"

"And Papa? Have you seen him, too?"

Her spine stiffened. "Yes, I've seen your father." The finality of who she was and what she shared with Rhys at last washed away the last vestiges of shock. Tristan was not just hers, but was a part of both of them.

"And you forgave him also when he asked?"

How hopeful Tristan sounded. How simple he made the insurmountable problems seem. How would she answer the boy? Should she lie and say yes, or should she dash his optimism? "We haven't had a chance to talk," she compromised.

Planting his small fists against her heart, he pushed back to look up into her face. "But you will forgive him, won't you?"

"If he asks." That statement was the truth. If he asks, which she sincerely doubted would happen.

"I'm asking."

Calypso twisted to find Rhys leaning in the doorway, the lantern light giving an aura to his body so lean yet solid, a magnet of charisma pulling at her heart with a forcefulness too strong to deny. "An what do I have to forgive you for?" She needed him to voice his crimes against her.

Their gazes met over Tristan's head, locked, and no power within her could make her tear her eyes away.

"For not listening, for not believing in you, but most of all, for turning my back and leaving without explanation."

"Yes," she replied, "you did all of those things." Her eyes began to water, but she didn't dare break the moment of understanding between them. "But I was no bet-

ter," she admitted. "I've done much to reg⟶
She held her breath in anticipation. Would th⟶
last end here?

"Then kiss and make up," Tristan piped in. "Is⟶
what grown-ups always do?"

Simultaneously they glanced down at their son, his innocent demand alleviating the tension crisping the air.
"Is that what you think of us?" Rhys asked.

"Yah. Big people are always kissin'."

"What terrible influences have you exposed my child
to?" Calypso demanded, her eyes twinkling.

"Oh, all kinds of dockside lowlife," Rhys supplied.

"I can well imagine."

"Can you?" He took a step toward her, the look of
desire in his gaze undeniable.

Calypso still clutched Tristan to her heart. Instinctively
she released him, and the boy wiggled from the bed,
dressed only in a nightshirt.

"Go to the galley and find Cook, Son," Rhys instructed him, never once taking his eyes off Calypso.
"Tell him to feed you breakfast, then to take you up top
and have Ferguson teach you to tie sailor knots. Your
mama and I have some talking to do."

"Sure, Papa," Tristan squealed, squeezing past Rhys
and out the door before Calypso could grab him to see
that he was dressed properly. He turned and squatted
down to stare back into the room between his father's
wide-braced legs. "You're gonna be kissin', not talkin'. I
know," he taunted.

"You imp," Rhys growled, angling to catch the boy
before he got away, but Tristan sped down the companionway.

"Honestly, Rhys," she scolded, "you sent him out in
his nightclothes."

He shrugged his wide shoulders. "It doesn't matter if

nothing at all." His mouth lifted in that infa-
ous smile of his. "In fact, I rather like the idea of
wearing nothing at all." The door clicked softly as he
moved nearer, so close she had to drop her head back to
see his face.

A warmth like melting wax oozed through her body.
She rather liked the idea of being naked, too. Shifting
forward, she attempted to rise, but he pushed her back
down on the bed, his knee pressing between her parted
thighs.

"Tell me, sweeting, how in the hell did you ever manage to land on English soil?"

She eased back against the pillow, allowing him access
to her body. "Wasn't so difficult being the Countess of
Flint."

"Ah, yes, the title." He ran his hand up under her
skirts along the soft inner skin of her legs. "And so,
love, you like the idea of being nobility?"

Did he think she didn't know he had renounced his
claim to the earldom? "Well enough. There's a certain
headiness to power."

"Power," he announced, drawing a finger up the side
of her waist to the fasteners of her gown, "can be gotten
other ways, you know."

"I know," she agreed, pushing at the front of his shirt,
easing buttons from their holders. "There's always
money."

For one second he froze, his body stiffening. Then she
giggled and leaned forward, nipping at the hollow of his
throat.

"You witch," he growled, grabbing her wrists and
planting them over her head. "You know."

"Of course, silly. I met your cousin." She wrinkled her
nose. "He's as odious as any earl could be."

He pressed her down into the bed. "Are you saying

I'm odious?" He took a deep breath, the curling hairs of his chest brushing against the tenderness of her exposed nipples.

"Only when you were an earl." Again she giggled, and the quivering of her breasts rubbing against his chest sent sparks of desire skipping through her.

His head lowered, and he explored her ear with his tongue. "You don't mind I'm a commoner now?"

She returned the caress by running her fingers over his shoulders and across the muscles of his back. "Remember you were only an American sea captain the first time I surrendered to you. I think a man who depends on his own wit and strength much more exciting than some simpering aristocrat."

"I never simpered." He placed his lips over hers, demanding she give freely of her passion.

She groaned in acquiescence, offering up her mouth and her soul to his desire. The kiss gentled, his tongue dipping into her mouth, then out again, until she grew dizzy with want. Then his face lifted, his warm breath fanning over her closed eyes.

"Look at me, Calypso."

Her lashes lifted to find her lifelong dream coming true. Adoration shone in his rich brown eyes—unabashed, unafraid—complete. "I love you," he vowed; then his hand moved to the back of her head, dragging her forward until their lips met again. "And nothing will ever make me change my mind."

A well of joy burst forth from somewhere deep inside of her. "Oh, Rhys, I've loved you for so long I—"

The kiss took charge, and her words were lost in her need to be as close to him as possible. The world about her was forgotten: the ship, the crew, the endless sea. There existed only the firebrand of his lips, the stirring touch of his hands upon her breasts, her hips, the very center of her being.

Her discarded gown was pushed to one corner of the bed; his clothing was strewn across the footboard and on the floor. Unadorned by anything except their hunger for each other, he stretched out beside her, his head propped in one hand as he drew lazy circles upon her skin.

The whirlwind of sensations he created drove her half out of her mind. Her breasts peaked as he scaled them with his fingers, her belly quivered as he traced the gentle swell down, down to the cradle of femininity between her legs. And when she thought the fireworks of completion would explode within her being, he rose above her, replacing his hand with the evidence of his desire.

She looked up to find him watching her, setting his pace to her response until the gentle rocking of his hips became hard, demanding thrusts that she met with eager lifts of her own. The waves of pleasure rolled in like the morning tide, washing away the tension, the past regrets that had muddled their lives, leaving nothing but the clean, undisturbed sand of the future before her.

"I love you, Rhys," she cried at the crest. "Nothing in my world or yours will ever come between us again."

Chapter Twenty-one

The rhythmic sound echoed again. Click, tap, shuffle. Calypso woke with a start, sitting up in the bed, a shaft of early morning light dancing across the coverlet. Her arm lifted, swiping at her forehead, and returned coated with sweat to her side.

Dear God, what had she been dreaming about? She glanced down at the pillow beside her. Rhys was not there, but that was to be expected. Like most mornings, he would take a predawn stand at the wheel in order to watch the skies for signs of turbulent weather.

Pulling her knees forward, she sat in a cross-legged fashion and tried to remember what had frightened her so about the nightmare. She had been back on Long Island in her father's home, crouched at the foot of a sofa. No, she had been hiding in the library like the day so long ago when Evan had discovered her eavesdropping. But somehow it had all been different. She was older, a woman not a girl, and her concern wasn't for herself but for someone else. But who? She couldn't remember. Then another person had entered the room, and she had been so afraid, but the reason why escaped her. The strange pattern of noise that had awoken her returned with crystal clarity. Click. Tap. Shuffle. Those sounds meant something, but what? Damn it, she just didn't know.

Feeling uneasy and not the least bit sleepy, she rose and slipped out of her nightgown and into a simple, lavender woolen dress. The need to find Rhys was so strong she didn't fight the urge, as if she had to confirm for herself he was safe and alive. Had he been the one she had been worried about in her dream? She couldn't be certain.

Her feet bare, she climbed the companionway stairs. On deck, a strong gust of cold tugged at her hem, belling her skirts about her hips and legs and whipping coils of fiery curls about her throat and face.

In the distance she could see Rhys, his legs braced wide apart, standing at the helm of his ship. How handsome and virile he looked, his light blue shirt beneath his vest billowing in the wind, his dark blue breeches snug on his hips, his long brown hair ripped from the leather binding it behind his head to curl around his neck. She paused, drinking in the sight as butterflies batted her insides.

His face angled, and he caught sight of her. Lifting his arm, he signaled to her to join him at the wheel. She moved across the deck, her bare feet making no sound against the cold planking. She should have donned her shoes, but she didn't wish to return for them. One hand clinging to his chest, she slipped under his arm, pressing her other palm against his back. As radiant as the early morning sun, she smiled up at him, and his free hand curled about her shoulder, holding her close.

"Good morning, sweeting. Did you sleep well?" He kissed the top of her vibrant red tresses.

"I missed you this morning," she offered up shyly, blushing.

"Not nearly as much as I missed you. A warm woman is a hell of a lot nicer than a cold winter wind." He glanced down at her bare feet. "Where are your shoes?"

Her right toes crept up her left ankle. "I forgot them."

He shook his head. "You're worse than Tristan, wench. I guess I'll have to send you back down below to retrieve them."

She clung to him. "Not yet." That strange feeling of unrest the dream had planted in her mind returned. It *was* Rhys she was concerned about. Something about him being in the Bahamas. Looking up, she watched his jaw tighten and relax over and over as he concentrated on his task of sailing his ship.

Chewing on her bottom lip, she battled within herself. There were questions she wanted to ask him, questions about why he had appeared at her father's house posing as a suitor. Why the secrecy? Why the deceit? Why was the American government spying on her father? What harm could one man do to an entire country?

"Rhys?"

He looked down at her.

"Can I ask you something? And if you can't answer me truthfully, don't reply at all."

His brow furled upward in curiosity. "All right."

"Why did you come to Long Island all those months ago? You weren't there to court the baron's wayward daughter."

"Wasn't I? I married the wench, didn't I?" His evasion was obvious to her.

She stared at him, waiting.

Glancing away, he shifted his position and released her shoulder, placing his free hand beside the other on the helm. "No, I suppose not."

"Rhys, why were you there?" she persisted.

"I was there because of my work."

"For the American government?"

His gaze shot down to hers. "How do you know about

317

that?"

"Eliza told me."

"How in the hell did she know?"

"Mr. Jefferson told her."

"I see." His hands flexed against the wheel.

"You still haven't answered my question."

"Calypso, I'm deciding if I can."

She waited, breath held. What would he say?

"I was checking out a rumor that an attempt to overthrow the American government was being plotted there."

"And my father."

"Was thought to be the ringleader. But I don't think that's true," he added.

"What *do* you think?"

"My opinions aren't important. Thomas Jefferson got my report, and he sent another man to investigate further."

"Another man? Who?"

Rhys didn't answer, and she realized he wouldn't.

"What will happen if my father *is* involved?"

"Nothing as long as he remains at home. However, if he attempts to move to the States . . ." The ominous reality dangled in the air.

"And what of me and Tristan? What if it's thought I'm a part of these plans?"

"Are you?"

His question took her by surprise. Would he believe her answer whatever she said? Clearly she remembered that fateful morning, her ear pressed against the sofa, her cat's claws embedded in the flesh of her arm, her father's and brother's declaration to see the Americans fall. And worse, their vow to commit assassination if they must. Did Rhys know about all of those things? Had her father's emotional declaration only been the an-

318

gry words of a disillusioned colonist? John Collingsworth was many things, but not a murderer. "No, I know only that my family suffered at the hands of patriots, and we were forced from our home."

"I'm sorry, Calypso." His arm returned to embrace her.

"You had nothing to do with it."

"And your father. Is he capable of hatching a plot to overthrow a government?"

"No, Rhys. I don't believe he could."

He hugged her gently, reassuringly. "Then there's nothing for you to be concerned about."

Pressing her head against his chest, she thought about what he had told her. She hoped he was right, but there was something that still bothered her. What important fact had she forgotten? The answer was there, just out of reach, but no matter how hard she thought she couldn't remember.

"Tristan, whatever are you doing?" Calypso watched in amusement as her son tried to tie a wooden pole to his kneecap.

"I wanna be a pirate." He hopped about. "With a peg leg."

"Tristan, that's a terrible thing to want to do." She snatched the pole and tangle of twine away from him. "A man can't help it if he loses a limb. 'Tis not something to joke about."

He looked up, his big eyes welling with moisture. "I'm sorry, Callie," he sobbed, falling into the circle of her arms when she knelt down beside him.

Her heart lurched. He called her Callie. Whenever his emotions took over, it seemed he always reverted back to calling her by her name.

"It's all right, Son," she reassured him. "I know you didn't mean any harm." The mother's need to discipline softened. Gently she pressed the broken broom handle back into his smaller hand. "Here. Why don't you pretend to have a limp? That's not nearly so bad. Use the stick like a cane."

His face lifted and his eyes lit up. "Will that be all right?" His sober concern brought a smile to her lips. "I won't make fun of anyone.

"I know you won't." She patted him on the back and gave him a shove toward the sun-drenched spot on the deck where he had been playing. Rising, she sighed as he closed his eyes and began tapping about with the stick as if he were blind. Children. Why this fascination with physical afflictions?

She turned to stare out at the sea, her hands sliding up and down the brass rail as she watched the gray winter water skirt around the ship.

Nightmarish images cast a shadow across her mind. The dream, as she had begun labeling it, refused to give her peace. For the last three nights she had experienced the horror, over and over, until she thought she would scream. But still the message, the warning it was trying to convey slipped past her.

Perhaps she should tell Rhys. No, he had told her she had nothing to worry about. He would probably find her fretting silly and unimportant.

Dropping her arms to her sides, she hugged them close to her body as she tried to fathom the nagging mystery.

Click. Tap. Shuffle. The sound came from behind her, stirring the acid in her stomach. Sweat trickled between her shoulder blades as she jumped and spun to face whatever was behind her. The dream.

Tristan moved across the deck, using the cane and

dragging one leg. Click, tap, shuffle. A lump so hard she couldn't swallow collected in her throat.

Click. Tap. Shuffle.

A noise somewhere between a gasp and a groan squeezed past the lump. Of course. Of course. The answer seemed so simple. Why hadn't she figured it out before now?

Her father had been visited by a man she had never seen, only heard, his raspy voice, his strangely gaited walk. Click, tap, shuffle. Seeing Tristan imitate a lame man brought the facts hidden in the deepest recesses of her mind rushing forward.

Only one man she knew walked that way and spoke in a voice she had found familiar the first time she had met him, but hadn't known why. She glanced about the ship looking for Rhys, but he was nowhere to be seen.

What would he say when she told him his friend, Jeremy Stickback, was the traitor he sought, the ringleader of the group wanting to overthrow the American government?

Pushing away from the railing, she hurried across the deck to the companionway stairs and took them as fast as she could. Rhys had to be somewhere below. Then remembering she had left Tristan unsupervised, she lifted her skirts and returned above, looking for one of the sailors she felt she could trust to watch the boy.

Ferguson was starboard, repairing a sail. Stumbling once in her haste, she approached him, heart racing, breath hissing in and out of her lungs, her gown still held high with her hands. "Tristan. Will you watch him for me?"

The sailor looked up, curious about her panicked state. "Yes'm, if you want."

She whirled, tore across the deck, nearly falling as she skittered down the steps. The first place below she checked was their cabin. One glance revealed it was empty. Where was Rhys?

Down the passageway she ran, checking behind every door she passed. She found him in the galley, sitting on an old stool and drinking from a thick ceramic mug.

"Rhys," she cried, then came to a halt in the doorway.

He jumped up, slamming the mug down on the table, taking in her disheveled appearance. "Calypso, what's wrong?"

At that moment doubts about what she planned to say crowded her reasoning. What would Rhys say when she accused his best fried of treason? Would he believe her? And worse, what did this imply about her family? Were her father and brother truly involved with an assassination plot? As cruelly as they had treated her, could she inform on them and see them thrown in jail? She didn't have the heart of stone they possessed.

Rhys's hands folded about her shoulders and shook her. "Dear God, woman, what has happened?"

Her head flopped back, and she stared up into his demanding eyes. She couldn't tell him, not if it meant betraying her flesh and blood. Swallowing hard, she lowered her lashes, blotting out his concerned face. Then an image of George Washington lying in a pool of his own blood shattered her family loyalties with the force of a bullet entering her conscience. The president had been more than kind to her. Could she turn her back on him as well?

"Calypso, damn it, tell me."

She looked up. "Rhys I know who's behind the plot against your Mr. Washington."

His brows lowered until his eyes were slits on his face. "How could you possibly know that information?"

"Because the person came to visit my father once, a long time ago. In fact the same day I met you." She

322

swallowed hard, unable to say the name. "Your friend
. . . Jeremy Stickback."

Rhys blinked, but not another muscle moved, until his
jaw clenched with a grinding sound.

"If that's true, Calypso, why didn't you tell me this
sooner?" Again he shook her.

"Because," she choked, "I didn't really see him, I only
heard him."

"You heard him speak, and you accuse him on so
little?" There was desperation in his voice.

She shook her head in denial. "No, there's more. I
was listening from a concealed place in my father's
study. I heard him walk. The way he uses his cane and
drags his lame foot. That sound has haunted me for
years, Rhys. I know it was Jeremy."

"What did he say?" When she didn't respond immediately, he shook her again.

"I don't know, Rhys. It was so long ago. I can't remember." Her eyes darted about the room seeking a safe
place to rest — anywhere to avoid the cold calculation in
her husband's gaze.

"You must do better than that. It's important."

How she wanted the truth to be something other than
it was. He was hurting, and her words were the cause of
his pain. "He talked to Father and Evan about being
prepared, that the king's Secret Society would call upon
them to do their duty. Then he said something about
helping the rebels destroy themselves. That's all, Rhys.
That's all I know."

He released his painful grasp on her arms. Spinning
about, he headed toward the companionway.

"Rhys," she whispered, fearing his answer no matter
what it might be. "What are you going to do?"

"I don't know, yet, but we'll change our course, and
I'll know by the time we reach Long Island."

"Long Island?" she mouthed. She wasn't sure she wanted to go back to the place that held such unpleasant memories for both her and Tristan.

"Damn you, Jeremy," Rhys cursed under his breath as he paced the confines of his cabin. "I don't understand your motives."

He sank down on the lone chair and buried his face in his hands. If what Calypso had told him was true, Stickback had used him time and again to set his devious plot in motion. They had taken that trip to Long Island together seven years ago to buy salt, but to his knowledge Jeremy had never left the ship and had never been to the island previously. Not once had he suspected the man used the stop to make contact with his cohorts. He slammed his fist against the desktop. "Damn it, I should have been more aware. I should have known it would come to this confrontation between me and you. I know now, you've been patiently waiting for me to uncover your part in this plot."

No wonder his friend so adamantly denied there was any truth in the report he had given to Thomas Jefferson a month ago. And when the secretary of state had sent Stickback to the Islands, he had given the man the very opportunity he needed to perfect his plans.

Was there still time to halt this Secret Society? He shot to his feet to reissue the order to continue on to Philadelphia. Then he brought himself up short. No, he had to check out the facts first. Calypso, if she was correct, still was coming to her conclusion with unsubstantiated reasoning. A person couldn't be convicted on the way he walked alone. If only she had seen him.

He pressed his forehead against the door. If only he could be absolutely sure. Who to believe—the woman he loved but knew so little about or a man who had been his friend for many years, even saved his life on one occasion.

"Rhys?" Calypso called softly through the door and attempted to release the latch. "Please, my love, I must talk to you."

Dragging his fingers through his hair, he took a deep breath and stepped away from the barrier. Calypso entered, slipping with elfin grace through the half-open door, her eyes searching his for answers.

"What do you plan to do to my family?"

How did one answer such a hard question, especially to a person one loved? "If your father and brother are still at the plantation, nothing."

"And if they're not?" she pressed.

"Then what choice have I, Calypso? I must go after them and stop whatever plot they're a part of, no matter what I have to do or who gets hurt."

"And Tristan. Are you not concerned for your son's safety? What if my father tries to take him away from us?"

Something inside Rhys tightened like a slipknot, squeezing until he thought he couldn't breathe. Did she have so little faith in him that she feared he was incapable of taking care of the boy? The internal pressure within him transferred to his arms as he clutched her to his heart. "No one will ever touch *our* son without my permission. Especially not John Collingsworth."

Chapter Twenty-two

Long Island, Bahamas
January 14, 1791

The Collingsworth docks looked more like a public harbor; vessels of every description and size crowded against one another, vying for a place to anchor near the wharf. Ladies dressed in cool summer gowns twirled parasols against their shoulders as their escorts guided them up the walk leading to the plantation house.

Calypso watched in total bewilderment. What was going on? Was her father having a celebration? She couldn't remember social guests coming to the Collingsworth manor since before her mother died. This entire affair made no sense whatsoever.

She spun about, seeking Rhys, wanting his opinion. In his place at the wheel he looked regal and in charge, and for one brief moment she was thankful.

"Drop anchor," he ordered, though they were still a distance from shore.

Crossing the deck, she waited until he accomplished his tasks; then she scooted close to grasp his arm. "What do you think this means?" With a sweep of her arm she indicated the gala on shore.

His jaw tightened. "I'm not sure, but whatever it is,

326

it's probably not good. If your father is celebrating . . ."

Calypso clutched her hands against her heart. She easily completed Rhys's unfinished remark in her mind. *Then he has something monumental to commemorate, something like the death of a president.*

Rhys stepped away, leaving her to her thoughts. "Lower the starboard boat. My wife and I will be going ashore."

She glanced his way, shaken with the reality she would soon face her father again. The last time she had seen him was the morning she had been arrested and taken to Fort Charlotte. What would his reaction be to her return? "Rhys, I—"

"Don't worry, sweeting," he offered, returning to her side and slipping his arm about her shoulders. "You're my wife, now. Collingsworth wouldn't dare harm you. Remember, he still thinks I'm the Earl of Flint and you're my countess."

She nodded stalwartly.

His finger slid under her chin and lifted her face. "You'll always be my countess—at least in my eyes."

A smile of appreciation bowed her lips.

"We must get going," he reminded her.

"I know. I'm ready."

He helped her down the rope ladder to the small boat bobbing beside the ship; then he took a seat directly across from her where he could watch her face and the shoreline behind her back. In no time the oarsmen navigated the skiff to the beach where a curious crowd gathered to see who the newcomers were. Was her father somewhere among them, waiting? More likely steaming at their intrusion.

She glanced about, seeking familiar faces. The few she knew watched her with mouths open even when she nodded and said hello. Then as she passed, she could hear them whispering among themselves.

They climbed the hill, hand in hand, and as they crested the top, she squeezed Rhys's fingers in gratitude for his unfaltering support. Expecting to find the lawns strewn with tables and party gala and greens edged out for skittles or John Bull, she instead discovered a crowd assembled about a large platform upon which rested many familiar household contents of the plantation.

Her heart skittered to a halt when she spied the bed she had used since childhood on one end of the platform. And there—she strained to see over the crowd—was Tristan's cradle. "Rhys, what does this mean?"

"Seems to be an auction taking place." He frowned and led her forward.

"Why would Father sell the household furnishings?" It didn't make sense to her. Something was wrong—very much so—and the prospects frightened her. "Rhys, I—"

"Hush, Calypso. Let's listen. Maybe we can figure out what's happening."

"Ladies and gentlemen," began the reed-thin man on the platform as he lifted his hand for silence.

The crowd obeyed. Calypso glanced about for some sign of her father or brother.

"As you can see, what we have here are fine pieces of goods, and the manor house, grounds, and acreage are impeccably maintained. The previous owner was a man of taste as you well know."

"The previous owner?" she hissed softly under her breath.

As if he anticipated her action, Rhys captured her arm, keeping her from rushing forward to deny the man's statement. "No, sweeting, wait," he whispered.

"But, Rhys."

"No, Calypso. There's nothing you can do. What we need to find out is why the estate is being sold. Stay here and say nothing." As soon as she nodded, he ambled away, blending into the crowd.

The man on the platform began the age-old singsong of auctioneers. In a matter of moments he shouted, "Sold," and her father's mahogany writing table that had occupied the library was carried off. Something inside of her pulled as if displaced, and her throat clogged with disbelief. She tore her eyes away as the damask-covered sofa was brought up on the platform next.

Unable to watch the dissolving of what she had always considered a solid part of her life—the family heirlooms that had been painstakingly brought from Maryland during their escape from the colonies—she concentrated on locating Rhys. Where was he? Why couldn't she find him? An uneasiness settled about her as she lifted on tiptoe, her neck craning to see over the crush of people.

The sofa was removed from the platform, and Tristan's cradle was brought forward. *Oh no,* she cried inwardly. *I can't watch.* She covered her face with her hands.

The bidding began, and her heart broke as the auctioneer again yelled, "Sold." How she would have liked to have that cradle—one small reminder of Tristan's babyhood.

Someone touched her arm, and she turned, expecting to see Rhys. Instead the kindly face of the old gentleman who had been so helpful and given her money in Nassau smiled down at her.

"Why, Miss Calypso, whatever are you doing here?"

"Mr. Hanson," she said with a slight lift of one side of her mouth.

"You didn't run away again, did you, girl?" He bent down and said in a conspiratorial manner. "To be quite frank, I haven't a crown to my name to help you if you have."

329

She reached out and patted his gnarled hands. "No, sir, I'm fine. In fact I'm here with my husband."

"Ah, good. I'm glad to know this time you made the young man marry you first."

Dear, kind Mr. Hanson. She guessed he had never found out she had escaped from the Fort Charlotte prison. He had always figured she had run away with a lover. Sliding her eyes to the side to watch him, she wondered if he knew the reason the Collingsworth holdings were being disbanded on the auction block. She took another glance about, seeking a sign of Rhys, but still couldn't find him. "Mr. Hanson," she queried, turning to face him, "can you tell me why my father's plantation is being sold?"

The old man cocked his head. "Where have you been, girl? Don't you know what John Collingsworth did?"

Her heart paused in midbeat. What terrible crime had her father committed? "No."

"He took several big loans from the bank, and then he and your brother, Evan, just up and disappeared. Left everything in the house, didn't even tell the servants they were going. But 'tis rumored they returned to the colonies—er, I mean the United States." He swept his hand in a wide arc. "The bank has taken over the plantation, my dear, trying to recoup some of their money."

She paled, and her breath came in short wisps.

"Miss Calypso, are you all right?" His shaking fingers gripped her arm, and he looked about, concerned.

She nodded mutely. If her father and brother went to the States, they were going for one thing, to carry through with their heinous plot to attempt to overthrow the government. "I must find my husband." Pulling from the old man's fingers, she rushed headlong into the crowd. She had to locate Rhys and tell him what she knew.

The auctioneer began again, but the drone of his voice was no more to her than the rhythm her feet must follow. When at last she spied Rhys near a table set up to collect monies and disperse goods, she called his name.

He started toward her, and what he held in his arms brought tears to her eyes. Tristan's cradle.

Her mouth lifted with a quiver, not sure if she should smile or cry. He scooped her into his arm and started toward the ship's rowboat waiting on the beach.

"Oh, Rhys," she cried, taking the cradle from him as he offered it up and clutching it to her. "My father and brother have gone to the States," she informed him, glancing his way to get his reaction.

"I know, and we haven't time to waste." Gently he retrieved the awkward piece of furniture from her grasp. "I'm sorry, Calypso, you had to see this." With his eyes, he indicated the auction going on behind her.

"You're not to blame." She touched one of the rockers on the small bed. "Thank you," she stated in a throaty whisper.

"It's not much." His fingers touched hers where they rested on the cradle.

"No, you're wrong. It's everything to me."

He helped her into the boat, and she intentionally took the seat looking out to sea. She didn't want to look back. Then her eyes snapped closed as the skiff rocked and entered the water. She didn't want to look forward, either. The future was just as frightening to contemplate as her past.

Calypso never thought she would consider a public house a welcome sight, but City Tavern was just that—home. Its canvas awnings, and large, individually paned windows spilling yellow light into the darkness beckoned from across the street as Rhys stopped them to judge the traffic before guiding them over the cobblestones.

For once Tristan followed meekly, allowing Calypso to hold onto his hand as if he sensed the urgency in his parents' steps.

"What are we going to do, Rhys?" she asked, looking up into his face illuminated in a window as they cut in front of the tavern.

"*We* are doing nothing. Take the boy upstairs and settle him in. I'm going to find out what information I can in the common room."

She turned and touched his arm as he stepped back to allow her to enter the front door first. "Then you don't plan to take any action until tomorrow morning?"

"I didn't say that, Calypso." Entering the crowded building, he placed his hand against her back, forcing her to move ahead.

The innkeeper, who stood behind the bar, looked up and smiled. "Your Lordship, Your Ladyship," he said with a grin. "Good to see you've returned, together." He jerked his head toward the stairs. "Your rooms are still waitin', and that Nanny woman has taken up squatter's right, refusin' to allow anyone, even the housekeeper, in the doors."

"Nanna," Tristan gurgled, pulling from Calypso's hand to take the stairs two at a time.

Torn, she glanced at Rhys as she called to her son. "Wait, Tristan."

"Go on. I won't go anywhere without letting you know," Rhys promised. Their eyes met, and he smiled wearily. With a nod, she gathered up her skirts and navigated the steps in pursuit of the boy who could be heard calling for Nannette as he raced down the upstairs hallway.

Why did she feel the way she did? Because Rhys had

said he would do whatever he must to stop an attempt to overthrow the American government. Just how far would he go? Would he work only as a breakwater to protect President Washington if in truth her father and brother were involved, or would he go further? Would he have them arrested, or worse, killed?

There was no love lost between her and her father or even Evan, she rationalized. So why did she care? No matter what they were or did, she didn't wish to see them die. She hesitated on the landing. But what if Rhys had no other choice? She pushed her unfounded fears to the side and forced her feet to continue their climb. There were always choices, she assured herself. Rhys would never go so far as to kill her family.

So many times on the trip from Long Island to Philadelphia she had wanted to ask him, to make him promise not to harm her father and brother, but he withdrew from her whenever she tried to bring up the subject. Was it because of Jeremy Stickback's involvement and the fact she had been the one to denounce him? And now, he wished to leave her behind when he went searching for those involved with the plot. She couldn't sit and wait to hear about the outcome secondhand. She had to be a part of whatever her husband planned. Rhys couldn't stop her from going.

Tristan's giggle of delight and Nannette's wail of relief as the two met in a doorway brought her attention back to reality. She halted at the far end of the corridor and watched as the little Scottish woman knelt and gathered the boy to her bosom.

"Who are ye with, laddie, your mum or da?"

"Both, Nanna. We're all together," he cried.

"Thank the saints above," Nannette sobbed, patting the boy's head and back as if she were afraid to let him go. She looked up and saw Calypso at the top of the stairs.

"Lassie," she exclaimed, rising to her feet, Tristan still clinging to her neck, and held out one arm. "You're home."

Feeling young and vulnerable again, Calypso rushed into the embrace, drawing in a deep breath filled with the smell of the rose water Nannette always wore. "Yes, we *are* home," she murmured, "for good."

"And the earl, lassie, where is he?"

Calypso looked down into the expectant face and wondered what Nannette would think if she knew about the task Rhys was setting out to do. "He'll be along shortly."

"And is all forgiven and forgotten between ye?"

She nodded, her lips parting in a slight smile.

"Ah, lassie, I knew the two of you would work out your problems." She turned and began leading Tristan into the room she shared with him. "Everything's here, laddie, just as ye left it."

"Wait, Nannette," she called. "I need your help to get ready."

"Ready?" The little woman turned back around to face her. "For what?"

"I'm not sure, but Rhys will be up soon, and I must be dressed to leave as well, no matter where he's planning on going."

Nannette frowned. "Very well, let me settle the boy in, and I'll order you up a bath."

"There's no time. I want to be dressed and waiting when he appears. No matter where Rhys says he's going, there's no way he's leaving without me."

"Are you sure, Francis?" Rhys stared down into the face of the bespectacled little man, Thomas Jefferson's secretary.

334

"Aye, Rhys. I heard Mr. Jefferson say he planned to attend."

"And Jeremy?"

"Said he'd be there to keep an eye on things."

"And the president, for sure?"

"So Mr. Jefferson said. Apparently there are British dignitaries in the city that Mr. Washington wishes to impress. What better way than the Powel House?"

"British?" His brow lifted in curiosity. "Do you know who they are?"

The other man shook his head.

An uneasy feeling akin to dread oozed through Rhys's veins. English dignitaries, and Jeremy Stickback saying he was going to a social event—something the man usually avoided at all costs. He stood and flashed a smile toward the secretary. "Thanks, Francis. I'm sorry to have disturbed your dinner."

He crossed the common room and took the stairs leading up to the guest rooms, moving as fast as he could without attracting attention. He must find Jefferson and tell him what he suspected. Instinct told him the conspirators might try to carry through with their plot this evening.

Tearing at the jabot at his throat, he loosened his cravat in the process. There was no time to waste. He would change his clothing and present himself at the Powel House, uninvited, and assume his standing in the political community would gain him entrance.

Calypso would be disappointed, most likely angry, when he had no time to wait for her to dress. She would have to understand and trust him as it was his intention that no one be hurt, but the president's life must be protected even at the risk of his own or anyone else's.

He pushed his way into the bedroom, prepared for the bombardment of questions she would ask. Instead she

335

turned to face him, and he caught his breath, one hand on the buttons of his waistcoat becoming still, the other holding his necktie dropping to his side.

"Calypso?" His surprise was evident in his voice.

Crimson velvet edged with wine-colored piping clung to her upper torso as if the gown had been stitched while on her body. The wide, full skirt dropped from her waist to trail on the floor in a small train. How regal, yet innocent she looked with the crown of flame ringlets feathering to fringe about her face, the rest of her hair falling long and curled at the ends to her waist.

"I wasn't sure where you'd be going, but I thought to be prepared. I'm going with you." The command was spoken so softly, he could find no reason to protest.

"You would put Eliza Powel to shame the way you look."

"Will I have a chance?"

"For sure, wench." He pulled his gaze away from her and tossed his neckwear on the bed. "Now move back from the mirror and give me an opportunity to get ready." He stripped his waistcoat and shirt from his chest and put them aside, then he donned fresh ones, more elaborate and dandified than the ones he had worn aboard ship. The last thing he did was replace his nankeens with gray cassimere breeches. Within moments he had transformed himself from sea captain to elegant gentleman.

He grabbed her lace-covered fingers and turned her so she must face him. "I must warn you, Calypso. I have no idea what will happen this evening, but you are with me strictly for show. I don't want you interfering with whatever I must do, nor do I want you to take it in your pretty head to do my job for me. Do you understand?"

She nodded, the ringlet curls about her face bouncing. For one moment he considered kissing the fullness of

336

her mouth, then changed his mind. Jeremy Stickback's involvement in this plot he could handle, and would take care of with whatever force was necessary. But Calypso's family—that was a different matter. As much as he despised the baron and his son, and as little as he cared about what happened to them, he could see Calypso was hurting, fearing what would happen to them, should they be involved. And in his heart he knew without a doubt they were a part of the plot.

Damn it, he loved this woman, and most likely she would be the death of him, as he would take every precaution he could to see her father and brother did not die because of their misguided political fanaticism.

Chapter Twenty-three

Ablaze with light and surrounded by coaches of every size and description, the fanfare at the Powel House left no doubt in Rhys's mind that tonight was the social event of the season, and anyone who was anybody in Philadelphia would be in attendance. His jaw tightened. If a public attempt on Washington's life were to occur, even if the plot was aborted, the United States could find itself obligated to another war, something the still financially crippled country could ill afford.

He returned his gaze to the interior of the carriage as Calypso strained forward, peering out the window. The illumination from the mansion shining into the vehicle reflected the anxiety squeezing her lips into a courageous line.

Leaning toward her, he grasped her fingers that were knotted in the crimson velvet of her gown and pulled them his way until they rested on his knee. "Remember, Calypso. Stay in the center of attention, keep circulating, and speak of me as if I've stepped no further away than the punch bowl. Make the guests believe I'm somewhere in that crowded ballroom." He pressed her hands, demanding a response.

"I understand," she responded, the timbre of her voice low and steady, belying the inner turmoil he knew churned within her.

Bending closer, he pressed his lips against the soft curls skirting her forehead. "Relax, sweeting. Chances are nothing will happen. There's the possibility your family isn't even here in Philadelphia." He didn't believe that, and he suspected she didn't either, but perhaps by keeping her occupied, she would never witness what would take place behind the scenes. President Washington must be secreted away from the gala, Jeremy Stickback cornered and arrested, and if the baron and Evan were there, they must be detained until Thomas Jefferson could decide what to do with them.

The Collingsworths were English citizens, not Americans, so the resolution of their involvement was sticky at best. The fledgling new country needed no international action taken against it because of a few insane conspirators. The British government would never be a part of a plot to overthrow another country but might turned blinders in the plotters' direction. They were like bullies, whipped in a fight and tasting their own blood. The slightest excuse, and the redcoats would begin the foray all over again.

Sighing, he angled back against the seat, releasing her hands. The coachman opened the door, and the urge to tell Saunders to close it again and return them to the inn struggled with his need to take care of his responsibilities. Damn it all to hell, how had he managed to fall in love with the enemy's daughter?

"Rhys, I'll not disappoint you." Her voice registered concern, and her eyes pleaded with him to believe her.

Realizing he was frowning, he forced his facial muscles to relax. "You could never disappoint me, my lady." He dropped his forehead into an open palm and rubbed his closed eyelids. "I just wish this evening over and done with. Somehow I've lost my taste for patriotic martyrdom. The need to free a nation all by myself doesn't seem so important anymore."

"No, Rhys. Don't say that." She slipped into the seat beside him and gripped his hands to press them against her heart. " 'Tis most important. This country is giving us a chance to be who we wish to be, not what tradition dictates we should be. But more important, it will give Tristan a chance to learn how to make his own choices without guilt."

Surprised at the fervor of her words, he lifted his head and raised one brow. "You little minx," he mused. "Soon you'll be singing 'Yankee Doodle' to me. When did you get so patriotic?"

She looked away, flustered.

Grabbing her jaw, he forced her to face him. "When?"

Her eyes leveled, assessing him. "The first time I saw you standing proudly at the helm of your ship," she replied, notching her chin higher. "And then when you married me—unashamed of who I was. The way these people"—she gestured toward the Powel House—"accepted me without question." She looked down at her hands nervously picking at her gown. "This country needs you, Rhys, but more important—you need this country." Her hands stilled, but her head remained bowed. "Do what you must to keep it strong."

As if a valve had been released somewhere inside of him, he felt the pressures of his responsibilities uncapped, spilling unexpected emotions into the back of his throat. The pain was unbearable, and he swallowed. Dear God, what would Calypso think if he broke down in front of her? She would see him as less of a man.

He forced down the rawness clawing at his gullet and

nodded stiffly, then captured her in the circle of his arm. "No more than I have to, I promise."

Then he straightened, remembering the coachman standing in the drive waiting for them to disembark from the carriage. Stepping down first, he offered her a hand and a crooked smile. "Come, Calypso, let the world see what a wonderful woman I married."

Candles planted in buckets of sand lined the walkway to the front door. The flames winked and nodded at her, and Calypso forced the well of tears threatening to cascade over her lashes to a standstill, as the pinpoints of light blurred into watery nothingness. She would not cry or demand he ignore her final statement giving him carte blanche to do what he must. But neither would the hollowness inside of her dissipate.

She forced her feet to take the stairs and then a smile to lift her lips as the front door was opened by the serving girl, Maggie, who had greeted her the last time she had presented herself at the Powel home.

"Yer ladyship," Maggie acknowledged with a dip. Spying Rhys standing behind Calypso, she opened her eyes wide. "Yer Lordship, too." The dip deepened. "Mistress Powel will be most pleased you both could come." She led the way through the front foyer archway and up the staircase to the ballroom on the second floor.

The guests overflowed into the hallway. Men in cassimere and silk and wielding walking sticks vied for the attention of velvet-clad ladies stirring the air with fans of every size and color. Rhys took Calypso's fur-lined cape from her shoulders, added his long coat, and deposited them in the serving girl's hands. Then stepping

341

forward, he ushered her into the crowd to announce their arrival.

Their hostess caught Calypso's attention from across the room where she stood under the Waterford chandelier, the brilliance of the light causing the diamonds in her blond curls to wink with a rainbow spectrum of colors. Dressed in royal blue, Eliza Powel made the majority of the women guests look plain by comparison. Standing proudly by her husband's side, Calypso took a deep breath of anticipation. *Please let the evening be uneventful,* she prayed.

"Easy, sweeting, just remember what I told you," Rhys whispered in her ear.

Her head nodded once, and she stepped forward, meeting Eliza halfway to take the woman's hands in warm greeting.

"Countess, you're back," the blonde said with a flashing smile. Her eyes swept up to Rhys, who stood a few steps behind. "I see you found that rascal of a husband of yours." She turned to Rhys and lifted her fingers, demanding recognition. "Your Lordship."

"Mistress Powel," he replied, taking her offered hand and bringing it to his lips. "Where might I locate Mr. Jefferson?" He released her fingertips.

"You men, all the same. Always business." Eliza wrinkled her pert, upturned nose. "Most likely you'll find him downstairs with my husband in his office."

"With Mr. Washington as well?"

"Of course not, Rhys." Lifting her fan, she tapped his upper arm, forgetting the formality of their speech. "You know George better than that. If he were here, he would be circulating among the ladies. He charms us all with his kind words and gentlemanly ways."

Rhys straightened. "And Jeremy Stickback?"

342

One arched blond brow lifted. "Not yet. 'Tis said he'll be bringing the English dignitaries. My, Rhys, why all this interest in the arrival of the guests?"

" 'Tis nothing, Mistress Powel. Idle curiosity." He turned to Calypso. "Something to drink, my dear?"

With a nod, she swallowed, and forced a casual smile. "Please." She turned away, knowing the play had begun and Rhys was walking into danger, but she dared not watch him go. Eliza must be mollified and kept from knowing anything was amiss. "Oh, Eliza, I've so much to tell you," she began, taking the other woman's arm and leading her in the opposite direction from the way Rhys had gone.

"However did you find him?" Eliza demanded. "When finally I discovered your husband had departed for Wales, you were nowhere to be found. Even that tight-lipped woman of yours would say nothing."

Calypso forced herself to concentrate on her friend's words. *Be careful, my darling.* She willed her thoughts to Rhys. *Please, God, see that my father and brother are nowhere to be found.*

Following Eliza's lead, she allowed herself to be carried away by the social whirlwind of the party, though her gaze continuously sought the doorway, looking for Rhys to reappear and confirm or deny her heartfelt prayers.

From across the study, Rhys waited for a reaction from the other two men in the room.

"How can you be absolutely sure, Rhys?" Thomas Jefferson's voice was level and low.

"I can't be. I realize the only facts I have are hearsay. But, damn it, man. What does it take? An actual

343

threat on the president's life to convince you? All I'm asking is to take precautions. See Washington to safety and question Stickback." He spun about, planting his fists behind his back. "Jeremy is my friend. I don't accuse him lightly."

"No, Rhys, I don't imagine that you do." Jefferson's words held no malice.

"What of the English dignitaries?" Samuel Powel's question hung in the air like thick, choking smoke.

The secretary of state looked to Rhys for his suggestion.

"I say they must be detained or at the very least interrogated."

"And if they are innocent, we will have an honor duel between nations on our hands. The British government will never stand by and allow us to mistreat one of their emissaries. No," Jefferson said with a shake of his head, "I can't allow that. It's too risky."

"Then let me take it upon myself, Thomas. If I'm wrong, the American government can claim they had no part. You could bring me up on charges. That should satisfy even Mad King George."

" 'Tis taking a lot upon yourself, man."

"Perhaps, but I could never live knowing I did nothing to prevent the death of an entire country because I was not brave enough to follow through with my convictions." His unwavering stare refused to allow Jefferson to contradict his statement.

Jefferson looked once at Powel, then back at Rhys. "All right. If there is time, I'll see that the president is informed and stopped from attending this evening. If not, I'll see he's protected. God help you, Rhys, I hope you're right for your sake." He put out his hand, and Rhys gripped it firmly. "You're on your own."

344

Without further comment, Rhys wheeled about, his mouth set in a determined line. He was damned by his country if he was wrong, and damned by his wife, no matter what she had said, if he was right. He wasn't sure which course of punishment was worse.

The strain of watching the doorway pulled Calypso's insides so taut she felt as if she couldn't breathe. Then the chatter of voices in the hallway stilled, and she along with every other occupant in the room turned to see what was going on.

Eliza rushed forward, her slippered feet hushed on the polished ballroom floor. As the three men entered, she dipped a bow, then offered Jeremy Stickback her hand in greeting.

Calypso thought a volcano had taken residence within her. Her wildest nightmare had come true. Standing beside Stickback and an aristocratic older man was Evan, her brother.

She sidestepped until she melted into the crowd, praying she would pass unnoticed. Once Eliza gestured in her general direction, and the men's eyes turned that way. Fearing her friend had unknowingly given away her identity, she scrunched down out of sight. Then she bumped into the table behind her and realized Eliza had only been indicating the refreshments.

Determined to work her way behind the new arrivals, she skirted along the walls of the room. Maybe she could find Rhys and tell him what she had seen. Don't interfere, he had warned, and don't try to do my job, but blazes to Satan she couldn't just stand there and watch.

Reaching the door unnoticed, she eased past the human overflow and down the long corridor leading to the staircase. Grabbing her skirts without considering how unladylike she must appear, she rushed down the steps to the first landing. There she paused when the serving girl opened the front door to George and Martha Washington.

Thomas Jefferson exited out of the study door and stopped the president and his wife before they reached the foyer archway. His words were muffled, but she could see Mrs. Washington pale and clutch her husband's arm.

The presidential party trailed behind Thomas Jefferson beneath the stairway where she stood unobserved. Indecision coursed through her. Should she follow them? No. She must find Rhys and tell him her brother was upstairs.

Waiting until the foyer cleared, she darted down the steps and rushed to the study, confident Rhys would be there. The room was smoke filled, the butts of two cigars still burning in a silver tray, but there was no sign of her husband.

Placing her fingers to her forehead, she tried to think. Where would he be? Perhaps he was waiting for the president. She remembered the time she had visited Eliza all those weeks ago. There was a back door that led to the gardens. Were the officials gathered there, deciding the best course of action?

Returning to the foyer, she worked her way to the rear of the house and found the exit into the gardens. From the ballroom the sounds of music floated down upon her as she followed an unlit path toward the conservatory. The winter chill was penetrating, and she wrapped her arms about herself for warmth, refusing to allow the cold to stop her search.

The path wound about like a maze, and soon she was thoroughly lost. She paused, listening for sounds, but only the faint rhythm of the pianoforte and the violin vibrated the air. She could hear evidence of no one else in the gardens.

Plopping down on a cold, marble bench, she tried to decide what to do. Maybe she should go back and search the mansion again. Rhys had to be somewhere.

Click, tap, shuffle.

Her head shot up; her breath hitched in her chest. Glancing about nervously, she waited for the sound to come again so that she could decide which direction it came from.

Click, tap shuffle.

From her left. She rose and slipped into a patch of rhododendron bushes to wait. Jeremy Stickback was close, close enough to hear. What would he do if he found her there alone? Her apprehension fluttered like a tiny sparrow pursued by a falcon.

The steps drew closer, and she realized they were accompanied by another pair. She pushed down a branch and strained forward to see, then pulled her head back, allowing the limb to snap into place when the two forms crossed directly in front of her.

"It's now or not at all, Jeremy. If what we were told is true, my sister will recognize me immediately. Chances are she'll suspect you, too. What were you thinking when you sent her on that wild-goose chase to Wales?"

"I was thinking the wench would get lost. I never thought she'd find him, damn it. I had thought to be rid of both of them."

Her breath quivered for release, but the two men were so close she could have reached out and touched them.

"You were a fool, Stickback. You should have killed Winghurst a long time ago. Because of your misguided friendship, the cause may be lost forever."

"No, Evan, you're wrong. Plant yourself somewhere close and shut up. George Washington will have to come this way, if they plan on sneaking him out the back."

Calypso crouched down as Evan entered the brush with nothing more than an ancient oak trunk between them. He would hear her, she was sure. What would her brother's reaction be when he discovered her presence? Her mouth went dry when she recognized the sound of a pistol being loaded and primed.

She couldn't just hide there and allow her brother to shoot President Washington. Her heart thumped out its denial of her mind's courageous thoughts. Then Evan angled the pistol so the moonlight reflected on the gun barrel as he waited for his target to appear.

Without considering the consequences, she snaked out her hand and grabbed the weapon from Evan's unsuspecting hand.

"What the hell?" he mumbled as he turned to find his pistol pointed directly at his heart.

"Callie?" he hissed, disbelief lifting his pitch to an unmasculine high note.

"Evan, 'tis good to see you again." Her mouth lifted at one corner as the thrill of being in charge of the situation raced through her. "Appears I've caught *you* for once, Brother dear." She cocked her head. " 'Tis justice perhaps." She tapped a finger on the pistol butt. "I'm not sure what punishment I'll extract. Any suggestions? You were always so good at blackmail."

He stepped around the tree, his hand reaching out to

take the weapon away from her.

Lifting the barrel a notch higher, she backed away. "I wouldn't if I were you, Evan."

"And tell me, Sister dear, what do you plan to do? Shoot me?" His lips curled in a sneer.

"If I must."

"But I'm your brother. Whatever would that counterfeit earl of yours think if you killed your own flesh and blood?"

"He's not counterfeit, and he would think I saved him the trouble." She stared into her brother's jade eyes that twinned her own and, for the first time in her life, felt pity. Father had made Evan what he was. He was right; they were kin. She would never shoot him. The gun wavered in her hand for one brief second of time.

With the speed of a cobra, Evan snatched the pistol from her fingers and aimed the barrel at her heart. "I knew you couldn't, Callie," he whispered softly as he pulled the trigger back. "No matter what Father said, I knew you would never turn on your own kind."

The tension strained between them. Knowing she couldn't shoot Evan offered no guarantee he wouldn't pull the trigger on her. She closed her eyes, fearing the answer.

With a click the hammer released, and he dropped the weapon to his side. "I know I've never said it, and most likely never shown it, but I did love you all those years, you know. I just needed Father's love more. You can understand, can't you?"

Her eyes snapped opened, shocked by the revelation. She had to stop him. Somehow she had to make him see how wrong he was in his actions. "Evan," she replied in a rasp. "Please, don't do this. If you quit now, nothing will happen. I'll see you have a place to go where you're safe." She choked on a sob as her hand reached out to deter him.

The sound of multiple footsteps echoed on the garden path, and they both turned to see who was approaching.

" 'Tis best, Mr. President," she heard the familiar voice of Thomas Jefferson. "If in truth our own agents are involved, I feel both you and Mrs. Washington should leave now and secretly."

"Please, George, don't argue with Mr. Jefferson." The soft slur had to belong to the president's wife. "Your life is at stake."

"All right, Martha, I'm going, but Eliza will be most disappointed."

"She'll understand," Martha replied.

"The cause," Evan hissed under his breath, and Calypso whirled to grab his arm to keep him from proceeding. The moonlight reflected in his eyes highlighted the bitter insanity embedded in his mind.

"No, Evan," she cried as he pulled from her grasp and crashed through the shrubbery.

The approaching party came to an abrupt halt on the pathway.

Her brother's crazed laughter rang out from the darkness. "Glorious revenge is ours, Father." The gunshot reverberated in the night.

Calypso screamed. So did Martha Washington. Fear clutching her heart with fingers of steel, she was afraid to open her eyes, knowing she would see the president lying dead in the garden path. The sobs of horror started slowly and built to a crescendo she had no control over. *I should have stopped him.* "If only I'd had the strength to pull the trigger."

"Calypso, no." Loving arms wrapped about her cold

shoulders and tucked her into the security of a warm chest. "It's all right, sweeting. It's all over."

"Can you forgive me, Rhys? He's dead, and it's my fault. If only I had stopped Evan, Mr. Washington wouldn't have been killed."

"Calypso listen to me. The president is unharmed."

Her eyes swept open, and she glanced about the garden, a multitude of candles lighting the walkway where a still form darkened the path.

"But the shot I heard. Who—?" Gazing up into the depths of Rhys's brown eyes, there was more than reassurance residing there. Much more. There was a mixture of dread, apprehension, and sympathy.

Her head snapped around to stare at the figure on the ground. The size was too slight to be the president. As she pulled from Rhys's grasp, he released her without resistance. Mouth suddenly dry, she couldn't swallow, as the truth thundered in her ears.

"Evan?"

No. It couldn't be.

She stumbled toward the facedown body and fell on her knees beside the lifeless hand thrown out across the pathway in defeat. The unfired pistol was still clutched in his fingers.

"Evan?" she repeated, her voice trembling with shocked disbelief. Pushing at the broadcloth-covered shoulder, she managed to turn him over. Her brother stared back at her with lifeless eyes.

Forgotten were her earlier self-condemning thoughts, the appalling reasons her sibling was there in the Powel gardens to begin with. All she could see was her brother, senselessly shot down, and one person could be held responsible.

"You killed him," she choked, angling her face to

351

look up at Rhys towering above her.

"Calypso, there was no way to avoid what happened. The servant did what he thought—"

"Did you have to kill him?" Sanity swallowed up by shock and hysteria, she cut him off, not caring to hear his excuses for what he had done.

His powerful hands gripped her shoulders and lifted her to her feet. "Calypso, listen to me."

"You murdered him." Her accusation rang out in the still garden.

He shook her until her teeth felt as if they would be jarred loose. "I didn't." He tried to pull her against his chest.

Pushing him away with all of her strength, she visualized the hands holding her pulling the trigger that had taken her brother's life. "Let go of me," she screeched, ripping at his fingers with her nails.

The sting of his palm cracked against her cheek, sending her own guilt spinning like a whirlwind back to the surface. Her hand flew up, covering her stinging flesh, and she gasped as the pain reminded her *she* had not stopped her brother—and could have.

"*I* wasn't strong enough. If only I had made him believe I meant what I said." A sob of confusion tore through her with the force of a bolt of lightning, the blame she so desperately needed to pin on someone clawing at her throat. "Damn you, Rhys. Did you have to shoot him down like a stray dog?" She turned pleading eyes on him.

"Evan's death was unavoidable." He stared back at her, anger and sense of betrayal setting his jaw and hardening his look to a glare. "You knew there was that risk." Without waiting for her response, as if he didn't care what she felt, he spun about, presenting his back to her.

She swallowed her acid response as the sound of a scuffle further down the pathway filled the air. The shuffle of heels grew closer, and she swept around, unsure what to expect.

Two men she had never seen before pushed Jeremy Stickback before them, his hands secured behind his back. Behind them came the tall dignitary she had seen enter the ballroom with Evan, an escort holding his arm. The group stopped before Rhys.

His eyes raked Jeremy's figure, his lips curling in distaste. "Why?" he demanded.

Stickback glared in return, and his head lifted in pride. "I'm true to my king." He spat on the ground beside Rhys's shoe. "You're a traitor of the worst kind, Lord Turncoat."

Rhys's body jerked as if he had been hit. His hands clenched at his sides, his fists turning bloodless. A crueler thing couldn't have been said to him, and Calypso sucked in her breath, unsure how he would reply.

"Take him away," Rhys said, his voice low and emotionless; yet when he angled around and the flickering candlelight reflected on his features, she could see the deep-rooted pain etched there.

"Sir, I demand to know the meaning of the way I am being mistreated." The English dignitary pulled his arm from his escort's grasp. "The British government will not like to hear of American bullying."

"This is not government business, but personal. How well do you know that man?" He pointed at Evan's twisted body.

"My association with an English subject is none of your affair."

"Sir Jameson. You can answer me now or answer me

353

later. The choice is yours, but you will remain in my custody until you do."

Jameson dusted his wrinkled sleeve. "This is an outrage. I don't appreciate your crude colonial manners, but if you must know, I met him this evening. That gentleman, Jeremy Stickback, your government's representative I would like to remind you, introduced us saying that Mr. Collins"—he pointed at Evan—"was a emissary sent by the governor of the Bahama Islands to negotiate salt contracts. Mr. Stickback indicated the gentleman wished my support in contracting a strong agreement. I consented."

"That's all?"

"My word as a gentleman, sir."

Calypso could see the indecision savagely spinning the wheels in Rhys's mind. What was he up to? Why did he deny his government connection? Instinct kept her from voicing her thoughts, though she watched her husband for some indication of his intentions.

He looked at her askance, then back at Jameson, as if seeking a sign of recognition from her.

"I've never seen him before, Rhys," she responded to his mental questioning.

He nodded, turned to the escort behind Jameson, and gave him a signal to release the dignitary. "My apologies, sir, for the abruptness of the interrogation. You are free to leave."

"You've not heard the last of this, Winghurst."

His mouth curled in irony. "No. I imagine I haven't." He pivoted and began walking away as Jameson returned to the house.

Calypso was left standing on the pathway with her brother, and her confusion rushed out in the shape of a demand.

"Where are you going, Rhys?"

His broad shoulders hunched forward as he paused, never once looking back at her. "I'm going to complete the task at hand."

Her heart thudded to a standstill. "Which means?"

"Your father," he replied softly. "He must be brought to justice."

"Justice, Rhys, or revenge? You told that man this entire affair had nothing to do with government business. You've stopped the conspiracy. My father can do nothing on his own."

He whirled about to face her. "Why, Calypso? Why do you defend a man who treats you worse than an insect under his shoe?"

"Wasn't my brother enough?" she choked, seeing the truth in his words, but unable to give up the need to find peace with the man who had sired her. "Please, Rhys, let my father go."

Never had she pleaded with Rhys Winghurst for anything before. She needed him to give in to her entreaty. He couldn't deny her. Her chin angled upward, her eyes softening with her appeal.

Pausing, he flicked his gaze over her, taking in the curve of her rising and falling bosom, the way her hand curled about her throat to come to final rest on her parted lips. "It would be best if you left now, Calypso. The carriage will see you home. I'll give Eliza your excuses."

She blinked. He was dismissing her as if she were no more than an unreasonable child. Clutching his arm, she forced her voice to remain calm. "Surely, you won't deny me this one small request."

He stared down at her fingers on his sleeves. " 'Tis not mine to bequeath, 'tis the requirements of my job."

"So you say now, Rhys. I don't believe you. As you told Sir Jameson, this has nothing to do with your work. In my opinion, it's your pride that must be assuaged. Blame not my father for your own misjudgment when it comes to trusting others. Jeremy was your mistake."

His jaw tightened, and his eyes glazed over, erasing all evidence of what he felt. "What you think will not change my mind. Go home, woman. Our son has need of at least one parent." Walking away, he never looked back.

"Rhys," she called into the darkness, but he was gone.

Chapter Twenty-four

Calypso's accusation stung Rhys with the venom of a swarm of hornets. Was there merit in her words? He watched the carriage pull away, taking her back to the City Tavern. God help them both if there was, but he was committed by the virtue of the fact he needed to tie up the loose ends regarding the assassination plot before Jefferson would be required to call him up on charges of misconduct. Sir Jameson was not the kind of man to make idle threats. The repercussions of his lack of diplomacy would strike as soon as the emissary could communicate with British officials. Damn! He wouldn't have long to find John Collingsworth. A few weeks at the most.

He tore his gaze from the receding vehicle and returned to the chore of seeing Evan's body removed from the gardens before any of the other guests learned of the affair. Though Samuel Powel had been made aware of the situation, Eliza had been kept in the dark, the president's nonarrival excused by illness, and the dignitaries' abrupt departure as political. The truth but vague enough.

Finally he had put down Calypso's and his departure to exhaustion from their long trip from Wales. No one would be the wiser, and, if they were lucky, news of the near assassination would never reach the public ear, and would remain one of those incidents unrecorded by history. For the sake of the young, struggling country, an image of stability was best.

Turning away from the drive, he worked his way to the stable to claim the mount Samuel had given him permission to use for as long as he needed. He blocked out the anger and disappointments, both his and Calypso's, and refused to allow the look she had given him as the carriage had taken her home to make a difference as he formulated his plan of action.

John Collingsworth couldn't be far away. The first place to check would be Jeremy Stickback's residence, a boardinghouse west of the Powel home on Walnut Street. Accepting the reins from the stablehand, he mounted. It wouldn't take long to reach his destination.

He pushed the horse into a canter until he crossed Willings, then followed Fourth to Walnut. Minutes later the three-story structure he searched for came into view, a whale-oil street lamp illuminating the cobblestones right in front of the house.

Bringing the roan to a halt, he studied his surroundings. A shadowed pedestrian crossed Walnut and entered the building beside the one he watched. In the distance he heard the whinny of a horse. A public stables, perhaps, or a carriage horse tethered to a hitching post. Collingsworth's vehicle maybe? He dismounted, secured his animal, and cautiously approached the boardinghouse, unsure of how he should proceed. Would the baron be on guard or leisurely awaiting the return of his son and Stickback? One could never tell with a man like John Collingsworth.

A plan began to take shape. If the assassination had been successful, would Evan and Jeremy have returned here? Most likely not; they would have sent a message to the baron proclaiming the deed done. A messenger. Why not?

He navigated the walk to the front door and knocked. Much to his surprise at this late hour, a servant answered almost immediately.

"I've a message," he stated, "for Mr. Collins." He used the name Sir Jameson had called Evan.

"Of course," the servant replied. "Mr. Collins is expecting you. Through the back. The last door to your left."

With a nod, he followed the directions down the back hallway. This was easy. Too easy, perhaps. He slipped a small pistol from the interior of his coat as soon as the servant was out of sight. Knowing he would have one chance, and one only, he cocked the weapon. The minute Collingsworth saw him, the older man would realize something had gone afoul. At the designated door, he knocked softly, his insides knotting with apprehension.

"Come," called a voice accustomed to being obeyed.

He hesitated only a moment, then pushed the door open with the barrel of the pistol.

John Collingsworth stood beside a small table, shuffling a stack of maps and documents. Before he looked up, he demanded, "The message please. What took so long?"

"My message is simple, Collingsworth."

The baron glanced up to find the gun pointed at his heart. "You," he hissed. "You have nerve coming here after—"

"After what? You're a son of a bitch who deserves everything that's happened to you."

Collingsworth straightened. "So what do you plan to do now?"

"Your English citizenship is the only thing protecting you from being dragged into the street and hanged. 'Tis what should be done with you."

The baron's face lit up with crazed delight. "Then the task was accomplished. The colonial dog who dared to try and be a king is dead. Long live King George." His fist lifted in emphasis.

"President Washington was untouched. It was Evan you sacrificed, you old fool."

His face a deadly white, Collingsworth charged forward, catching Rhys off guard. "No, you lie," he accused, tearing down the hallway.

Rhys lifted the gun and took aim at the baron's retreating figure. His finger on the trigger, an image of Calypso's pleading face caused him to hesitate for a split second.

Then it was too late. A man stepped from one of the other rooms, obviously curious about the commotion. From another, a small boy poked his head out the door. Both intrusions prevented Rhys from getting a clear shot.

Ignoring the growing audience, Rhys raced down the hall in pursuit and out the front door. In the distance Collingsworth ran around a corner and out of sight. He followed, determined to keep the man from escaping.

A shot rang out from ahead. Rhys ducked behind a picket fence, but didn't fire back. The risk was too great he might injure an innocent party.

Studying his surroundings, he tried to gauge exactly

where Collingsworth had gone. Damn, why had he hesitated when he had had the opportunity to shoot the man? Never had he allowed a personal problem to interfere with his duties. Never, that is, until he had fallen in love with Calypso. He had not been alert enough to realize the baron had a gun. A mistake of that caliber could have cost him his life. He was losing his touch now when he needed his instincts to be at their sharpest.

Pushing away from the protection of the fence, he followed an alley leading back to the rear of the boardinghouse where it came to a dead end. Collingsworth was returning to the house, most likely for transportation. Should he go after his own mount or wait here for the man to ride by?

Before the decision could be made, a wild-eyed steed flew out of the darkness directly in his path. Sidestepping to keep from being run over, he braced his legs, aiming the gun, but several people had entered the streets, curious about the commotion and blocking his access to the mad baron. He had no choice except to allow the horse and rider to continue on their way.

"You'll pay, Winghurst," the baron cried as the mount's flying hooves clattered against the cobblestones. "You and that traitorous daughter of mine. I'll see you both in hell."

Rhys lowered the gun and dropped his head. He had made a big mistake in allowing John Collingsworth to escape. Hopefully it wouldn't be a fatal one for the president or himself or—God forbid—Calypso.

Calypso draped her arm about Tristan's coated shoulder as they stared down at the freshly covered grave. Bare. Not one flower to signify a man had lived and died. She knelt and placed the single lily flower in her hand on top of the raw dirt. *No matter how misguided you were, Evan, we loved you,* she vowed, fighting back a sob as she reenacted in her mind one more time the nightmare scene that had taken place in the gardens two nights before.

"Mama," Tristan asked with the childish bewilderment. "Was Evan bad?"

"No, not bad, just confused. He did what he did for the wrong reasons."

"He was always nice to me. Even bought me a pony, remember?"

Still on her knees, she turned and pulled the boy into the circle of her arms. "I remember. Don't you ever forget that fact, either. No matter what he did to others he was good to you." *Including myself,* she thought. He had treated her abominably over the years, she couldn't deny, but he had loved her son. That one point was what saved Evan in her mind's eye, their shared love of Tristan.

Rising to her feet, she turned them away from the grave site. There was nothing more to be done here. Perhaps Evan would find peace at last, free of their father.

Father, she thought, her eyes narrowing to slits. What had become of her father and her husband's vow to see him brought to justice? Since the night of Evan's death, she had not heard a word from Rhys. Nothing. Almost as if he no longer existed.

To make matters worse, no one seemed aware of what had taken place in the Powels' gardens. Even Eliza chatted on about the disastrous party where the presidential couple had failed to arrive and the special guests had departed all of a sudden. No one appeared to know Evan was her brother or that he had been slain.

Her mouth clamped tight. How had Rhys managed to conceal the facts so well? Without a doubt, he was responsible, and she probably wouldn't see him until he had accomplished his goal of arresting her father.

"Mama?"

She glanced down at her son walking beside her as they approached the carriage.

"Where is Papa?"

For two days now she had been expecting this question from Tristan. She still hadn't formulated a good answer during that time. "Your father's work has taken him away for a while."

They walked on a few steps as the boy considered her answer. "Now that Papa's not an earl, what does he do?"

How much could she tell him? Though she would never forgive Rhys his part in Evan's death, it wasn't necessary for Tristan to know of his involvement. That information would crush the boy.

"Your father does very important work for the president."

"Why doesn't he come home?" he pressed. "Doesn't he love us anymore?"

She urged him up into the carriage. "Don't be silly, Tristan. Of course your father loves you. Dearly."

"When will he be back? I miss him." He gazed down at her expectantly.

How could she tell the boy she had no idea when he would return or even if he would? How could she express her desire to never see him again? Rhys had refused to listen to her, denied her request to let her father go, had chosen his obligations to his job over his loyalties to his family. Entering the coach, she settled back on the seat and lowered her lashes.

363

"Tristan. I cannot lie to you." She looked him straight in the eyes. "Your father and I have had a disagreement on how something should be handled. I'm not sure when he's coming back or even if he is." She took a deep breath.

The carriage began to move forward, the pace the horses set ringing in her ears. *Damn you, Rhys. Why must you be so determined to singlehandedly set the world to rights?*

"Callie?"

Her eyes snapped open when Tristan called her by her name. Before her sat not a boy of six, but an ageless soul who seemed to read her most intimate thoughts.

"Why do you and Rhys fight so much?"

His perception startled her. His maturity left her speechless. "I don't know, Tristan. Honestly, I don't understand it myself."

"Do you love Papa?"

Did she? No matter how hard she tried to deny the fact, she did. Chewing her lip, she nodded.

"Then why don't you tell him that?"

"Because, Son, I don't know where to find him."

Tristan settled back on his seat and crossed his arms over his chest, apparently satisfied with her answer. With a sigh of relief, she turned her attention inward. She had chased after that man once, she would not do it again. This time *she* had their son. Let Rhys come to her.

Across the street from City Tavern, Rhys waited for the stableboy to return with the information he had requested. For two days he had been scouting the countryside around Philadelphia, seeking the whereabouts of John Collingsworth, and had so far come up empty-handed. It was almost as if the man had disappeared into thin air. Every agonizing moment he had spent away from the city, he had worried about Calypso and Tristan as the baron's threat of retaliation had not been digested easily. The need to confirm his family's safety had gnawed at him day and night. He glanced at the building's front entrance. Why didn't the boy return?

The door opened as if to his command, a slight figure stepping out into the late night air. Rhys straightened, expecting the messenger to hurry across the street to where he stood. Instead the heavily coated form darted around the corner to Walnut Street and out of view.

Damn. Rhys shuffled his feet in impatience. Why didn't the stableboy appear?

A few moments later the door opened again. This time the person, a boy slightly larger than the first figure, crossed over to where he waited.

"They're fine, sir. Master Hamer says to tell you not to worry. He'll keep an eye on 'em for ya."

"Good," he replied, slipping the money from his pocket into the lad's waiting hand. "Now you go back and tell the innkeeper if he needs me, he can contact me through Thomas Jefferson. Understood?"

The boy nodded and hurried back across the street, stopping only long enough to count the bills he clutched. He flashed Rhys a grin and reentered the tavern.

Thank God his family was safe for the moment. Perhaps the baron's threats were idle, and he needn't be so concerned. Regardless, he planned to spend every moment he could spare planted here across the street keeping vigilance. His goal to find John Collingsworth was no longer business but a personal one. His family meant more than anything to him and he would not allow anyone to harm them.

"Calypso. Calypso." Fists pounded on the door, refusing to allow the blissful escape of sleep to remain undisturbed.

Calypso forced her eyes opened and looked around in the darkness of the room she now occupied by herself.

"Lassie, wake up and unlatch the door."

She sat up straight. Something was wrong. Dreadfully wrong. Nannette would never disturb her in the middle of the night otherwise.

"Rhys," she whispered. "Dear God, something has happened to Rhys," Tearing off the covers, she rushed to the door and fumbled with the lock, her fingers as unproductive as an unwound clock.

"He's gone," Nannette sobbed from the other side.

Just as she had feared. Rhys had been killed going after her father. Why hadn't he left well enough alone?

At last the door opened, and she fell into the nursemaid's outstretched arms, knocking the older woman's nightcap askew. "Oh, Nanna, what will I do? I was such a fool to be so bull-headed."

"No, lassie, 'tis my fault. I only left for a few moments to get a cup of tea from the kitchens. I thought he was asleep. I never imagined he'd disappear."

"Disappear?" Relief rushed through her like a gale wind. "Then you mean Rhys was here and left before I could see him?"

Nannette looked at her blankly. "His Lordship? You think he took the boy again?"

Calypso stared back just as confused. "Tristan is

366

gone?"

The Scottish woman nodded, her head bobbing like a cork.

Calypso pushed Nannette out of her way and hurried into the quarters adjoining hers. "Tristan? Where are you?" she called, confident he was somewhere in the room. "Answer me, boy." She bent to check beneath the bed.

"I looked, lassie. Everywhere. Even under there."

Calypso straightened, her complexion pale with worry. "Do you think Rhys might have taken him?" Would he do that to her again?

"No, lassie. I'd be thinking the boy left on his own. He's been talking all day about finding his da for you. This evening I told him not to worry so, and I thought the subject closed. I never figured he'd actually try to follow through with his intention."

"You mean he's on the streets alone this late at night? Where would he go?" She hurried back into her room and began throwing on her clothing. "I must find him before something happens to him. He's too young to be out there on his own." Drawing on her fur-lined cape, she prepared to leave.

"Wait, lassie. I think I might know where to look for him. Seems you mentioned to him his da worked for the president. I think he's gone to look for Mr. Washington."

"Oh, Tristan," she muffled into the back of one hand pressed against her mouth. "What a brave, but foolish thing to do." Without considering the lateness of the hour, she ran down the stairs to the common room. She must find Tristan, and she wouldn't stop searching until she did.

* * *

"Thank you, Mr. Secretary. I appreciate you meeting me so early this morning."

"No problem, Rhys. 'Tis best this way." Thomas Jefferson settled back in his chair and propped his feet on the hearth to warm them. "Jameson is screaming for your head, and as long as it's unofficial we'll do nothing. However . . ."

"I know. Once the English government demands satisfaction, you'll have no choice but to take official steps against me."

"I'm sorry, Rhys, it must be this way."

He nodded his understanding. "How much longer?"

"A few weeks at the most. Apparently Jameson sent a report the very next day after the incident. Fortunately, he knows nothing of what really happened that night. I'm sure you agree 'tis best we handle the affair with utmost secrecy."

Rhys clenched his jaws. "Absolutely. But it doesn't give me long to complete the job. John Collingsworth is out there somewhere, but damn, if I can uncover a clue to his whereabouts."

"We've men watching the grave site of young Collingsworth, thinking his father might try to visit there. No one so far except your wife and son."

His mouth thinned into a narrow line. His wife's reasoning was beyond him. "I'll find Collingsworth, Thomas, and bring him in," he assured with determination.

"Alive would be best. I think the British government would agree to a conspiracy trial since Stickback was involved as well, and we can prove the baron's connection."

"Alive," he repeated, relieved he could avoid doing more.

A light tap on the door brought the conversation to

an abrupt end. Mr. Jefferson's secretary stuck his head through the opening. "Excuse me, sir, but there is a young man out here. Says he has a message for Rhys Winghurst. Says Master Hamer from the City Tavern sent him over."

Jefferson glanced at Rhys, who nodded his assent. "Let the boy in."

The stableboy Rhys had paid last night to check on his family stepped into the secretary of state's office, his face awash with awe. "Beggin' your pardon, sir. But Master Hamer says it's most important."

"What is it, boy?" Rhys asked, a feeling of apprehension bubbling in his insides.

"The lady, your wife, sir, came in this morning. Been out searching all night. Your son has disappeared from the tavern. She seems to think he's run away."

His heart accelerated in fear. "Tristan? Are you sure?"

The messenger nodded.

An image of the small figure darting from the front entrance of the tavern and around the corner filled Rhys's mind. Had that been Tristan? Calypso must be frantic by now. No matter how they felt about each other, she needed his husbandly support. He turned to Jefferson with a stiff bow. "Mr. Secretary," he asked with formality. "By your leave."

"Of course, Rhys. Let me know if I can be of any help."

He left the office, his mind trying to figure out where the boy might have gone. Damn the child for his willfulness. He was too much like his mother. His mouth lifted ever so slightly. Perhaps that was why he loved the tyke so completely.

* * *

369

Calypso buried her face in her hands, squeezing shut her weary eyes. "I don't know, Nannette. I've looked everywhere. Mr. Washington has notified his servants at his home and his staff at his offices to keep a sharp watch for Tristan, but so far—nothing." The last word was almost a sob. "What could have happened to him?"

"We'll find him, lassie. He couldn't have gone far."

"I came back here thinking he might have returned." Something inside screamed to place the blame somewhere. "Oh, damn you, Rhys Winghurst. Why aren't you here when I need you?"

The staccato drumming of a fist against the door brought her head up sharply.

"Tristan," Calypso cried, pulling up and stumbling to the entrance. "Thank God."

Her anger melting into relief, she anticipated dragging the wayward child into her arms and smothering him with kisses. She jerked the barrier open.

One of the maids stood before her, taken aback by her exuberance. "Mistress," she offered with a small curtsy. "This letter came for ya." The girl handed Calypso a missive.

She flipped it over and spied the seal. Her heart thudded against her rib cage when she recognized the Collingsworth stamp. Her father.

With trembling hands, she ripped open the envelope and extracted the single sheet of paper. A small whimper lodged, unexpressed, in the back of her throat when she read the one sentence:

If you want to see your bastard son alive, you'll meet me at clock's high, alone, in the abandoned barn on the Great Road just before you reach Germantown.

She crushed the letter to her bosom. Dear God, what was her father's motives? How had he gotten hold of Tristan? She prayed he hadn't hurt her son in any way.

Did she dare go—especially alone? Of course she did; what choice did she have except to do what her father demanded?

"Lassie, what is it?" Nannette frowned down at her.

"I know where Tristan is, and I'm going after him." She started up and quickly changed into a riding habit, deciding she would have one of the carriage horses saddled up for her. How hard could it be to locate the barn indicated in her father's letter?

"Wait, lassie, ye canna mean to go alone?"

"Oh, but I do, Nanna. 'Tis the only way to get him back."

"But where are ye going?"

She paused and considered confiding in the other woman; then her lips clamped shut. "That I can't tell you. Trust me. I know what I'm doing is right. I can't allow Father to harm Tristan." She hurried from the room.

"Your father . . . ?"

Nannette's voice of concern trailed after her, but she didn't stop. As it was, she barely had enough time to get to her destination. There was not a single minute to spare explaining to the nursemaid what she must do.

The spent roan gratefully halted at the stable doors, his wide sides heaving in exhaustion. Rhys tossed the reins to the groom. "Cool him down properly; he's run a long way."

"Yes, sir."

Sprinting through the stables, he caught sight of one of his carriage horses, and was relieved to see the coach parked outside the door. At least his wife was still here, and hadn't run off unprepared to search further for the boy.

He reached the tavern door, pushed his way past a group of men gathered in front of the entrance chattering idly, and stormed into the building.

Glancing around, he sought Calypso. Alarmed to discover Nannette sitting in a corner, her hands moving in a wringing fashion as she muttered under her breath, he crossed the room to confront her. He had seen the old woman act that same way in the past, which meant only one thing. The situation was much worse than he had been told.

"Nannette," he demanded, looming over her, his face frowning, his chest still rising and falling with the exertion of his efforts to reach Calypso as quickly as he could. "Where is my wife?"

"Oh, sir," she wailed, coming to her feet as her hands twisted about each other faster. "The lassie's left."

"Left? Where in the hell did she go now?"

The harshness of his words set the little woman to sobbing harder. "She went after the bairn. I'm so afraid he'll hurt her, harm them both."

Rhys grasped the nursemaid's trembling shoulders. Foreboding shadowed his reasoning. "Who? Who's going to hurt them?"

The woman swallowed so hard, the sound was audible. "Lord Collingsworth."

He shook her, trying to dislodge the vital information as quickly as possible. "Where did she go?"

"I don't know. She wouldna tell me."

He released the nursemaid, and she dropped back to

her seat. A sinking feeling squeezed his insides. If John Collingsworth had his hands on either Tristan or Calypso, the insane man would never let them go—not unless they were dead. His shoulders sagged as he closed his eyes in frustration. How would he find the two people who meant more to him than life if he hadn't a clue as to where to begin his search?

Chapter Twenty-five

The Great Road to Germantown wound through the Pennsylvania countryside like an endless ribbon leading nowhere in particular. Calypso groaned. Her bottom hurt, and her thighs clutching the animal's sides in order to maintain her balance were beginning to cramp in the unfamiliar position. On Long Island she had always ridden sidesaddle, and had taken it for granted she would never have a need to do otherwise. But the stablehands at the tavern didn't have a lady's saddle available, and she was not about to wait until they located one. The urgency of her mission was more important than propriety.

Philadelphia would most likely be scandalized by her riding astride through the city streets, much as the old men sunning themselves on the street corner had been when she had stopped and asked directions to Germantown, but her notoriety was irrelevant compared with the life of her son. Be damned what society thought. She would have ridden Godiva style if that had been what was needed to save her child.

Sawing on the reins, she brought her mount to a halt. A feeling akin to desperation assaulted her. Had she missed the place her father had indicated as she had ridden along? Maybe she should turn back and recheck behind her? Shading her eyes with her hand, she glanced up at the sun, trying to judge the time. It was nearing midday; she didn't have a moment to waste searching fruitlessly for the meeting place.

She turned the horse so she could look back the way she had come; then she swiveled her head to inspect the unknown road ahead. Which way? Uncertainty lumped like an underleavened dumpling at the bottom of her stomach. What would her father do if she didn't arrive promptly?

The animal sidestepped in the direction of Germantown, expressing its impatience to move on.

"All right, horse," she said, bending low to pat its sweat-sheened neck. "Ahead it is." God, she prayed she wasn't making a mistake.

Setting off at a lope, she gritted her teeth against the pain radiating along her inner thighs. She watched the horizon, looking for the deserted barn the baron had indicated, deciding she would check every building she passed that remotely fit the description. The minutes ticked by, and she estimated she had traveled another mile at the least.

Damn it, she wasn't going to locate the barn. Her lips pressed painfully against her teeth as she forced her fear to remain bottled up inside her. She wouldn't stop until she reached Germantown; then she would consider turning about and retracing her steps.

The road curved and angled up an incline. She lifted in the saddle in order to see around the bend and caught a glimpse of a peaked roof. The barn? Her heart skipped in a mixture of relief and dread. What would she say to her father once she found him? What would he demand of her in return for Tristan? She didn't doubt he wanted something. Please let the terms be ones she had the power to grant.

The horse slowed to a walk, then halted fifty yards or so from the building entrance. Ominous silence greeted her as if the ramshackle barn were a sleeping giant. As she dismounted, she glanced about and saw no sign of activity in the distance. Was this the right location?

Tugging the reins over the mount's forehead, she led him forward to an outcrop of dormant shrubbery and tied him to a branch. She patted his rump as she skirted him, not sure who she was trying to reassure, the animal or herself. "Easy, boy," she whispered.

She stepped forward, approaching the building, a nerve-racking feeling slithering down her spine. Somewhere a hinge squeaked, and the courage lodged into her throat, threatening to escape. She forced herself to swallow and her foot to take another step.

The double-door entrance was soon an arm's length away. Still she saw no sign of life. Then she spied the trumpet vines that had once sealed shut the opening. They were broken, the top half of the creeper dangling unattached, swinging like hangman's nooses. No doubt the baron was inside, watching her through the one dirty window, judging her mental state.

Pausing, she took a deep breath, pressing her shoulders back. For years her father had intimidated her, but no longer. She was a woman full grown, and wouldn't give him the satisfaction of seeing her afraid, though her insides threatened to dissolve like a sand castle before the onslaught of an incoming tide.

Wedging her fingers between the doors, she separated them enough to squeeze inside. The only sound she heard was the curious snort of a horse munching hay deep in the interior of the barn.

"Father," she stated matter-of-factly, anticipating the response sure to follow.

"Daughter." The hissing reply filtering from the darkness made her jump. The baron stepped into the thin ray of light fingering its way through the dirty window.

"Where is my son?" she said, pleading with her eyes.

"Where is mine?" he countered so quickly her heart skipped a beat.

She frantically glanced about trying to see through the dimness. Dear God, Tristan couldn't be dead. She studied the man before her, looking for a clue to the boy's welfare. The baron's clothes were dirty and disheveled, his hair matted with straw. A sob of disbelief lodged in her throat. What had happened to the proud man who had confronted the angry mob as they demanded he change his allegiance to a rebel cause? Where was the father she had known and loved—yes loved—when only a child? He had gone, she realized, a long time ago, and in his place was a man possessed with the need to hurt others the way he had been crippled.

"Father, please, where is Tristan?" The plea burned as it ripped from her aching throat.

"Why care so much for the little bastard?"

"He's my son, and no matter what you label him, nothing can alter that fact."

He smiled, and his teeth gleamed whitely with an evilness that made her shudder. "For a while I managed to keep the truth from you, didn't I? You didn't know the boy was yours, for ever so long, did you?"

"No." She should despise this man for all the wreckage he had created in so many lives, but she couldn't. Only pity whipped like a whirlwind in her soul. In his weakness he had destroyed himself and annihilated the

377

lives of those closest to him: his wife, his children, his grandchild . . .

She stepped toward him, her hand reaching out as if to a wayward child. But no more. She would save herself and Tristan from this destruction no matter the cost to her father. "I want my son. Return him to me."

He eased back, the sunshine that had highlighted his features splashed against the barn floor. "An eye for an eye, girl." He turned and fled.

"Father, no," she sobbed, losing sight of him in the darkness.

From deep in the bowels of the building, she could hear the shuffle of his feet as he climbed a ladder upward. She rushed forward, only to slam into a support post, hitting her head. Putting her hands in front of her, she stumbled on ahead. She would not be defeated by the mere lack of light. Tristan was somewhere in that barn, and she would find him.

From above her the baron laughed; then another sound, a whimper of sorts, followed. Tristan. She pushed forward, tripping over a partially eaten roll of hay.

Lying in the acrid, moldy fodder, she fought tears of frustration. No. She didn't dare give in. Pushing up on hands and knees, she ignored the pieces of hay adhering to her hair and palms as she crawled forward, seeking the ladder her father had to have used. Tristan. Tristan. She had to reach her son.

A phosphoric stick flared, and she glanced up, focusing on the pinpoint of light. The clink of a lantern glass followed, the illumination haloing a loft overhead. Teetering on the edge of the boarding stood her father, Tristan, bound and gagged, suspended from his arm.

The child's frightened eyes clung to her, begging to be

378

rescued. In helpless frustration, she fumbled with the decision as to the best way to reach the boy before his grandfather harmed him. Her eyes darted to the lantern dangerously close to the hay stacked all around the man and boy above her.

"Father, let him go."

"Only if you arrange safe passage for me out of the country." He hung the boy dangerously over the ledge, the small feet swinging freely in the air.

"I can't." Of all the demands for him to make of her. She had no political influence. Rhys hadn't even honored her simple request to let her father alone. "I have no power to—"

"Don't lie to me, girl." He clutched the dangling child as if he was incapable of feeling pain. Tristan's eyes bulged in fear and agony. "I know of your connections with the rebel bastards. You and Winghurst plotted for years against me, didn't you?" He shook the boy, who cried out beneath the muffle of the gag. "Didn't you? You plotted and bedded with my enemy, and this is what you gave me for all I did for you." He grabbed Tristan by his hair and shoved him on his knees before him in the hay. "This spawn of the devil himself."

Wisps of straw drifted down on her upturned face as the boy's legs slipped precariously to the edge of the loft. "Father, no, you're hurting him," she cried.

From inside his overcoat he produced a pistol, which he placed against the boy's head. "Then let's put the changeling out of his misery."

"No, Father," she screamed. "Anything you want I will get you, just let my baby go."

* * *

379

Following Second Street beyond Christ Church and Elfreth's Alley, Rhys stopped before a group of old men playing dominos. According to the stablehands, Calypso was riding astride and had headed this general direction. Perhaps the players had noticed the unusual sight of a woman with her skirts hiked up about her calves, riding a horse like a man.

He slid from the saddle and approached the group. "Excuse me," he said with a quick bow. "I'm looking for a phenomenon one of you sharp-eyed gentlemen might have spied."

One old man looked up in curiosity. "Aye, sir. There isn't much that passes this way we miss."

"A red-haired wench astride a carriage horse."

" 'Tis funny you ask, sir. She did come this way. In fact she asked the direction to Germantown."

"Germantown." He grasped the bit of vital information if it were a living, tangible object. "Are you sure?"

"As sure as I'm Ned Holiday. I told her how to reach the Great Road. With nary an explanation she took off in a cloud of dust enough to choke a strong man, much less a pretty little thing like her."

"The Great Road. I thank you." Taking his watch fob from his pocket, he cursed the hands pointing straight up. He vaulted into the saddle and raised the crop to the rump of his mount. Germantown was hours away, and it would probably be late afternoon before he reached the outlying community. Maybe if he pushed the poor beast beneath him, he might close the gap between himself and his headstrong wife. But where in Germantown had she gone?

Lifting the whip again, he aligned his body against the animal's outstretched neck. He would have to keep his wits about him and pray there were more idle old

380

men along the way with nothing better to do than watch the riders traveling on the road. Not much to bank on, but what more did he have? A slim chance in hell, he decided, refusing to acknowledge the futility of his pursuit. Yet, when the situation involved his wife and son, he wouldn't consider the option of giving up. Not as long as he drew breath into his body.

"Please, Father. Let me come up with you. We can figure out a way to get you to safety." She swayed, her neck arched to the extreme as she watched the play of emotions network across the old man's face. Yes, old, she decided. Old and struggling like an ancient oak battling the gales of nature.

The barrel of the gun never wavered where it pressed against Tristan's temple.

"We'll talk," she reinforced as she edged her way toward the ladder to her left, moving with cautious deliberation. More than anything she wanted to rush up the steps and grab her son from his grandfather's arms, to protect him, to comfort him, to erase the abject fear that left his brown eyes wide and unblinking, his knees where they pressed in the hay shaking uncontrollably.

"Come then, girl," he ordered, the familiar tone of authority she knew so well returning for the moment as he dropped back on his haunches, stationing his prisoner between his sprawled legs.

She took each rung of the ladder with slow precision, her heart pounding so hard she thought for sure her father would hear the sound and correctly interpret her fear. Her palms sweated, her grasp slipping as she moved her weight upward; her mind spun with the hard-pressed reality she had no idea how her dilemma would be resolved. The next move she made could be the one to send the last vestiges of sanity her father possessed spiraling to the heavens.

Tristan, hang on, boy, she thought. *Don't do anything to upset him.*

Her eyes drew level with the loft floor. She could see her father's silver-buckled shoes, the soles now worn, the metal tarnished. One vein-laced hand circled Tristan's middle, forcing the boy to sit at an awkward angle, his brown hair, which he had so proudly styled after his father's, loose from its binding and spilling across his slim shoulders. The gag dwarfed his young face, leaving nothing but his eyes exposed. Catching them with her gaze, she tried to convey a confidence she didn't feel. The evidence of her son's fear upset her more than the instrument that caused it, the pistol draped across the baron's knee. Appearing deceptively at ease, at any moment he could again raise the weapon against Tristan's head.

Please, God, if you must take someone, take me—not my son.

"Father," she began again, forcing her eyes to travel upward to meet the hardened gaze of her sire. "I'll find you safe passage. Just turn the boy loose and keep me."

His arm tightened about the boy's chest.

"I'll not slow you down, and I'll give you my word I won't try to escape." Her foot moved up another rung, bringing her chest level with the loft.

Behind the muffle of the gag, Tristan protested.

My brave son, she thought, then shot him a stern look demanding he be still.

"I'll see you safely aboard a vessel bound for England if you want." She slipped up another notch. One more, and she would be able to crawl into the loft. "I went to Liverpool, you know. There's a captain in Philadelphia harbor who'd be willing to take you, too," she lied. Captain Langley most likely was hoisting a sail on an English frigate, cursing her at the moment. "We'll ride back together." She waited for his response. Fearing he would accept her bluff, she dreaded more he wouldn't.

He considered the offer. She could tell by the way his eyes glanced down at the boy, then back up at her.

"You'll be on your way to freedom in only a few hours, Father. All you have to do is release Tristan and take me." At last on her knees in the hay, she inched toward the man and boy.

"No." His arm squeezed his hostage as he raised the gun and pointed it at her. "I'll keep you both." Using the pistol as a signaling device, he waved her away. "Get below. We'll try your plan, but you two are going with me."

What could she do? In utter frustration, she scooted backward toward the descent. Searching for every possible reason to delay, she pointed at Tristan. "His hands are bound. How do you expect him to crawl down the ladder?"

The baron glanced at the boy's wrists secured behind his back. For one breath-held moment she thought he considered disposing of the child, and she cursed herself for bringing the problem to his attention. Then he shoved Tristan toward her, the barrel of the gun aimed in their direction seemingly growing larger by the moment. "Untie him and take him below."

Her heart raced with joy for the one small concession, as she gathered the precious child into her arms. She pressed her lips to his temple, the same spot the cold metal of the gun had touched, and she attempted to kiss away the fear she could feel pumping through his body. "Don't worry, Tristan. We'll be fine," she assured him, wishing there was merit to her promise.

"I'm sorry, Mama," he sobbed when she tore the gag from his face. "I thought to locate Papa and make things right. Then I found Mr. Washington's house. But it was dark, and I didn't think the president would like me to wake him. I fell asleep on the steps to wait for morning."

The baron laughed. "And that's where I found him. Imagine my surprise to discover the waif, my ticket to freedom, just waiting to be scooped up."

"You were lurking about the president's house? What had you planned to do?" She held Tristan close and pressed the back of her free hand against her mouth.

"Avenge Evan." A fervant fire of conviction lit up his eyes. "And Cathleen, your mother, as well." His face lifted as if expecting the blessing of heaven to rain down on him.

Glancing at the gun, she was surprised to see it drift downward against the flooring. His attention absorbed in his passion, was there a chance she could overpower her father? Did she dare try?

The muscles in her legs tensed as she leaned back away from her child. Then in one motion she pushed the boy aside and out of the line of fire and threw herself bodily upon the gun.

"Mama, the lantern," Tristan cried, but the words were meaningless to her. All she could think of was the hard metal pressed against her rib cage.

Would she die? Most likely. And Tristan? Not if she could help it. She would do whatever was necessary to protect him.

"Run," she screamed at the boy, as she grappled to take the pistol from her father's hand.

"Ungrateful bitch," the baron bellowed, as her teeth sank into his exposed wrist. He grabbed a fistful of her flame-colored hair, attempting to drag her off. The flash fire of pain brought tears to her eyes.

Sweat trickled down the edge of her hairline. She was hot, but why she couldn't understand when moments before the damp chill in the barn had been unbearable. The gun, pressed against her bosom, seemed to have a will of its own as her fingers battled with her father's, each trying to keep the other from gaining control of the trigger.

From somewhere far away, she heard Tristan's cry of fear. "The fire, Mama. The fire."

She continued to struggle, clawing at the baron's fingers, as an alarm clamored in her brain. What fire? What was Tristan screaming about?

Her fingers curled about the trigger guard, dislodging her father's grasp. Using every ounce of strength she possessed, she ripped the weapon from his hands and stumbled backward to the very brink of the ledge. Lungs rasping, heart pumping, eyes stinging, she leveled the gun at her father and glanced at her son.

In his panic, he was throwing armsful of hay onto a moldering circle where the lantern lay shattered. Smoke billowed as the flames were temporarily snuffed, but the fire then burst into a hungry ring of fire devouring the fuel the boy had unwittingly fed it. He gathered up more hay and again cried, "Mama, the fire."

"No, Tristan," she objected, "back away, Son. You're only making the situation worse."

Tristan stood, blinking as he looked at her and followed her instruction. For the moment she forgot the struggle for dominance between herself and her father. They were family now, and they needed to work together in order to save all their lives. She lowered the gun. "Hurry, boy. Down the ladder."

The child hesitated.

"Quickly now, Tristan. We'll be right behind you. Help him gain his footing, Father." She turned expectant eyes on the older man, who now stood closer to the ladder than she did.

The baron moved to block the exit. "No. You and your devil's spawn will not escape God's righteous wrath."

In disbelief, she raised the weapon, pointing it at her parent. "Move, Father."

He ignored her. The flames inched closer to where she stood. Already the fire had reached the supports against the far wall which snapped and crackled with the heat. Glancing down at the barn floor far below, she considered telling Tristan to jump. But the distance was too great. He would hurt himself in the fall. Raising the pistol, she took aim at the center of the baron's chest. "Damn you, you foolish old man, move. I'll not let my son die."

Her father's manic laughter overshadowed the hungry sounds of the fire as he dared either one of them to come a step closer. "I'll kill the boy with my bare hands if he comes any nearer."

Arms stretched out, she leveled her aim at his chest rising and falling with insane determination. Her father. Her flesh and blood. Taking a quick glance at Tristan, she fought to keep her resolve strong. Her son. The joy of her life. Her hands began to shake. Could she do it? Could she shoot her own father down in cold blood even to save her child? Her mind screamed "yes," but

386

her finger wrapped about the trigger refused to respond.

God help her, whatever decision she made would make the rest of her life, whether short or long, a living nightmare, a hell she wasn't sure she could reckon with.

Chapter Twenty-six

As exhausted as the animal beneath him, Rhys realized neither of them could keep up the grueling pace he demanded much longer. Reluctantly, he pulled the horse to a halt by the side of the road, dragging out his watch fob to check the time. They had only been on the road a couple of hours and had made good progress. Germantown wasn't much farther. Lifting his head, his eyes scanned the curve in the road, a sensation of helplessness balling in the pit of his stomach. Once he reached the settlement, just where would he begin his search? The lack of an answer accentuated the hollow, vulnerable feeling gnawing at his insides.

He snapped the cover on the watch closed. No time for diffidence. He had solved situations much more complicated than this one over the course of his career working for the government. Perhaps, he thought, setting his mouth in a grim line, but none had involved the lives of his wife and son. None had seemed so personally pressing. There was no way he could separate himself from the outcome. If he failed, his family died, not some obscure names on a piece of paper, but the woman who was more to him than life itself and a boy who represented the dreams of his future. He couldn't acknowledge a chance he might be unsuccessful. Too uch was at stake.

Jabbing his heels into the sides of his mount, he
ook off at a steady pace. He would push on until he
ound Calypso and Tristan or he and his horse
ropped. He wouldn't give up; he didn't dare.

The road curved to the left, taking a sharp incline,
nd he slowed to a walk. A thin curl of smoke drifted
n the horizon ahead. Not thinking much of it, he still
ound his eyes incurably drawn to the white haze that
as beginning to turn darker and heavier.

Rounding the steep corner, he discovered a dilapi-
ated structure, the smoke streaming from the seams in
e roof. Careless vagabonds, no doubt, had set their
efuge afire. The urge to stop and investigate twisted at
is conscience, but there was no time. He had to find
is family.

Reaching the crest of the hill, he lifted his heels to
ur his mount to a faster pace. Then he spied the
orse tied to a clump of brush, fighting to free itself
om the restraint as the smell of smoke descended
pon it. His carriage horse, the one Calypso had taken.

Relief somersaulted in his stomach; then apprehension
agged the feeling of elation, bringing it to a sickening
alt. Calypso was inside that burning barn, and most
kely Tristan as well. Were they alive or dead, coherent
r unconscious? Where was John Collingsworth?

Before his horse came to a complete stop, he vaulted
om the saddle. Bending low, he took no other precau-
on as he raced to the great doors of the barn. *Please,
t them be alive,* he prayed.

He forced the doors open. A stench of burning hay
ushed toward him, the whinny of a frightened horse
ssaulted his ears, the bright glow of the fire overhead
rought his gaze up with a snap.

Highlighted in the eerie flames of death were hi
wife, his son, and his father-in-law. The pistol Calyps
held in her hands aimed at the baron's black hea
trembled, and Rhys held his breath, his hand slippin
into his coat to retrieve his own weapon, waiting fo
her to fire the gun.

Calypso felt the tears of necessity and regret cours
down her cheeks. "Please, Father," she pleaded, prayin
he would listen, "move." In her heart she didn't kno
how, but she must pull the trigger.

"Mama," Tristan shrieked, huddling close as th
flames snaked nearer.

Glancing down, she reached out with one hand whe
she saw the terror in her son's eyes, and knew she ha
no choice. Her father's life was nothing compared wit
Tristan's. But in those few seconds it took to come t
that decision, the weight of a body hit her, wrenchin
the pistol from her unprepared fingers.

She screamed as the edge of her skirts fluttered i
the flames, igniting. Dropping to her knees, she beat a
the hemline until the fire was snuffed out, the materia
blackened and smoldering. A sick feeling dawned o
her with soul-wrenching reality. She would die soor
and so would her child simply because she had no
been strong enough to do what she must.

Tristan threw himself against her chest, clutching he
with all his might. "Mama," he sobbed.

She soothed him as best she could, glanced up t
find her father, pistol in hand, next to the ladder, refus
ing to give up his vigilance. What a fool she had bee
not to shoot him when she had the chance.

How much longer did they have? Minutes at th

most until the agony of the flames would claim them. Enveloping Tristan with the protection of her body, an inner well of resolve bubbled forth. She couldn't watch her child die such a tortured death.

Straightening, she stood her full height. She would appeal to her father one last time. "Think of what you do. If we all perish, what will become of the Colingsworth blood? Let Tristan go. He is innocent of any wrongdoing."

Waiting for his response, she glanced behind her at the waves of flames, then ahead to the long distance below to the floor of the barn—to Rhys standing at the foot of the ladder, his pistol aimed at her father's back, seconds from pulling the trigger.

Their eyes met, his demanding she understand what he was about to do, hers pleading for a moment to think. A moment she knew couldn't be spared, but she needed it nonetheless.

"No, girl," her father's crazed reasoning intruded. 'Tis best this way. The sins of our family will be scorched clean from this earth." His voice broke with a jagged sob as he aimed his weapon at the child.

Throwing herself in front of her son, she heard the thunder of the gun. Would the pain be unbearable when the bullet slammed into her body? Feeling no regret for her action, she closed her eyes and waited to meet death.

"Mama," Tristan cried, his small hands pushing at her back, attempting to skirt the barrier of her body.

Where is the pain? She thought for sure the bullet would have struck by now.

"Calypso, help Tristan down the ladder."

That wasn't her father's voice—her eyes snapped open—but Rhys's. For one crazed moment she had forgotten he was there.

Her eyes swept the loft. Crumpled in front of the ladder was the baron, unmoving, as Tristan attempted to climb over his body to escape. The unfired pistol lay beside him. The gun she had heard had been Rhys's.

She stumbled forward, kneeling to help the boy position himself on the ladder, her hand grasping his shoulders. Then Rhys was there on the rungs, circling the boy about the waist to haul him below. "Hurry, Calypso, there's not much time before the fire—"

"But Father. I can't leave him here."

"He's dead, Calypso. There's nothing more you can do." His gaze hardened with impatience.

"No, he's not dead. He can't be."

"Get down here and take Tristan to safety. I'll see to the old man."

Tears of self-incrimination streamed from her eyes as she obeyed his order and scrambled over the baron's prone body to the ladder. As her feet touched the barn floor, the inferno that had once been the loft came crashing down. She screamed, unable to accept the finality of what was happening.

Taking Tristan from Rhys's arms when he thrust the boy at her, she followed his orders to get out, confident he would find her father and bring him to safety as well.

Coughing, her lungs burning, she pushed through the open barn doors. She hurried to reach cover, then dropped her precious burden onto the ground. Kneeling beside Tristan, she ran her hand over his smoke-blackened face and was relieved to feel the warmth of his breathing caress her fingers.

"Rhys?" she called, turning her head and fully expecting to find him right behind her. The barn doo gaped open, smoke billowing from the interior of the burning building, but he was nowhere to be seen.

"Rhys," she screamed, coming to a swaying stance as she stumbled back toward the flaming barn, her hands shielding her face from the intense heat of the fire.

"Mama," Tristan choked behind her, his head raising as he coughed, unable to catch his breath.

She spun, pulled in both directions. Tristan needed her comforting, but Rhys? Where was he? Did he require her help to escape?

"Mama, where are you?" Fear spasmed in his child's voice.

Which way to go? She pivoted and returned to Tristan, grasping his face in her hands. Forcing him to look at her, she had to make him understand. "Tristan, you must stay here and not move. I'm going after your father. Understand?"

The terror remained in his eyes, but he nodded, and she knew he would obey. Rising to her feet, the thought she might not find Rhys or escape herself once she returned to the building brought her fears full circle. What would happen to the boy in the wilds by himself, in life alone—an orphan?

But what if Rhys needed her and she didn't go in after him? Pulling her cape over her head, she darted back toward the barn.

When she reached the open doors, she could hear Rhys struggling in the interior.

"Rhys?" she called, relieved to know he was still alive.

"Get away, Calypso. There's nothing you can do. Go back to Tristan."

What was he insinuating? Was he trapped but refusing to allow her to take a risk in saving him? If he died, it was because she had insisted he not leave her father behind. She couldn't stand there and allow him to sacrifice himself.

She rushed into the interior, the wall of smoke nearly knocking her backward. Rhys cursed as he grabbed her arm and spun her about. A horse whinnied in terror. Her father's horse. She had completely forgotten its existence.

"Damn it, Calypso. I've got my hands full. Get out of here and out of the way."

She stumbled toward the doors, confident of her father's rescue. Falling to her knees a few feet from where Tristan huddled sobbing, she turned to check Rhys's progress.

He keeled forward from the billowing smoke, leading the terrified mount from the barn, his coat slung over the horse's face to blind it. She strained to see through the haze. Was her father draped across the animal's back?

Rising, she rushed forward to help him lead the reluctant beast forward, and ease the baron to the ground. Hope soared. Her father was alive. There was the chance she could help him see how misguided he had been and turn around his life.

She stopped dead in her tracks. The horse's broad back was empty. Then, as if to corroborate the horror of her discovery, the roof of the barn came crashing down, the entire building engulfed in the flames of hell.

"Rhys, my father." Her head ached with the intensity of her scream and the suffocating heat.

Securing the rescued horse beside the others, he turned and grasped her by the shoulders, the blaze behind him silhouetting his body as if it were something straight from hell. "He's dead, Calypso. I told you that.

There was nothing we could do to help him."

"You promised you'd rescue him for me."

"I said what was necessary to make you get out of the structure before it collapsed. Damn it, woman, I would have said anything to save your life."

"You lied to me." Her fingers clawed at his where they gripped her. "You never even checked him to make sure, did you? Instead of my father you saved that stupid animal." She swung about, pointing at the horse.

"The stupid animal, as you call it, was alive and innocent of crimes, Calypso, which is more than I can say of the beast that sired you." He spun her back around to face him.

The world came to a crashing halt as they stared at each other. "Let go of me, Rhys. My father was many things, but you are more of a beast than he ever was." Twisting away, she was surprised when he released her without a struggle.

The tears were there, stuck in the back of her throat, but she couldn't cry. The pain in her heart accompanying them demanded recognition, but she ignored it. Falling to her knees beside her child, she gathered Tristan up in her arms.

Rhys moved to stand over her. She could feel his presence but refused to look up at him, and instead clasped Tristan harder, pressing kisses to his sooty cheeks.

"Let's go home, Calypso. There's nothing more we can do here."

Rising to her feet, she lifted Tristan's exhausted form in her arms. Rhys extended his, offering to take the burden, but she shouldered past him.

She hadn't loved her father for a long time, but there had always been a chance he might change. First her brother and then her father. Rhys had shot him, then refused to try and save him. She couldn't live with, much less love, a man who could do something so cold-blooded.

Placing Tristan in the saddle, she hoisted herself up behind him, then turned her mount toward Philadelphia, not once looking back to see if Rhys followed. As of that moment, she no longer cared.

Chapter Twenty-seven

March 1, 1791

The cold wind whipped in off the Delaware River, a fitting usher to the fatalism sweeping through Rhys as he stared down at the missive in his hand, official notification of his discharge from the state department. His country—the land he had chosen to serve, not inherited—no longer "required" his services. Sir Jameson, the English diplomat, had quite efficiently seen to that. With both the baron and Evan dead and through political necessity Jeremy Stickback's involvement concealed, the American government's hands were officially tied. He had had to face the review board alone, and his own testimony had damned him.

His mouth lifted on one side in ironic amusement. The worst disappointment was the lack of response to the request he made several weeks ago. Most likely the president felt he couldn't jeopardize the nation as a whole to see justice done for one citizen. He had dedicated his entire life to standing up for his principles, and what had his actions gained him? A country that publicly shunned him as a political embarrassment, and a family who would be better off without him.

He balled the notification in his fist, dropped the

paper over the railing of *The Oceanid,* and watched the white speck disappear into the river's depths. Then his empty fingers lifted and adjusted the collar of his coat to better protect his neck from the freezing cold. Not much to be proud of after thirty-five years of life.

Resignation lifted his shoulders in a shrug as he buried his numb hands into his pockets. Who gave a damn anyway? There was more to life than love, honor, and loyalty. Money and power? No, he had had that once, and it hadn't made him happy. Then what was left?

Racking his brain for an answer, he came up empty-handed. There wasn't one thing he could think of that was more important than those three intangibles—love, honor, and loyalty. How had he managed to lose them all? He snorted in disgust. The process had been easier than he had ever imagined.

To his irritation, a voice penetrated his musings. "Beg pardon, sir."

Without enthusiasm, he turned his attention to the intruder, staring at the man in blank askance.

"Jim Graver, sir. Your first officer."

"Mr. Graver, of course. What do you want?" Calmly he laced his fingers behind his back.

The seasoned sailor looked at him with suspicion. No doubt the man thought his disheveled captain a bit of a loon. Perhaps Jim Graver was right. A man who no longer cared what happened next probably should be classified crazy.

"The navigator is wantin' to plot our course." The sailor looked down and away. "And you've yet to give him our destination, sir."

The "sir" had been an afterthought on the officer's part, Rhys could tell. Damn. Had he lost his touch that completely? "Ask Mr. . . ." What was the navigator's name?"

"Jackson, sir," Graver supplied.

"Yes, Jackson. Ask him where the last course he plotted took him."

"Sir?" There was genuine confusion on the sailor's face.

"Where his last commission took him. Ask him. Then tell him to chart us there as well."

"But, sir," the man protested, "don't you want to decide where we're goin'?"

"Does it matter to you, Mr. Graver? To me it doesn't. Wherever he takes us in as good a place as any other." He turned away, dismissing the man. Jesus Christ. He was losing his mind. The evidence was obvious, even to himself.

"Graver, wait. There's one thing I need you to do for me, before we leave port."

"Yes, sir," came the reply.

"In my cabin on my desk is a packet I need delivered to my wife."

"Your wife, sir? I didn't know you had one."

"I don't anymore. But nonetheless, you'll see the correspondence taken immediately to Mistress Winghurst at the City Tavern."

"Aye, sir, I'll see your orders carried out personally."

He heard the man walk away, yet his face registered no emotion. He was leaving Philadelphia, and most likely wouldn't return. The last time he had left Calypso behind, he had sworn he would never do it again without telling her. The packet fulfilled his obligations, both to himself and to her.

At last his mouth curved into a semblance of a smile though no rush of inner warmth accompanied the expression. What he had sent her would say it all, and

399

perhaps leave her with a few pleasant memories of a man who had found her impulsiveness irresistible, and her limitless pride something he would always cherish.

"I care not, Nannette. There's nothing more to discuss. Tristan is simply suffering from the trauma of that horrible ordeal in Germantown. The lack of his father's presence has very little to do with his emotional distress." She stared back down at the book in her hands, and though she appeared at ease, the words on the page before her eyes were no more than blur.

A foul curse formed on the tattered edges of her mind, but she squelched the thought before it had a chance to become full-blown. She was beyond needing to call Rhys Winghurst names for what he had done.

Clearing her throat, she repositioned the book and forced her gaze to focus.

"Lassie, how can ye dismiss his obvious stress so easily? Canna ye see the bairn's hurtin' and confused by your lack of understandin'? Regardless of how ye feel about the boy's sire, he loves him, and has a right to see him."

Calypso's mouth buttoned in anger. "No, he doesn't, Nannette." Her hand squeezed the spine of the book so hard her fingers ached. "I don't want to discuss Rhys Winghurst anymore. Is that clear?"

"Aye, there's plenty clear to me, lassie. The mention of Rhys Winghurst disturbs ye so because you're feelin' the same as the laddie. Ye miss him, but you're too stubborn to admit it, even to yourself."

The open book crashed down against the arm of the chair in which she sat. "Stop it, Nanna." The tears came gushing forth, and using the back of one hand, she brushed them away. "I'll not have you speak to me that way." The command came out more like a plea.

"Lassie, don't you see what you're doin'? You're punishin' the lad for somethin' that has nothin' to do with him. Just like your da did to ye."

"No!" Calypso covered her ears with her palms, refusing to accept the terrible truth.

"You're blamin' him for how the Master handled the situation with your father and brother." The nursemaid grabbed her wrists and forced her hands down. "Ye know what I'm sayin' is right."

"Don't call Rhys Winghurst 'the Master,' at least in front of me. He was the cause of their deaths. That was not 'handling a situation' as you called it; that was murder."

"Lassie, listen to yourself." Nannette stationed her aging bulk at Calypso's feet. "Hear your false accusation. Rhys was only protectin' those he loved. Besides, he didn't shoot your brother; a well-meanin' servant did. And as far as your father—tell me truly, girl, had the situation been reversed, had Rhys and Tristan been in danger—what would ye have done?"

The bottled-up emotions she had corked for so long pushed like shaken champagne against the restraints in her heart as she buried her face in her hands. "Oh, God, Nanna, I don't know. I've asked myself that question so many times I want to scream." Her eyes darted up, looking for understanding in the Scottish woman's face. "I've relived the nightmare of that afternoon so often, but I don't know the answer."

Nannette curled a protective arm about her shaking shoulders. "But ye do, girl. Didna ye tell me ye threw yourself between the baron and Tristan when ye thought ye had to?"

401

She nodded, the tears leaking past the cup of her fingers pressed against her eye sockets.

"Ye were willin' to die to save someone important to you. Rhys did no less. Don't ye think he knew there was a possibility of losin' your love if he killed your father. Perhaps he's sacrificed something more precious than life." Nannette forced her to look up. "If ye asked him right now, I bet without reservation he'd tell ye he'd give his life for the return of your love."

"No, Nanna, you don't understand. There were terrible words between us. I . . . I . . . said things to hurt him. I refused to listen to what he had to say in his own defense. Then I—"

"Ye've made mistakes, ye may have even burned a bridge or two, but I'd be thinkin' he's hurtin' as much as ye are."

She realized Nannette waited for a response, but her thoughts were much too confused to express verbally. She did know the terrible grief created by the loss of her father and brother still existed, but there was another pain vying for a position in her heart, the separation from Rhys.

"Did ye know he was dismissed by the government for his actions?"

"Dismissed?" The hollow agony intensified, and her face tilted upward. "Are you sure?"

"Aye, lassie. I've heard the talk in the tavern's long room."

"They couldn't have. Right or wrong, he did what he thought he must to protect the president."

"Are ye defendin' his actions to me?" Nannette gave her gray head a knowing shake.

"His country was everything to him. How could they forsake him so?"

"How could you?"

"That's different," Calypso defended, striving to maintain the status quo of her convictions. "He destroyed my family."

"No, he didn't, lassie. Your husband and son are your only family. You're destroying them all by yourself."

Calypso stared at Nannette, amazed at how easily the wise old woman had rooted out the truth. Sliding from the chair, she crumbled to the floor beside her lifelong companion. "Oh, Nanna, what am I to do?"

"Bring Tristan his father back."

"But what if he refuses to listen to me?" She swallowed hard, the thought of just rejection sending a shiver down her spine.

" 'Tis a chance ye must take, lassie."

Calypso shook her head. "No, Nanna. How can I make you understand?" Bending forward, she clutched the dear servant, whose loyalty was more the labor of love than necessity. "I went after him once. My pride will not allow me to do so again. Perhaps, with time, we can meet on common ground."

How righteous and noble her words sounded. They would meet again, they would, she reassured herself. Somehow, some way, on a street corner, at a gathering. Wasn't that the way "happily ever after" occurred in the many novels she had read? He would sweep her up and carry her away to a world where the harsher realities in life didn't exist. That was the promise of love, wasn't it? Forcing back bitter tears, she was afraid to seek the answer.

A sharp rap tattooed against the door. Both women's heads snapped up, and Calypso pushed to her knees.

"Are we expecting someone, Nannette?" For some

crazy, unspecified reason, her heart pounded in anticipation as she brushed the unshed emotion from her eyes.

The Scottish woman shook her head as she turned to answer the door.

Calypso strained forward, catching the masculine voice as it spoke softly to the servant. Disappointment knifed through her. Whoever had come, it wasn't Rhys. But then, what had she expected? The proud stubborn man she had married to come begging for her forgiveness? She looked down at her hands, admitting to herself how much easier her task would be if he did.

"Lassie," Nannette said, stepping forward to offer an unmarked package to her.

"What is it?" The smooth, brown paper crackled beneath her fingertips.

"The messenger said it was from Captain Winghurst."

"Captain?" A sense of alarm rushed through her, but she suppressed the urge to rip the paper away from the contents. Slowly she unknotted the twine holding the small bundle together, her fingers trembling so hard she found the process nearly impossible to accomplish.

When at last she succeeded in unwrapping the package, a folded letter dropped into her lap. Around it was a silver chain divided by a broken link, a silver crown strung on its length. The silver crown that had passed between them so long ago.

Where had he gotten the coin? A flash of his lean body lying across her bed spiraled through her mind. The night she had lured him to her bedroom on Long Island.

Why had he kept it all this time? She had thought the coin lost, an omen that the debt between them was filled. Clearly she recalled the passionate outburst that had passed between them that night as well as the fated meeting at The King's Ransom. She had accused him of being a cad, of taking advantage of her. Now she understood he had only been a man accepting what had been offered. In return he had given her something more precious than life itself, her son.

Would the message declare the battlelines drawn between them again? Grasping the paper, she eagerly sought an answer. She knew how to confront Rhys Winghurst and win if only he would challenge her. Unfolding the piece of paper, she spread it out across her lap.

"My lady," the missive began. "This coin has passed between us twice, if I remember correctly. Once from a misjudgment of identity and again from a misjudgment of ability. I return this symbol of fair play to you, payment for giving me a chance to know the love of a son and a woman whose loyalty and honor rises above all else. I sorely misjudged your character.

"Remember me as unerringly as you did so long ago, as I shan't forget you. Farewell. Perhaps it's best this way."

Farewell? She blinked, as the meaning sank into her brain. He was leaving? No, he couldn't give up on her, not now.

She scrambled from the floor and raced across the room to the door, the silver crown pressed to her heart, the chain dangling between her splayed fingers. Be damned her romantic pride and her visions of what love ought to be, she must stop him, no matter what she had to do or say, for if he set sail, she would never see him again. That wasn't what she wanted for herself and especially not for Tristan. Of that much she was absolutely sure.

"Excuse me, Captain." Graver stuck his head around the door of Rhys's cabin and cleared his throat.

Rhys looked up from his log book, a frown of displeasure twisting his features. "What is it, mister?"

"We just got under way, sir," the man stammered.

"You aren't telling me something I don't already know."

"Yes, sir, I understand, but, sir, there's a woman running up and down the pier screaming your name. I wasn't sure if you wanted us to heave to or not."

"A woman—are you sure?" He pushed up from his seat so quickly the chair crashed to the floor behind him. *Calypso. It had to be Calypso.* He had hoped she might come but never dreamed she would.

"Aye, sir. I've been at sea most my life, but I know a female, especially one as pretty as this one, when I see one."

Taking the companionway steps two at a time, he stopped short of reaching the deck. If the woman was Calypso, he didn't want her to witness his overeagerness. If it wasn't, he didn't wish to appear a fool. Straightening his collar and running his fingers through his mussed hair, he emerged into the sunlight.

She was there, just as Graver had described. Her flame-kissed tresses were unbound and flying about her face as she cupped her hands about her mouth, calling his name.

"Rhys, please hear me. I love you."

For the briefest of moments he considered sailing on out to sea. Maybe his lifelong friend, Luther, had been right. Marriage to Calypso would never be easy, the ups would be ecstasy, but the downs would be the pits of hell. There would never be a steady middle ground, an easy comfortableness in their relationship.

His mouth lifted in a smile that set his eyes to sparkling. He didn't desire a spiritless love, but one that kept his blood afire. He wanted Calypso, his green-eyed siren who kept him off balance just enough to keep him alert, anticipating—alive.

"Heave to, helmsman," he ordered.

It was no easy task turning the ship about in the river and returning to the wharf. By the time the feat was accomplished, a crowd had gathered on the Philadelphia docks to watch, an assortment of wharf officials, shopkeepers, street urchins, and tavern patrons standing along the landing.

The gangplank was barely settled in its grooves when among the cheers of encouragement, both dockside and shipboard, the two of them rushed forward to meet in the middle. Like a flag of courageous surrender, her red hair whipped about them, binding them in the privacy of its richness as they kissed, their arms clinging to each other.

"I love you, Rhys," she whispered.

At that moment the throng about them ceased to exist for him. There was only Calypso, her full lips offered up for his tasting, her passionate eyes clinging to him in adoration, her knowing hands exploring the contours of his back.

"Are you sure, sweeting? Our life won't be easy, you know."

"I know. I'd not want it any other way."

"And what of the lonely months when I'm at sea? You've no choice except to stay behind with Tristan; he needs an education so he can do better in life than his father." His mouth lifted in irony. "Perhaps he'll be a

407

professional man, a doctor or man of the law."

"I'll miss you." She clung to his every word.

"And will you wait?"

"Forever, if I must."

He swept her up into his arms, returning to the ship's deck. "As soon as we can afford it, I'll build you a house with a captain's walk so you can watch for my ship to return. Will that please you?"

"We sound so Third Estate, don't we?" She giggled, and her finger lifted to outline his jaw. "And, yes, my love, a place to scan the wide-open seas for you will please me."

"No fancy balls or silk or satin for a while, you know." Carrying her below by the companionway stairs, he paused in front of his cabin door.

"That doesn't matter. I know you well, husband. You'll not stay subdued long." She circled his neck and lowered his face to meet her. "You never have."

The kiss was gentle, as soft as down upon his lips, but he could feel her longing, the need for more as she closed her eyes.

Was love enough to sustain them? For a while, more than enough, he decided as he laid her upon the bed and stretched out beside her.

But what of all that had passed between them, the misunderstandings, the loss of her family that had cost them so much, almost their love? Would those memories come round about to haunt them after the peaks were scaled and the valleys confronted them? Would it tear them apart again? He must know the answer.

He rolled to his back, putting a space between them as guilt speared him with its razor sharpness. He had to know, now, if she still blamed him for her brother and father's deaths.

"Calypso. I want your honesty."

She lifted upon one elbow, her hand feathe. his shirt to release the buttons. "I have never g. less, Rhys. The truth as I see it."

"Your father, do you still blame me?"

She angled over him, pressing her mouth to his, squelching his question. Then she pulled back and rested her cheek against his furred chest. "I won't deny the pain is still there. I don't know if I'll ever divest myself of it completely, but I'll try. With all of my heart, for you—for us. I know now you did what you had to do." She twisted her neck so she could look at him. "Had I been in your place, I would have done no differently."

His arm circled about her, dragging her as close to his body as he could as a surge of relief washed over him. He was forgiven, but more important, understood.

But what did the future hold? Of the time they'd spend separated without the strength of the other to bind their hearts together? Would their love endure? The need to brand her with his claim before he put to sea knotted in the pit of his stomach. Rising above her, he pushed aside the gathered bodice of the simple muslin day dress she wore and encompassed her heated flesh with his lips. She was his, all his, and he would leave her with a memory to sustain her through the long, lonely nights.

His lovemaking, slow and thorough, focused on his desire never to be forgotten. He caressed her everywhere, adorning her soft skin with feather-light kisses. God, he would miss her during those endless months at sea. He would make this final day together last eternally, for by the morrow *The Oceanid* must be on her way.

.....erless to stop time, he made each second count. .....racing the curve of her ear, he whispered, "You'll not forget me. I'll not permit it."

Tightening the circle of her arms about his shoulders, she pushed until she lay atop him. "And what of you? I remember our first meeting. The captain's bed in room nine needed warming. What if I had not been naive enough to come? Would you have accepted any woman?"

He grinned at her. "Most likely."

"And now when your bed grows cold over the months, what will you do?" she demanded, straddling his hips and pinning his wrists to the mattress, her fingers barely circling them.

"Why, wench, what any hot-blooded man would do." He didn't resist her domination.

She pressed her weight into him, a threat of a teasing kind. "Hot-blooded perhaps, but married with a child," she warned.

With one smooth motion he twisted from her grasp and flipped the two of them back over, him on top between her thighs, her arms spread wide and pincered to the bed by his much larger hands. "I'll think of these last few hours with my winsome wife until my tortured senses can take no more . . ."

"And?" Her chin jutted at a proud angle.

"I'll take a cold dunk in the sea."

She giggled. "And you'll stay there until your waterlogged skin is wrinkled and puckered."

"Would you have me drown?"

" 'Tis better death than infidelity."

He pressed his hips against her and growled. "Just don't you forget those profound words either."

Her hand slipped between them to caress him in a

most intimate way, then she guided him forward until they fit together as man and woman. At first, his movements were leisurely, testing, teasing, awakening her sensuality until the electricity of tension hummed in the pulse of her throat beneath his lips. Still that wasn't enough.

Grabbing her about the waist, he rose to his knees and settled back on his haunches, dragging her forward into his lap as he guided her in the rhythm of love.

At long last her cries of fulfillment washed over him, and he allowed the building pressure to take control. The tidal wave of release rushed in, and he savored the moment, memorizing each nuance of pleasure and storing it away for those times he would be without her.

Draped across him in sated languor, she pressed her face into his neck, her silent tears mingled with the heated beads of moisture gathered there. Lifting his hand, he stroked her hair, and lowered his head to kiss her bare shoulder.

In his heart he knew she felt the same as he did. They had finally discovered the true meaning of love, the sacrifice, the understanding, the trust, only to be torn apart by fate. With eyes open, he had given up his heritage for the sake of freedom, a freedom that now demanded they sacrifice even more. When they needed the time together most to solidify their relationship, there would be nothing but solitude.

With a sign of regret, he eased her back against the pillows and stretched out beside her. His departure was only hours away. And though he could postpone the inevitable an hour, a day, a week, eventually he would have to leave. Would their love survive without the ability to touch, to constantly reconfirm their commitment, not of the body but of the mind? He fervently prayed it would.

Standing beside Rhys, Calypso lifted her face so she could etch his features permanently in her mind. Over the long months would she forget the way his eyes possessed her, the way his mouth spoke volumes simply by quirking up one side? No, never, she assured herself. One always remembered something so important.

"But Papa, why can't I go with you?" Tristan threw his arms about his father's neck, his small legs dangling from the crook of Rhys's arm where he perched.

" 'Tis as I said, Son. You must go to school. Education is most important if you're to make something of yourself when you grow up."

"I want to be a general like Mr. Washington. Must I still go to school?"

Rhys hugged him closely. "More than ever. Generals must know a lot about everything to be good at what they do."

Tristan's face sobered. "Then I shall go to school and learn everything quickly so I can go with you next time."

"Next time," Rhys echoed.

And the next time, she thought to herself, *what will you tell him then?*

As if he read her thoughts over the boy's head, he smiled at her with a shrug of his shoulders. *I couldn't crush his hopes,* his expression defended.

"Tristan," she instructed, reaching out her arms to the child clinging to Rhys. " 'Tis time to turn your father loose. He must leave."

Something inside rebelled against her own words. *No, he can't go. Please, God, do something so he doesn't have to sail away.* Pressing her lips tight, she checked the tears scalding the back of her throat.

She swung Tristan to the deck and took his small hand in hers. Together they turned and walked toward the gangplank. He squeezed, she reciprocated. As much as she wanted to spin back around and confront Rhys with her desires, she kept on moving forward. Was this how a condemned felon felt as he marched to the gallows? Resigned to fate, unable to fight the inevitable?

Her hand slackened its grip on the boy, and Tristan pulled away.

"Papa," he cried.

She came to a halt, but dared not look back. She would never allow Rhys to go if she did.

"I love you, Papa."

"And I you, Son."

He was right behind her, she could feel the heat of his body beckoning to her.

"Calypso?"

He wanted her to look at him. No, no, she couldn't. "Yes," she replied, her voice harsh and edged with pain.

"I love you."

How precious were those three words. "And I you, Rhys," she choked, fearing she would never make it to the end of the pier, where Nannette stood waiting for them, without breaking down.

Rhys's warm fingers took hers and returned Tristan's hand to her protection. "Look for me with the turning of the autumn leaves."

She nodded and hurried forward, crossing over the plank, the connection between the land and ship, him and her. Only then when she heard the squeal as the crossing was removed did she turn about.

"Cast off," she heard him say. He was going, really going. Her heart twisted until she thought the pain would cut off her breath.

The pounding of horses' hooves and squeak of racing wheels brought her head about. From the corners of her eyes she spied Rhys straining to see also. Did he look for a miracle as she did? But what could save them? Nothing.

Pivoting back around, she stared out into the river. Yet Rhys didn't move, just held his ground, waiting.

The sound of someone rushing up the pier could not be ignored. She glanced at Rhys; he was smiling and ordering the seamen to replace the gangplank.

"Mistress Winghurst," puffed the winded voice behind her. The bespectacled little man's face was red with exertion as he crossed in front of her. "Captain Winghurst. Where is he? I've documents from the state department."

Without a word, she pointed toward the ship.

The stranger crossed the gangplank with the awkwardness of a landlubber, his hand waving a beribboned scroll. "Captain. You got it. The papers have come through."

The papers? What papers? She released Tristan's hand to Nannette's care and gathered up her skirts to follow in the wake of the messenger. Who was this man, and why did Rhys seem so pleased to see him?

"Good to see you, Francis," Rhys announced. "I'd given up on you."

"Rhys, what is it?" she asked, craning over his shoulder as he untied the tube and unrolled the paper flat.

"Our salvation, sweeting." He angled the document so she could see it.

She blinked, unable to believe what she read. A deed.

414

Ownership of the Collingsworth plantation in Maryland that had been politically confiscated during the rebellion.

"Father's land? But how?"

He handed her the ornately lettered note that had been rolled up inside the document. Her eyes widened as she read the presidential words.

"Rhys, for your patriotic dedication from a country that owes you more than it can repay. Live well, my friend. George Washington."

"What does this mean, Rhys?"

"This mean, my love, the Winghursts have a home. I'd much rather plow the land than the sea any day." He knelt down and called, "Tristan, come here, Son."

The boy rushed into his waiting arms, and he lifted him up so the three could press their heads together.

"Let's go home," Rhys whispered.

"Home," she repeated, her heart expanding with the joy of love and belonging to both a family and country that would only grow stronger over the years.

**TURN TO CATHERINE CREEL — THE
REAL THING — FOR THE FINEST
IN HEART-SOARING ROMANCE!**

CAPTIVE FLAME   (2401, $3.95)

Meghan Kearney was grateful to American Devlin Monta-
gue for rescuing her from the gang of Bahamian cutthroats.
But soon the handsome yet arrogant island planter insisted
she serve his baser needs — and Meghan wondered if she'd
merely traded one kind of imprisonment for another!

TEXAS SPITFIRE   (2225, $3.95)

If fiery Dallas Brown failed to marry overbearing Ross Kincaid, she would lose her family inheritance. But though Dallas saw Kincaid as a low-down, shifty opportunist, the
strong-willed beauty could not deny that he made her pulse
race with an inexplicable flaming desire!

SCOUNDREL'S BRIDE   (2062, $3.95)

Though filled with disgust for the seamen overrunning her
island home, innocent Hillary Reynolds was overwhelmed
by the tanned, masculine physique of dashing Ryan Gal-
lagher. Until, in a moment of wild abandon, she offered
herself like a purring tiger to his passionate, insistent caress!

*Available wherever paperbacks are sold, or order direct from the
Publisher. Send cover price plus 50¢ per copy for mailing and handling to Zebra Books, Dept. 2569, 475 Park Avenue South, New
York, N.Y. 10016. Residents of New York, New Jersey and Pennsylvania must include sales tax. DO NOT SEND CASH.*